# Rookie Mistake

## On the Board, Book 1

### Anna Zabo

### L.A. Witt

This is a work of fiction. Names, characters, places, and any incidents are either the product of the authors' imagination or are used fictitiously. Any resemblance to actual persons, living or dead, to business establishments, events, or locales is entirely coincidental.

Rookie Mistake

First Edition

Copyright © 2022 by Anna Zabo & L.A. Witt

Edited by Mackenzie Walton

Cover design by L.A. Witt

All rights reserved. No part of this book may be reproduced or transmitted in any form or by any means, electronic or mechanical, including photocopying, recording, or by any information storage and retrieval systems without written permission from the authors, and where permitted by law. Reviewers may quote brief passages in a review. To request permission and for all other inquiries, contact L.A. Witt at gallagherwitt@gmail.com

Ebook ISBN: 978-1-64230-128-1

Print ISBN: 979-8-80461-661-9

# Acknowledgments

Thank you to Bey Deckard for checking our Quebecois! Any mistakes remain our fault, and not his.

# Content Advisory

This book contains discussions of and trauma associated with sexual and emotional abuse. Also some brief allusions to suicide.

Additional notes:

- Consumption of alcohol.
- Brief physical violence (hockey fights).
- Mentions of vomiting.
- Explicit rough sex and light kink.
- Intense fear of flying

# Chapter 1

## Isaac

Julien Landry was fucking *hot* when he was pissed.

I mean, he was hot anyway. I'd had a crush on him long before I'd ever been signed with the Griffins, and now that we were teammates, I was lucky I could walk around him, never mind skate. People always told me rookies could get a bit starstruck by their teammates, especially the top dogs, but it wore off quickly. That had been the case with Nikolai Sidorov and Elias Karlsson; a handful of weeks into my rookie season, we were almost like drinking buddies now.

Landry, though. Fuck.

I was beyond starstruck with him. Sure, he was one of the best and most badass players in the league, but it wasn't his stats, trophies, medals, or titles that screwed with me. It was *him*. He had an energy about him that could make me forget how to speak. Something about that swagger on and off the ice. About the way those dark eyes looked at you like he *knew* something about you. Or how his slim lips always seemed to be *this close* to a mischievous grin, an arrogant smirk, or a ridiculously charming smile.

And when he was mad... Holy shit, be still my heart. So. Fucking. *Hot*.

Except tonight.

As we all changed in the locker room after that trash fire of a game, Landry was livid, and I was just hoping he forgot I existed.

"What the fuck was that?" His French-accented tirade cut through the noise of post-game activity. "That was bullshit! Fucking bullshit!" He threw his helmet into his locker, which was three down from mine, and he snarled something I didn't catch. I didn't even know if it was in French or English—he switched between the two a lot when he was fired up—because I was quietly unlacing my skates and trying not to be noticed.

Most of the time, I was like a stupid school kid with a crush thinking, *Notice me, notice me!* Sometimes he did, and those moments were gold, but right now, the less he was aware of my existence, the better.

I didn't want anyone aware of my existence right now. The press and all the armchair captains on Twitter were probably talking up a storm about me, and I was grateful as hell that I wasn't getting shoved in front of a camera tonight. Three of our teammates had already been herded out so they could go answer questions from reporters who expected profoundly quotable explanations for things like "they scored more goals than us" and "they played better hockey than we did." Like, what did they want from us?

There'd probably be questions tonight about that idiot rookie who was in way over his head and clearly needed to go down to the minors for a while. After all, what kind of shit player fucks up and gives the other team a two-minute power play during the crucial final minutes of the third period? We'd been down a goal with time running out, and I'd been cooling my heels in the penalty box instead of helping my team tie up the score. They'd had to pull our goalie just to even out the men on the ice so they had some hope of keeping us alive, and that had given Ottawa the opportunity to send the puck into the back of our empty net with twelve seconds left on the clock.

We could have gone into overtime. We could be out there right now, fighting for that win, but no, we'd lost by two while I'd been in timeout like the useless kid I was.

The whole team was pissed. I was pissed.

And Landry…

Let's just say that right now I was starting to understand where the metaphor about "spitting nails" came from, because I was genuinely surprised he *wasn't*.

Three lockers over, he slammed his skates down and stalked off to the showers, still snarling and gnashing his teeth about tonight's loss.

As soon as he was gone, I exhaled and put my own skates aside with considerably less force. It didn't help that this was game five of a demoralizing losing streak. We'd all been pumped and ready to break that streak tonight, and then…

*"Twenty-nine, Pittsburgh,"* the ref's voice still echoed in my head despite being nearly drowned out by the cheers of the other team's crowd. *"Two minutes for hooking."*

I'd caught a glimpse of Landry as I'd headed to the penalty box, and he'd been fuming. He hadn't looked at me, but the fury in his expression—that pissed-off cat energy that the fans and I both loved—had left nothing to the imagination. He hadn't looked happy after I'd whiffed two *easy* shots during the first and second periods, either. Or after that one that *would* have been an easy goal if I'd actually, like, caught the puck Ozzy had passed to me. God, I'd been on a roll tonight.

With a sigh, I gathered my things to head for the showers, hoping I could slip in without Landry seeing me.

I'd had fantasies involving Landry, me, and an unrealistic

amount of privacy in the showers, but not tonight. I didn't want to face him alone. I didn't want to face him around our teammates. Shower or not, this one time, I hoped he didn't notice me. Not until he'd had a chance to cool off, and maybe for good measure, until I'd finally scored a damn goal and redeemed myself a little.

It was usually kind of fun to watch him get mad, especially on the ice. He didn't fight often, but when he did, the other guy almost always ended up regretting his life choices. And there was something painfully sexy about watching Landry, helmet gone and long, sweaty hair flying while he threw his fists at some jackass who'd fucked around and found out. I wasn't the only one who thought so—there were YouTube compilations of his angriest moments and most ferocious fights on the ice, and no, I did *not* have them all bookmarked.

Safely in the shower, rinsing away the sweat and shame, I closed my eyes and exhaled. This would pass. I'd seen Landry almost go to blows with Sidorov one time, and they'd been back to chirping and bantering the next day. Of course, they were friends and longtime teammates. As familiar and even affectionate as they could be with each other, I'd actually wondered more than once if they were secretly dating, assuming Sidorov wasn't with Karlsson. Dating or friends or whatever, the point was they were close enough to fight hard and bounce right back to normal.

I didn't have that background with Landry. I was just the rookie who occasionally got a "Nice play, Rivera," and then clung to it for days afterward because holy shit, Landry had complimented my hockey.

So God knew when this would blow over.

I just hoped it didn't end with my hockey idol telling Coach to punt me down to the minors to unfuck myself.

For once, we weren't leaving at the ass crack of dawn to catch a flight. We'd go to the airport early tomorrow afternoon, and we'd have one more game on the road before we headed home.

Still, I needed to sleep. I was vaguely jetlagged thanks to the time change coming here from...from...wherever the fuck we'd played before tonight. These road trips were brutal. I was definitely looking forward to being home for a few days before we headed out again.

I was tired, but I was too keyed up to sleep, and my roommate wanted to FaceTime with his wife. He didn't usually stay in the room for that since he didn't like booting people out, but I needed to go walk around for a bit anyway, so I left him to it.

The hotel bar was open, and outside, so was the patio. Not that there was anyone out there—it was cold as balls, so not really inviting for anything other than a smoke break. The perfect place to be alone as far as I was concerned.

I strolled out to the concrete railing that overlooked the river. For a moment, I just closed my eyes and enjoyed the peace out here. I'd always gravitated toward water; kind of came with the territory of growing up at the ocean's edge in Oregon. There was nothing in the world more soothing than the roll of the tide. A gentle river wasn't quite the same, but it was something. It was moving water. Fountains, streams, lakes —even a shower would do in a pinch.

The river didn't do much tonight, though. Sighing, I opened my eyes and watched the city lights dance along the ripples in the dark, swirling water.

I'd get past this. Hockey was a fast, intense game, and no one was immune to physics or just plain fucking up. Everyone turned over. Everyone spent time in the penalty box. Everyone lost an edge when the camera was right on them and it could be replayed over and over on Twitter by people who'd probably never even worn an ice skate. Penalties happened. Shots missed. Teams lost.

But it was hard to swallow, especially when I'd worked *so hard* to get to this level and was afraid at every turn that I was going to get traded or sent down. Being on the same team as some of my hockey idols—especially *that* hockey idol—was a double-edged sword, because while playing with them was amazing, it also meant they had a front-row seat to my fuck-ups. It meant they were *affected* by those fuck-ups. That turned out to be a lot more pressure than I'd anticipated, especially while my first pro goal still eluded me. All I'd given this team so far was a pair of assists and a badly timed penalty.

Exhaling a cloud into the cold air, I chafed my arms.

*Coach is going to ream me tomorrow. The guys are probably pissed. They're going to—*

"It's warmer inside, you know."

That smooth, low voice stopped my breath in my throat. There was no mistaking who it was. Not with that accent.

I turned around.

Oh. *Fuck*.

Julien Landry was sitting at one of the otherwise abandoned tables on the patio, still in his suit with a glass on his knee. Ice water with lime, knowing him. The light from the hotel bar cast a soft, warm glow across his features, illuminating him just enough to pick out the shadow of a few days' worth of scruff darkening his jaw and framing the emotionless line of his lips. His long hair was swept back, no longer sweaty or mussed like it always was after a game, and his eyes were fixed right on me.

"Hey." I leaned against the railing and tried not to look intimidated. Or starstruck. Or whatever it was I felt whenever I was alone with him even when I *hadn't* cost his team a much-needed win. "I didn't realize you were out here."

He shrugged, the bespoke jacket barely lifting with the subtle motion of his broad shoulders. "No one does. That's why I'm here."

Oh. Well. Okay. I could take a hint.

"Um." I cleared my throat and pushed myself away from the railing. "Sorry. I, uh... I didn't mean to—"

"Stay." He took a drink, then rose. My heart sped up as he crossed the patio to where I was standing. There was a touch more light over here, so I could see him better as he pressed his elbow onto the railing and put the glass down between us. The cool wind played with a few strands of hair that had fallen over his face. Fatigue had smoothed some of the intensity out of his features. His tie was gone, the top two buttons of the gray shirt undone beneath his unbuttoned jacket. It was one of those looks that could either be breathtakingly stylish or embarrassingly sloppy. Landry, of course, pulled off stylish, looking tired but deliberately mussed; the suited equivalent of artfully tousled bedhead.

Under normal circumstances, I'd be quietly drooling over him. Tonight, I was way too tense. Bracing too hard for whatever he was going to say. Because he was *going* to say *something*. He hadn't just walked over here to stand in silence. Or was he expecting me to speak? Shit, maybe he was.

I cleared my throat again and blurted out, "I blew it tonight."

One of his sharp eyebrows flicked up. "Come again?"

"I..." Looking at him was too much, so I shifted my focus back to the river and searched the water for its usual comfort. No luck. "I gave them a power play when we needed all the advantage we could get. And every shot I took was—"

"Rivera." Landry's voice was surprisingly calm, given the circumstances. "That penalty was horseshit."

"I know." I shook my head. "I never should have—"

"I mean the call. It never should have been a penalty."

I turned to him. "What?"

"I saw what happened, and I saw the replay." Landry brought up his glass for another drink, and he gave a quiet growl from the back of his throat, a tiny hint of the fury from the locker room. "It wasn't hooking. I don't know what the fuck the ref saw, but...that *wasn't* hooking."

I stared at him as he swallowed some water.

Apparently sensing my incredulousness, he sighed and lowered his glass. "Tonight was tough. For all of us. We played better than we have recently, but we didn't play well enough, and the refs..." He muttered something in French before adding with a faint laugh, "The hockey gods didn't want us to win it."

"Oh. I thought..."

His eyebrows rose, and there it was—that look that said he knew something about me. That said he was reading something I didn't even know I was saying. Probably my imagination—after all, it did run wild where Julien Landry was concerned—but it beat the hell out of being convinced he was blaming me for tonight's loss.

He set the glass down on the concrete between us. "Tonight wasn't on you."

Oh. Shit. Maybe he could read me.

"I guess?" I shrugged, shaking my head. "Just seemed like I was fucking up at every turn. The penalty, but also when I shot..." I groaned. "One was *wide* open. And the other...just. Fuck. I should've made those goals."

"The team made twenty-nine shots on goal tonight. We got two into the net." Landry chuckled softly and gave my arm a firm clap. "Don't carry all that weight on your shoulders because you missed your two."

I stared out at the river again. He was right, and I knew it. The vast majority of shots didn't go in, or else hockey scores would regularly be well into the thirties instead of single digits. It was just killing me that I hadn't racked up even one goal as a pro. Especially not when my team *needed* me to.

"Rivera. Look at me."

If he only knew how much I wanted to do that *all* the time, and how hard it was to do it right now, but I did.

"You're a rookie." He said it without judgment or condescension. "Every rookie wants to be at the top of the game right from the start. There's a ton of pressure. I get it. I've been there."

Sometimes it was difficult to remember that he'd been a rookie at one time too. That he hadn't fallen from the sky as the league's top defenseman.

But he had been a rookie, and he'd had his struggles. His second season had famously been a disaster—something commentators were in no hurry to let anyone forget despite his success. Yeah, he'd been there. For all I'd convinced myself tonight that he'd blame our loss on me, and that our next interaction would be him tearing into me, he was the one who was talking me down.

And right then, in Landry's eyes, I found exactly what I'd been looking for in the gently flowing water of the river—calm. Permission to breathe. Permission to move on from a few mistakes instead of pulling the weight of an entire loss onto my own shoulders.

I swallowed. "Thanks. I, uh...I needed to hear that tonight."

Oh God. That smile. A little asymmetrical. A lot sexy. Full of all the reassurance I hadn't believed I'd deserved until it had come from the beautiful lips of the hottest player ever to touch the ice.

He clapped my arm again and jerked his head toward the hotel. "Go get some sleep. We've got a losing streak to break."

I managed a quiet laugh. "Think we can break it next game?"

Landry just grinned, all arrogant and gorgeous. "Of course we can."

And I believed him.

# Chapter 2

## Julien

I patted my pockets before letting the hotel room door close. Phone and room key. That was all I needed for the team breakfast. Coach told us to be there by 9AM. When I walked into the hotel banquet room at 8:58, he merely rolled his eyes. "Landry."

He knew me well by now. Team meetings and meals? I always walked in at the last moment. "Hey, Coach, did I miss anything?"

He glanced over at the buffet. "Maybe the eggs with cheese."

"Well, as long as there's bacon..."

There was that long-suffering sigh. I gave him a grin, and headed to see what my teammates had left me to eat.

Turned out there was plenty, including eggs with cheese, several strips of bacon, fruit, meats, cheeses, plus some of those gluten free muffins that were so popular. I did try to keep the carbs down, but I also had limits, so I stuck to protein and fruit, plus coffee, then scanned the room for the guy I'd spent the better portion of the night thinking about.

Isaac Rivera.

Not hard to spot. Rivera wasn't tall—his stats said five foot eleven inches, slightly shorter than my six feet, but he was closer to five nine. His shoulders, though, were broad, and next to Elias's bright blond hair, the rookie's short dark mop stood out. It was getting longer, and had picked up a bit of curl.

Rivs, the other guys called him. It was good to see his tentative smile this morning, especially after how much weight he'd piled onto himself last night. As if he'd been the sole reason we'd lost. Hell, that bullshit penalty hadn't been the reason—just an insult to our already injured pride.

Refs. What can you do? They see what they see.

All the metrics said we'd be fine. Sure didn't feel like it now, but I'd been here before. Rivera? He hadn't, not on this stage. It was eating him alive.

Glad he was sitting with Elias. He got along well with both him and Nikki, which was good. When he wasn't a pile of nerves, Rivera was easygoing.

Lately, he'd been that pile of nerves, and I felt for him. Reminded me of—well, me. At least a little. I'd been more shy, so quiet, very naïve, and starstruck by exactly the wrong player.

Ah, no. I wasn't going to think about my rookie year. There was no point, and those memories weren't ones I was willing to drag up. All of that? C'est fucké. Hockey was a game of the here and now—you couldn't hold on to the past, and I had no desire to comb through that particular collection of my greatest mistakes. There were enough people on the internet that regularly catalogued my faults and declared me a pretty, but ultimately empty-headed fool with no understanding of the game. That shit was *poison*.

Suffice it to say, I empathized with Rivera on some level. That's probably what'd pissed me off so much last night when the ref had called that penalty. The look in the rookie's face, like his entire heart had gone missing.

When Elias saw me, he leaned back dangerously in his chair. "Oh, there you are. Finally." He tipped forward, then slapped my shoulder as I slid my plate onto the table. "Last one to breakfast. It's why he's so good-looking. Got to get his beauty sleep."

I saluted our captain with both a middle finger and a smile, then took my seat. "I'm not late."

"You're never late. I was just telling Rivs." He plucked a grape off my plate, popped it in his mouth, and spoke around it. "Barely on time, but never late."

Rivera looked down, those full lips of his trying—and failing—to hide his smile. When he looked up and met my gaze, I wanted to tell him to cut it out.

Puppy dog eyes. Big brown ones. Idol worship. If there was a player on this team who shouldn't be *anyone's* idol, it was me. I'm an awful role model. But I gave Rivera a smile and focused on those eyes of his. "Did I miss anything interesting?"

He looked down, and I swear those lips got fuller when he smiled. "Not really." He fiddled with his fork. "Except for everyone giving Larry crap about the giant hickey on his neck."

Our goalie, David Larfield, was a bit of a lady's man. Didn't blame them for flocking to him at all. He was six foot four with that lanky goalie build, rugged good looks, and a habit of showering his sandy brown hair with his water bottle during stoppages. Man looked good both dry and wet. If he weren't straight, even I might've hit on him. If I fucked teammates. Which I didn't.

Not anymore.

"Good for him," I said. "He stood on his head last night. Deserves a little fun."

"What about you?" Elias raised his eyebrow. "Work out your aggression last night?"

Crisse. The look on Rivera's face. That blush. Those dark wide eyes. I couldn't decide if I wanted to smack Elias or thank him for provoking that. Instead, I chuckled. "Me? Not that way, no. Spent some time cooling off outside, then took me and my pride to bed."

There'd been a hot minute when I'd brought up Grindr on my phone, but I knew better than to even look. I'd been too angry in the wrong way for sex with someone I didn't know. Hell, for a while now, hookups hadn't touched the itch I wanted scratched. Sex was fine, but I wanted a connection. Someone to see beyond my looks and my reputation as an airhead. That's one of the reasons why I hadn't used any of those apps in a long time. Water, cold air, and some time and space to stare into the darkness had been the better plan.

Then Rivera had stepped out onto the patio, the one person I shouldn't even be thinking about.

I kicked Elias in the shin. "You?"

He laughed outright but didn't say anything.

Heavy hands descended onto my shoulders and I nearly choked on the eggs I'd been eating.

"King making jokes again?" Nikki's voice was deep and rumbly. Nikolai Sidorov was one of our alternate captains and one of my best friends. I was the only person who could get away with calling him Nikki. He was the only one who ever called me King. He dug his fingers into my shoulders, working out some of the tension I'd been carrying there.

"Fuck."

He laughed, then smacked me on the back. "Too tense."

Maybe. Nikki read people well. The press thought he wasn't that smart because his spoken English was a little choppy under pressure. Some of that was an affectation, some nerves. Around us he was as sharp as a fresh skate blade and he knew that I, like Rivera, could carry shit on my shoulders.

"He didn't get laid last night," Elias said.

"Too tense," Nikki repeated.

"Will you two assholes fuck off?" I said it with a smile, then went back to trying to eat my breakfast.

Rivera was pushing the remnants of his food around on his plate, his brow furrowed. He must have sensed me watching him, because his gaze drifted up to meet mine. "Are we that screwed?"

Both Elias and Nikki froze, because there was an unspoken rule of not discussing games—either past or future—over breakfast. Not unless Coach was the one doing the talking.

"No." We weren't at all. We'd had a stretch of bad bounces and our timing had gotten off. Rivera should know that. I studied him, all that worry and eagerness and concern. "Why do you ask?"

He shrugged. "You're stressed. You're never stressed."

That gave me pause, as did Nikki's grunt of agreement. Elias gave me a questioning look, too.

Well, fuck. Guess I hadn't managed to shed all of my frustration from the previous night. "It's not stress. I was pissed last night, that's all. I'm over it."

Rivera gave me a dubious look.

"We're *fine*." All three of them jumped a little. I'm not usually that vehement, but someone had to get everyone on the same page, and I wore the other A, so if it wasn't going to be Elias or Nikki, it had to be me. "Fast. Smart. Good." I pointed my fork at Rivera. "Especially you, Rook. Believe it."

Those lips of his, goddamn it. They parted, then curled into the sexiest smile I'd seen in a long time.

"Okay. I'll believe it." Then he rose. "Thanks. Gotta go get my shit together."

Didn't know if he meant figuratively or literally. Maybe both. I watched him wind his way to the exit.

Nikki's hand pressed down on my shoulder again. "You're good with Rivs."

Ah, shit. I was. I wanted to be. I studied the food on my plate and went back to shoving it into my mouth so I didn't say anything. Rivera *idolized* me. I shouldn't be encouraging that. Or my own interest in those big damn brown eyes.

Oh, the chuckle from Elias. "Ah, Julien." That tone with the use of my first name—I hadn't heard that in a while.

"What?" I met my captain's amused stare. "He's putting too much on himself. Not going to help him or us if he's that way."

"That's familiar." Nikki slapped me on the back again, then gripped Elias's shoulder. "You done?"

A nod from Elias, though he didn't stop studying me. "Lans, it's good." He rose.

Nikki nodded in the direction Rivera had taken. "Have fun." Then he and Elias headed out of the room.

I carefully set my fork down, leaned back in my chair and closed my eyes. All the curses I knew went through my mind before I blinked and stared across the room.

Nikki knew my unspoken rules and why they were in place, and he'd suggested I break them. With Rivera. What the *fuck*?

Wasn't happening. But maybe he and Elias were right about one thing: Rivera listened to me. If I could use that to get him to relax a little on the ice? Maybe I should. The rookie was good. *Really* good. Strong legs, protected the puck well. Great sense of the game. The plays he could make when he stopped thinking too damn hard? Top notch.

So if I could help him with that? Good. There was an A on my jersey, after all, and not just so I could bitch at the refs. I was a leader in the room, and despite public opinion that I was an arrogant fool, I took my role seriously.

Any other *fun,* as Nikki put it, was completely off the table.

After boarding the plane, I settled in at the club table next to Elias. Nikki was across from him, as normal. Sometimes Larry joined us, sometimes Jackal, but they'd both opted to nap on the flight to Winnipeg. Larry looked happily wrung out, and so did Jackal, so I suspected he'd gotten lucky, too.

Probably a good thing I hadn't opted for that route last night. Yes, the tension was still there, but it wasn't anything a nap and a good hard practice couldn't shake out of me. Bad luck was a strange beast and being upset about it only begat more.

Okay, maybe I was stressed after all.

Just then, Rivera boarded the flight, and his gaze flicked all around the cabin. Us older players had our set spots. The newer guys jostled for the rest until the team settled into a routine. We hadn't quite gotten to that point in the season yet.

Even from where I sat, I saw the dismay in Rivera's expression. Guess his favorite place had been snatched up. "Rivera."

His head snapped in my direction, those eyes wide once again.

I nodded to the seat across from me, the one next to Nikki. "Join us."

He paused for a second, then came striding down the aisle. "You sure?"

"King says sit." Nikki smiled up at Rivera, and patted the seat. "So sit."

He sat, and pushed his backpack under his seat. "Thanks." But a hint of tension lingered, and his eyes flicked between Nikki and me. "Um, can I ask you guys something?"

Nikki shrugged. I said, "Sure."

His attention shifted to Nikki. "Why do you call him King?"

"Oh, God," I muttered as both Elias and Nikki burst out laughing.

Rivera's cheeks heated. "I'm sorry… I just…"

I waved his concern away. "No, it's fine." I gave Nikki a look. "Do you want to tell him?"

Of course Nikki grinned back. "No, no. You should. It's your name."

Fucker had even managed to get the equipment folks to put it on my stick somehow, and no amount of my pleading had ever changed it. At this point, all I could do was laugh. "My nickname on the ice since Bantam has been Lans. But this guy…" I crossed my arms and glared at Nikki. "He starts calling me King the year after I come up. I thought he was fucking with me, because my second year was—"

I cut myself off before the memories came flooding back. Fucking nightmare, that year and the one before. I should have been bounced down to the minors. Hell, I should have been thrown out of both leagues. Part of me wonders what miracle kept me in and allowed me to recover from all the foolish mistakes I'd made.

Nikki's voice was soft. "Wasn't fucking with you. You *are* a king. You just needed time. Friends."

There was one half of the miracle right there: Nikki. The other half was Elias. "Anyway," I snapped at him. "I was more —volatile—back then."

Elias snorted, and silently air-quoted the word "more," so I gave him a shove.

"His name is Jules," Nikki said. "Kings have jewels. He's a king." He settled back in his seat and grinned at me.

"No one called me Jules," I said. Not my parents. Not my siblings. Even Travis— *Non*. I shut my brain down as soon as it hit that name. "No one."

"Except me." Nikki's grin was as wide as the sun.

Rivera took that all in, his head cocked to one side.

"So I started calling him Nikki. Figured maybe he'd cut the King thing out." Everyone else called him Sido, or Nisha if he said they could. But I was a cocky bastard.

"And here we are," Elias said. "Seven years later."

Rivera nodded absently, and I wondered what that was about. "So I should stick to Landry?" His foxy little grin took me completely by surprise.

*Have fun*, Nikki had said. And in that moment, I wanted to. Thankfully, the announcement that we were departing blared over the speakers, shattering that thought. We belted in and put everything where it needed to go. The roar of the engine during takeoff filled the silence that had descended over us.

I hated this part of flying. Hated flying in general, but especially takeoff. The noise. The rumbling and shaking. The way my head and stomach felt as we rose into the air. Elias patted my leg, as he always did, and I smiled faintly at him, my other best friend.

Across from me, Rivera seemed more relaxed than I'd seen him before. Serene, even. He stared toward the cabin windows. I wished I had that calm. I never did, but especially not while climbing into the air in a metal tube with wings. No matter how many times I'd done it before.

But when the plane leveled out, I could breathe again. We got our drink orders—including my gin and tonic—and our favorite snacks, and settled in for the flight.

Rivera eyed my glass but said nothing. The question, though, was in his eyes. Everyone on the team knew I didn't drink much. A glass of wine here, maybe a beer there. Most of the time, it was water, like Rivera had now.

But I'd found over the years that one somewhat strong gin and tonic made me care a whole lot less about flying, so that's what I had every damn time we had to go up in one of these things. I'd tried anti-anxiety meds, but I didn't like how those made me feel afterward, so I stuck to gin.

Nikki dug out a pack of cards and tossed them on the table. "Spades?"

That too was tradition. Nikki didn't wait for Rivera to agree. He took the cards out and started shuffling.

I nudged Rivera with my foot. "You play?"

He nodded and raised his eyebrow. "Are we partners?"

The alcohol had kicked in, because I liked that look a little too much. I leaned back in my seat. "We are."

Elias dusted his hands together. "Fair warning. You'll lose with him as your partner."

Nikki pursed his lips and shook his head side to side as if only half agreeing with Elias's assessment, then dealt the cards.

I'd never seen Rivera look that incredulous. "Are you that bad?"

"He's not," Elias said. "But people can't read him." He grabbed a handful of mixed nuts. "Well, Nisha and I can, but..."

I tapped Rivera with my foot once more. "You're my partner. Not them. Let's see what we can do, eh?"

There was that blush again, but also a fiery look in his eyes. "All right." His grin was devilish, and I knew right then and there two things: we were about to decimate Nikki and Elias at Spades, and Isaac Rivera would score multiple times during our next game.

An hour later, Elias threw his last card into the pile on the table and groaned dramatically.

Three rounds of Spades. Rivera and I had won each one. He'd read me perfectly, and I him. We'd captured trick after trick. I only had to stare into those deep brown eyes of his, look for the subtle crinkle, the twitch to his lips, and I knew what card to throw. Or he knew. Magical, almost. Better than with Nikki, which was something.

Nikki cursed in Russian.

I snorted. "Well, you do call me King, after all."

"Wasn't you." Nikki pointed a finger at Rivera. "You can read his mind."

The rookie looked down at the table, a brilliant smile spreading across those tantalizing lips. "He's not that hard to read." Then he looked up.

Oh *fuck*, there it was. That soft smile, those hooded eyes. A little lick of his lips. He wanted me. Badly.

Maybe it was the gin—I get loopy with gin—but I returned that smile. Long and wide. Then I leaned back in my seat, bumped him with my foot, and closed my eyes. Wouldn't be too bad to flirt a little, would it? Felt safe enough.

"Nap time for Julien," Elias said.

"Like you two don't pass out after cards, too."

Rivera laughed, and I liked that sound. When I opened my eyes, I liked how relaxed and happy he looked. Wanted to keep that going. "Join us. Then you can say you slept with three hockey players."

The blush and the fit of giggles Rivera fell into was stunning. God, what a beautiful man.

For the fourth time, I nudged him with my foot. "Seriously. Get some rest. It'll be good. Promise."

"Yeah," he said, meeting my gaze. "I believe you."

Good. I leaned my seat back, closed my eyes, and let the heady warmth from my drink, the card game, and Isaac Rivera's smile pull me into sleep.

# Chapter 3

## Isaac

*It was the gin talking. It had to be.*

I tried not to stare at Landry while he slept. Most of our teammates were either asleep as well or occupied with something else. Eating. Reading. Playing on phones. Playing cards. Talking with whoever was closest. Paxton, Landry's defensive partner, brought his stepson along on road trips sometimes, and he was quietly helping him with some of his second grade math homework.

No one was paying a damn bit of attention to me, but that didn't stop me from being sure that if I let my gaze linger too long on Landry, everyone would notice. Including him. Especially him.

So I buried my face in one of the paperbacks I always kept in my carry-on, and I stared at the words. They didn't mean anything, though. I may as well have been looking over Sidorov's shoulder and trying to parse the Cyrillic he was reading for all I understood what was on my own page.

But it was something to point my eyes at and throw everyone else off the scent that maybe, just maybe, Julien Landry was fucking with my head.

He *had* been flirting with me, right?

Except, no. Gin. Landry was a lightweight, everybody knew it, and nobody let him forget it, so yeah, one gin and tonic was definitely enough to dissolve what little filter he ever had. Enough to flirt with me, though? Really?

I thought about when we'd played cards with Karlsson and Sidorov, and I couldn't stop myself from shivering.

Sidorov turned to me. "Cold?"

The laugh came before I could stop it. I was the opposite of cold right then, and now he was looking at me like I was a complete tool. Clearing my throat, I shifted in my seat. "No, I'm good. Wouldn't be much of a hockey player if I didn't like the cold." Aw, fuck. That was stupid. Yes, the sport was played on ice, but if anything, I was more likely to get too hot. Since it was a sport. A fast one. Played under five hundred layers of gear.

But Sidorov just grunted, returned his attention to his book, and let the subject go.

I definitely wasn't cold now. Not with the warmth rising in my cheeks over that painfully awkward interaction.

And not with my mind wandering back to that Spades game again.

Karlsson and Sidorov had been frustrated that I could apparently read Landry better than they could. If I was honest, I couldn't believe I'd remembered how to play at all. I'd played Spades millions of times with my college teammates, so I knew the rules back to front, but exchanging those silent looks with Landry had all but scrambled my brain.

Because yes, I *had* been able to read him.

And he'd been able to read me.

And there'd been this feeling like we were completely in sync.

I'd been on the same wavelength as Julien Landry? How fucking cool was that? It had been a hell of a thrill, and it was something I hoped we could get on the ice as well, because having a connection like that with a talented player would create some *serious* advantages.

Marking my page with my thumb, I closed my eyes and imagined catching Landry's eye on the ice. I'd been intimidated and fascinated from the start by how he'd look at me like he knew something about me, and after today, I was painfully curious about how that could carry over onto the ice. Non-verbal communication was as critical in this sport as verbal, and I'd be the first to say I was damn good at it. So was Landry.

But sometimes players were so in sync, it bordered on telepathy. They could communicate an entire play through nothing but glances. Whenever I'd had that connection with a teammate in the past, we'd been unstoppable.

Today, if only for a little while, I'd had it with Landry.

And then, with just as much gin in his system as when we'd been on that perfect wavelength during our card game, he'd flirted with me. Hadn't he?

I opened my eyes again and watched him sleep. Intense features had smoothed out. The vent above him was teasing a few strands of his long hair, and the dark fan of his eyelashes intrigued me even from this far away. Scruff darkened his sharp jaw and made him unreasonably sexy. How was he so hot? Who gave him the right?

And that guy…had flirted…with *me*?

Oh, fuck.

Forget non-verbal communication.

I was never concentrating on the ice again.

---

THE CLOSER WE got to our next game, the more our *last* game loomed over my head. Despite everything Landry and some of the other guys—including Coach—had told me, all those mistakes nagged at me like throbbing bruises. Was that how my (presumably brief) professional career was going to go? Flipping between drooling over my stupidly sexy teammate and berating myself over my inability to carry my own weight on this team? Because even Landry drunkenly flirting with me couldn't keep me from obsessing over everything I'd done wrong and how much I was going to let my team down tonight.

Okay, so the hooking penalty had been bullshit. I'd watched the replay at least two dozen times, and it wasn't even accidental hooking. Theories among my teammates ranged from a simple error on the ref's part, some money changing hands to make sure we ended up on the wrong end of a power play (though why they'd pick me as the sacrificial lamb and not Landry or one of the other solid players, I had no idea), or —my personal favorite—a ref's coffee spiked with a powerful hallucinogen.

So I believed now that I hadn't deserved the penalty and that my teammates hadn't given up on me because of it.

But I still couldn't convince myself that I'd exactly *helped* my team that night.

In my hotel room before we left for tonight's game, I watched and rewatched the various replays from the other night, sinking deeper and deeper into the pit of *I don't belong here*. If I'd shot two seconds sooner, that forward would've been too far away to easily deflect the puck before it went anywhere near the goalie. If, instead of hesitating, I'd passed to Paxton when there'd been nothing but wide-open ice between us, that turnover wouldn't have happened and Ottawa wouldn't have scored that goal. And holy shit, what was I thinking when I had three people I could've easily passed to, but instead decided to shoot into a dense screen of opposing players who were happy to relieve us of possession?

God, I sucked. I'd been so fucking convinced I was hot shit in college. And when multiple teams were openly courting me and I'd been one of the top draft picks? Oh. Yeah. Ego to burn, right here.

These first few weeks in the league had been a lesson in humility, that was for sure. Maybe I wasn't that good. Maybe I was like that kid who kicked ass in junior varsity, only to have his own ass handed to him the second he advanced to varsity—promoted to his own incompetence. Maybe I was—

"Hey. Rivs." Benson, my roommate, waved a hand in front of my face. "Bus is waiting. We gotta go."

"Right. Right. Sorry." I pushed myself up off the bed where I'd been sitting and tucked my phone into my inside pocket. Buttoning my suit coat, I said, "Ready when you are."

He looked at me kind of like Sidorov had on the plane yesterday. Like I'd said or done something stupid. Which I probably had. Story of my life now that I was in over my head.

He didn't comment on it, though, and in silence, we headed downstairs to join the rest of our team.

I was more than a little disappointed—and kind of alarmed—when I didn't see Landry join us. There was no way he'd slipped past me. He wasn't a scratch tonight, was he? Though he'd still be coming to the game. Unless he was sick? Or hurt?

As casually as I could, I turned to Paxton. "Hey, where's your buddy tonight? Did he finally come down late and actually miss a bus?"

Paxton laughed, glancing up from helping his stepson with his bowtie (which matched his—holy shit, those two were cute). "Nah, remember? He and Karlsson had that promotional thing today. The..." He paused to adjust Chase's bowtie. "That photo thing or whatever with the local youth team."

"Oh. Right." I chuckled, pretending not to be at all

relieved that Landry's absence had a perfectly reasonable and not at all disastrous explanation. Seeing him may have screwed with my ability to play hockey, but being out there without him wasn't quite right either. I'd been playing since I was a toddler, and the time I'd shared a roster with Landry could be measured in weeks, but he'd already become one of those fixtures whose absence was like a stadium light going dark—it just threw everything out of whack.

Plus he would be one less hyper-talented player to distract people from the fact that I probably had no business at this level.

He was coming, though. Nothing to worry about except myself.

*I can get my shit together tonight. Right?* Right?
*Oh fuck. I hope I get my shit together tonight.*

I focused on that. Concentrated on it. Obsessed over it. All the way to the arena, and whenever I had any downtime, I was watching those replays again, mentally running through everything I'd do differently tonight. If I had a shot, I'd take it. If I had the puck and someone else had a better shot, I'd pass it. All common sense stuff that I knew anyway, but I pounded it into my own head like I was a novice instead of a rookie pro.

*I am not going to fuck up tonight's game, damn it.*

Even when we headed out onto the ice for warm-ups, my brain was still in "strategize until no one notices my incompetence" mode. Ironically, I was so fixated on that, I kept losing track of what the whole team was doing. As if our warm-up routine varied even a little bit from one game to the next. Hockey players were way too superstitious for that. So it should've been as automatic as skating, but—

"C'mon, Rivs!" Ozzy gave my skate a tap with his stick as he sped by. "Get them *in* the net!"

I laughed and fired a puck at the goal like I was supposed to do. This one actually went in, so maybe there was hope for me yet...if I was standing still and shooting casually at an empty net.

"Saving all your energy for the game?" Karlsson skated up beside me and looked down at me from six-foot-God-knew-what. "It's warm-ups, kid." He tapped my skate like Ozzy had. "Get moving so you're loose."

"I just didn't want to get in the way of all you old guys who *need* the—"

He huffed a laugh, rolled his eyes, and gave me another smack with his stick before he skated off.

I chuckled too, but I also got my ass to work. Skating. Stretching. Taking a few shots. My teammates had obviously noticed I was off, which meant I needed to unfuck myself. Ideally in the next—I glanced up at the clock—nine minutes and forty-seven seconds.

My teammates weren't being unkind about it, but that was because we were out in the open. Warm-ups weren't broadcast like the game would be, but there were thousands of people in the stands, and most people had camera phones these days. I could read between the lines: "Get your head in the game, or you're going to hear about it in the locker room as soon as there aren't any cameras nearby."

So, as best I could with my head all over the place, I made it through the rest of warm-ups like normal.

At least, I thought I did.

I hadn't even made it all the way to the locker room when one of my teammates halted me.

No, not "one of my teammates."

*That* teammate.

As soon as we were alone, Landry faced me.

"Rivera." He put his hands on my shoulders. "Look at me."

I did, grateful for the gloves and pads that kept him from making actual contact. As much as I'd have sold my soul for him to touch me for real, there was no way I could deal with it right now. Not with my head all over the place and my gaze now locked on the dark eyes of the most intimidating man I'd ever met.

This close up, he was as gorgeous as he was intense. His hair was damp (some from sweat, but mostly from his water bottle) and tousled from his helmet, and some wet strands hung in front of those eyes that were fixed right on me. There was a subtle furrow in his brow—the same one he always had when a camera snapped him in deep concentration during a game. Or when he was pissed. Oh fuck. Was he pissed?

Except he didn't seem to be. He wasn't smiling, but nothing about him really telegraphed anger—just intense focus.

Voice even and discreet, he said, "You're still hung up on the other night." It wasn't a question.

I gulped. "You're good at this."

Expression serious, he shook his head. "No. But I was a rookie once too. I know about the pressure you're under, and if you're anything like me, you're putting most of it on yourself."

I wanted to laugh bitterly at the idea that I could be anything like him, but in this instance, he was right. I dropped my gaze because I couldn't hold his anymore.

"Listen," he said. "I know how easy it is to fixate, but you can't. You can't focus on the past in this game. Once the buzzer goes off, it's over. Clean slate. You can't even wait that long—you fuck up, and then you pick yourself up and move on before someone uses your distraction as an opportunity to score." He gave my shoulder a firm smack before withdrawing his hands. "Mistakes you've made before—they don't matter."

I did let go of that humorless laugh this time. "Except in our stats, right?"

"Do you think about your stats while you're playing?"

"I..." Okay. He had me there. "No, I don't."

"And you shouldn't. All we can do is keep doing our job. When you're out there, the numbers don't matter, and neither does the past."

I swallowed and made myself look up at him. "So how do you shake that off? Because I did for a little while, but then it all..." I flailed a gloved hand. "It all just came crashing right back in."

"What did you do that helped you shake it off?"

I met his eyes. Did he actually want me to spell it out?

For a split second, Julien goddamned Landry looked caught off guard, and even a little flustered. Clearing his throat, he shifted his weight, skates scuffing on the floor beneath us. "What do you think would get you out of your funk?"

"Besides finally scoring a goal?"

At that, Landry smiled. "Would that do it?"

"I think so." I absently prodded at the floor with my stick. "I haven't scored yet this season, and it would make me feel a hell of a lot more like I belong here instead of in the minors."

Landry's smile turned to a lopsided grin, and he smacked my padded shoulder. "Well. Get out there and do it." Jerking his chin toward the ice we'd left, he added, "Score."

"You make it sound so easy."

"What's stopping you?"

Nerves? Confidence? Fear? Incompetence?

But maybe he was right. Maybe that was what I needed.

"Okay." I grinned. "Maybe tonight will be the night."

"That's the spirit." He started to head toward the locker room, but paused. "By the way, I meant what I said—we all fuck up. There are literally video compilations out there of my worst turnovers. Compilations. Plural."

I stared up at him. I knew about those videos because there wasn't a Landry-themed video on the internet that hadn't at the very least gone across my *Recommended For You* bar—including some I absolutely did not need to be thinking about right now—but I played stupid anyway. That wasn't difficult when I was looking at him. "There are?"

He nodded. "Yes. I'm pretty sure there's also one out there from a spectacular fall I took in major juniors." He gave a little self-deprecating laugh. "That was embarrassing enough without being the reason our opponents got the puck and tied up a critical playoff game."

I swallowed, not sure what to say.

And then that became a moot point, because Coach poked his head out of the locker room and barked, "Landry, are you coming in here or not?" His gaze darted to me, and he gave one of those "Dad's down to his last nerve" sighs. "You too, Rivera."

"Coming, Coach." Landry turned to me. "You good?"

"Yeah." I smiled, and though I was still nervous about tonight, I meant it when I said, "I'm good."

# Chapter 4

## Julien

This game was an absolute shit show. Osti d'marde.

The whole team was a mess right now, from Elias on down. Couldn't get our legs, couldn't get to our game. The only reason we were down a single goal in the second was Larry. Once more, he was saving our bacon while we got our heads out of our asses.

We needed to get our heads out of our asses.

When your star center is out of whack, things tend to go badly, and Elias was not having a good night. Coach was bent over, talking into his ear, and he was nodding along.

Nikki was out with his line, trying to make things happen. I was sandwiched between Rivera and my D partner, Paxy. Rivera was talking, a stream of commentary coming out of his mouth. Probably didn't realize he was doing that, either. "Shit," he said when our guys got hemmed into our end. "We can do better than this."

He was right. Especially since the other team wasn't playing spectacular hockey, and the refs were pretty even-handed tonight. But the home team was getting the bounces and juice from the crowd. The arena was loud and raucous, and it was hard to hear your teammates even when you were sitting next to them.

Paxy bumped my shoulder and spoke into my ear. "Someone needs to make something happen."

No shit. I nodded and watched. A minute thirty left. We needed to tilt the ice so we could come out next period with our heads up. Scratch out a win or at least a tie. Get a point.

One of their big defensemen checked Nikki into the boards, and I swear I felt Nikki's irritation come off him in waves. Good. Piss the Russian off. See what happens.

I nudged both Rivera and Paxy. "Here we go. Watch."

When Nikki wanted a puck, it was nearly impossible to stop him. When he was pissed off, magic happened. A couple of nifty moves at the boards, and the puck was flying to our D and Nikki's line was heading north through the neutral zone, full speed, catching the other team's line flat footed in our end. Three on one.

"That's it. That's it!" I was on my feet because I knew. Felt it in my bones.

"Oh shit." Rivera was up too, his glove landing on my shoulder. "Fuck me." Glee in his voice.

I would have fucked anyone in that instant, or fought them. Anything, because energy surged through every one of us.

Sure enough, our D got it up to Ortiz and there was that tic-tac-toe play we could execute so well when the other team was on their heels. Not a fucking chance. Nikki tapped it in past their goalie, and we all reacted like it was a freaking cup game.

Nikki had the widest grin when he came by for fist bumps.

"Lans, Paxy, you're out!" Coach called, and we went over the boards, along with our shutdown line. Just over a minute to go. Only needed to hold the tie, then we could get into the room and build off of Nikki's goal.

Nothing got by me, not a puck, not a player. Coach left me and Paxy out the entire time, but sent Rivera's line out to finish the period. His gaze met mine, and I knew he wanted more. That we had more.

Later that night, they asked me during the media scrum about the play, and I gave some bullshit answer about wanting to get the puck out, then seeing Rivera open, and lucky bounces and all that. Truth was that in those brown eyes, I saw the play. Knew *exactly* what he wanted.

Maybe it was foolish, but when the puck hit my stick, I shoved the guy on me out of the way, wound up, and flew up the ice. There were times when I did this, and it went badly, but tonight? Tonight I knew Rivera was there. Felt exactly where he was on the ice.

I snarled at the goaltender and faked the shot. The goalie moved right and I passed left without looking.

A moment later, the puck sailed into the gaping empty space behind the goalie and the horn sounded. Isaac Rivera's first of the season. First in the league.

Rivera flew into my arms. "You're fucking amazing!"

All I managed to get out before our linemates crushed us in hugs was, "Told you. Welcome to the big time."

With twenty seconds left in the second, we took the lead on Rivera's goal.

After the hugs, I made sure to grab the puck and tossed it to Tavish, our equipment manager, behind the bench. I always made sure the rookies got their first pucks. They *meant* something. They were special. I ignored the sharp stab in my heart and tried to forget that my own first goal puck had been taken from me. Yet another painful memory from my rookie year that I wouldn't dwell on. I caught a glimpse of the word tattooed on my wrist. *Now*. Past was past. Forget it.

The energy in the room during intermission was exhilarating. Coach must have thrown out his scolding speech, because all he said was, "That's how you fucking play the game. Go out there and do that again."

I downed an entire bottle of cherry-flavored electrolytes. When I was done, Nikki slapped me on the back. "Hail King!" The team cackled and laughed.

"Wasn't me. Rivs wanted it. I gave it to him."

Rivera's winger, Ozzy—Valdis Ozols—shoulder-checked him. "Getting it from Lans, now. Lucky you."

Red spots bloomed on Rivera's cheeks, and oh fuck. Those lips and eyes. Those sweaty curls. I was lucky Elias shoved me, because I was probably about to lick my lips or something ridiculous like that.

"Mind reader," he said, quietly.

Maybe. I hoped not, because what I read in Rivera in that moment heated everything in me. The conversation from before the game came back. The one time he hadn't been worried about the game was on the plane. When we'd been playing cards and the gin had loosened me up enough to flirt a little with him.

Idolization and desire. Fuck my life. No time for that—none at all. I shook it off and set about retaping my stick.

"Rivs gave us the lead. Let's go hand the other team their asses."

We did, too. Killing off two penalties (fucking refs) and adding an empty net goal for insurance in the dying minute of the game. That snapped our five-game losing streak and finally got us some goddamned points again.

Rivera's smile at the end of that game was the best thing in the world.

---

THE BUS RIDE to the hotel was loud—the flight home would be very early the next morning—but we all piled into the bar anyway. Too much energy, too much happiness to even think about sleeping yet. An hour later, my brain zinged in that peculiar way it did when I'd immersed myself in too much noise and light and people, so I grabbed my glass of water, tapped Nikki on the shoulder and inclined my head toward the patio balcony.

He nodded, and I slipped free of my teammates and out into the cold night.

The wind was sharp and bitter as I made my way to the railing. For an instant, I was transported back to my childhood in Saguenay. Those long, dark winters. The backyard rink. A far cry from suits and hotels and chartered flights. This was the dream I'd chased as a kid. And here I was in Winnipeg, still chasing dreams and cups. Nothing had changed at all. Still the fool. Still the brat.

Fuck. Maybe I should have gotten a glass of wine after all, if my brain was going to twist into melancholy on me.

Non.

This was only a crash, a comedown from the high of the win. I downed the rest of my water, set my glass down on a nearby table, then leaned against the iron rail. I bowed my head and let the strange stillness of the city on a frozen night sweep over me, let the silence loosen the thoughts I'd stashed away.

Isaac Rivera. Centerman. Dark hair, dark eyes. Looked lanky at first glance, but I'd seen enough in the showers to know the thickness of his thighs and legs and just how muscular his arms and back were.

Fuck.

Wasn't going there. I'd been Rivera, long ago, and had nearly ruined my career when a veteran player had taken interest in me. I pulled out my phone and swiped at the screen until I was staring at my collection of hookup apps, but the shiver that pulsed through me was more biting and bitter than the breeze, so I crammed the phone back into my pocket.

"You know, it's warmer inside."

Maudit.

Of course he'd find me. "I don't want to be warm." A lie, but that's what came out. I was desperate for warmth, for the camaraderie inside that'd been overwhelming. Now I was a crashing, aching mess when I should be happy and cheerful, and the absolute last thing I needed was the friendship of this man. I wouldn't become my own nightmare.

Rivera joined me at the rail. I caught a glimpse of his black pants and suit jacket, but I kept looking down, focusing on the street below. The heat from his body warmed my side, or maybe that was my imagination.

"You know, we won tonight." Low voice with that soft American accent. "Because of you."

I coughed out a laugh. "Not me. Was you, and Nikki. He got us going. You scored the goal." I raised my gaze a fraction. "I know we won."

Rivera was quiet for a handful of breaths. "Then why are you out here?"

"Aucune idée." I had no idea if he understood French, but he didn't deserve two lies from me, so I turned and met the concern in his eyes. "Sometimes, it's too much. The noise. The people. The way my head feels when we win like that. It's..." I searched my English vocabulary for the words to explain how full my head felt, how I thought it might crack apart, and came up short. I shrugged. "And now I'm crashing, so I'm a fucking nightmare to be around." I gestured toward the bar. "They don't need that."

His smile brought a warmth I hadn't felt in a long while. "Yeah, but maybe you do?"

I couldn't do much other than stare at him. He was right, of course. That was the paradox of the moment. I needed to flee because I needed them all too much. My life was this team, these men.

And here was Isaac Rivera, throwing a fucking rock against my carefully constructed glass box.

"Look," he said. "I wanted to thank you. For talking to me. For believing in me." There was a sly little tilt to his grin. "And for passing me the puck."

"You called for it."

"You know I didn't."

But he had. With that look when he'd stepped onto the ice for his shift. I gripped both his shoulders, and stared into those dark, dark eyes. "I knew what you wanted."

His expression shifted, smoldered, and I studied those lips, reading the tension in his body. The glint in his eyes.

"What about now?" Husky voice, so low it wouldn't carry beyond where we stood.

Would be so easy to step into his heat. To give him the kiss he desired, the one I longed for with the same sudden homesickness I'd felt earlier.

I huffed out a breath. "I know now, too."

"And?" He lifted an eyebrow and there was a challenge there, one that lit a fire in me.

*Non, Julien.*

Such a bad idea. I searched his face once more and gave his shoulders a squeeze.

"Not tonight," I whispered. I couldn't say no, didn't want to. But tonight was not a night for yes, not with my head like this. Not with the entire team just inside those doors. I hoped he could read me. Hoped he understood.

God, that smile. No puppy dog eyes this time. I let go of him, and he clapped me on the arm. "Let's go inside. I'll buy you a water."

That drew out a laugh from me, and I let Rivera draw me

back to the team I loved. Later, Nikki patted me on the back. "He's good for you."

*Fuck.* I glared up at him. "What?"

He set down his empty glass. "You always go away. Leave us. Bad game. Good game, you know? You stay for a little bit, then..." He mimicked walking off. "Not good for you or us, Jules. Rivs brought you back out of the cold."

Despite knowing I shouldn't, I glanced around for Rivera. He was over chatting with Larry and Paxy, but the moment my gaze skimmed over him, our eyes locked, and he smiled. Warmth to my toes.

"I don't know if that's a good thing." Rookies were off limits—or they should be. I knew that more viscerally than most.

Players get traded. Young ones. Old ones. I'd heard the rumblings about my own trade value a few times this off-season. Fooling around with a teammate was fine—as long as that's all it was. Chances were, you'd not stay teammates forever. A couple seasons, maybe, between trades and free agency.

That Elias, Nikki, and I had been together eight years? Unusual. Especially since we weren't superstars. Elite, yes. Generational? No.

"Julien, Julien."

Nikki rarely used my full name. I snapped my gaze up, but he shook his head, that mix of amusement and worry that was entirely Nikolai Sidorov written all over his face.

If he had more to say to me, that was interrupted by Elias. "Shit, I'm tired. We should wrap this thing up, or we're all going to miss the plane tomorrow."

Trust our captain, even with a couple beers in him, to be the responsible one.

So we broke the party up. Of course, Rivera ended up in the same elevator cab as me. Luckily, three other guys entered, too. The chatter was about sport cars and soccer. When we got to our floor, we all headed toward our respective rooms. I took three steps, then spun. "Rivera."

He turned halfway toward me—he'd been heading the opposite direction.

"Sit with us on the plane." I had no fucking clue what I was doing. None. But in the now? This felt *right*.

That smirk again, as if he'd caught me, as if he really could read my mess of a mind. "See you tomorrow, Landry."

Tomorrow, too damn early, we'd all be on the bus to the airport, then finally—finally—home. What the hell was I going to do about Isaac Rivera then? What was I doing now? "Night, Rivera."

I turned, dragged myself to my room, shucked my suit off, and fell into bed.

Problem was, I knew exactly what I wanted to do, and I'd already set the wheels in motion. One thing the press got right? I was a stubborn bastard sometimes, including to myself. Reckless, too. Didn't think things through all the way.

Ciboire, I was *fucked*.

## Chapter 5

### Isaac

Landry and I couldn't win at Spades.

The first time we'd played, we'd mopped the floor with Sidorov and Karlsson, but this morning, while our plane sat on the tarmac—delayed, of course—our teammates cackled with glee as they won again and again.

"Maybe we should be playing Gin," Karlsson mused, gesturing at Landry's glass. "At least until you finish that."

Landry responded with a scowl that should not have been that hot, and then a sarcastic grin accompanied by flying the bird.

"You wish." Karlsson kicked him, narrowly missing Sidorov.

"Hey." Sidorov didn't miss Karlsson, driving a pained yelp from our captain. "That'll teach you."

"Hey, come on," I said, sounding almost as nervous as I was. "Let's not hurt him right before our first home game in a while, yeah?"

Sidorov muttered something in Russian. In English, he said to Landry, "Maybe you should finish that, then?"

Landry fixed a glare on him that was decidedly less good-humored, and he held it as he took a long drink from his glass.

I watched the interplay, but said nothing, and our club table was quiet except for the sound of Karlsson shuffling the deck.

The banter between the three of them (and me, to an extent) was sharper than usual this morning. Edged in a way that didn't seem right the morning after a win. I didn't think anyone was mad at anyone else. It was probably just a side effect of being up at are-you-fucking-kidding-me-thirty to make this early-ass flight, which was still on the ground fully two hours after it was supposed to take off. Weather, from the sound of it. I wasn't sure if it was weather in Pittsburgh or between there and here, only that Winnipeg looked clear from my window. Not that I could see much, since it was still dark.

Well, whatever. I was eager to get home and sleep in my own bed. At the same time, I wasn't going to complain about hanging out with these three. Especially Landry. Even if they were all bitchy like kids who'd been dragged out of bed and shoved onto the school bus.

Karlsson finished shuffling. Landry finished his drink.

And we still couldn't get our shit together.

"So the mind-reading was a fluke!" Sidorov smacked Landry on the back, earning him the kind of glare I usually only got from my mom's cat.

"It *wasn't* a fluke," Landry informed him. His gaze slid toward me, and the glare softened to something less feline but decidedly more feral. "I can read him just fine."

"Reading *him* isn't the problem." Karlsson pointed emphatically at Landry. "It's reading you that takes... I don't know. Magic or some shit." He eyed me. "*Was* that a fluke?"

I held Landry's gaze. No. No, it wasn't a fluke. I couldn't read a single thing in his face right now that had to do with cards, but I could absolutely read him. Instead of figuring out which cards he'd throw during that last game or which cards I should throw, I read things that had me grateful for the table hiding my lap from the other guys. And from him. Especially from him.

Could I still read Landry? Uh-huh. And everything I read was pornographic as all hell. Which probably meant I was seeing things, and I should really—

The upward flick of Landry's eyebrow told me I'd been staring at him stupidly for a beat too long while he and our teammates waited for my answer. I quickly cleared my throat and turned to Karlsson. "Of course I can." I laughed. "I don't get why it's so hard for you guys."

Karlsson scowled and rolled his eyes, muttering something I didn't catch.

I slid my gaze back to Landry, and the corners of his mouth had risen in a grin. One that was probably meant to tell me I'd said the right thing, but all I could see was...

No. I was imagining that.

*God. Get a grip, Rivera.*

I shook myself. "So are we going to play another game, or what?"

We did, and they handed us our asses again.

Sidorov had just finished explaining how terrible we were at Spades and how our near-telepathy on the last flight clearly *had* been a fluke when the announcement finally came that we were about to take off. A collective sigh of relief went through the cabin...except for Landry.

After we'd put up the table, he tilted his glass back to catch whatever precious gin might be lurking at the bottom, then closed his eyes and pressed back against his seat. His jaw worked and his knuckles were white as he held on to his glass.

He definitely wasn't hard to read now, and not in the flustering way he had been all morning. It was no secret that Landry hated flying. Once we were in the air, he'd be better, and I silently pleaded with the pilot and the control tower and the ground crew and whoever else had a hand in things to get this plane off the ground *stat*.

My pleas were answered, and for once it wasn't a "hahaha, no." Within minutes, we were taxiing toward the runway while the flight attendants gave the usual safety spiel. Then they sat down, and in no time, the plane had taken off.

As we ascended and my ears popped a couple of times, some of the tension unwound in Landry's features. The line of his mouth softened. His jaw wasn't so tight. His neck, his shoulders, even the fingers around his glass.

The more he relaxed, the more I did too. I hated seeing him like that. I had to wonder, too, if he'd been even worse about flying early in his career. Like if time and the frenetic regular season schedule had desensitized him a little. Or if something had happened during that time. A rough flight, maybe. I was curious what it was about flying that fucked with him.

As if there was anything about this man that hadn't piqued my curiosity, but now wasn't the time to be thinking about that. Not until they let us put out the tables again. Sidorov and Karlsson would never let me hear the end of it if I got an inflight hard-on. And God help me if Landry noticed.

The announcement finally came that tray tables could come out, and the flight attendants started coming through to serve breakfast. Breakfast? Was it still morning? Probably. Maybe. I didn't even want to know what time it was. Food had been served at the hotel before we'd left, but that had been at oh-God-o'clock and I hadn't eaten much. Plus I was pretty sure that had been like nine hours ago. Okay, five. Whatever. Point was, I was starving, and unlike commercial airlines, the team's charter had *spectacular* food.

Landry didn't order another drink. He never seemed particularly drunk on flights, so I guess that wasn't much of a surprise. And unlike when we were flying into another city, we had to get ourselves home after we'd landed. So he must've wanted to sober up enough to drive safely.

*Which is a good thing, Rivera, and not a missed opportunity to offer to drive his drunk ass home.*

Our food came, and the four of us fell into some banter that was more chill and less sharp-edged than earlier. That must've meant we were all waking up and not quite so bitchy over the early morning and late flight. We were on our way home. After a much-needed win. This was how we *should* feel and sound and interact.

After the dishes had been cleared away, Karlsson smacked the cards emphatically in the middle of the table. "Let's see if Nisha and I can make it a clean sweep."

Landry smirked, leaning his forearms on the table and looking right at me. "Well, Rivera? You up for it?"

I couldn't make any promises about my Spades prowess or my ability to read him, but why the hell not? "Sure." I sat up. "Let's do this."

True to form, I read Landry like a book. Every thought that could be hidden in the upward flick of an eyebrow or the knowing lift of the corner of his mouth, I read it loud and clear. From the subtle way his lips would tighten or his chin would dip, he saw and heard everything going on in my head too.

Unfortunately, none of it had a damn thing to do with Spades, and our teammates made mincemeat of us. Again.

Karlsson fist-bumped Sidorov across the table. "A shutout!"

Landry huffed a sharp laugh as he collected the cards into a stack. "Shame you're not a goalie and this isn't hockey."

Karlsson rolled his eyes and muttered something. Landry must've caught it, or at least caught the undertone, because he chuckled as he handed the cards back.

The early morning and recent breakfast were starting to catch up with us. The cards went back into Karlsson's bag. Sidorov settled in to catch a nap. Before long, so did Karlsson. The flight was only like two and a half hours, and a lot of the guys were grabbing power naps so they'd be awake enough to drive once we made it back to the training facility where we'd left our cars.

I managed to doze for a little while. When I woke up, we were still in the air, Karlsson was still out cold beside me, and Sidorov was snoring just loud enough to carry over the low, steady noise of the plane.

And Landry...

Landry was wide awake.

And watching me.

He had a glass in his hand that was about three-quarters full. Probably just water, since he had to drive soon.

Then he put the glass down on the table between us and picked up his phone. "The in-flight WiFi is incredibly fast."

From anyone else, it would have sounded like a random bit of small talk. Except there it was—that subtle eyebrow flick. The look that said he wasn't actually marveling at the speed of the plane's internet.

I took the hint, pulled out my phone, and logged into the WiFi.

When I looked up again. Landry was typing.

Then my text app pinged, and I opened it to find a message from him.

*That first time playing Spades—it wasn't a fluke.*

The words sent heat rushing through me. We were doing this? We were doing this. Right here at thirty-some-odd thousand feet, surrounded by our oblivious and/or unconscious teammates, we were going to look this thing in the eye.

I was pretty good at typing on my phone. Fast and

without errors. This time, not so much. It took an embarrassingly long time to write out and send, *You don't think so?*

I didn't think it was either, but I didn't want to put my skate in my mouth, so I took the spineless route.

Landry read the message, then looked at me through his lashes, and that grin made me forget the rules to not just Spades, but every card game I'd ever played. Probably hockey too. He started typing. My heart started pounding. What was he writing? Where was this going? And why was I absolutely convinced Sidorov or Karlsson were going to wake up, look over one of our shoulders, and know what was happening? Or that the WiFi would fritz out and send our messages to every phone on the plane and on the ground for good measure?

I liked to think I was a pretty rational and reasonable person (outside of the rare occasion when I threw gloves), but when it came to Landry, that all went out the window.

My phone chirped, startling me so bad I fumbled it onto the table.

Across from me, Landry chuckled, though I doubted anyone else heard it. When I met his gaze, there was something sly in his expression, but also...not? Nerves, maybe?

Then I read the message.

*It's like trying to play hockey when the other team's fans are too loud.*

I read it a couple of times, letting the words sink in. I knew exactly what he meant. Even when it was our own fans, it was still hard to hear each other.

*So too much noise,* I wrote back. I hesitated, then added, *How do we shut off the noise this time?*

Before I could stop myself, I sent it. Heart still pounding, I watched him. And I waited.

Landry read my messages. More than once, I thought.

He put his phone facedown on the table and looked right in my eyes. Just like during the Spades games, I could read him, and this time I wasn't trying to concentrate on anything else. My attention was fully fixed on him and on everything we'd been trying and failing to ignore while the cards were on the table.

This wasn't wishful thinking. I knew how Julien Landry looked at me on the ice, across a breakfast table, over cards. The way he was looking at me now, that had only happened recently, and right now, he wasn't even trying to hide it. Neither was I.

Jesus Christ. If eye-fucking counted, Landry and I would be in the Mile High Club by now. Probably in the hall of fame.

*"Not tonight,"* he'd said while we'd been outside the hotel bar.

My heart sped up again, and I broke eye contact so I could type something out on my screen. By the time I sent the message, I was dizzy with nerves and God knew what else.

*What did "not tonight" mean?*

Phone down. Gaze up.

Landry didn't immediately look away as his phone vibrated beside his hand. No, he held that stare just long enough to screw with my head even more than he already had. Then and *only* then, he picked up his phone.

The surprise that registered on his face gave me a zing of excitement, but also a cold rush of panic. Had I gone too far? Been too direct? Shit. Was it too late to unsend the—of course it was, since he'd read it and was apparently reading it again. Oh, fuck.

And was that...

Was Julien Landry *blushing*?

Oh my God. He was. Holy crap, that was cute. And hot.

Then he started typing.

Paused.

Backspaced.

Started typing.

Paused.

Muttered something under his breath and—I thought—cleared away what he'd already written.

Damn. Had I gotten him flustered? Or was he trying to gently explain that "Not tonight" was Landryspeak for "Keep dreaming, kid"?

Right then, the pilot came over the speaker and informed us that we were about to start our descent. The WiFi would be going off in five minutes. Landry hissed a curse. All around us, our teammates began to stir. Tables stayed out for the moment, but guys started shuffling things into bags and finishing drinks. Karlsson got up and shuffled toward the lavatory. Sidorov rubbed a hand over his face and grumbled in that grouchy way he always did when he didn't want to be awake. That would usually prompt some ribbing from Landry about "Well, good morning, Sunshine," but not this time.

Seemingly oblivious to our teammates or even our surroundings, Landry chewed his lip and he stared at his screen. I gnawed the inside of my cheek. Had I overstepped?

Before I could send another message and try to do some damage control, he started typing again, faster this time. Then he sent it, and before my phone had even vibrated, he'd pushed his into the inside pocket of his jacket.

With absolutely no idea what to expect, I looked at my screen.

*Do with this what you will.*

Below that, an address.

It took me a second to put the pieces together. The address was in Sewickley Heights, which I'd been told was one of the wealthier towns outside of Pittsburgh. It was also fairly close to our training facility in Cranberry Township. For that reason, a lot of my teammates lived out there.

Including Landry.

Which meant...

Oh. Fuck.

My head snapped up, and his expression was a clash of emotions. More apprehension than I'd ever seen in him. Some playfulness and some challenge. And an unmistakable hunger that easily matched my own.

*Well, Rivera?* his eyes seemed to ask. *What's it gonna be?*

---

BEFORE I KNEW IT, we were all getting off the bus outside the training facility in Cranberry. Some of the guys were talking about hitting up the golf course while the weather was still halfway decent. Others were going to pick up their kids after school and spend an evening doing family stuff. I was behind Landry when Sidorov asked him about his plans for the rest of the day.

"Don't know." Landry shrugged. "I might spend it in bed."

If I'd been drinking right then, I'd have spit it all over the back of Landry's suit jacket. Fortunately, my water bottle was safely capped and in my hand...so it just went flying when I stumbled.

Karlsson caught me by the arm. "Easy, there. Let's not put you on the injured list right after you scored your first goal."

I laughed, a little rush of excitement cutting through the warmth of embarrassment. I had scored my first goal, hadn't I? A game-winning one, too! How cool was that? I wondered if they'd all think I was a dork if they knew I'd spent a good half hour just staring at that puck in my room last night. Turning it over and over in my hands, reading and rereading the handwritten words on the white tape:

*Isaac Rivera. First Goal. From Julien Landry.*

My first pro goal. Holy shit.

And it had come off a pass from Landry.

Landry, who had stopped and was now looking at me like I'd lost my mind. I wondered if anyone else noticed the mischievous sparkle in his eyes.

Sidorov picked up my water bottle. "I believe you dropped something, rookie."

"Uh. Yeah." I smiled sheepishly as I took it from him. "Thanks."

He nodded. He cut his eyes toward Landry. Back to me. Back to Landry. Then he rolled them, shook his head, and kept walking, muttering under his breath.

Landry snickered and fell into step beside him.

I wasn't sure I wanted to know what that was all about, or if Sidorov had half a clue what Landry had meant by spending part of the day in bed.

We all kept walking, and I was grateful the media guys weren't hovering around with their cameras to get footage of us for the hype videos they posted before games. I doubted they'd include me tripping over my own feet and throwing my water bottle, but I'd just as soon that footage didn't exist at all.

In the parking lot, everyone dispersed and headed for their cars. I looked around for Landry, but he and his bright red BMW were gone.

Settling into my own car, I started the engine but didn't put it in gear yet.

*Do with this what you will.*

Landry's words echoed in my ears as if he'd whispered them to me instead of texting them.

So...now what?

I tapped my thumbs on the wheel. Go home? Go to Landry's? What the hell was I supposed to do?

I definitely knew what I *wanted* to do. There were all kinds of reasons I shouldn't—something, something, make things weird on the team, something, something, risk my career—but it was hard to hear them over the reasons I wanted to put the pedal to the floor and get my ass to Sewickley Heights.

Squeezing my eyes shut, I exhaled. I could tell myself we shouldn't cross this line, but really, hadn't we crossed it already? Were things ever going to get un-weird between us if we let this tension keep crackling as if we had any hope of ignoring it?

And what if I disappointed him? Because Landry's reputation wasn't exactly a big secret. I'd seen most of what he had to offer long before I'd ever shared a locker room with him because of that, ahem, video that leaked onto the internet a few years back. The one with Landry and another couple, where the guys definitely hadn't been *solely* focused on *her*. I hadn't watched it all—I'd closed it as soon as I'd realized what it was, since it seemed intrusive as hell to watch something like that, though I heard rumors later that Julien himself had leaked the video. And there were plenty of *other* rumors of him with—he got around, is the point.

Me? I'd been so focused on hockey that I could count the number of times I'd slept with someone on one hand. Not the number of people—the number of times. Well, and the people too—both of them.

I didn't imagine I was going to do much to impress he of the multi-notched bedpost and at least one bisexual threesome.

But he *had* given me his address.

Maybe he didn't want to hash this out via texts while we were on a plane surrounded by our teammates. Maybe he wanted to let me down easily in private. Maybe—

*"Don't know,"* he'd told Sidorov. *"I might spend it in bed."*

I gulped. Okay. So he had something in mind. All I could do was follow his lead and hope I caught on to how he liked things before he figured out that the ice wasn't the only place where I was a rookie.

Fuck it.

I took out my phone, punched the address into my GPS, and headed out of the mostly empty parking lot. As the GPS counted down the miles to the exit, my heart raced and my dick insisted on being uncomfortably hard. What could I say? The anticipation was killing me.

In my mind, I tried to imagine how things would go, same way I envisioned plays on the ice before they happened. Where we'd be. What we'd do. Small talk to break the ice. Then someone would move in and get physical. And then... Jesus, I couldn't help the goose bumps every time my brain got to this part.

I had no clue what Landry might be like in bed, or what he might want, but it was hard to imagine him being bad at sex or kissing or anything that could happen once I reached his house. That was quite possibly because I'd never seen him do anything badly. Hockey. Spades. He even effortlessly held his own in the press scrums, though we all razzed him because while his answers were always professional, his eyes could never hide the sarcasm or the cattiness. Like no one else's, that man's eyes could convey, "Are you fucking kidding me?" or "Really? *Really?* You're going to ask me that in front of a camera? Seriously?"

I chuckled as I drove. His interviews were always so entertaining, and not just because I'd been crushing on him since forever. His unspoken answers were hilarious.

And now I was suddenly on the receiving end of Landry's non-verbal communication. And on my way to his house. And...

I gripped the wheel tighter and took a few slow, deep breaths. Once again, I ran through how I thought things would go down when I arrived. Go to the door. Go inside.

Exchange some small talk. Feel each other out a bit. Probably wait for him to make a move physically, if only so I could be absolutely sure I was reading him right.

The GPS told me to get off the interstate. The directions got a little convoluted from there, and it didn't help that I was still running through the play in my head.

*Door. Inside. Small talk. Wait for a physical move. Go from there.*

I turned off the main drag and into a neighborhood that looked familiar. Didn't Sidorov live out here? I was pretty sure he did. I'd been to his house for his annual pre-opening-night barbecue, and...yeah, this was definitely the neighborhood. In fact, that was his house. I wondered how many of my other teammates lived out here.

According to the GPS, at least one lived half a mile up the road.

I took another deep breath.

*Door. Inside. Small talk. Wait for a physical move. Go from there.*

The GPS directed me onto a road that went out of Sidorov's neighborhood and into what looked like rich people farm country—huge houses on enormous plots of land. Some were surrounded by fences or brick walls with wrought-iron gates. Others were tucked back behind trees.

And there was Landry's driveway.

I gulped.

*Door. Inside.*

The driveway wound through some trees.

*Small talk.*

It snaked around and cut a path through a manicured lawn toward a large white house.

*Wait for a physical move.*

"You have arrived at your destination."

*Go from there.*

With my heart hammering in my chest, I parked in front of the four-car garage, got out, and headed up to the porch.

*Just breathe. Remember the play.*

*Door. Inside. Small—*

The door opened before I'd cleared the last step, and somehow I didn't trip for the second time today.

He'd taken off his jacket and tie, and he'd unbuttoned the first couple of buttons of his shirt. Just like the night he'd startled me outside the hotel after that abysmal loss, he looked perfectly stylish and sexy, and...oh fuck, I couldn't believe he was looking at me like *that*.

"Hey." I swept my tongue across my lips as I stopped in front of him. "I, um... I hope I'm not..."

The grin broadened. Landry stepped aside and gestured for me to come in.

*Door. Inside—*

*Fuck it.*

Landry shut the door behind us. "I wasn't sure you'd—"

I shoved him up against the door and kissed him.

Landry tensed, but he didn't even give me a chance to worry I'd made the wrong move before his arm slid around my waist and his other hand went up into my hair. Oh God, was that a moan? From him? Yeah, it was. And pressed together like this, there was no avoiding the fact that we were both hard, but I was mostly caught up in how he kissed, because...oh...*wow*.

He wasn't as aggressive as I thought he'd be. I mean, he grabbed on, and he returned my kiss with feverish intensity, but he didn't take over. If anything, he kind of...melted? As if he wasn't just *letting* me take the lead—he *wanted* me to take it?

I'd fantasized before about running my fingers through his long hair, and I decided, why not? Still keeping him against the door with my body, I combed my fingers through his hair, marveling at the softness and the warmth.

"Pull it," he murmured, barely breaking the kiss.

"Pull—wait, what?"

His lips curved against mine and his hand tightened in my hair. "*Pull*. It." The subtle sting of my hair tugging at my scalp sent goose bumps all the way down my spine.

I gripped his hair tighter. "Like that?"

"Harder," he growled, rubbing his erection against mine. "When I say pull it, I mean—ooh, fuck." The shudder that went through him when I pulled his hair turned every fantasy I'd ever had about him to dust. "Fuuuck, Rivera."

"Isaac."

"Huh?"

"Call me... Call me Isaac."

Landry drew back enough to meet my gaze, and holy shit, his eyes were on fire. "I'll call you anything you want as long as you get these clothes off."

I shivered, which inadvertently tightened my grip on his hair, and the choked little moan that escaped his lips almost made getting naked a moot point. "Clothes off. Sounds good."

He licked his lips and nudged me back a step, and as we started to untangle, he said in a low, needy voice, "Upstairs."

I didn't argue.

# Chapter 6

## Julien

Fuck *going to*—we were doing this. Finding Rivera—Isaac—on my porch, still in his suit, had sent my pulse skyrocketing. Him slamming me against my door and kissing me? That had been sublime. And the way he pulled my hair when ordered? Yes, please. I was rock hard, needy, and wanted out of these damn clothes.

We shouldn't be doing this. *I* shouldn't be doing this, but maybe one night would get this out of our system. I ignored the scoffing in my mind, and led Isaac up to my bedroom.

The sun streamed in from the balcony doors. I'd left my suitcase by the entry to the walk-in closet. My jacket and tie were tossed on a bench by the bed. Normally, I loved wearing my suits, but right now? I didn't want anything on me but Isaac.

When I faced him, some of the hesitancy he'd had on the plane and at the practice facility had returned as he took in the bedroom—but only some.

I could work with that. I cocked my head and stared at him, undoing another button on my shirt, and a moment later he was walking me back toward my bed, and knocking my hands out of the way of his. I hit the bench, which forced me to sit on my jacket. He straddled my legs with those thick thighs of his and worked my shirt open.

"Clothes off." Isaac's voice was low, almost a rumble, as he pushed my shirt from me. I looked up, saw the fire I felt in his eyes, and once more we were in sync. He reached down as I reached up, and he had my mouth. His fingers tangled into my hair again, and—

Ah, fuck. I moaned into Isaac because the sharp pain against my scalp was so good. When we broke the kiss, he looked a little dazed, but as hungry as I felt.

I leaned back and grinned up at him. "Lose *your* clothes if you want to fuck me."

He peeled off his suit jacket, tie, and shirt in short order, placing them neatly on a nearby chair. That was glorious to watch, with those dark brown eyes focused on me, and his gaze flicking between my tattoos, then lingering on the stylized smoke from the firebird that disappeared under my waistband.

"Pants," he said. "Get them off." He stepped back to unbuckle his belt.

I didn't break eye contact when I pushed myself to standing. "Thought you'd never ask." Pants, underwear, socks, I shucked them all, even as Isaac did the same.

We'd seen each other naked, of course—locker rooms, showers. There was no privacy, really. The team staff got eyefuls of naked players every practice and every game. But seeing Isaac like this? Ruddy from wanting me? His cock full and hard? An absolute delight.

I needed this man inside me. Screw the rules. Fuck my past. I didn't care.

He breathed out. "God, I don't even know where to begin." He coasted a hand over my chest, sending shivers down my back. I stepped closer, my hand landing on his hip.

"Well, I'm here. The bed is there. There's condoms and lube in the table to the—"

He crushed my mouth against his, hand tight in my hair. This kiss was more demanding than the last, and I melted and moaned as he tightened his hold on my hair and dug his fingers into my ass.

I didn't know how much experience Isaac had, with men or otherwise, but the way he kissed me...he'd at least done this part before. Maybe not the hair-pulling, but the way his lips moved over mine, the little bites, the sweep of his tongue.

This man could kiss.

And yes, he could pull hair well, too. His latest tug nearly sent me to my knees, and I whimpered against him.

When he came up for air, he stared at me, breathless. "You really like that?"

I rolled my hips, rubbing our dicks together. "Whatever gave you that idea?"

Isaac rolled his eyes. "Fuck you."

"Well, yes. I'm trying to get you to do that, but you're—"

Isaac pulled me away from the bench at the foot of the bed, rotated me enough to clear it, then pushed me hard onto the mattress. "Do you ever stop talking during sex?"

"This isn't sex yet, and no, not really, not unless I'm moaning or crying or—"

He crawled on top of me, took my dick in one hand, then kissed me so hard, I could only close my eyes and groan.

"Like that?" he murmured against my lips, amusement licking his words. He lazily stroked my shaft, his hand so warm against me.

I stretched under him. "That's a reasonable start." I probably should have warned him I was a complete brat in bed. "Bet you can do better."

"God, you're like a fucking housecat. Unrepentantly demanding."

I hooked a leg around him and ground up, trapping his hand between our cocks. "Do you mind?"

His laugh was a little high. "No, but this isn't anything like I expected." His hand was free now, his weight an exhilarating press against me, and the thrill of his dick against mine momentarily stole my senses, then Isaac's fingers were in my hair, pulling and tugging. He thoroughly kissed my mouth, then my neck, and I was putty in his hands. I liked sex rougher, but we could work up to that. This? This was fine. "Oui, Isaac. That."

"God, Landry." He pressed his forehead against my chest, then licked at one of my nipples. "Shut. It. I can't *think* when you talk."

"Julien," I whispered. No one had ever called me Julien during sex, but I wanted Isaac to. "It's Julien."

"That's not any better." He stared down at me. "You and your damn accent." Then he yanked my hair again, harder than any of the times before.

I cried out and thrust against him. "Fuck, please," I babbled, because words weren't going to stop spilling from my lips until he had me writhing in pleasure. Too keyed up. Too into him. When was the last time I'd actually known the person I'd fallen into bed with? "Isaac," I hissed. "Please make me stop talking."

He stared down at me, his gaze drilling into my skull, then those perfect, full lips rounded into recognition, and heat blazed through me.

Finally. Finally.

"Stuff's in the nightstand?" His eyes were pure fire.

I nodded, and so did he.

Then his mouth was on mine again, almost brutally, and we rutted and frotted against each other, wrestling for purchase. God, I was going to come like this, his cock rubbing against mine, his mouth brutalizing my lips, then raining surprisingly gentle kisses down my jaw. Teeth sliding delightfully over my chin.

I wanted bites and scratches. Domination.

Isaac caught my hair again and yanked hard. That was just as good, and I was gone, a moaning and writhing mess as he tugged and cursed and fucked his dick against my thigh. The fingers of his other hand dug into my ass cheek hard enough that I'd probably have marks tomorrow.

So good. I could only moan and thrust, my climax hovering somewhere just beyond my reach. Needed more. So much more. I struggled against him, wanting his strength, needing to be manhandled and crushed and—

"Fuck," he growled, low and deep. "You little fucking—"

Câlisse, Isaac was strong. Stronger than me. His grip, his arms and legs. I wasn't weak in any sense of the word, but he was compact and thick and damn, could he use that. He flipped me over on the bed, caught my wrists, and had them clamped at the small of my back, all his weight holding me down. Fuck, I was going to come.

"Isaac!" I heard the desperation in my voice. "Please, I need you inside me."

He slapped my ass. Not enough to hurt, but I yelped anyway.

"Getting there," he gritted out. "God, you're a handful."

"You think?"

This time, the smack did sting. "Don't you dare move."

I didn't. I wanted what was coming, and given the thighs on Isaac, hopefully I'd get it hard and strong.

He didn't waste any time finding my condoms and lube. "I haven't done this that often. I hope—"

"Fucking stick your fingers inside me."

Next thing I knew, Isaac had me pressed hard against the mattress. "God, I should tie you up."

Maybe next time. I didn't say that, but I laughed until the

lube hit my crack and Isaac plunged a finger inside me. My vision twisted, and I moaned.

"Oh, damn, you're tight."

"Been a while," I managed.

His laugh was breathless. "You really don't shut up, do you?"

I couldn't answer because he found my prostate, heat raced to my balls, and I lost all words. English. French. What came out was a long moan of pleasure as Isaac held me down.

"There we go," he said.

I could only whimper in agreement.

He took his time opening me. I would have protested, but I still couldn't make my brain or my tongue work. Felt so damn good, I was on the edge of coming, and scrabbling at the comforter.

Given the chuckle, he was enjoying himself. "You're so damn hot. Goddamn, I never imagined *this*."

*Please just fuck me already.* What came out was a sob.

He must have figured the meaning out, because a wrapper tore, and a moment later he gripped my hip. Then he was pressing into me, and I was going to lose what was left of my mind.

"Oh fuck, Julien." His other hand found my hip, and he thrust in deeper, his strokes slow and obnoxiously careful.

I pushed up onto my hands, levering myself back against him. "Isaac," I warned. "If you don't fucking *fuck* me I'm going to—"

Those fingers dug into my hip, and he thrust hard. "I'm trying to be gentle."

"Fuck gentle!" I gasped when he started to rail me, then sobbed as he pulled me back against him using my hair.

"Fuck your mouth." I'd never heard Isaac growl so deep. Perfect. Absolutely perfect.

"Next time," I whimpered. "Please."

He groaned, pushed me over, and whatever inhibitions he'd had about pounding into me vanished. I was gone, too, a fucking sobbing mess as Isaac rode my ass hard and fast, stripping me of every coherent thought. There was only light and heat and pain and my orgasm approaching like a six-foot nine enforcer intent on ramming me into the boards.

Isaac wrapped a hand around my cock and jerked me off until I was screaming and crying actual tears, then he was shouting in my ear, and we both fell hard against the mattress, his weight crushing me into the soft surface.

"Câlisse," I murmured when I could think enough to make words again. Been a while since I'd been fucked like that. Come like that. My whole body hummed and ached, and Isaac was a pleasant weight on top of me. Heavy. Solid. I shivered, wanting more of him. So much more of those lips and that cock and those strong hands and thighs pinning me down.

Could I get him to bite me? We had all day to find out. I sighed and melted into the mattress.

Isaac stirred. "Are you okay?"

"Oui."

"I should—" He shifted and pulled out, and I sighed again.

Rustling sounds. Tissues, probably. A soft thump. Into the trashcan, most likely. The bed bobbled, and Isaac's warm hand stroked my back. "I didn't hurt you, did I?"

I could only laugh. "Ouin ça va." I rolled on my side and smiled up at him. "Pourquoi?"

Isaac furrowed his brow. "Um, my French is kind of limited."

Right. Oregon. Crisse, I was out of it. "You didn't hurt me at all. Why do you ask?"

Isaac slid down next to me, and I pulled part of the comforter over us before wrapping an arm and a leg around him.

He swept fingers over my tear-damp face. "You were crying, and...I was kind of rough."

"Kind of, yes." I couldn't help teasing him.

When those sweet eyes of his met mine, there was annoyance, frustration, and a little hint of fear. I traced the line of his jaw. Despite him being a rookie, he wasn't that much younger than me. A handful of years only. Our paths to the league had been vastly different, and I'd ended up here before he had. Still... "Have you been with many people?"

That got me a sigh. "A couple of guys. I—hockey was more important."

"There's nothing wrong with that." I pushed his sweat-dampened curls off his forehead. "Hey. I was curious, that's all. No judgment."

His groan was all frustration, and he didn't meet my gaze. "I know you have more experience."

I snorted. "Lot of good it's done me over the years." The one thing that debacle with Travis had taught me: Nearly every person who'd ever fucked me was only doing so because I was pretty. Or famous. Or both. Very few people wanted me for my personality. Especially since my reputation for a lack of one preceded me.

Vapid and vain Julien Landry. A fantastic fuck, but that was all I was good for. No brains in my skull. That had bled over into how people spoke about my hockey. Low hockey IQ. All flash, no grit. Yet another reason I'd stopped sleeping around over the last year or so. I'd had a few hookups during the off-season while overseas, where less people knew me by sight, but none since then. A change from my early years when I didn't care as much about my image, or at least not in the same way as now. I'd even leaked a video of a threesome partly as a way of coming out as pansexual.

I nuzzled Isaac's nose, then gave him a quick kiss. "You're more clever than me in that regard."

This time Isaac did meet my gaze. "I don't want to hurt you. Or make you mad. Or—disappoint you."

"Do I need to roll you over onto the spot where you fucked all my cum out of me?" Oh, the red cheeks at that. "I'm not disappointed. That was perfect, I promise."

The blush remained and was joined by a fiery glint in his eyes. "So, not too rough."

I grinned back at him. "I'm a defenseman, you know."

He laughed. "Wait, do you like being thrown into the boards?"

"Not the *boards*, no."

Ah, there was his ability to read me, come back to life. The wide eyes, the sudden comprehension.

Walls. Furniture. Doors. The floor. I liked things rough. Wasn't always easy to get. Or safe. "People think I'm soft."

His bark of laughter held disbelief. "How?"

I shrugged. "Toxic masculinity? How can someone with a pretty face and pretty hair be *strong*?" I ran my fingers over his jaw again, then settled my hand on his hip.

He was quiet for a long moment. "That's such bullshit." Vehemence there. Anger. "I've seen you fight. You're a *defenseman*, for Christ's sake."

"I know. I know." I searched his eyes, hoping I wasn't about to make a huge mistake. "You're the first person I've had sex with in a very, *very* long time who I know and *like*. Who I'd like to know better. Have more than one night with." I paused and glanced toward the doors to the balcony. "Well, day, but—"

Goddamn, those eyes. Like he actually saw me. Only two other people came close to that, and in that moment, Isaac surpassed both. "You want to date?"

I wanted to date. I huffed out a high laugh. "I'm not sure I'm datable. I'm—a loose cannon. I have a reckless streak. Also, you're a teammate." And he was a rookie. Sure, older than I'd been—he was twenty-two rather than my just barely nineteen—but he was still new to the league. I'd been here eight years now. A veteran, a leader.

He shrugged. "We can see where it goes?" He pursed those miraculous lips of his. "I never got the sense you were a loose cannon or reckless, though."

I laughed outright at that. "Oh my God. I really am. Especially when it comes to sex. I'm so lucky only a couple things have leaked out on the internet." Granted, I'd been the one to do the leaking on one of those. The others? Not so much.

That renewed blush and that sheepish look told me he'd found *those*.

Well, *well*. I chuckled, pulled him close, and kissed his forehead. "Let me tell you a story. Then you can decide what you want to do."

He propped himself up on his elbow. "Okay."

"There's this blogger who hates me. Truly *hates* me. Claims to be a fan of the team, but every other comment is about how I'm soft and weak and lazy. Not worth my contract. Totally useless to the team." I snorted. "Noise. I ignored it, but people kept bringing it up, and he tagged me in his shit, and sometimes it would leak through the filters."

Isaac's face hardened suddenly. "Oh. *That* guy. He—doesn't do that anymore."

"No, he doesn't." I ran my hand over Isaac's thigh, then returned it to his waist. "A few years ago, he came to our charity casino night."

I enjoyed those events. Looked forward to them, even. Fans were generally well-behaved, and it was fun to meet people in a controlled environment like that. They're happy. Excited to meet the players. Plus, the money raised was given to children's charities. What more could you ask for?

"Oh shit. Did he give you trouble?"

I shook my head. "Not in the way you mean. Didn't come

near me. He merely stared at me the entire night. Always in my view, no matter what I was doing. It was irritating, because I was trying to be a good host. Banter. Smile. Have fun. But there he was." Both Nikki and Elias had spotted him too, and tried to engage, to keep him away from me. Didn't work.

Isaac combed his fingers through my hair, slowly and gently now. "What happened?"

"At the event? Nothing. But I noticed the way he looked at me, you know? Like he couldn't *not* look."

I rolled onto my back and peered up at the wooden beams that led to the peaked ceiling. "I always get a hotel room after those nights. I'm too exhausted from being on for hours. I don't want to drive all the way back here to collapse."

"You fucked him."

Perceptive. I waved a hand. "I wanted to prove a point to that jackass about strength and stamina, and who I was. So yes. At the end of the night, he was at the bar, still watching me, so I went over."

Elias had started toward me, but Nikki had stopped him, and they'd had a short but intense conversation. I'd given both a "calm down" gesture. Wasn't like I was going to punch the guy out or anything. What I had done, once I'd gotten close enough, was cock my head and check him out, unabashedly.

That had made him stiffen in more ways than one. "All I said to him was the name of my hotel, my room number, and that he should wait two hours. Then I walked away."

"He showed up." Isaac flattened his hand against my stomach, then drew circles around my belly button.

I shivered, both from his touch and the memory. So many things could have gone wrong that night. "He did. So, I threw a box of condoms and a bottle of lube on the bed, then said, 'You think I'm weak. Here's your chance to prove it. See if you can fuck me hard enough to get me off.'"

Isaac went still. "Shit, Julien. He could have hurt you."

"Like I said. Reckless." When I'd told Elias and Nikki about it later, Elias was beside himself, and even Nikki was upset with me. I'd learned exactly how "You goddamned fucking fool" was pronounced in Russian, because Nikki had repeated it about twenty times. Loudly.

Silence, then Isaac stirred. "Did he? Get you off."

I huffed. "No. Not at all. Tried three times. He came, but I didn't. I didn't even get hard, honestly. I kept wondering why the hell I had gone over to him." I rubbed my forehead. "In hindsight I shouldn't have, but..." I waved a hand, then thumped it against the bed. "Some of the stuff they write about me is true."

Isaac shifted so he could look me in the face. "So, what happened?"

That hadn't been my finest hour either. "Well, he threw the box of condoms at me and said something like, 'How hard do you fuck if that's not enough?' and I asked him if he wanted to find out."

"Jesus."

Yeah, that was about right. "He said he did. I made sure he knew that he could tell me to stop at any point, and I would." That had confused him.

*Look*, I'd said. *You're an asshole and a jerk, and yes, this is a hate fuck, but you're still a human being. You tell me to stop, I'm going to fucking stop, okay?* I sometimes wondered if that, more than the sex, had been the thing that had screwed with his head.

"So, I fucked him. Not as hard as I could've, not nearly as hard as I like, but enough to give him an orgasm that blew his mind and was probably on the edge of painful. Four times in one night? That's...a lot.

"When he'd recovered, I handed him a bottle of water, told him I could have gone a hell of a lot harder, and that I could literally deadlift more than he weighed. I wasn't weak or soft, and then I asked him what his problem was. We ended up sitting down and talking about that for a while." I waved a hand at the ceiling. "In retrospect, we should've started with talking. Guy had issues. I was lucky nothing came of it, other than him finally leaving me the hell alone."

Isaac wheezed out a thin laugh. "Okay, maybe a little reckless."

That was an understatement. Hell, he and I in this bed was probably the very definition of a bad idea. "You shouldn't date me," I said.

"Hey," he said. "Look at me."

I did, and damn, he was gorgeous. Serious and concerned, but stunning, especially with that dark dusting of scruff coming in.

"You didn't invite me over here to throw me out."

*Shit*. Isaac could actually read my mind, because I knew exactly where this was going. Fear and hope bit into me. "No, I didn't."

"And you want me here, right?"

I nodded.

"You said that you like me and want to know me better."

"Oui." Yeah, he was going to make me explain myself. I hated that. Nikki and Elias did that shit too. Got me to face my emotions. My thoughts. Sometimes my past.

He leaned in closer, so I couldn't escape those eyes. "And you *want* to date me."

"Yes." That came out as a whisper.

"Then let's see where this goes before you write me off?"

My laugh was more nerves than anything. "I'm not writing you off. I'm trying to warn you that I'm a difficult man with a bad reputation who likes being thrown around and fucked."

Isaac rolled his eyes. "You know, I just had the best sex of my life. I'd kind of like to do it again." Then he pinned that stare back on me. "And you absolutely need to be thrown around and fucked, it seems." With that, Isaac got up and dragged me out of bed.

He fucking *got it*. Maybe it was the story, maybe he'd figured it out from the way I'd come when he'd let loose and really rammed into me, I didn't know, but this time? This time he had me up against the wall, then bent over a chair, then on the floor. My scalp hurt gloriously from the way he hauled me by my hair.

By the time we made it back to the bed, I was in heaven. One thing could make it better. He was pounding my ass from behind, those hands of his digging into the bruises already forming from our previous round, and I was so close, so gloriously close to oblivion.

"Bite me, Isaac. Please please—just. Bite me." God, I hoped that had been English. I had no idea what was coming out of my mouth most of the time.

He hauled me up by my hair, his thrusts not stopping. "God, Julien." There was wonder in that voice.

Then he bit my shoulder hard, and I was gone. Coming and yelling and trembling in his hands. The two best fucks I'd had in years had come in rapid succession from the one person I shouldn't be sleeping with.

Isaac Rivera. My rookie teammate.

When I could see through the haze of my tears and my over-stimulated brain, I stretched an arm out. "Fuuuck." My bruises were going to be spectacular.

He laughed. "Better?"

Isaac sounded entirely too pleased with himself. I peered over my shoulder and goddamn, that sexy, foxy smile. Something in my chest flipped over and over. Fuck the sex. I wanted to do everything in my power to see him smile at me like that again. "Yeah."

He laughed. "Noticed you didn't talk as much."

And I thought I was a brat. I shuffled up the bed, snatched one of my pillows, and tossed it at him.

He caught it, of course, then buffeted me with it. Then we were tussling and wrestling in a mock pillow fight that devolved into kissing and cuddling. Gentle, this time.

He liked that, I think, and maybe I did too.

"So," he said. "Dating? See how it goes?"

I huffed a laugh. "Yeah, okay." Because there was no other answer I could give.

Everything seemed brighter with Isaac in my arms.

# Chapter 7

## Isaac

I'd seen Julien naked before, and I'd seen him asleep before. Came with the territory of sharing locker rooms and airplanes.

What was new this time was Julien naked *and* asleep, and he had his head resting on my chest. His tattooed arm was draped across my stomach. His long hair was damp from the shower we'd shared, a few strands separating perfectly to frame the darkening bite mark I'd left on his shoulder. I had a momentary flash of regret, worrying I'd bitten him too hard and he'd be sore and annoyed later, but the way he'd begged for it? The way he'd come? Okay, no, he wasn't going to be bothered by that mark. Quite the opposite, I suspected.

*I wonder what the guys will think when they see that.*

A laugh tried to bubble up, but I tamped it down. Tried to, anyway. As funny as it was to imagine our teammates ribbing him about getting laid—and they would—I didn't want to disturb him. Despite my best efforts, I did chuckle a bit, which probably jostled him.

Julien didn't stir, though. He stayed right where he was, completely still against me.

That was a new experience too—Julien being still. A lot

of hockey players were high-energy and twitchy, but Julien took it to a whole other level. Even when he slept, he moved a lot—shifting in his seat, bouncing his knee, crossing and uncrossing his arms. Whenever Coach had us all take a knee on the ice so he could talk to us, Julien would be in the back, switching knees, rocking back and forth, just…always moving. Sometimes he even got up, as if he couldn't deal with his nervous energy while he was kneeling. Coach never seemed to mind the way he would with the rest of us; I wondered if he just understood that there was no stilling Julien for longer than the duration of the pre-game national anthems.

Except, apparently, after a couple of brutally hard fucks.

Two rounds of the most spectacular sex I'd ever experienced, and now Julien was practically in suspended animation apart from his slow, steady breathing. As if today could possibly get any more surreal.

*I can make you calm? Whoa.*

The longer I lay here thinking about that, the more surreal it was. And the more anxiety prickled along the back of my neck. Julien wanted us to date. Not just screw around—*date*. I wanted that, too. A lot. But holy hell, I had no idea what I was doing. I could pick up cues well enough during sex, especially with someone as expressive as Julien. Relationships, though? That sounded like a minefield full of things everyone else started fumbling through when they were like fifteen while my stupid ass had been focused on hockey.

*What if I fuck this up?*

Shit. What if I did? Because by some ridiculous stroke of luck, my hockey idol—the larger-than-life man I'd crushed on for years—had become my teammate, and then my friend, and now he wanted to be with me, and oh my God, I did not want to fuck this up. I did not want to lose this man.

I stroked Julien's hair.

*Would you still want this if you knew I have no idea what I'm doing?*

Maybe. Maybe not. But the best I could do at this point was probably the same thing I'd done in his bed—follow his lead. Watch for his cues. Hope like hell I could read him as well as I could for hockey and Spades.

One step at a time. See where it goes. Hope for the best.

I closed my eyes and exhaled. I could do this as long as I didn't overthink it. Which I would. Because I always did.

My arm and shoulder were starting to fall asleep, so I shifted just enough to get some blood flowing again without disturbing Julien. I was aching in a few places—some from hockey, some from...not—but I was comfortable. After the early morning and the rowdy sex, I would have happily lain here for the rest of the day. My stomach, however, had an opinion on the matter, and growled audibly.

I winced, hoping Julien didn't hear. There were too many things I still needed to process before I was in his intense crosshairs again.

But Julien stirred. He lifted himself off me with a quiet groan and met my gaze through long strings of damp hair. "Hungry?"

Heat bloomed in my cheeks, and I gave a self-deprecating laugh as I rolled my eyes. "Apparently so, yeah."

He smiled a smile that was somehow every bit the Julien who'd intimidated and intrigued me, but also sweet and even a little serene. That was almost more satisfying than the sex.

"I could eat too." He came up and kissed me softly. "I hope you won't think I'm lazy if I suggest we order in."

I slid a hand up his arm just because I could. "Ordering in sounds great. Then only one of us has to put on pants."

The laugh that broke through was relaxed and easy. Another new experience—Julien laughing when there was no pressure and no clothes.

With a grin, he said, "In that case, I volunteer, because I'd just as soon not cover any of this up." He trailed light fingertips down my thigh, making my breath stutter.

"You're a dirty man, Julien Landry." I cupped his neck and dragged him roughly down to me. "Never change."

He purred into a kiss, and when we separated, he bit his lip. "We're going to get started again. We should... We should eat."

Oh, I wanted to get started, but I was going to follow his lead here, if only because he *had* to be sore. Even if he enjoyed it rough and painful, I imagined there came a point where it started getting less fun. And we did still have to practice tomorrow morning and play tomorrow night.

I tucked his hair behind his ear. "Let's go eat."

There was relief in his expression, as if he'd actually worried I'd push for more right now.

"Downstairs." He got up, moving a little gingerly. "In all seriousness, if you want to put something on, I can get your things out of your car."

My things... Out of my...

Oh. Hell. I'd been wearing a suit when I'd arrived, and I hadn't even thought to grab anything else out of the car.

"Thanks. That...that would be great."

He flashed me another smile, one that I'd definitely never seen before. Who knew Julien Landry had a sweet and subdued side if someone fucked him hard enough?

He put on a pair of faded sweats with the logo from his major junior team. Not that I knew every detail of his journey to the league or anything.

My car keys were in my jacket pocket, and after he'd fished them out, he left the bedroom. Alone for what would probably only be a minute or two, I pushed out a breath and raked a hand through my hair, which was as damp and messy as his.

I'd had sex with Julien. Twice. It was nothing like anything

I'd ever done with anyone before, and now we were dating, and... This was all going to fit into my head, how?

I laughed into the emptiness of Julien's enormous bedroom. The day I'd learned I was signing with the Griffins, that I was going to be the pro I'd worked so hard to become, I'd known my life was going to be turned on its ass. More money. More pressure. Busting my ass to keep living the dream.

Fucking Julien Landry so hard he literally cried? Nope. Hadn't seen *that* coming.

He returned a moment later with my suitcase and keys. I fished out a pair of black sweats, and since Julien didn't bother putting on a shirt, neither did I.

"Isn't it a little cold out there to be wandering around shirtless?" I asked as I pulled on the sweats.

"Nah. It was only for a moment. If this had been February or something..." He grimaced.

I fixed my best puppy dog eyes on him. "But if I asked you really nicely, you'd go out shirtless in February to get my clothes, wouldn't you?"

He arched an eyebrow, the same look he gave when he was going to answer a reporter's question professionally but couldn't keep the "*you fucking tool*" out of his expression. "If you're still leaving your clothes in your car in February, you're on your own."

"That's cold, Landry."

"Uh-huh. That's why you're going out to get your clothes."

We glared playfully at each other, then laughed, and I followed him out of the bedroom. I may have taken a bit of pride in the way he was walking with extra care. And in the way that bite on his shoulder stood out even more prominently than other new-looking bruises on his back. His sweats sat just right to reveal some marks on his hips; Christ, how hard had I been holding him? And why was that so hot? Getting rough was new, but so far, I liked it a lot. Both in the moment and after the fact when he was marked to hell and back because of me.

*The second you want to do it again, Julien, say the word.*

In Julien's living room, which could probably fit most of my new apartment, we settled onto his enormous, cushy sofa to browse food delivery apps.

"Okay, so..." Julien tucked himself into my side and held his phone so we could both see it. "What are you in the mood for?"

Arm draped around him and fingertips gently drawing circles on his skin, I watched him slowly scroll through the available options on GrubHub. "That depends—are we taking full advantage of a night off, or are you going to rat me out to Coach if I eat something I shouldn't?"

He twisted around to look up at me, again with that expression he liked to direct at reporters. Then he rolled his eyes and shook his head. "Yes, Isaac. I'm going to send Coach an email with the words, 'So after Rivera and I fucked like rabbits...'"

I snorted. Beside me, he vibrated with laughter.

"Okay, okay," I said. "So, pact of silence. Got it." I craned my neck a little. "Any decent pizza in this town?"

"Define 'decent.'"

"Um. I can taste the difference between the pizza and the box?"

He huffed a laugh as he switched to another app. "I know just the place."

He ordered us a couple of larges from a nearby restaurant. Apparently it was locally owned and "even Elias can't find a reason to complain about it." That was all the endorsement I needed, given our captain's snobby palate.

While Julien entered the order into his phone, I stole the

opportunity to really look at him. I was familiar with his tattoos, but it was a trip to see them up close like this. There were entire Tumblr blogs devoted to the full sleeve, with people speculating about the meaning of all the various designs that intertwined from his wrist to his shoulder. I was deeply curious, but even here and now, after we'd fucked and were lounging half-naked on his couch, that seemed too intimate. Like something I should let him volunteer. Maybe because a number of journalists had pressed him over the years, and he'd always been politely cagey about it in a way that said it was none of anyone's business.

"They tell a story," he'd said during one interview without going into detail about what that story was.

"They remind me of certain moments in my life," he'd told another without elaborating. "People. Places." A dismissive shrug, a knowing smile, and nothing more.

The firebird on his thigh, tail feathers and smoke curling all the way up his hip and onto his chiseled abs, had been in a magazine once, too. One of the sports journals did an annual issue celebrating the physiques of various athletes via artistic and tasteful nudes, and yeah, I had a copy of that one from three years ago. Okay, a few copies. Because holy fuck.

On the inside of one wrist, written in a prominent scripty font, was the word *Now*. I was definitely curious about that one, especially since a lot of those Tumblr fans had noticed him gazing at it or thumbing it when he didn't think anyone was looking. So much ink. So many questions.

I kept those to myself for the moment, though. I didn't want to make things awkward or earn myself one of those "mind your business" side-eyes that he sometimes gave intrusive reporters. That, and I was still too blown away that now, today, somehow, there was a bruise forming under the bird's smoke and feathers. A bruise that my hand would fit over perfectly.

How? *How?*

Unaware of my brain spinning out over my proximity to his famous ink, Julien exhaled and put his phone on the coffee table. "Finally. Jesus. They're lucky they have good pizza, because their app fucking sucks."

I laughed to mask my nerves. "Guess they're making sure you *really* want it."

He just chuckled. "Guess they do. And it says about forty-five minutes, so we can relax until then." He shifted so his back was against the armrest, and he draped his legs over my thighs. I hesitated before resting my arms on them but then decided to go for broke and curve one hand under his nearer thigh. From the way he bit his lip, he didn't object.

I wondered if he was even aware of the way he was rubbing one bare foot against the other, or if it was just second nature to be constantly moving somehow.

He took a breath like he needed to pull himself together. Then he met my gaze. "You said you haven't done this often. Hooked up."

Now I wanted to fidget and squirm, but there wasn't much range of motion with a defenseman's legs across my lap. I settled on running my thumb along the seam inside the knee of his sweats. "No, I haven't. Like I said—too focused on hockey." I laughed with sudden nerves, alternately watching my fingers and his feet instead of holding his gaze. "Just, um... I was just so focused, I never really looked up from the ice long enough to connect with anyone."

Without even turning to him, I could feel his gaze on me. All the questions. The curiosity. I'd grown more embarrassed of my inexperience as I'd gotten older, and I hated discussing it. Hated admitting that I'd made it this far in life without trying much with men. It hadn't really bothered me as a teenager—there'd been time—but then one day I was twenty-two and wondering where that time had gone.

"Isaac?" Julien prodded gently. "Listen, I'm not asking you to put all your cards out on the table. But I'm already pushing you into something that's clearly new territory. So I'd like to know if there's something I should be careful of. So I don't push you too hard."

I laughed nervously and turned to him. "I think I'd be the one pushing you too hard, wouldn't I?"

"I doubt that. But giving what I'm asking for... It's not a small thing. Some people don't like it. You clearly did today, but especially if you don't have a lot of experience, we can tap the brakes."

"I don't want to tap the brakes." I looked down at my fingers again, staring intently at the way my middle finger ran along that seam. "I've already lost so fucking much time, and I..." Sighing, I shook my head. "If anything, I want to make up for *lost* time."

"I get that," he said evenly, "but there is such thing as swinging the pendulum too far in the opposite direction." He slid a hand over my forearm. "I don't want to do that to you."

I lifted my gaze again, meeting those dark eyes that were so full of gentle concern. "I don't think you will. What we did up there—I liked it. A lot. You might have to guide me sometimes, but I *want* to. I just...don't really know what I'm doing yet."

Julien laughed softly and squeezed my arm. "I don't think you need to worry about not knowing what you're doing." When I looked at him again, he grinned. "Trust me—I was more than satisfied."

Warmth settled in my chest along with renewed desire. I knew we weren't going to fool around again for a while, but the promise of more heated my blood. "You did seem satisfied."

"Understatement," he said dryly. "But yes, I was. Very much so. Question is, were *you* satisfied?"

I had to laugh at that. I'd fucked the man I'd been crushing on for years, and the reality had blown any fantasy I'd had out of the water. I felt a lot of things afterward, but unsatisfied wasn't one of them. "God, yes, I was."

"Good." He squeezed my arm again, then let it go. He leaned back, stretching his arms before resting his hands behind his head. Didn't matter how much of my life had been spent around fit, sculpted hockey players—or, hell, how long I'd *been* one—I couldn't help staring at his six-pack when the muscles tightened like that.

"Jesus, you're hot." The words tumbled out before I could stop them, and my cheeks burned.

Julien just smiled, though, and the way he raked his eyes down my chest and abs made my heart flip. He didn't say a word. I supposed he didn't have to.

After a while, he sobered. "If you don't mind sharing, I would like to know how much experience you do have."

"Not much."

"Mmhmm." There was a prompt in that. An unspoken *go on*.

Annoyance surged in me, but I didn't think it was really directed at him. He had a right to know. And maybe if he did know, he'd understand when I inevitably did or said something that only a complete novice would.

I tilted my head back and stared up at the high ceiling. "Like I said—I was focused on hockey. School, too. My parents kept reminding me that I might not make it into the league, so I needed to have a backup plan."

"They didn't believe you had the chops?"

"Oh, no, they totally did." I lowered my head but didn't look at him. "They just wanted me to be set in case it didn't work out. The thing is, my dad was bound for a professional baseball career when he was young, and he didn't have a backup plan. He and my grandpa thought backup plans were just setting yourself up for failure. Nothing drives a person to succeed like knowing there's no Plan B."

Julien snorted. "Mmhmm, and we all know about the best laid plans."

"Exactly. So in my dad's senior year in college, right about the time he was being scouted by several major league teams, he was in a motorcycle accident."

Julien's feet stilled, the sudden cessation of movement startling me because I'd all but forgotten they were moving at all. Voice quiet, he asked, "How badly was he hurt?"

"I mean, he obviously recovered—this was before he and my mom got married. But his right knee was never the same, and he still has problems with it to this day."

Some of the tension in Julien eased. "So, he was all right, but no major league baseball career."

"Yeah, which is why he was adamant that I have another career in mind as a backup plan. He *begged* me, said even if the league wanted to pick me up at eighteen or something, he still wanted me to go to school. Study on the buses and planes if I had to, but be able to land on my feet if hockey suddenly wasn't an option anymore."

"Your father is a smart man." Julien's feet started rubbing again. "Even if he had to learn it the hard way, he passed it on to his son and made sure you were prepared."

I nodded. "He is, and I'm glad he did it. But it's one of those things where you don't realize how much it cost until you look back. I put my nose to two different grindstones, and I forgot to live along the way, you know?"

"That can happen," he said with genuine sympathy.

"Yep. And that's a really long way of explaining why I never touched another guy until I was twenty-two."

"Twenty—" Julien's feet stilled again. "You're twenty-two *now*, aren't you?"

The heat in my face was almost unbearable, and I didn't

look at him as I nodded. "Yep. Like I said..." I laughed humorlessly. "Not a lot of experience."

"How much experience *have* you had in that time?"

I swallowed. "Uh. Well, my college roommate and I fooled around a few times. And then I went out to celebrate after I signed my contract with the Griffins, and I hooked up with some guy."

Julien was stock-still, which was seriously weird. I turned to him, and his eyebrows had climbed. Voice cautious, he asked, "And after them?"

I gestured at him.

Julien's eyebrows rose even higher. "You've... I'm the third man you've been with. And that's all been within the last year."

"I know, I know, it's pathetic. I should have—"

"Isaac." He reached out and took my hand. "I'm not judging you. If anything, I'm amazed you handled *me* so well when sex is so new to you."

I eyed him. "You're not that hard to handle."

"Oh, I am." He laced our fingers together and brought my hand up to his lips. He pressed a kiss to my knuckles, then lowered our hands onto his chest. "You fuck with a lot more confidence than I would have expected, given your experience. That's all." He frowned. "Though maybe we should have had this conversation before we went to my bedroom. I realize now how much I could have overwhelmed you and—"

"Don't." I shook my head. "To tell you the truth, I'm glad we didn't."

His eyes widened.

"If you had known, you'd have held back. But you didn't, and it was amazing, and I want us to keep fucking like that."

Julien swallowed hard. "But if it's too much, you'll tell me? Promise me you will?" He squeezed my hand. "Don't ever think I'll be upset. I'd never forgive myself if I pushed you too hard."

I smiled, rubbing my thumb along the back of his. "I will. I promise."

He relaxed again. His feet started moving again. It was funny how there were apparently two types of stillness in Julien—when he was completely relaxed and when he was seriously tense. The twitchy fidgeting seemed to exist in the space between those two extremes.

"So, in the experiences you've had," he said, "have you always topped? Or have you bottomed?"

"I tried both with my roommate."

"And?"

I shrugged. "Bottoming is all right, but I get way more out of topping. Not the position itself, but at least my roommate was way more responsive when I was on top."

Renewed interest gleamed in Julien's eyes. "So it isn't so much a matter of who's doing the fucking—you want to do more for the other person."

"Exactly. Yeah." I couldn't help squirming, and slid my free hand between his powerful thighs just because I could. "That's why being with you is so much fun."

Julien also shifted a little. "I'm a pretty loud top, too. Just FYI."

"Oh yeah?"

Nodding, he licked his lips. "I prefer to bottom, but—"

"But if you're on top, I'll still have to work to shut you up?"

He threw his head back and laughed, raising goose bumps all over me. God, he was so damn pretty. "Somehow I don't think you'd back down from that particular challenge."

"Not on your life."

"I'll have to keep that in mind." From the way his eyes sparkled, he wasn't kidding.

"We, uh... Maybe not as rough at first, though? If I'm bottoming?"

Julien's humor instantly vanished. "I'll always follow your lead. I'm not in this to hurt you. I promise."

I nodded. "Okay. Okay, good." This conversation had the potential to shift into incredibly frustrating territory (since we weren't going to get naked again for a while) or on to heavy subjects, so I redirected us: "So, if we're dating, how exactly do we, uh, handle this with the team?"

He pursed his lips. "We should probably keep it to ourselves."

I wasn't sure how I felt about that. He was right and I knew it, but stupid insecurity elbowed its way in and said he was embarrassed of me or something.

"Isaac." He rubbed my arm. "We've only just started. Once the cat comes out of the bag, there's no putting it back in. You haven't been with the team long, but I'm sure you've seen us all in action enough to know that keeping cats in bags for as long as possible is...smart."

I laughed, because okay, he had a point. "I think Sanders is still kicking himself for letting us find out about his girlfriend."

Julien snickered wickedly. "Oh, he is. And if those two end up getting married, he's probably going to ban any of us from giving speeches at the wedding just like Paxy *wishes* he did."

"Wait, what happened with Paxy?"

He just grinned. "Ask him sometime. He'll tell you. And then you'll understand why discretion is probably our best friend for the time being."

My insecurities died away. Keeping this quiet wasn't a bad idea under the best of circumstances, but when we shared locker rooms, planes, buses, and hotels with relentless pranksters and gossips... Yeah. Good call. And that was to say nothing of the media.

Julien turned serious and looked right in my eyes. "It's also not a bad idea for us to get a handle on it first. Figure out what it is. What it isn't. It's much less complicated without our teammates breathing down our necks." His expression softened even as a grin came to life. "Don't think this is because I don't want people to know Isaac Rivera is helping me destroy my furniture."

Laughing, I nodded. Trust him to read me like a book yet again. "Okay. Point taken."

He smiled flicker-fast, then checked his phone. "Pizza should be on its way soon." He pulled his legs off my lap, swung his feet to the floor, and stood in one smooth, fluid motion. "I should find us something to drink. Do you like beer with your pizza?"

I rose too. "Uh. Beer depends on if I'm driving any time soon."

He cocked his head. "Are you planning on leaving any time soon?"

"It's your house." I shrugged. "You tell me."

Julien studied me for a moment. Then he nodded and gestured for me to follow him into the kitchen. "Beer, it is."

# Chapter 8

## Julien

Sitting at my kitchen island, shooting the shit over pizza and beer with Isaac, seemed the most natural thing in the world. Like he belonged here, even more than Elias or Nikki when they visited. The three of us were in and out of each other's houses all the time.

But Isaac? He didn't feel like a *guest*.

Good fucking God, I'd been the third person he'd ever had sex with. That still had me reeling, even as I listened to Isaac ramble about the new fantasy show everyone was streaming these days. He'd read the books. I hadn't.

"...but what I'm really waiting for is when—"

I sat bolt upright and slapped my hand against the cool marble of the kitchen island. "Don't! Oh my God, don't spoil it!"

That irresistible blush spread across his cheeks. "Sorry. I'm just—passionate about these books. They were the only thing besides hockey that kept me sane in high school, you know?"

I gave him a gentle shove to break the sudden tension. "Sure, I get that. But I can't stand when people spoil plots and stuff."

When Isaac smiled, his eyes sparkled. "Happen to you a lot?"

Maybe it was the beer that had me warm, but I didn't think so. Drunk on Isaac. I pushed the pizza crust on my plate around. "Nikki loves to spoil things. I got so angry a couple years back—enough that both Elias and Coach told us to get our shit together because our constant sniping was affecting the team and our game."

Isaac placed one of his hands on my bouncing knee, and I huffed out a sigh, warmed at his touch. I didn't drink much, but this wasn't the beer at all.

God, I hadn't felt this good and relaxed after sex in years. Too many hookups, I guess. No chatting. No meals. Nothing but an empty hollowness afterward when I wandered through my house or paced my hotel room alone.

I twined my fingers in his and drank in the moment. Isaac fit this room, this house. That should've scared me. Instead, I pushed aside every reservation I had so I could bask in his presence, in these precious moments. In this now.

Isaac gazed at me through those lashes of his. "I have to say, I have a hard time imagining you and Sidorov fighting for very long."

Certainly had been an uncomfortable month. Nikki meant the world to me. Facing his cold unforgiving side had been rough. "We were both too stubborn to sit down and talk."

"What?" He mocked surprise. "An opinionated Russian and an opinionated Quebecois? Stubborn? You don't say!"

Isaac had enough wherewithal to dodge my kick to his shin, and his grin lit parts of me on fire I'd forgotten existed. Wasn't entirely sexual. That was there, but our earlier bouts had drained much of that. This was—more. A desire I hadn't felt in years.

Isaac understood me, somehow.

I leaned back in my chair and tapped my foot against the island. "In the end, Elias collared us both, dragged us into a room, and made us talk it out. Turns out, for Nikki, knowing what was coming before it happened didn't diminish his enjoyment of a story. He'll read the ends of books first, even. It's the journey he likes. For me—" I paused to work out what I wanted to say. "I like the journey, but if I know what's coming, I can't focus. The story turns dull. I need all the twists, turns, and surprises, the discovery, those emotions, or the whole thing is ruined. He didn't understand how I process things, until I explained."

Isaac nodded. "I'm more like Sidorov, I think. But I see what you're saying." The concern in Isaac's eyes caught me off guard. Few people look at me like that. "Do you like rewatching things? Rereading?"

"Yeah, especially if it's something I loved. I'll remember the feelings and enjoy them again, you know? But I have to *have* those feelings for that to happen." I untangled my hand from Isaac's, pushed back from the island, and stood, needing to burn some of my excess energy and to calm the emotions churning inside me.

Isaac Rivera gave a damn about me. I wanted to dive into that brain and find out all I could about him. Outstanding sex and someone I liked who seemed interested in me *beyond* my looks or salary? There had to be a catch.

*Yeah, he's your teammate, a rookie, and you're the third man he's ever fucked.*

Esti. "Do you want another?" I pointed at his beer.

He wrinkled his nose in contemplation, and even that was annoyingly attractive. "No. I need to drive later."

I didn't want him to leave, but I grunted in acknowledgement, pulled two cans of seltzer out, and slid one across the marble top of the island to him. "You can stay the night, you know," I said, even as I ticked off all the reasons he shouldn't. I opened my can and took a swig.

He cracked open his, and leveled a smoldering look at me. "Do you think you'll be in any condition to skate tomorrow if I stay tonight?"

I nearly choked on my fizzy water.

His toothy grin was wicked. "Julien Landry is out day to day with a lower body injury."

"Oh, Coach would love that," I sputtered breathlessly. Given the way I ached now, another round would probably interfere with skating, and in turn, the game. "We need the points."

Seriousness had returned, and he nodded. "I know. And you're right about not telling anyone."

I hated that. Hated hiding. Plus, I shouldn't be this into Isaac yet, but I only had two settings: on or off. I took another sip to ease my throat, then started putting the few slices of pizza that remained away.

"There's a chance Nikki or Elias might figure it out." A lie. Nikki would know as soon as I stripped. The boys would give me shit about the marks—they always did—but Nikki would *know* who made them. "They'll keep quiet, though."

Nikki wasn't the one I was worried about. Elias, however... Yes, he was a good friend, but he was still my—our—captain. Pretty sure he wouldn't be pleased.

When I turned back from the refrigerator, Isaac was deep in thought, absently picking at the skin on his arm. He looked up. "Are Karlsson and Sidorov together?"

I didn't know how to answer that. I'd known the two of them for eight years. They'd known each other for ten. They were my two closest friends. But the answer to this? "Chais pas," I said. "I don't know."

Both Isaac's eyebrows were up in disbelief.

"Sometimes I think yes, sometimes no. They're extremely

close. Came here at the same time, two years before me. Hell, it was rocky when I got here, but when they did?" I blew out a breath. "Team was bad and unlucky. There was very little leadership." The year they'd drafted Elias and Nikki, the Griffins had lost the lottery for the top player. Thankfully, they'd still ended up with two picks from the first round—Nikki and Elias. Me? Two years later, I'd been toward the end of the third round. "Those first two years were rough for both of them, and created a bond that I'm not sure I understand."

"Even though you have a bond with them, too."

Perceptive, perceptive. I nodded. "Different circumstances." I wouldn't be getting into that. Isaac didn't need to know about Travis and the near disaster I'd caused, or the way Elias and Nikki had pulled me out of the mire—especially the way Nikki had. Explaining the night I'd slept with Nikki meant explaining Travis, and—no. Isaac would drop me like the hot-ass mess I was, and I was selfish enough not to want that to happen.

Past history served no place in the present.

Isaac digested what I'd said. "I'm not sure why I asked, except that they seem like an old married couple half the time."

Laughter poured out of me. "Well, that's accurate. They are, at least around hockey." Always in each other's business. Bickering the way partners did.

Nikki was one hundred percent pansexual, and pretty much out. Elias? He was like Isaac—didn't look up from the ice much. But there was no doubt in my mind they loved each other fiercely. I just didn't know if that spilled over romantically or sexually. I did know, out of the three of us, I was the odd man out, even if Nikki was my best friend.

I waved at our plates and the pizza boxes on the island. "I should finish cleaning this up."

Isaac rose. "Let me help you."

I did, grateful for the extra set of hands and the company, even if the task was light. Gave me a chance to run a hand down his back, and steal a kiss here and there. In turn, he looped an arm around my waist and kissed the back of my neck.

I could get used to this. I wasn't in love yet—but this was the companionship I'd craved, what I'd wanted with— Non. Nope. I was not treading down that path.

I pulled Isaac close. "Let's go watch TV."

Rather than answer, he kissed me. When he'd finished stealing my breath, he murmured, "Watch TV, huh?"

Maybe it was our earlier conversation about his experience, but I didn't want to get near the thought of pressuring him for anything else. "It's good background noise."

"What, for you moaning?" I caught a glimpse of that impish smile before he had my mouth again. His fingers slid against my scalp, and I shivered.

I could drown in this man. Between kisses, I managed to say, "Living room or bedroom?"

He laughed, grabbed me by my hips, and tugged me out of the kitchen. "Living room. I had a thought."

Fuck me. Isaac had a *thought*. Meanwhile, those were in short supply in my head. When he pulled me down onto the couch next to him, I finally spoke. "A thought?"

That look was going to ignite me from the inside out. "Do you know how many times I've fantasized about you sucking me off in the showers?" The tips of his ears were red, as were his chest and cheeks, and there was no mistaking the tenting of his sweatpants.

Or the tenting of mine, for that matter. "Oh?"

He nodded, but didn't say anything more.

I leaned in, nuzzled my face against his and whispered in his ear, "Order me."

Isaac's breath stuttered. "Order..."

I stared into his eyes. "Tell me what you want, then make me do it."

Fucking hell, the way he looked at me, like he was about to devour me whole, like I'd just unlocked a door to a treasure.

"Get on your knees, Isaac growled, low and deep, and I slid off the couch.

My back hit the coffee table and I reached around and shoved it out of the way. Isaac's gaze flickered to the table, then locked on mine again. He opened his impressive thighs and pushed down his sweats to reveal his hard cock, head already glistening with precum.

I licked my lips. Couldn't help it.

"Fuck," he groaned, then started jacking himself. "Could come watching you like that."

"If that's what you want." I slid my hands up his thighs, feeling the heat through his sweats.

"What I want." His gaze turned sharp, and he sat up. "What I want is your lips around my dick."

God, that voice. All lust and gravel. Of course I gave him that, taking his dick between my lips and circling his head with my tongue.

"Oh my God, Julien. Fuuuuuck." Isaac's fingers scraped through my hair, and my balls ached at the thought of what was coming. Sure enough, his grip tightened. My scalp burned and I moaned around his dick.

That got another breathless "God" out of him.

Isaac tasted fantastic, all musk and salt. I loved giving head, so I settled into a rhythm of sucking and licking, my hands braced on those powerful thighs of his, and looked up, right into his eyes.

He promptly squeezed them closed. "Oh fuck, I'm not gonna last if you look at me like that."

Couldn't help the chuckle, which didn't help him any, given his groan and how his hold on my hair tightened.

It was a fucking joy to turn him inside out. I was so hard, so close myself, but I didn't want to—couldn't—let go of Isaac's trembling thighs to jack myself off. Probably would have come instantly anyway. Between Isaac's moans, the way he fucked my mouth, and the strength of his hands in my hair, urging me on—that was as good as a dick in my ass, honestly.

"Oh, fuck. Julien." That was the only warning I had before Isaac was spilling down my throat.

When he'd finished, he didn't even hesitate. He pulled me up into his arms and kissed me. I couldn't think. His taste, his smell, and now his lips and tongue had my every sense overwhelmed. In that moment, I'd have given anything to this man —anything at all. This was heaven, and I wasn't sure how I'd gotten here from a small conversation on a hotel patio a couple nights ago.

Isaac thrust his hands into my sweats, wrapped the same strong fingers that'd been in my hair around my shaft, and stroked me until I was gasping, moaning and coming. He didn't stop kissing me while he turned me to absolute jelly. When he finally rolled me over onto the couch cushions, I could only stare up at the ceiling, my heart thudding in my chest and my brain completely shattered. I tasted Isaac with every swallow, and pleasure hummed through my veins.

"God, you're stunning." Isaac was breathless. "Fucking hell."

Somehow, I managed to look over. Incredible smile. Shining eyes. "You, too," I said, because he was.

There was that self-deprecating laugh. "No one's ever gone down on me like that. Better than my fantasies."

My laugh was high and short. "No one's ever jacked me off like that, so I think we're even."

Disbelief sketched over his face. "Really?"

"Really." I reeled him in for a kiss, this one gentle. "But now I'm a mess. Let me go clean myself up?"

He held up his right hand and my jizz was drying on his fingers. "Not a bad idea."

Isaac headed for the kitchen while I hauled my sorry ass up to my bedroom to grab another pair of sweatpants.

The bed was a mess and Isaac's suitcase lay on my floor. In the bathroom mirror, a wild-haired, debauched version of myself looked back as I cleaned up. Already, a livid bruise was rising on my shoulder.

We shouldn't be doing this. I hadn't felt this good, this alive in *years*.

When I returned to the living room, Isaac was over by the patio doors. "It's getting late."

Wrapping my arms around Isaac from behind felt like a dream. He shifted his weight to settle against me, his bare back against my equally bare chest.

"It's still early enough." I wasn't ready to let this day go, so I pulled him to the couch and covered us up with a throw. That led to a leisurely session of kissing and snuggling on the couch, and that devolved into both of us falling asleep, worn out from travel, sex, and food.

By the time we woke, the living room was dark. Moonlight leaked in through the windows and the patio door, but out here, there wasn't much to break the darkness.

"Shit," Isaac said. "Now it's actually late."

I grunted. "Going to turn on a light. Beware." I rose and worked my way around the room, relying more on memory than anything, and flicked a switch on.

Isaac groaned and blinked into the suddenly bright room. "How late is it?"

No fucking clue. I leaned into the kitchen to check the clock on the microwave. "Nine twenty-seven."

Isaac rubbed his face, then dropped his hands heavily to his thighs. He didn't want to leave.

I didn't want him to go. "Stay," I whispered.

God, the look he gave me, all conflict and passion and need. "I want to." He licked those gorgeous full lips of his. "I do. But I shouldn't. You know that."

"Oui." He was right—if he remained, neither of us would be in any shape to skate tomorrow. Hell, we probably wouldn't make it to the rink. That would get us both scratched and disciplined, and where would that leave the team? "I know."

He rose and joined me in the entryway to the kitchen. He leaned in, his hand on my chest, and kissed me. "You get into things fast, don't you?"

"Non." I didn't get into things like this at all. I searched his face. "This isn't normal for me. Would it bother you if I told you this frightened me?"

His chuckle was a little high. "No. Makes me feel better, believe it or not." He stilled and stared at me. "I'm not alone in this."

"You're not."

He caught my hand. "But I should go home."

I didn't want to say yes, so I nodded. "We should be responsible, professional athletes and show up on time tomorrow."

"Even if we do want to spend the night breaking furniture." He grinned up at me.

Oh my God, I was so fucked.

Isaac laughed and kissed me, and I surrendered to that, letting him press me against the slim bit of wall between the rooms.

Eventually he relented. "I need to get my bag, but I'm not sure how to get to your bedroom. This place is a maze."

"It's not that big." I kept hold of his hand as I led him upstairs, turning on lights as we went.

"I have a loft you could fit into your living room." He

didn't sound awed, just factual. "Seems like a lot of house for one person."

"My parents and my siblings and their kids come down at least once a year, so the extra rooms come in handy."

Back in my bedroom, Isaac dug a sweatshirt out of his suitcase, then zipped it back up. "You have a brother and a sister, right?"

"Did your research, eh?" He reddened at that, and I chucked, waving his concern away, and we returned to the first floor. "I'm the youngest, if you can believe that."

"Was it hard, being away from your family?" Curiosity there. "I mean, going from a full house to being alone."

A sliver of sadness wormed its way up my chest. "I got used to being alone." I glanced over my shoulder when I hit the ground floor. "I'm six years younger than my brother. Eight younger than my sister. Spent a lot of time on my own at home, then when everyone realized my hockey talent, I went to prep school, then billeted while I was in major juniors." I'd been a handful for everyone. Teachers, coaches, billet parents. Never still. Always moving or talking or both. So nervous most of the time. I learned to be quiet first, then learned to be alone with my thoughts.

Isaac set his bag down by the front door, then took hold of my shoulders. "But was it hard?"

That sliver cracked open. My lips pressed shut, and I nodded. It'd been excruciatingly hard. But hockey was everything, and being out on the ice almost made up for the pain. Making the big league? That had soothed the rest.

Isaac drew me into a hug. "I'm glad your family can share this with you." He pulled back. "And you have the team, too."

I had Isaac. Unexpected, beautiful Isaac, who somehow had chosen to flirt with me, of all people. "What about your family?" My voice cracked from the emotions I didn't want to show.

He rolled his eyes. "I'll be here all night if I try to explain them."

I drew him in for a kiss that lasted a little too long for goodbye. When we came up for air, I spoke. "Some other night, then?"

Oh, that smile. "Absolutely." The grin dimmed when his gaze settled on the door. "If I don't go now, we're not getting to practice tomorrow."

I had to laugh at that truth. I opened the door and ushered Isaac out into the cold.

Halfway to his car, he spun around. "We're going to win tomorrow," he blurted out. "You're going to score a goal for me."

In that moment, I believed him. "Anything you say, Isaac."

"Anything?"

Fucking hell, that look. I swallowed. "Anything within reason."

I loved when he laughed, loved that smile and those dimples. I knew better than to give my heart to anyone at all, but watching Isaac climb into his car and drive away, my resolve to never fall in love again started to crumble.

# Chapter 9

## Isaac

*Why does my partner want me to pull his hair? Search.*
*Why do people like rough sex? Search.*
*How do I dominate my partner? Search.*

I rubbed the back of my neck as I stared at the long list of results on Google. It occurred to me now that if anyone ever got their hands on my laptop or even my browser history, things could get a little awkward, but whatever. It wasn't like they'd know my questions had anything to do with Julien. Oh my God, my face burned just imagining the media scrum if *that* got out.

"Isaac, how does your relationship with Julien Landry affect your interactions on the ice?"

"Do your plays include safe words now?"

"Is there a penalty box in your bedroom?"

I laughed aloud, the only sound in my apartment besides the small fountain trickling on the coffee table, and I leaned my head back against the couch and stared up at the ceiling. I was ridiculous and I knew it. Today had been overwhelming. *Julien* had been overwhelming. Had it really been this morning that we were playing cards on the plane with Sidorov and Karlsson, and then exchanging the text messages that led us into his bedroom? Holy shit.

I wiped a hand over my face and exhaled. I should've been sleeping. The whole reason I'd left his place had been so we wouldn't be dead on our feet tomorrow, and now it was almost one in the morning and I was still sitting here with my laptop. My eyes were burning from reading the screen. My head was swimming from all the information I'd crammed into it over the last few hours. And of course, my body was still aching from everything I'd done with Julien. I was in damn good physical condition, and I probably could've gone at least another round with him, but a few muscles were definitely letting me know this was new and different.

I could handle it, though. With enough practice, my body had gotten used to all the ways hockey taxed it, and it would do the same when it came to sex with Julien. More practice. That was all I needed.

Closing my eyes, I chuckled again, then lowered my gaze to the screen. On the page, were a few of the literally millions of hits on my last search. In the almost three hours since I'd come home, I'd read dozens of articles and blog posts, and I'd even watched a few videos, trying to understand exactly what it was that Julien craved. I mean, I could ask him, and I probably *would* ask him, but a primer couldn't hurt so we could skip the basics and get to what he needed and wanted.

The primer had helped. It had also raised questions I wasn't even sure how to ask. Oh my God, I was so clueless.

And...kind of...really...*seriously* turned the fuck on.

I'd vaguely heard about stuff like this over the years. I'd absorbed it about as well as I'd absorbed anything that wasn't hockey, but I was definitely paying attention now. The more I read about dominance and submission, the more I fantasized about driving back to Julien's and being non-functional on the ice tomorrow.

*"To submit is to relinquish control to a trusted partner,"* one article had explained. *"This allows the submissive to let go of the reins and lose themselves freely in pain, pleasure, or other stimulation, all the while knowing they are safely in the hands of a caring, loving Dominant who is focused on them and no one else, and who will see them gently back to earth when it is over."*

I shivered, shifting a little on my sofa. I'd never thought of myself as a Dom—hadn't even really known that was a thing—but at least with Julien, I definitely could be if that was what he needed. I wanted to be. It sounded like some Doms liked the power, but what had me getting hard all over again was the idea of being the one to take Julien there. He'd always been wound tight and vibrating with the need to move, both on and off the ice, and today I'd seen a completely different side of him. I'd seen him boneless and blissed out after I'd given him everything he'd begged me for. I'd seen him *still*.

*"Isaac. Please make me stop talking."*

*"Bite me, Isaac. Please please—just. Bite me."*

*"Order me. Tell me what you want, then make me do it."*

I pushed out a ragged breath. "Oh, my God." Apparently I *was* wired to be a Dom, at least for this man, because all of this was heady as fuck. Julien pleading with me. Giving him what he wanted. Turning him into someone I had never seen before. Wow. Yes. I might still need some guidance from him —I *would* need some, let's be real—but I was in. Completely the fuck in. Julien Landry wanted me to take him there. He wanted me. Period.

The exhilaration and arousal started to ebb in favor of panic.

Julien Landry wanted me to take him there.

He wanted me. He wanted to *date* me.

Ooh fuck, I was in over my head. The pressure kicked in hard, almost like one of those nightmares where I'd signed my league contract and instead of going to practice and games and all of that, I'd been handed my skates and shoved onto the ice for a shootout. Without my stick. During a playoff final. So much pressure and absolutely no confidence or competence to pull it off.

*What if I screw this up? What if I do the wrong thing?*

All the articles I'd read about sub drop and injured subs and straight up traumatized subs crashed through my brain, and oh, yeah, I was absolutely standing on that ice, holding my skates without a stick in sight with the outcome of the playoffs on my idiot shoulders and—

I needed to talk to someone and get my head straight, because sitting here in my living room with all these browser tabs open, I was going to drive myself insane.

Too bad it was 1:22 in the damn morning.

Though I did have people on the West Coast, some of whom were night owls. Worth a try, right?

I logged onto social media and—jackpot. One of my friends from Oregon was shit-posting on Twitter and trolling people who were obsessed with cryptocurrency, which meant they were awake.

I sent them a DM: *Hey, could use a few minutes on FaceTime. You around?*

Unsurprisingly, the response came quickly and in the form of a FaceTime request on my phone. I indulged in a relieved sigh, shut my laptop, and accepted the request.

Darian's face appeared, their pale complexion blanched by the harsh glow of their screen in an otherwise dark room. Their glasses were perched on their nose, and though it was hard to tell in the weird light, I thought their long, ink-black hair had streaks of bright red this time. The streaks were never the same color for very long. I loved it.

They lounged back on their bed. "Hey, Puckster!"

I chuckled at the nickname, which I hadn't heard in way too long. "Hey, yourself. How are things?"

They shrugged. "Same old, same old. How's life as a superstar athlete?"

Heat rushed into my cheeks. Darian had been calling me that since we were in elementary school, and they took great delight in reminding me at every turn that their prediction had come true. Smug little shit.

"It's good," I said. "The travel and the pressure take some getting used to, but it's good."

"Yeah?" They cocked their head. "So why the S.O.S. in the middle of the night?"

I sighed, avoiding their gaze. "Yeah. Uh..."

"Everything okay?" Their breezy, playful tone was gone.

I swallowed. "It's... So, I started seeing someone."

The sound on the other end made me think Darian had choked on something, but when I looked at the screen, they were just staring right back.

"You?" They sounded genuinely surprised. "Isaac Rivera. Seeing someone. When did *that* happen?"

"Well..." I chuckled. "It's a pretty recent development."

Darian whistled. "Pittsburgh definitely agrees with you, doesn't it? Or just being a famous athlete?"

"Something like that." I didn't want to tip my hand too far. I trusted Darian like few others on this planet, but I didn't want to betray Julien's trust either. Keeping some details vague here seemed like the best approach. "It's really new, though. And I've never dated anyone before, so—"

"You don't have to tell me." They weren't mocking— they'd wondered aloud many times if I'd ever date or even hook up, or if I was asexual or aromantic. I wasn't, but making actual connections with people took work that wasn't hockey, so it didn't happen. Darian studied me. "So, what's going on with them? I'd ask if everything was okay, but since you're pinging me this late..."

I exhaled, pressing back against the couch. "It's... I mean, everything seems to be going great. But it's new. Like, really new. And he has way more experience than I do."

"Well, that's a good thing. The experience, I mean."

"Except he's experienced enough that he'll know when I'm being a clueless dumbass."

Darian rolled their eyes. "And if he's worth giving the time of day, never mind dating, he'll understand you're inexperienced and he'll guide you."

Okay, they had a point. Julien had definitely guided me plenty today, mostly by way of begging or outright demanding I do something to him. He hadn't seemed annoyed by that or frustrated with me, especially when I did what I was told. Or when I made *him* do something, I thought with a shiver.

"I guess?" I rubbed the back of my neck. "But like, what if I do something wrong?"

"In the relationship or in bed?"

"Either. Both? Probably at the same time, knowing me."

Darian shrugged. "So what if you do? Everyone fucks up in relationships, and some of my best sexual partners are the ones who could laugh with me when one of us fucked up in bed."

"Really?"

"Dude, yeah. This isn't porn. It's real life. If you can't laugh when someone's dick slides out at the wrong time or someone gets cum up their nose, then what even is the point?"

I snorted. "Cum up their nose? That sounds, uh…"

"I don't recommend it." They grimaced. "That shit burns."

"Uh. Good to know?"

"It happens, though. A lot of things do. My ex's St. Bernard joined us in bed at an inopportune moment." They waved dismissively. "You just laugh it off and move on. We all laugh shit off with our friends and family—why should it be different with a partner?"

That...was a good point. One I hadn't thought of. "I swear, every movie makes it seem like a disaster if someone sneezes or looks at a stranger for two seconds."

"God, I know." Darian groaned and rolled their eyes. "It's all just ridiculous drama, and normal, grownup relationships roll with it. There's no reason you and your guy can't do the same. Honestly, most people put too much pressure on relationships. They're more intimate than friendship, but they kind of operate the same way, you know? Like if you're in a good relationship, you should be friends with the person, so why would it be any different?"

I furrowed my brow. "That... Are you sure you're not oversimplifying it?"

They shrugged. "Are you sure you're not overthinking it?"

"Touché."

"Seriously, though." They sat back, sliding a hand behind their head on their pillow. "Think of all the things you do when a friendship goes wonky. Like when we've been... Okay, we've never really fought or anything, but sometimes we're not on the same wavelength, right?"

I nodded.

"Right, so what happens then?"

"I worry myself stupid that I've fucked everything up and you're not going to forgive me?"

Darian laughed softly. "Uh-huh. And then we talk, and we listen, and everything is fine. Right?"

Chewing my lip, I nodded again. "Yeah."

"Relationships don't have to be any different. Communicate with him. Listen to him. Don't be a dick to him."

I barked a laugh. "That last one—nice."

"Am I wrong?" Darian shrugged unrepentantly. "Because that's been the big deal-breaker with most of my exes."

Sobering, I thought about it, and they were right. Their

last few exes really had been dicks, especially toward the end. "So it's just that easy? Talk, listen, don't be a dick?"

"It's that *simple*," they said. "It's not always easy, especially when you need to talk about things that are hard to talk about or listen to him say things you don't necessarily want to hear. But that's how you make it work, you know?"

I nodded slowly. "I think I can handle that."

"Of course you can." They grinned. "And from the way this guy is making you smile, I don't think you'll have any trouble not being a dick to him."

My cheeks heated, because of course they did. Well, all that was encouraging. Maybe relationships didn't have some secret that everyone knew but me. Talk. Listen. Don't be a dick to him. I could do all that.

I sighed, pressing back against the sofa. "Okay. So I *am* overthinking it."

"You overthink everything," they told me like they had thousands of times in the past. "Hon, here's the thing. If it's going good with him, then let things progress on their own. Ask him if you aren't sure. Tell him if you want something. Talk about it if one of you or both of you fuck up. Communication really is key."

I nodded, chewing my lip. All those BDSM articles I'd read had hammered that point home, too. And the kinky side of things was another part I really needed input on, but I didn't want to tip my hand too far. Or rather, tip Julien's hand. Even if I didn't mention him by name, there was always the chance the public could find out we were dating. Even if my friend was a steel trap, I'd feel awful knowing someone out there knew intimate things about Julien that he probably didn't want anyone else to know.

Which meant I couldn't ask Darian a lot of the things I really needed to ask *someone*. Vague reassurances that I needed to communicate with Julien were the best I was going to get tonight without violating his trust. Damn it.

"I guess I'm just worried about screwing up," I told Darian. "I've never done this before, and I really like him. A lot."

"I bet you do." Darian smiled, a hint of playfulness in their expression. "If he turned your head when you're surrounded by all those hockey gods, he *must* be amazing."

I coughed a laugh. "Uh. Yeah. Something like that."

They cocked a brow. "Unless you managed to bag one of your team—"

"What?" I laughed a little too enthusiastically. "Come on. They're all hot, but I'm pretty sure I'd get the boot if I hooked up with a teammate."

"Shame," they mused. "The things I'd do to that one guy. Landry? God*damn*."

I suppressed a shiver, which lit up all the aches and twinges from the things *I'd* done with that one guy Landry. *Oh, Darian, if you only knew.* "I know, right?" I sounded nervous now. Shit. "But I'm pretty sure all he'll ever give me is the puck."

"Like he did the other night. Awesome goal, by the way! Congrats!"

"Thanks. Kind of wild getting my first professional goal from the player I idolized all through college."

"Idolized." Darian guffawed. "Is that what kids are calling it these days?"

I rolled my eyes. "Shut up."

We chatted a little while longer, but then I really needed to get some sleep so I didn't pass out on my skates tomorrow. As it was, I'd have to bust my ass to keep Coach from noticing how hard I was dragging in the morning.

I did feel better after talking to Darian. We hadn't been able to discuss everything I'd wanted to discuss—not without slicing my conscience to ribbons in the process—but apparently I'd just needed to hear someone tell me to let things progress naturally and to communicate with Julien. That it was okay to screw up in bed and in the relationship, and that it wouldn't spell disaster if I did. It made me feel like we weren't as precarious as I'd somehow imagined we were.

Which actually meant I could dip my toes into both a relationship and this dominance thing Julien apparently wanted. As long as I was careful and watched for signs that he wasn't enjoying it or that I was actually hurting him, we'd be all right. A mistake wasn't a point of no return. We could course-correct. Without even telling Darian what Julien and I were into, they'd told me what I'd needed to hear more than anything else.

And I did sleep pretty well that night.

Partly because I was exhausted, but mostly because of that orgasm I had while imagining the things I wanted to do to Julien next time we were alone.

All my worrying and overthinking aside...

I couldn't wait.

# Chapter 10

## Julien

As expected, I got shit from the team the moment I started changing. Hoots and hollers. Larry yelled, "Someone got laid!"

The bite mark Isaac had given me was prominent on my shoulder. When I stripped off my pants, Paxy whistled low. "Jesus, Lans, did you fuck or get into a bar fight?"

The bruises on my hips weren't *that* bad. There were some scratches on my back, but nothing too outrageous. At least, I didn't think so. I glanced over my shoulder to reply, but Nikki beat me to it.

"You think he goes to bars?" He mock punched my shoulder. "Spent all day in bed, huh?"

That got a round of laughter out of the group. I hoped Isaac was chuckling along. Thankfully, he tended to blush whenever the banter turned to sex. I didn't dare look his direction.

"Eh, some of these are from pucks, you know. Or the boards." Even with the protective gear, we still got banged up. When a puck hits you at a hundred miles per hour, or a huge player rams you into the dashers, it hurt no matter what. "And

I don't kiss and tell, so..." I let that trail off as I put my base layer on.

Thankfully, they left it at that, and in no time, we were hitting the ice for practice. Line combos, some special teams work. Nothing really strenuous, since we'd be back in gear and out here in a couple of hours. Being on the ice did give me a chance to finally watch Isaac in between line rushes. He was focused and sharp. Serious. When he caught me staring? He curled those lips of his into a devilish smile.

I was the one blushing. Fuck me.

Isaac *had* fucked me. We were *dating*. Oh my God.

Coach blew the whistle, and I pushed all of that out of my mind to focus on the puck. Easier than I'd expected. When me and Paxy were out with Isaac's line? Absolutely seamless. Crisp passes. All five of us reading each other. In sync.

Granted, this was practice. The test would be tonight, but when I locked gazes with Isaac, this time his grin was all pucks and sticks. He was moving well, seeing the ice and the plays. If he did that tonight, there'd be no stopping him. Or us, because that same confidence infused the team, from Elias on down. Coach must have felt it too, because he cracked a bunch of smiles.

I would've said practice was perfect, except I caught Elias watching me, and his cheerful expression faltered into concern.

Didn't help that Nikki kept slapping me right on Isaac's bite mark. I pushed him away, and he glided a little before stopping and giving me an exaggerated shrug. "What?"

"There's a bruise there, you asshole," I said, with a smile in every word.

"You've got shoulder pads on." He was positively gleeful.

I couldn't help laughing. "Still hurts!"

"Pffft." He waved that away, then came closer, speaking low so only I could hear. "I'm glad. You look happy."

The relief in his eyes caught me off guard. "I'm always happy."

Oh, did *that* get me the patented Nikolai Sidorov look of incredulousness. I spun away from his next shove. He followed, though, and draped an arm over my shoulder. "It's a good look, eh? Keep it."

I *was* happy. More than normal, even if I didn't want to admit that. My face hurt from grinning most of practice.

All my other teammates probably thought I'd gotten a good piece of ass, and that had settled my temperament. Nikki knew better, and he knew who I'd been with. In fact, he circled Isaac like a proud uncle. That meant Elias knew, too. Hopefully, he'd let it slide.

No such luck there. As practice ended and we all stretched out, Elias gave me a pointed look. We'd been friends and teammates long enough that I read what he was saying.

*We're having a conversation later.*

I rolled my eyes at him, and that didn't help. He narrowed his, and underneath that concern, there was anger. Shit.

I let my shoulders droop and tried to look contrite. *Please don't get on Isaac's case.* No idea if Elias understood—probably not. But in any event, Isaac didn't notice, thank God. He and Ozzy were talking about something—probably hockey plays, given the way Isaac was waving his hand.

I got up, headed for the nearest net, and started shooting pucks into the twine. Needed the practice, and stretching never did me any good anyway. Besides, I always helped pick up the pucks after practice. That had been my role as a rookie, but I'd never stopped, though often the younger guys helped. Sometimes Nikki and Elias.

It was the latter who skated over this time. I didn't say anything, and neither did he, but I knew that look, knew he was reading my expressions and gauging my mood. He and Nikki both had a bead on me. After my horrible first year, and during my disastrous second, they'd taken me under their wings. Protected me. Elias had even housed me, but also chastised me when I needed it. Now?

We were friends. The team's leaders. But some habits never died.

Once we'd showered, we studied film and ate, and started all of our game day routines. So when Elias clapped me on the shoulder, I knew what was coming.

"Leadership meeting," he said.

That happened before games often enough that none of the guys, not even Isaac, blinked. But I knew.

Nikki rolled his eyes, and we both followed Elias into one of the small meeting rooms off the lounge for some privacy. Elias closed the door, crossed his arms, and glared at me. "Did you fuck Rivs?"

Nikki snorted. "Of course he did."

Heat blazed through me. I didn't want to say yes, I didn't want to say no, so I shrugged and said nothing at all.

Elias had two good inches on me, and he seemed to grow an extra inch with his ire. "For fuck's sake, Landry! He's a rookie!"

Not good when he reverted to my last name. "He's twenty-two." I spit the words out, trying to keep my volume down. Last thing the team needed was to overhear the three of us fighting.

Well, two of us. Nikki just chuckled. He had this placid smile on his face like the whole thing was utterly hilarious to him. Maybe it was.

Elias rounded on him. "Don't you start, Nisha."

Nikki pushed out his bottom lip in one of his quirky smiles. "King knows what he's doing."

Except I didn't.

I groaned and leaned my ass against the table, rubbing my face with my hands. "Look, I know it's not a good idea."

"It's a great idea," Nikki said.

Elias threw his hands up and turned away from the both of us. When he spun back around, he pinned me with the icy stare he was known throughout the league for. "You, of all people, should know better."

In an instant, I'd closed the distance between us. "Don't you fucking *dare* say that to me." I didn't need Elias throwing *that* into my face.

Fear flashed over Elias's features, and he put both hands up.

"Hey hey, Jules." Nikki grabbed my arm, his calm voice cooling some of my fury.

I didn't yank away from Nikki, but I didn't back down either. "I know it's not a good idea," I repeated. "Believe me, I *know*." Such a bad idea, for all the reasons Elias had dragged me into this room, and for all the other ones I'd already tumbled over in my head.

Except one fact stood out from all that, like a black puck on a fresh sheet of ice. "I like him."

"You like a lot of people." That was Elias at his most exasperated.

Nikki shook his head. "He doesn't like the people he fucks."

Ouch. I sat my butt back against the table. "I don't *dislike* them. But—they're one night stands."

Elias froze. "Wait. All of them?"

I met his gaze. Whatever was in my face was answer enough, because a look of horror took up residence on Elias's.

"Eight years of one night stands?" His voice was faint, but his words sharp.

"Seven," I spit out. Because that first year? I'd been with exactly one person.

That didn't help. Elias paled and slumped back against the wall. "Julien."

"He knows what he's doing," Nikki said again.

I choked out a laugh. "I have no idea what I'm doing."

Nikki gripped my shoulder. "You do."

"Fuck my life." Elias raked both hands through his hair. "Nisha, don't encourage him!"

Nikki snapped something in Russian that I didn't catch, and Elias gave him the finger. That led to louder Russian, then they were yelling at each other.

Fuck this. "Stop! Just fucking *stop*." My voice shook. Hell, my hands shook.

The room was suddenly very quiet. Glancing between them, I saw the shock and the worry, and wondered how loud we'd gotten. "I haven't felt like this about anyone since..." I waved my hand, not wanting to say Travis's name. "And it's different with Isaac." I met Elias's stare. "I know everything that can go wrong with dating a teammate, believe me."

Nikki placed a heavy hand on my shoulder, right over Isaac's bite mark.

"Ow, fuck!" I pushed him, but he didn't move an inch. Didn't lift his hand either.

"Dating." I couldn't read Elias's expression at all. Might have been exasperation, but there was a tiny smile there that made no sense at all. "What the fuck am I going to do with you, Julien?"

I shrugged. "Let me be?"

Elias chuckled. "Yeah, probably." He pulled me into an unexpected hug, breaking the hold Nikki had on me.

God, I needed that. I sagged into Elias. "Don't tell the team? We want to keep it quiet for a while."

"We'll keep it quiet, but Julien, be careful? He might be twenty-two, but he's still a rookie. Still new to the league. And you—" He opened up space between us. "We need you. If we're going to get to playoffs, we need you, too."

"Sure." I gave a flippant shrug.

That got me a gentle shake from Elias. "I mean it, Julien Joseph Alex—"

I laughed, cutting him off. "Fine. Jesus. You don't have to be an asshole. That's his job." I jerked my thumb at Nikki.

Who found my bruise again. With *his* thumb.

"Ah, fuck!" I pulled away from both of them.

Elias rolled his eyes. "Nisha, I said we need him. Please don't break him."

"It's a bruise. He's fine." He patted my back. "You fine?"

The spot ached, especially because of Nikki's torment. "If you can stop poking me there, I'll be fine for the game."

"We should talk about tonight," Elias said. "Since this is supposed to be a leadership meeting."

That brought back the memory of Isaac standing in front of my house, telling me we'd win, and that I'd score a goal. "Detroit is fast, but their defense is young. We get behind them, keep down the odd man rushes, we'll be fine."

Nikki nodded. "Five-man units."

Elias shrugged. "So, the clichés. Pucks deep. Battles on the wall, all that."

I huffed out a laugh. "I mean, they're clichés for a reason."

We bounced ideas back and forth about some set plays, then headed out to the lounge, all jokes and smiles. No one on the team batted an eye. Maybe they hadn't heard the Russian shouting match. Hopefully, they hadn't heard me.

We were going to win tonight. I was going to score a goal, just like Isaac said.

# Chapter 11

## Isaac

I WAS HALF RIGHT—WE did win that night, but Julien didn't get a goal. He had two assists, though, including on Sidorov's goal that gave us the lead with a minute and a half left to play. The other team fought like hell to answer that with another point to tie up the score and push us into overtime, but we weren't having it. Larry barely had to do a thing in the net for that last ninety seconds since Julien and Paxy wouldn't even let the puck into our zone, and my wingers and I made drive after drive for their goal until the buzzer finally sounded.

It hadn't been a perfect game, and I'd made some mistakes I wasn't proud of, but no game was perfect and it hadn't been all mistakes on my end. And I'd picked up a point with an assist in the first period, so hopefully that balanced out some of my other bullshit. Enough that tonight's fuck-ups wouldn't come back to haunt me when I was lying awake at night like that missed goal in the peewee championships or that really awkward thing I'd said one time when I was fifteen.

Overall, it was a great night. The energy of the hometown crowd was amazing—I would never stop loving the way the crowd roared to their feet every time we scored—and that energy stuck with us in the locker room after. That losing streak was definitely behind us now. We couldn't rest on our laurels, and we had to keep playing this hard going forward, but it felt less like we were about to be *that team*—the one that sucked so bad it was embarrassing to lose to them. We probably hadn't even been in any danger of getting to that level, but losing streaks were demoralizing and I wasn't rational, so there it was.

Eventually, everyone started filtering out to the parking garage. Sometimes I'd go with some teammates to a nearby bar to hang out with fans for a while, especially when we were pumped after a good game. Most of the time, though, I was one of the players who'd call it a night and go home. Downtime—the kind that was actually quiet and granted me the luxury of being alone—was hard to come by these days, and I grabbed it where I could.

Tonight, I didn't want to be alone, and I didn't want anything quiet.

On my way to my car, I took out my phone and wrote out a text:

*Here's my address. Be there in 20.*

I felt ballsy as hell, telling him to be there instead of asking. No question marks. No *hey, if you want to...* Or *if you don't have anything going on* or *if you don't want to, that's cool* or even a, *do with this what you will*. For a solid thirty seconds, I hesitated with my thumb over the Send button. Too much? Too forward? Too presumptuous? It wasn't like we'd interacted more than normal in the locker room or between periods. Did that mean he'd lost interest since yesterday? Or was he just trying to lay low so our teammates didn't find out?

After all those articles I'd pored over last night, and after my conversation with Darian, I decided it was worth the risk. If I'd misread Julien or stepped over a line, we could talk about it and adapt going forward. It wouldn't be a deal-breaker. Julien might've been a hothead, but he was reasonable, and we were both grown-ass adults.

*"And if he's worth giving the time of day, never mind dating,"* Darian had said, *"he'll understand you're inexperienced and he'll guide you."*

So, why not stick my neck out a bit?

Without another thought, I sent the message.

Then I shoved my phone into the inside pocket of my jacket, continued toward my car, and headed home.

My apartment was close to the arena. Along with the view of the Monongahela River, that had been one of the biggest selling points, especially since by the time I left, post-game traffic had nearly always cleared out. It took under five minutes to get from here to there. Not very long, but definitely long enough for me to work myself up and consider every imaginable way that text could blow up in my stupid face. I came up with a few more disastrous outcomes when I glanced at my phone in the elevator.

Julien had read the text. He hadn't responded.

Oh. Fuck.

By the time I keyed myself into my apartment, I was a shaky mess. The whole time I was unsteadily changing into a T-shirt and a pair of jeans, I swore at myself for being so stupid and presumptuous and awkward. Everything Darian had told me went out the window. I *had* screwed up. This *would* ruin everything. We *were* going to—

The doorbell rang.

I was still pulling on my jeans and actually stumbled because my idiot brain wanted to bolt for the door before Julien had a chance to change his mind. Fortunately, I only took one or two ridiculous steps, didn't fall on my ass, and was completely out of anyone's sight except my own. That big mirror on the closet gave me a nice view of the whole shit show, though. Awesome.

Still red in the face, I hurried down from the loft, shoving my arms into my sleeves as I did. At the door, I paused to take a quick breath and compose myself.

Then I opened the door.

Oh my God.

He was still in his suit, the jacket unbuttoned and his tie MIA, and nothing about his expression said I'd misjudged the play. The subtle upward tilt of his lips. That knowing, needy look in his eyes.

The only thing that kept me from putting my nerves on display—no shifting, no swallowing—was something I'd read last night. Something about how the more confident the Dom, the more at ease the sub.

Without a word, I stood aside just like he had when I'd been on his porch yesterday. He came in. I shut the door. He didn't push me up against it like I had, though, and I understood why. *He* wanted to be controlled and manhandled.

*Don't mind if I do.*

I stepped right up into his space and looked in his eyes as if I'd never in my life been intimidated by this man. "You came."

In a husky whisper, he said, "It's what you wanted, yes?"

I curved a hand behind his neck and then up into his hair. "It's part of what I wanted."

Julien swallowed. "Part of it?"

"Mmhmm." I closed my fist around his hair, and he gasped as his whole body tensed up. In a low, quiet voice, I said, "Down."

He met my eyes, his full of surprise and...oh yes, there it was: lust. Hunger.

I tugged downward, and his knees buckled. I'd imagined shoving him to his knees, but he was an athlete and this was a hardwood floor. Not all pain was good pain, and those would be bruises he didn't need. So, I let him kneel at his own speed.

Once he was situated, he gazed up at me, and I had a feeling it was only partially because I had an iron grip on his hair and was *making* him look at me. From the pure, molten desire in his expression, he wouldn't have looked away if I let go. And for as talkative as he'd been yesterday, he was completely silent this time. And still.

Holy shit, this was all heady as hell.

With my free hand, I started undoing my jeans. I didn't say a word, just unbuttoned and unzipped my fly, all the while watching surprise and anticipation and desire roll across Julien's face. His eyes flicked toward my hard-on, but then came right back to meet my gaze, and I had never seen so much unspoken *want* in my life.

Still gripping his hair tight, I pushed my cock against his lips, and I had a split second of worry that he was going to decide this was too much or not what he wanted or... I don't know... *Something*.

But then his lips were around the head of my dick, and his moan said I had absolutely nothing to worry about. He steadied me with a hand around the base, and with the other, he grabbed a handful of my jeans and pulled me forward, drawing me deeper into his eager mouth.

"Holy shit," I breathed. I had to rest a hand on the wall to keep my balance. He kept tugging at my jeans and pulling at the grip I had on his hair, as if he wanted me to pull harder, or—

*"Fuck your mouth,"* I remembered growling at him.

*"Next time,"* he'd whimpered. *"Please."*

I rocked my hips experimentally. Julien groaned around me, the sound full of *lust* and *yes*. Head spinning and heart thundering, I gave him more, thrusting into his mouth. Not hard, not too deep, but enough that he knew I meant it, and he rewarded me with more groans and some mind-blowing magic with his tongue.

I had to widen my stance a little to keep from dropping to the floor in front of him, and the hand on the wall kept me from wavering as the room spun around us. "Goddamn, Julien. Oh, fuck..."

His eyes flicked up to meet mine, a hint of tears on his long lashes, and oh my God, he was so damn sexy like this, on his knees in a suit with my cock sliding in and out of his mouth. Every fantasy I never knew I had, all coming to life with the man I never thought I'd have.

*How is this real?*

"Don't stop, Julien," I moaned, loving the way it felt to say his name while I was this turned on. "I'm gonna come. You—" I stopped myself from asking if he wanted it, and instead I went with, "I'm going to come in your mouth and you're going to swallow it all. You hear me?"

It felt weird to talk like that, but the moan he released had me right there on the edge.

"Jesus, Julien." I gasped as my balance tried to falter. "Keep—yeah, that's it. Get me there. Get me off and swallow it."

It took him mere seconds to do exactly that, and my shout of pleasure echoed off my apartment's high ceilings as I came in his mouth. He pumped me with his hand and kept teasing me with his tongue as if he were eager for more, and he didn't stop until I let go of his hair and took a shaky half-step back. By some miracle, I found the coordination to fix my pants, but that was about all I was good for.

"Oh, my God," I breathed.

Julien gazed up at me with fire in his eyes as he wiped an unsteady hand along his swollen lips. We stared at each other for a moment. I wondered if he was as speechless as I was, or if he was waiting for me to say something.

I had no idea what to say. I did know what I wanted, though, so I extended my arm. He clasped his hand around it, and I helped him to his feet.

And then, just like I had in his foyer yesterday, I shoved him against the wall and kissed him hard.

He didn't miss a beat. He opened eagerly to my kiss as he wrapped his strong arms around me, and when he dragged his fingers through my hair, I shivered with the prickle of goose bumps running down my back. His lips curved into a grin against mine, as if he enjoyed getting that reaction out of me. He drew back and inhaled like he was about to speak, undoubtedly ready to fire off something smartass, but the palm of my hand over his hard, clothed dick shut him up. Eyes closed, lips still parted with his remark unspoken, he let his head fall back against the wall.

"What's wrong?" I purred, leaning down to kiss his neck. "You're usually so"—I teased him through his pants—"talkative."

"And you're usually..." Julien made a choked sound as he rutted against my palm. "Who *are* you?"

I grinned against his throat. "The man who's got a whole head full of ideas for making you scream."

"A whole—" He tensed. "Wait a second..."

Alarm shot through me, and I pulled back to meet his gaze. "What?"

His eyebrow arched. "A head full of ideas? Have you been...reading about this?"

The heat in my cheeks had to be a dead giveaway. "Uh..."

"Did you?"

I dropped my gaze as I pulled my hand back. "I...didn't want to fuck this up. And I don't know a damn thing about what we're doing. The rough stuff, and the domination, and... So I..." Christ, I had to be scarlet by now. "I googled it, okay?"

Silence hung between us for a few mortifying seconds.

Trust me to say something to throw the night off the rails before I even got his pants off.

"Isaac. Look at me."

I didn't want to, but I did.

Julien was grinning. It took me a second to realize he wasn't laughing at me, though. Not at all. Sliding his hand behind my neck and drawing me in, he whispered, "If this was a taste of what you've been reading"—he brushed his lips across mine—"then by all means, keep reading."

And then we were kissing again, deep and long and perfect. Julien took my wrist and guided my hand back to the front of his pants, and I reveled in the way he gasped as I started stroking his thick erection. He was right back to rutting against my hand the way he'd been doing before I'd made things awkward, and okay, maybe Darian was right—we *could* recover if I said or did something stupid at the wrong moment. Especially since this apparently hadn't been as stupid or the moment as wrong as I'd thought.

I broke the kiss and met his smoldering eyes. "I hope you weren't planning on staying this dressed the whole time you're here."

Julien bit his lip. "I'll stay as dressed as you want me to." The words were half plea, half challenge.

"I don't want you dressed at all." I jerked my head toward the stairs. "Go up to the loft and strip." I kissed him again, brief and hard. "I'm going to fuck you until my neighbors complain."

Julien whimpered softly. "Yes, please."

I stepped back and nodded toward the stairs again.

He leaned down to untie his shoes, which was probably a challenge when he was that hard. Then he toed them off and pushed them up against mine beside the door.

And without another word, he headed for the stairs, unbuttoning his shirt as he went.

One of these days, Julien and I would have the chance to spend the night together, but at this rate, it was probably going to have to wait until the off season or something. He stayed late enough for us to go a couple of rounds, and then headed home. After all, we had to be at the training center in the morning to once again go to the airport and fly off to... wherever it was we were going. Florida, I thought.

I got to the training center early, because of course I did. Julien didn't, because of course he didn't. Knowing him, he'd pull in right about the time someone was ready to text him and tell him to meet us at the airport. I'd have to ask him sometime if he was really chronically almost late or if he just enjoyed antagonizing the powers that be by showing up at the absolute last possible moment. I was pretty sure I knew the answer.

Most of the guys were shooting the shit and drinking coffee. Larry had basically fallen asleep in a chair, and some of our teammates were conspiring to punish him for that by drawing dicks on his face, messing with his phone, or something equally hilarious. Even I knew better than to fall asleep around teammates when they were awake and bored; my university team had pranked me enough times to break me of that habit. Larry had been around long enough that he should've known. He probably did, but knowing him he'd also gotten laid last night and hadn't had much sleep.

I suppressed a grin and buried my nose in a book on my phone. I'd gotten laid last night too. Also hadn't had much sleep. The less my teammates knew or suspected about that, the better.

They also didn't need to know that Julien and I had spent a little time perusing reading material in between screwing, and a couple of books had interested him. The reviews were decent and the blurbs had sounded good, so I'd bought them, and while they'd downloaded, I'd fucked him against my bedroom wall before finishing him in my shower. Afterward, he'd mentioned that my bathroom counter was the perfect height to bend someone over, and the view in the mirror would be sexy as hell. I'd tucked that away for another night, because oh fuck yes, I wanted to watch myself fuck Julien Landry until he cried.

I squirmed in my seat, willing myself not to get a badly timed hard-on. Then I focused again on the chapter I'd been reading about Dom/sub dynamics. It was still pretty basic stuff, but I was less embarrassed about diving into it now that Julien knew and had given his enthusiastic blessing.

"I want things that a lot of people aren't comfortable giving," he'd explained. "If understanding it academically helps you be comfortable doing it..." He'd trailed off into a shrug as he'd offered up a sweet, genuine smile that had melted my heart.

So, yeah, I was going to dive into this side of it, and hopefully then I'd be able to give him what he wanted and needed. So far, so good, if last night was anything to go by. Though I was definitely intrigued by the idea of tying him up and—

"Rivs." Sidorov's voice pulled my attention away from my book.

I quickly shut off the app so no one caught a glimpse over my shoulder. "Hmm?"

He gestured for me to come with him.

My heart jumped into my throat. A one-on-one with Sidorov? Oh shit. Was this about that ridiculous turnover I'd had last night? I mean, I'd had several, but there'd been one where Sidorov had set me up to pass to Ozzy, who'd had a perfect shot behind the distracted netminder, but I'd hesitated just long enough for an opposing player to snatch the puck away. He'd fired a shot at our goal that only the crossbar and dumb luck had prevented from being a game-changing goal.

Well, an inopportune hard-on definitely wasn't going to be a problem now. I stood, tucked my phone in my pocket, and sheepishly followed Sidorov outside. The morning was brisk enough to keep our teammates and staff inside, but not so uncomfortable that we couldn't stand out here for a little while to get some privacy. Uh-oh. Ass-chewing? Fuck my life.

I slid my hands into my pockets and tried not to cringe as I waited for my teammate to speak. Sidorov looked around the parking lot and at our teammates' various cars.

"Listen." He met my gaze. "I've debated whether to say anything at all. Maybe it's none of my business, and..." He waved a hand and shook his head. He seemed frustrated, as if he couldn't quite find the words. Then he settled on simply, "Julien."

My heart stopped, and not because he'd gone for Julien's given name over his usual nickname. "What about him?"

"He's been a friend of mine for a long time. Not just teammate. *Friend*. You understand?"

Mute and confused, I nodded. Everyone knew Sidorov, Karlsson, and Julien were tight, and it wasn't for nothing I'd not only wondered if Sidorov and Karlsson were or had been a couple, I'd thought the same about Sidorov and Julien.

Sidorov exhaled, wiping a hand over his face, and he suddenly seemed tired. Not angry, not frustrated, just...tired. "I know about you and him."

I swallowed. There probably wasn't any point in playing stupid. If he knew, he knew. "Okay? Are you going to tell me to keep it on the down-low? Because that was the plan."

He studied me. "No. I don't have to tell you that. You're not stupid. I only know because I know Julien." With a dry, almost sad laugh, he shook his head. "He couldn't hide anything from me if he tried."

I didn't say anything. I had no idea what to say.

Right then, an approaching car engine turned both our heads, and we watched as a bright red BMW M4 pulled in the parking lot. My pulse surged. Only one member of the Griffins drove that particular car.

Sidorov faced me again. "You're not stupid, Rivs. And as far as I can tell, you're a good man. Just..." He nodded toward the red sports car, and his expression was pleading in a way that Julien's absolutely *hadn't* been last night. "Be careful with him. Please?"

My stomach turned to lead as alarm sent my pulse surging. Be careful with him? How? Why?

But Julien was getting out of his car. He was heading this way with his suitcase on his heels. Almost within earshot. There was no time for Sidorov to explain.

"Jules." Sidorov brightened as if nothing were out of the ordinary. "Right on time, as always."

Julien laughed. "Eat a dick, Nikki."

Sidorov grumbled something in Russian. Then, "Come on. Let's go before Coach sends a search party after all of us."

We followed him inside. As we walked, Julien touched my back, but only for a second. I glanced at him, and we exchanged smiles. His seemed perfectly normal, as if nothing were amiss. Hopefully mine did too.

All the while, though, my mind was racing and my heart was right there with it. I knew about Julien's questionable history—at least as much as he'd told me, like when he and that blogger had hate-fucked—but was there more to the story? Were there entirely different stories I knew nothing about? Julien was an enigma. A closed and guarded book in a lot of ways, jarringly open in others, especially if the rumors were to be believed about him leaking that sex tape.

I was afraid to ask him to show me more cards. Communication was key and all—Darian had driven that point home loud and clear—but this felt like a "don't ask questions unless you're sure you want the answers" type of situation. I wanted the truth in the sense that I wanted to know who this man was who I'd just started dating, but I was afraid he'd turn over a card that would make me look at him differently. I was also afraid that card would blindside me at the worst possible time in the worst possible way. I was better off knowing, right?

Probably. As we joined our teammates and started making our way toward the bus, I couldn't shake the feeling that I was going to find out sooner or later. Sooner if I had a spine, later if I was a complete coward who'd get what I deserved for ignoring my teammate's warning.

I needed to know, but I didn't *want* to know.

*What are you hiding, Julien?*

*And why the hell does Sidorov think I need to be careful with you?*

## Chapter 12

Julien

*What the fuck is going on?*

I sipped my gin and tonic as the plane leveled out from its climb and my heart ticked down from its *oh-fuck-we're-in-the-air* pounding pace, and took stock of the three men I sat with. Nikki had his nose in a book—an honest to God hardcover, too. Looked like it might be a mystery novel, but it was difficult to tell. Russian book covers were different than anything in North America, more illustrated, more abstract. Made guessing the genre hard sometimes.

Isaac was staring at his phone. Both he and Nikki were tense and neither had looked up since we'd sat down and gotten our pre-flight drinks. My gaze snagged on Elias's—he sat across from me—and he lifted a questioning brow. I gave him the suggestion of a shrug and flicked my fingers at Nikki and Isaac, and mirrored his expression.

*What's up with these two?*

Elias wasn't as close to me as he was to Nikki, but we'd been friends for the same number of years, so he knew me well. A sharp shake of his head and a shrug, then his lips twisted into a quick frown. *I have no idea* was what he was saying.

Well, shit.

At the training facility, Nikki and Isaac had been standing outside and talking when I'd driven up. Nothing had seemed amiss between them. On the bus to the airport, we'd all sat with different people, but that was normal. Sure, I'd rather have sat with Isaac, but that would've given everything away, because I doubted I could keep my hands to myself. I wanted to hold him. Touch him. I ached for him. His voice. Those fingers in my hair. His dick in my mouth. Or ass. I shifted in my seat and looked out the window. Great start to a relationship if we were already at the awkward-silence-after-banging stage.

I took a peek at Nikki and rewound the interaction between those two when I'd joined them.

*Jules.* Nikki had called me Jules, not King. I cocked my head and took a harder look at my best friend. *What did you say to him, Nikolai?* Something had gone down, and now it was killing the vibe we all had, the one we all needed. Three games this trip, including one with Carolina, our—and my personal—rival. I downed the rest of my gin and tonic. Crisse, I needed to fix this, and quickly.

When I faced Elias again, his other brow was up. He looked rather pointedly at my glass.

Yeah, I didn't normally chug my drink. Nor did I order more than one, except on flights to the West Coast. Florida wasn't a long flight, but when the attendant came by, I asked for a second.

That had Nikki looking up from his book. "Are you okay?"

"Me?" I snapped. "I'm fine." Pissed, but fine.

Right. Nikki looked chagrinned. Great.

In the seat next to me, Isaac shifted. "Uh, should we play cards or something?"

I didn't answer right away because the attendant returned with my drink. No one else ordered anything, and Nikki still wasn't meeting my gaze. Neither was Isaac. His flicked between Nikki and Elias.

I took a sip and finally spoke into the silence. "Yes, let's play cards."

Elias nodded, so Nikki put his book away, got out his deck, and started shuffling. He dealt the cards for Spades without naming the game.

Isaac finally made eye contact with me, and I raised my brow. *Well? What's it going to be?* I didn't like this at all. If we needed to talk, we should talk, not Nikki...shooting off his mouth.

Isaac looked down at his hand, then back at me, and there was worry and apprehension there.

I sipped my drink, then spoke. "Why don't you partner with Nikolai for this round?"

"Julien..." That from Elias.

I turned my stare on him. "You don't think you can play with me?"

He set his jaw. "Of course I can play with you. I've been playing with you for eight years."

"Let's go, then," I said, and downed another swallow of the gin and tonic before setting it aside.

The game was close, but Elias and I won in the end, reading off each other and trusting our instincts. Elias was cool and collected as always. I was buzzed.

The game obviously wrung both Nikki and Isaac out, but they'd played well, despite the situation I'd thrust them into. From what I could tell, confusion simmered in Isaac, while guilt and anger burned in Nikki. I'd be hearing from both of them once we were on the ground. Or rather, they'd be hearing from *me*. Enough of this shit.

My brain buzzed and my inhibitions were gone from the second gin and tonic, so I snatched Nikki's cards and started shuffling, despite all the warning lights blinking in the back of my head. "My third year on the team, we had a ton of injuries on the blue line. You remember that, Elias, yes?"

He nodded carefully, eying me like I'd grown antennae. Hell, maybe I had. "I do," he said.

"Do you remember what you told me when I complained about having a different defensive partner every night?"

Elias froze, and I saw the moment he realized what I was doing. His nod was smoother, and a hint of a smile curled his lips. "I told you that you needed to be able to play with anyone on the team, at any time, no matter what was going on. Because this was hockey and every game mattered."

"So, this game, Nikki and me. Elias and Isaac." I dealt the cards and studied my hand. Not bad. Two of the four aces. King of spades. Two queens. Some high cards in other suits, and then a bunch of low cards, including five spades.

I looked up into a fiery set of eyes. "Oh, is it Nikki again?" he said.

He was pissed, but so was I. "For now. We'll see how it goes."

He narrowed his gaze, glanced at his cards, and sneered. "Six."

Either he was bluffing or we both had fucking good hands. One thing I knew for sure, Nikki cared about me. Even when we fought, that was done with love. Maybe it was the gin, maybe our past, but I chose to take him at his word. "All right. Six for me as well."

Isaac made a choking noise, and Elias shifted in his seat. Twelve tricks out of thirteen possible tricks. Nikki's smile was sharp and full of barbs.

We won eleven tricks that hand, but managed to lose the game by blundering another hand completely when Nikki didn't believe me, and we bagged too many tricks. Isaac and Elias were ecstatic at the win, high-fiving each other over the club table.

"Trust is an interesting thing," I said to no one in particular.

Nikki's fury had abated somewhat, but he scowled at me. I grinned back.

Isaac gathered the cards at the center of the table. "So, you and me, and Karlsson and Sidorov—Sido?"

I'd never seen Elias roll his eyes quite so hard. "It's Elias, or Karly."

Isaac's sheepish grin was lovely. "Okay."

Nikki leveled another glare at me before shifting his attention to Isaac. "You can call me Nisha here." He gestured to the four of us.

Isaac nodded, then started shuffling. God, his hands were mesmerizing. Crisp. Careful. Rhythmic. I wanted them on my body again. "You've played cards a lot."

"Poker. In college." When he met my gaze, there was worry there, uncertainty.

*Trust me*, I thought. *I don't know what he said to you, but trust me.*

He looked away and dealt the cards while I took another sip of my drink. Exhaustion crept in at the edge of my mood, that heavy feeling I got from alcohol mixed with flying. After this round, I'd probably pass out until we landed.

My cards were a mixed bag of nothing. Not even a single spade. The highest card I had was an eight, and only one of those. "Nil."

Nikki whistled. "Five."

"Four," Elias said, crisply.

Isaac arranged his cards. "Six."

Fuck. Someone was wrong. When I met Isaac's gaze, he had a wicked smile, one that burned right through my gin-infused haze. "Game on, then."

Not only did we win the hand—with me taking no tricks—we won the game, the same way we had the first time we'd played. Isaac and I were in sync again.

Nikki was silent as he gathered his cards and put them away.

Elias huffed a laugh. "You're something else, Julien."

"That's why you love me." I finished my drink and set the glass down on the table. My eyelids were heavy and space was gently turning repeatedly to my right. I attempted to focus on Nikki. "We're having a conversation once we land."

He looked away and grunted.

I closed my eyes and touched Isaac on his knee. "Then we're going to talk."

"Julien," he said, his voice shaky.

"No. Non. None of you get to fucking 'Julien' me. I'm going to sleep, and we'll deal with this later." I leaned my seat back, curled into myself, and let my swirling mind pull me down.

Just before I lost consciousness, I heard Isaac ask, "Is he always like this when he has two drinks?"

I didn't stay awake to hear an answer.

---

BY THE TIME we reached the hotel, I was sober but still pissed. I didn't like Nikki interfering in my relationship with Isaac. After we got our room keys, I caught Nikki by the arm. "My room. Ten minutes." Then, I showed him the number on the envelope.

I was hanging up my suit for tomorrow when a knock sounded on the door. Nikki was punctual even when he knew he was about to get reamed out. He slinked in, impressive for someone as tall and broad as he was.

When the door clicked shut, I turned, crossed my arms, and leveled him a look that must have worked, because he ran a bashful hand through his hair. "Jules..."

"Nikolai."

That had him meeting my stare with a sharp one of his own. "So, back to that."

"Maybe. I want to know what the *fuck* you said to him."

"Nothing!" He held up his hands. "I told him to be careful with you."

Oh fucking hell. I let out a stream of curses, then threw up my hands and stalked over to the balcony door. Then I spun around. "You told him?"

There were only four people who knew anything about what had happened between me and Travis Canterbury, and that included me and Travis. Nikki and Elias were the other two. I doubted Travis would tell anyone—he knew exactly how it would look from the outside.

"I didn't tell him. I told him to be careful, that's all. He should hear about that from you." Nikki pinned me with a glare of his own. "You should tell him."

"God, I am not telling Isaac about history that's over and done with." The very thought of explaining Travis to Isaac tumbled my stomach and filled me with loathing. "It's not important."

I couldn't take the look Nikki was giving me, so I spun again, and stared out the window. In the reflection of the glass, Nikki approached, and his hands landed on my shoulders. "I won't tell him. But that's a part of your life, and if Isaac becomes what I think he will for you, he needs to know."

I didn't answer. Didn't shrug off Nikki's touch, either.

"You're many things, Julien. But you're not a fool. You

weren't then, and you aren't now. Don't let that shithead hold you back."

I'd been both a fool and naïve. "I'm not," I murmured. "He's nothing. I don't think about him anymore."

Nikki snorted in obvious disbelief.

Before I could take his head off, both our phones buzzed. Nikki dug his out first.

When I got mine out, I found a group text from Elias: *Isaac and I are going out to dinner in 20. Steak. You two joining us?*

"Well?" Nikki jiggled his phone at me.

My stomach growled and my anger softened. When you burn as many calories as we did, you couldn't skip a meal, and Nikki? Well, he was trying to help.

"Fine," I said, then texted *Count me in.* Then I flipped over to Isaac's number and typed out, *My room, in 10* and gave him the number. I pocketed my phone.

"So, are we good, King?" Nikki grinned at me.

I couldn't help the laugh. "Yeah, we're good, you jerk."

I punched him in the shoulder, and he pulled me into a hug. "You be careful with you, too."

When he let me go, I saw him to the door. "I'm a hockey player, Nikki, not porcelain."

He rolled his eyes. "We're all porcelain inside, Jules." Then he was out the door and heading down the hall.

I turned over Nikki's last words in my head as the door clicked closed, then stripped off my button-down, which joined my jacket on the bed, and I headed into the bathroom to freshen up.

When a knock sounded on my door, I'd finished shaving, but I still needed to put my hair into some amount of order—that involved wetting it down and working the tangles out. I'd gotten as far as the wetting down stage.

Towel in hand, I answered the door. No surprise that it

was Isaac on the other side. He was dressed in a dark blue suit with a white shirt and gray tie. Plain, but it fit him well. I stepped aside to let him in.

His gaze raked up my bare chest, but when it landed on my face, there was only apprehension there. "You shaved."

"I do that occasionally, yes." I gestured at the room. "Have a seat. I need to find my brush."

Took me a minute to dig that out of my bag and to finish toweling off my hair. Then I was back out and Isaac was staring at me, this time with a hint of lust mixed in with the nerves. "I—did I screw up when I talked with Nisha? Cross a line? Julien—"

I waved those words away. "No. If anyone did, it was Nikki getting involved. Or maybe me for not giving you enough about me. I don't know. This is going so fast."

His deep brown eyes were so guarded as he looked at me.

God, I wanted him. I wanted to be the one sitting on the bed with Isaac looming over me in that suit. Except there was no time, and there were things that needed to be said first. Trust to be regained. I swung to the mirror and started working out the tangles. "Nikki told me what he said to you. You don't have to worry about me."

I met Isaac's gaze in the mirror, and after a moment, he glanced away. "There's a lot I don't know about you."

"Honestly, there's not that much to know. It's probably all out there on the internet, anyway." I grimaced as I worked a knot undone. "That threesome, for instance."

Isaac's sudden shifting and blush told me he'd seen those photos. That video. "You have a lot more experience than me. I—I'm not sure what I'm doing a lot of the time."

I set down my brush and turned to face Isaac. "That's not why you were ignoring me on the plane."

He pierced me with his gaze and I wondered if he knew how much he could still me with that intense look. "Is there anything I should know about your past? Any reason I should be worried?"

Nikki's admonishment wormed up my spine, but Travis was history. A bad memory. "No. I haven't screwed anyone over or anything like that. No secret children." I paused. "That I know of. I've always used protection, and I assume by this point someone would have come to me for support, you know?"

He hadn't looked away. Same intense brown eyes meeting my own.

"Isaac, please trust me."

He swallowed, then spoke softly, and there was a tremble to his voice. "Come here, and get on your knees."

I moved without thought, the hunger inside me making me sink before him on the carpet in front of the bed. I didn't get hard because this wasn't sexual, for all that it was desire and need.

Isaac tucked back the strands of wet hair that had fallen into my face. The blush was there, the closed off expression. "I don't want to fuck this up. Tell me if there's something I need to know."

"There's nothing," I whispered. I couldn't read a damn thing in those eyes, as guarded as they were. We sat like that for a long moment, me staring up at him.

Isaac sighed, and there were all the emotions: the worry, the fear, and the relief. "All right." He cupped my jaw and drew me in for a kiss.

Kissing him made my head spin worse than gin. Always did. When he came up for air, he skimmed his fingers over my clean-shaven jaw, and smiled. "You going to go shirtless?"

"Bet you'd like that."

Isaac laughed, and my heart finally eased to where it belonged. "A little too much." He patted my cheek. "Get dressed. I'd rather not have to fight everyone in this city for your attention."

I rose and grabbed my shirt. "You wouldn't have to. You won't have to. I'm all yours."

That made Isaac look down, a sexy wicked smile twisting his lips. "Good to know."

A few minutes later, now wearing a shirt and tie, I shrugged into my jacket, and we headed down to the lobby to meet up with Nikki and Elias.

We were exactly on time, too.

# Chapter 13

## Isaac

"And then this idiot"—Nisha jabbed his fork at Julien—"decides he's fucking bored, and he starts trying to do doughnuts with the golf cart."

"What?" Julien shrugged with mock innocence. "I *was* bored! We'd been out there for hours!"

"It was the second hole!"

"Exactly!" Julien huffed as he reached for his drink. "Sixteen more of those and I'd have clubbed myself to death."

"Not with my clubs, you wouldn't have," Elias groused. "Those were expensive."

"And you use them to hit *grass*." Julien rolled his eyes. "Golf isn't a sport. It's a punishment."

"I don't think you're supposed to hit the grass," I said.

"Hey, cut him some slack," Nisha said. "At least he could hit the grass. Those little white balls?" He grimaced and shrugged.

Julien made an exasperated noise and flipped him off.

"You can't hit a golf ball?" I snorted. "But you hit pucks all day long. And they're moving. And so are you. Golf balls, you just stand there and—"

He turned that middle finger on me, which had all of us—including him—laughing.

"It's boring," he declared, still chuckling. "Where's the fun? Where's the challenge?"

"Where's the challenge?" Elias barked a laugh that was loud and boisterous for him. "Says the man who went eight over par on a three-stroke hole."

"Is that what you call it now?" Julien cocked a brow. "A three-stroke hole?"

Elias's laugh turned to a glare, and now he was the one rolling his eyes. "For fuck's sake..."

"You kind of walked into that one, bro," I told him.

There was a time in the not too distant past when a pointed look like that from our captain would've triggered an *oh fuck* butthole clench. Ever since I'd been brought into this little group, though, Elias had become just one of the guys. No, that wasn't right. *I'd* become one of the guys. I was *friends* with Elias Karlsson and Nikolai Sidorov. The kind of friends who could talk shit and use first names and even nicknames. Whoa.

And that was to say nothing of the way things had evolved between me and Julien. Every time my thoughts quieted during dinner tonight, they slid right back to that moment when I'd put him on his knees in his hotel room. When he'd been trying to reassure me that he wasn't hiding anything, and he'd knelt at my feet and looked in my eyes and—I was absolutely certain—told me the truth.

I believed him. I'd misread Nisha's warning before our flight, and while I was still jittery over being out-of-step with Julien for a few hours, and still sure I knew next to nothing about him, I didn't think he was hiding anything like I'd tied myself in knots over today. Nothing nefarious. Nothing that I should keep my guard up for or run away from.

No reason I should break up with him.

Which, holy shit, the reason that was even an option at all was because *Julien Landry was my boyfriend*.

I wondered how long it was going to take for that to completely settle in. I mean, it kind of had. Most of the time, I forgot that he was Julien Landry at all. He was just Julien. And he was just amazing. And Jesus Christ, I was still so worried I would screw this up. Julien could do so much better than an awkward almost-virgin who had to google everything we did.

"What about you, rook?" Nisha's words jostled me back out of my thoughts, and he eyed me across the table. "You golf?"

I laughed as I started to cut another piece of my steak. "*Fuck* no."

"Oh, come on." Elias tsked. "You too?"

"I grew up in the Pacific Northwest." I shrugged. "It was always wet."

"Pfft." He shook his head as he stabbed a piece of salmon. "I know lots of people from up there who golf."

"Okay, okay, you got me. It wasn't always wet, but it *was* painfully boring and meant like four hours of being bored off my ass and listening to my dad and uncle talk about boring dad and uncle shit." I skewered the cube of steak. "No thanks."

"You wouldn't be listening to dad and uncle shit with us," Nisha protested. "It's a lot like hockey, except—"

Julien almost spat his drink across the table onto Elias. He sputtered a few times, then cleared his throat and wagged a finger at Nisha. "That, my friend, is a fucking lie."

"What?" Nisha put up his hands. "There's just as much chirping when we—"

"My grandmother's bridge club has as much chirping as hockey," I said. "I'd still rather clean the locker room showers with my tongue than join her."

And that, of course, was the precise moment when our server appeared beside the table.

"Uh." She stared wide-eyed at us. "Can...I...get you gentlemen anything else?"

My face was on fire and I cleared my throat. "Uh. Sorry. I'm good."

"Are you sure?" Nisha asked. "You look like you could use some cooling down."

I groaned into my hands. The other guys laughed, but Julien nudged my leg under the table. I glanced at him, and he winked, which didn't help at all. I was pretty sure he knew that. Asshole.

I kicked him, which made him laugh. Of course.

We didn't need anything from the server at the moment, and she was probably more than happy to leave us be for a little while. I suspected she'd heard worse—probably even tonight, since we were hardly the only hockey players in the dining room—but still. I'd tip her well. Knowing the other guys, they would too.

Dinner continued in that vein, with me and Julien finding camaraderie in our mutual hatred of golf and Nisha and Elias accusing us of being philistines for the same. By the time we got the check, they'd given up trying to persuade me to join them for a round to "prove that golf with hockey players is actually fun."

"No the fuck it isn't," Julien had grumbled.

"You're outvoted," Elias had said.

"Nope." I'd shaken my head. "I'm listening to the guy with the same taste as me."

"Oh for fuck's sake," Nisha muttered. "No one wants to know what either of you tastes like."

Elias and Julien both kicked him under the table.

And yeah, I blushed again. Goddammit.

After we'd tipped our server more than generously and thanked her for putting up with us, we Ubered back to the hotel. I was pretty sure our driver was a hockey fan, too. He did a double take in the rearview when Julien and Elias squeezed into the SUV's backseat beside me, and when Nisha took the passenger seat, I thought the driver made a little squeak. The same kind of squeak that had nearly escaped my throat the first time I'd been in the company of these men.

*I feel you, dude,* I thought. *I feel you.*

As we walked into the hotel, Elias and Nisha went to the bar where some of our teammates were hanging out.

"You want to join them?" Julien asked.

"Do you?"

He watched them disappearing into the loud, semi-packed bar, and I could almost feel the exhaustion start to weigh him down. As if the prospect of even walking in there made him want to drop to the floor and pass out.

I brushed his elbow with mine. "Let's call it a night."

He turned to me, forehead creased.

"I'm tired as hell." I grinned. "And I think what little energy I have left, I'd rather devote to one person than a crowd."

Julien's eyes widened, and a tiny bit of life slipped back into them. "Would you?"

"Mmhmm." I jerked my head toward the elevators.

He didn't say a word, but he followed me to the elevators, and we rode up to his floor. The hallway was deserted, fortunately, so no one saw us ducking into his room.

We didn't start pawing at each other or making out, though. Julien leaned against the door, hands on my waist, and met my gaze with apologetic eyes. "I can't promise much tonight. Not if I'm still going to play tomorrow."

"I just stuffed my face and chased it with a beer." I slid my palms up his chest and kissed him lightly. "Trust me—there won't be much tonight."

Julien exhaled, and he seemed to simultaneously come back to life and pull the veil off of exactly how tired he really was. As if he'd been holding himself up with sheer willpower, but now he could finally relax and let it show that he was ready to collapse.

"Come on." I gently tugged him away from the door. "Shoes off. Jacket off."

He blinked, but he did as he was told. We left our shoes beside his suitcase, and I carefully draped my jacket over the desk chair while Julien tossed his over the back of the couch as if it wasn't a bespoke piece of art. I wrinkled my nose, but didn't say anything. Instead, I loosened my tie, lay back on his still-made bed, and gestured for him to join me. I thought he might protest—maybe he was relaxed with me, but he was still Julien, and Julien was stubborn.

Instead, he lay beside me and rested his head on my chest. I wrapped my arm around his shoulders, and for a while, we were still. I wondered if he might fall asleep. I wondered if I would.

That thought actually jerked me fully awake. "I should set an alarm. So I don't stay too late."

Julien grunted. "Probably."

I slid my phone out of my pocket and set the alarm for ten-thirty, which was about an hour from now.

"You don't have to leave that soon." Julien kissed under my jaw. "Neither of us is going to be up for much, but I'm not in a hurry for you to leave."

"Oh. Um." I thought about it, then set it to midnight. When I showed him the screen, he nodded, and he relaxed against me as I put aside the phone.

"Did you have a good time tonight?" he asked.

"I did." I chuckled. "And I'm with you—golf sucks."

Julien's whole body shook with quiet laughter. "It does. What the fuck is the point? It's like they took hockey, cut out everything that makes the sport fun, put it in a field, and called it a day."

"I know, right? It's just so slow and boring. I mean, I get bored watching football. Golf is..." I wrinkled my nose.

"Ugh." He groaned. "Larry had a Super Bowl party one year, and I almost suggested we go play golf instead."

I snorted. "What? Football sucks, but it's still not as boring as golf."

"No, but I'd rather *play* golf than *watch* football."

"Fair. Still—either one sounds like a punishment to me."

Julien nodded. Then he pushed himself up and eyed me. "Don't you get any ideas."

"What?" I laughed. "What kind of ideas?"

"Punishments." He tapped a finger in the middle of my chest. "We ever get to doing shit like that, golf is a hard limit."

I burst out laughing. "Oh, come on! You take the fun out of everything!"

He grumbled something in French and rolled his eyes. "Sadist."

"Nah." I tugged him back down. "I wouldn't be that mean to you." I paused. "Mostly because I'd have to be there with you, and then I'd be punishing myself. Though I suppose I could have Elias or—"

"Oh my God," he groaned. "I've created a monster."

I snickered and kissed his temple. Silence fell between us again, and just as they did whenever a conversation hit a lull, my earlier worries started digging their claws in again. I *hadn't* fucked this up with Julien. It was a little miscommunication, more between him and Nisha than him and me, and it was settled. It was fine. We talked. We listened. We weren't dicks to each other. Everything was *fine*, even if I'd probably replay everything over and over like I did my greatest mistakes on the ice, or when I said something embarrassing and—

"Isaac?" Julien's soft voice nudged me back into the present, and when I met his eyes, there was concern in his. "Where did you go?"

"Nowhere. Nowhere." I shook my head and laughed nervously as my cheeks undoubtedly gave me away. "I'm... I didn't—"

"Hey." He pushed himself up on his elbow, a few dark strands tumbling over his eyes. "Talk to me."

Talk to him. Listen to him.

*"It's not always easy,"* Darian had said, *"especially when you need to talk about things that are hard to talk about or listen to him say things you don't necessarily want to hear. But that's how you make it work, you know?"*

I exhaled, gazing at the ink on his wrist because I couldn't look in his eyes. "Just... this morning. The whole thing with Nisha. It's..."

"Still bothering you?"

"Yeah." I laughed self-consciously. "I overthink everything, so—"

"You're not overthinking it." He caressed my cheek. "You're worried you went behind my back."

I considered it, then shrugged. "Kind of? I think it's more that things were off between us afterward. Before we had a chance to sort it out." I finally met his gaze, and his eyes were soft. "I don't like that feeling. Being out of step with you."

Julien winced. Then he pushed himself up farther and brushed his lips across mine. Drawing back enough to look in my eyes, he ran his thumb along my cheekbone. "I don't either. And I'm sorry. I didn't know what was going on. What he'd said. What..." He bit his lip.

"What I'd said?" I offered timidly.

Another wince, subtler this time, and he nodded slowly. "I

should have known. Things were weird, and I..." Trailing off, he sighed. "I'm not good at this. It's all new. But I don't want to fuck up with you."

The sound of my own words rolling off his tongue brought me up short. "I... I don't either. And it's all new to me too."

He studied me, worry in his beautiful dark eyes. That blew my mind—that Julien Landry was as nervous and uncertain about this as I was. Oddly, it settled something in me. As if we were on a level playing field, in a way. This was new for both of us. Maybe we were both overthinking it.

My friend's words came back, and I clasped my hand over Julien's on my cheek. "So I guess we just... communicate? Listen?" I laughed softly as I added Darian's immortal words, "Don't be dicks to each other?"

That got a burst of laughter from Julien that mercifully broke the tension. "Don't tell me you found that gem on one of your google searches."

Chuckling, I shook my head. "No. A very wise friend."

Julien's humor faded but the smile lingered. "Very wise." He dipped his chin for a soft kiss. "I'm sorry again. For today. I should have..."

"I'm sorry too. I should've cleared the air with you before things got weird." I held his gaze, then shrugged cautiously. "Chalk it up to both of us learning how to navigate this?"

He nodded. "Growing pains."

"Growing pains." I lifted my head for another kiss, and then Julien settled on my shoulder again. Closing my eyes, I let the calm wash over me. I still cringed at how this morning had played out, but it felt resolved now. Something I could file away until one of those sleepless nights when I needed to beat myself over the head with everything I'd ever done or said wrong.

For tonight, I was good, and Julien seemed to be too. In

fact, I was surprised neither of us drifted off. Julien wasn't nearly as restless as he usually was, but from the way he was breathing, he was still awake.

If we stayed like this much longer, though, I was going to pass out, and despite how tired I was, I wanted to be awake for this. There was no telling how much alone time we'd have between now and when we were back in Pittsburgh next week.

I thought for a moment, searching for some way to get a conversation moving, and finally settled on, "You and the guys are close." Instantly, I cringed. *Way to be awkward, Rivera.*

Julien tensed slightly. Then he pushed himself up again and met my gaze. "Elias and Nikki, you mean?"

I nodded, sure I was blushing like I always did. "Yeah. I mean, I know teammates get close. But the three of you are tight."

"We are." He watched his fingers tracing the edge of my tie, running them up and down as if he liked the way the material felt. "We've been teammates a long time. We've seen each other through a lot, on and off the ice."

"The rough couple of years when you all first joined the team?"

"Yes, but also in the years since." He looked at me through his lashes and his long hair. "There's a lot of life in that many years. A lot of things happen. When they do, it's good to have people like that."

"I bet. I've always envied you guys." I paused, then softly added, "Even before I joined the Griffins."

Julien's eyebrow flicked up.

I swallowed and half-shrugged. "It isn't like it's a big secret." I didn't bring up the sheer volume of fanfiction I'd read about "the Triple Threat." Or the fanart. Oh God. He would die. "There are a lot of pictures of the three of you out there. Articles. Things like that."

"There are," he acknowledged.

"You guys have always seemed inseparable."

With a subtle smile, Julien nodded. "They can't get rid of me no matter how hard they try."

I scoffed. "Please. If they wanted to get rid of you, they'd go golfing. I'm pretty sure they like having you around as much as you like having them around. It shows."

His smile was so sweet, I wished I could snap a picture of it right then. Oh well—my memory would have to do.

A stupid grin was forming on my own lips, so I quickly added, "And then there's all the videos you guys have done together. The ones for the team's website?"

Julien studied me, and I thought he might've been creeped out that I was that aware of his online presence, but instead, he chuckled. "The things the staff comes up with for videos. I swear they get high before they brainstorm them."

"They have to. How else does someone come up with making hockey players do tricycle races in the parking lot?"

"Oh my God." Julien grimaced. "That was such bullshit. But I did have an advantage over Nikki and Elias, so..." He grinned.

"Uh, yeah. My knees hurt just from watching them try to pedal those things."

Julien laughed for real, making my heart flutter. "Being two of the tallest men on the team isn't always an advantage."

"Thank God for that." I quirked my lips. "Maybe I should volunteer for trike races if they do it again."

He shot me a challenging look, though he was still grinning. "You think you can beat me?"

I arched an eyebrow. "You think I can't?"

"I'm three-for-three!"

"Against giants who hit themselves in the chin every time they turn the pedals!" I playfully thumped his chest. "Let's see you beat the short guy!"

He clasped his hand around mine. "Game on."

"Yeah?"

"If you're up for it, I mean." That eyebrow rose again, this time in a challenging look.

"You know I am." I curved my hand behind his neck and drew him down to kiss me. He grinned against my lips but then relaxed and let the kiss linger.

Which meant he let his guard down just enough…

He landed on his back with what sounded like a French curse, and he stared up at me.

Grinning down at him, I said, "Game on."

He blinked in surprise but then laughed, wrapped his arms around me, and pulled me down to him. There was no way we were fucking tonight, but this? Sinking into Julien's arms, drawing out a long kiss as he carded his fingers through my hair? Oh, I could handle this.

"We should have fucked earlier," Julien murmured between kisses. "While it was still early and we hadn't eaten so much."

"Eh. Next time." I leaned down to kiss his neck. "I don't mind this."

"Mmm, neither do I." He stroked my hair. "But I do love when you can throw me around and fuck me."

"Me too. And when we have the time and we're both up for it, I'm going to make you scream again." I nipped the side of his neck.

"Promise?"

I lifted my head and grinned at him again. "Would I lie to you about yanking your hair and slamming into you so hard you can still feel me a week later?"

The way his eyes widened and he shivered under me had me hot all over. Whatever he said next might've been French or English or fucking Russian, but all I understood was him pulling me down into another kiss.

God, yes, I wanted him so bad. And there was still a part of me that was relieved we'd settled things earlier. That it was just a miscommunication, not a crisis. I was so afraid I might say or do something and lose this amazing connection with him, or that he'd get tired of me if I couldn't or didn't want to have sex one night when he did.

But maybe I didn't need to be so worried after all. He and the guys argued and fought, and they were still tight. Neither of us was in any mood for the usual rough-and-tumble sex, though it was definitely on the horizon when time, privacy, and bodies lined up. Today's flight had been awkward and uncomfortable, but then everyone had talked it through, and we'd spent half the evening bantering effortlessly over an amazing steak dinner. Julien and I had unpacked it a little more after we'd come back here. The tension was gone. Everything was easy with them and between us.

I still wasn't quite sure what Julien and I were doing. This was, after all, entirely new territory for me, whether it was with him or anyone else.

But as we lazily made out in his bed tonight, knowing sex was off the table for the moment and this morning's tension was gone...

I felt a whole lot less like the clueless rookie on the brink of screwing it up.

# Chapter 14

## Julien

For all that Miami was supposed to be a cup contender this year, we waltzed into their arena, and walked out with two points in a five to zero game. Larry got his first shutout of the season, and I got my first goal and picked up two assists, one from a feed to Elias and a secondary assist on a goal from Jackal. Isaac got a point as well, and rang two off the iron. The game in Atlanta, however, had been a fucking grind. We'd pulled off a two-to-one win over the Wolverines, but we'd had to fight for every inch of the ice, and both goals had been lucky bounces.

You took what the hockey gods handed you. We'd showered, changed, and headed to the airport for the short hop up the coast.

Now our bus was pulling up to a hotel in Charlotte, North Carolina, home of the Carolina Seadogs, a perennial favorite to win the cup. They'd made it to the playoffs ten years in a row and won twice during my time in the league. I fucking hated them.

Well, no. Some of the players were okay. I hated one player in particular, who'd also won two cups with the Seadogs:

Travis Canterbury. Thirty-eight. Six-foot-four. Sandy blond hair that now featured a charming dusting of gray. Veteran player. He had an easy smile and a smooth voice. The camera loved that motherfucker, and so did everyone else.

He'd been my goddamned idol when I'd come to training camp eight years ago. Hell, I'd turned nineteen at camp. That night, Travis had shown up at my hotel room across from the training facility with a twelve-pack of beer, praised my playing and my skills, had gotten me drunk, told me how impressed he'd been with my maturity, and then he'd fucked me senseless.

I'd thought I'd found heaven. I'd been so very, *very* wrong.

He'd texted me before the flight to Charlotte, like he always did. I should've blocked his number years ago, but I'd never had courage when it came to Travis. Same text as always, different details. *I miss you. Let's talk.* Then the address of a restaurant and a time.

"Hey." Isaac nudged me. "Are you okay?"

I'd been staring out the window, not moving as everyone else filed off the bus. Isaac must have stopped at my seat.

"Yeah." I smiled up at him, and forced the painful memories of my past back down where they belonged. "Just tired, I think. Long day. And Carolina is always...hard."

"So everyone keeps telling me. You know, I watched the games before I came into the league. I know the history."

He didn't know *my* history, and my connection here was nothing I ever wanted to explain, so I laughed, grabbed my bag and followed Isaac off the bus. "You'll understand when you get on the ice."

Even though it was late—past midnight—there were a bunch of autograph hounds at the hotel, but also some people who were obviously fans. Nikki had stopped to sign a few things, and that lifted my mood. Like Nikki, I avoided the hounds and skipped to the fans.

One person in a Griffins jersey and a rainbow ballcap clapped their hand over their mouth and stared at me, wide-eyed.

Next to me, Isaac bumped my shoulder again. "Wearing your number."

Thirteen. Not a normal number for a defenseman, but the equipment manager during my first year in major juniors had handed it to me. "It's lucky," he'd said somewhat sarcastically, so I'd kept it, determined to make my own luck.

"Hi, do you want me to sign that?"

The fan's eyes got improbably wider. "Ohmygodcouldyou?"

I nodded and dug into my bag for a Sharpie, and had the fan turn around, then signed the middle bar of the three.

When they spun back, their hands were on their cheeks, their eyes still wide, but the smile—oh, those were the best. "You're my absolute favorite player. I can't believe you—" Then they slapped their hand over their mouth, again.

I gave them my brightest smile. "Thank you for being here. It means a lot." Then we headed down the small line of fans, stopping to sign a few other items.

"Isaac?" a voice called. "Isaac Rivera?" A woman stood close to the door holding a T-shirt with Isaac's number, twenty-nine, on it. "My son plays hockey at the University of Denver and he loves you. Wants to get into the league someday."

"Oh shit, really?" Then Isaac covered his mouth much like the earlier fan. "I'm sorry. I just..."

I clapped Isaac on the back, then held out my Sharpie for him. "He doesn't know how good he is yet." To Isaac, I murmured, "Get used to this." He was on his way to becoming a star. I sensed it. We were lucky to have him. *I* was lucky.

The university connection must have helped settle Isaac's

nerves. They chatted for a moment about her son—Devon—who was a freshman and a natural center like Isaac. "Tell him to have fun," he said. "Really was one of the best times of my life, and I learned so much from the coaches."

Once more, I wondered what it might have been like to come up through college. It meant starting in the league later, especially if you ended up in the minors first. Then again, Isaac was a better player as a rookie than I'd been. Three extra years of playing. Three extra years of maturity.

I shook off the chill that sank into my bones. I hadn't been mature at all.

After he'd finished with her, we hustled into the hotel, where we got our room assignments and key cards. "Breakfast at nine, boys," Coach said. "Don't be late, Landry."

I smiled sweetly at Coach. "I'm never late."

He rolled his eyes, then poked his chin at Isaac. "Don't start taking pointers from him, son."

Isaac raised his hands. "Coach, I'm listening to you. I'll be there early."

Coach raised an eyebrow and pointed at Isaac. "See, Landry?"

"Fine. I'll be there before Rivera."

"That'll be the day," Isaac muttered, so I elbowed him.

That got us a dad sigh from Coach. "Get out of here." He pointed at the elevators, and we went.

Once the door to the car closed, Isaac wrapped a hand around my neck and drew me into a kiss. "You know, these things have cameras," I murmured.

"Don't care." He let me go as the elevator slowed, then stopped. "You really think you'll be at breakfast before me?"

The doors slid open to our floor. "Probably not." I laughed. "But it gives Coach something to be grumpy about."

"As if your playing isn't enough?" He gave me a playful shove as we stepped out.

"Hey, fuck you," I replied through my laughter.

Isaac's grin turned sly. He didn't have to say it. I heard it, loud as rain on a glass roof: *I already have.*

God, was I falling for this man? I shouldn't be.

I stopped in front of my room's door, and Isaac paused for a second. "Hey, see you at breakfast."

I nodded, suddenly choked up. I had feelings for Isaac. We were about to play Travis's team. My brain and heart were tied up in knots. "Tomorrow," I managed.

Isaac gave me a curious look, but I turned and unlocked my door, a sudden panic rising in my chest. When I pushed the door open, I looked over my shoulder. "You know, it's going to be fine. The game."

Isaac's smile carried me into my room and through getting ready for bed. Sleep came hard and fast after the grind of the game earlier that night. One thing I loved about hockey: I slept, even when my brain wanted to chatter on forever. There were some things that could shut it off. A day of grueling workouts. Winning a long, hard fought game. A good fuck. Some combination of the three.

But as morning crept closer, I found myself suddenly awake, my heart in my throat and the memory of Travis's voice in my ear and his hands on my body. God, that year. I hated thinking about that year. Travis had been everything for me at first, then my every fear. More so than pleasing our coach back then, I'd done everything in my power to please that asshole.

When he left—traded to Carolina—he let me know just how much I'd meant to him.

Nothing.

I'd meant absolutely *nothing*. I was a shit player who'd never be any good. A warm hole that had been slightly better than a sex doll.

I threw myself out of bed and stuffed myself into workout gear. Then I found the hotel gym and started doing intervals on the bike. Didn't entirely chase the memories away, but forty minutes later, I was more settled. When I checked the time, it nearing seven thirty. After a quick shower and a change of clothes, I beat Isaac to breakfast after all. I beat everyone. The staff wasn't even done setting up the room, so I took a seat outside in the hall to wait.

When Coach arrived, he stared at me. "Landry."

"I'm not late." Which is what I said at every team breakfast.

He stared harder. "It's *eight fifteen*."

I shrugged. "Woke up early."

The look that crossed his face was one I'd never seen from him before, and I didn't know how to read it. Then he shook his head, and slipped into the banquet room. A moment later, he opened the door. "Get in here, Landry."

By the time I entered, Coach was over by the coffee station, getting himself a mug. Seemed like the best plan, so I joined him.

"So, is this your over-competitive nature?"

I shook my head. "I was going to let Isaac beat me, but I couldn't sleep."

That strange look again. "Carolina, then?"

Closer to the mark. "They're not my favorite team."

That got me a grunt. "Canterbury likes to target you, Sidorov, and Karlsson."

I tried hard not to flinch as I added cream to my coffee. "Anyone who played with him, yes." Anyone I was friendly with. Last year, he'd tried to take out Paxy. Failed, because Paxy has eyes in the back of his head and danced away from the check. Hell, Travis had bowled over Larry and taken an interference penalty that had cost Carolina that game. "It's been seven years. I don't know why he's such an ass."

Coach studied me. "That was before my time here. I've

never asked, but do you know where the bad blood comes from?"

I managed to choke down a sip of coffee before I answered. "No idea. I was a rookie his last year."

Just then Jackal and Ozzy entered, and I was saved from having to talk any more about Travis fucking Canterbury. It wasn't only bad blood with Travis—it was spite, head-games, and cruelty. It was me. Travis targeted *me*.

I found a seat nearby, sank into it and drank my coffee. There were moments when the irrational side of my head whispered that I needed to leave the team, that I was dragging them down. Ruining them. This was one of those times. Shaking that shit off was especially hard in Carolina.

All the stats said I was an amazing player. I'd broken a ton of team records and always held spots close to the top of the league board when it came to defensemen. We'd made the playoffs the last four years. Everyone said we could go deep this year.

Around Travis, though... I was nineteen again, feeling like a piece of shit, and wondering why the man who praised my play one night tore into me for the same play another. Usually while fucking me.

*You're a trashy little tramp. The only good thing about you is your mouth.*

"I thought you were letting me win?"

I opened my eyes and peered up at Isaac. "Brain had other plans. Woke me early."

He eyed my coffee cup. "You having food, or are we going to have to scrape you off the ice later?"

Just like that, I felt a million times better. Only took Isaac's smile to put everything right. "I'm eating. Let's go." I nodded to the buffet.

We sat down with Nikki, Elias, Paxy, Larry, and Davy, our backup goalie. No one gave me grief for being early, and we spent most of the time ribbing each other and laughing. That eased much of the rest of my worry from my soul.

To hell with Travis. We were going to win the game tonight and go home from this trip with six points.

---

THIS *FUCKING* GAME.

A puck was in the back of our net, but the goal had been waved off, thank God, because that would have put Carolina two up with four minutes left.

I grabbed Paxy by the back of his pants just as he was about to fling himself over the boards to go take out a Carolina player when *another* scrum broke out by Larry's net. Last thing we needed was a penalty or Paxy getting himself thrown out of the game.

"Fucking asshole cheap ass dirty shithead ass*holes*!" Paxy yelled.

Larry had his mask off, and the way he was sitting on the ice didn't look good. Mike, our trainer, was out with him and someone was helping the doc out onto the ice. The refs were all over Elias, who had a hold on Dubois, a Carolina center. Elias was screaming something at him as he tried to break free from the refs. Isaac was out there, but thankfully not in the scrum. He stood over Larry.

This period had been a complete shit show, and for once —*somehow*—I wasn't in the thick of it. Yes, I'd had my run-ins —literally—with Travis tonight, but I'd either rolled out of his checks or taken them without so much as snapping back. I was *not* losing my shit. Not over that fuck, and not in front of Isaac.

Keeping a firm hold on Paxy, I craned my neck up to watch the replay of what'd happened. From our angle on the bench, there'd been too many people in the way to see. But now? God.

Dubois had crossed in front of the crease, intent on distracting Larry as that shot from the point had come in. But rather than passing in front, he'd clipped Larry's head, snapped it to the right hard, and bounced it off the iron.

The shot had sailed into the net after that. No goal due to goaltender interference. Even the situation room couldn't fuck that one up. Dubois had been so far into the blue paint, he might as well have taken Larry's place.

Over on the far side of the bench, Davy tossed his baseball hat down the tunnel and picked up his mask.

Yeah, there was no way Larry was staying in. He was off to sit in the quiet room. Concussion protocol. Fucking hell.

Like Paxy, I wanted to kill someone. Everyone on the team did, but that was Carolina's game. Of course, there was no penalty. Why would there be when a player concusses the goalie? Fuck.

Davy took the crease. We were the next ones out, with Nikki's line.

"Paxy, keep your cool."

My partner shot me a glare. "*You're* telling me that?"

"I know, I *know*." If anyone was going to go off in a game like this, it was me. "One of us needs to, and you're better at that than me."

That got him smiling, and we set up.

Nikki won the faceoff, Paxy got me the puck, and we were breaking out. The best revenge was a goal and a win, always. We didn't get the goal our shift, but the pressure we put on them had them on their heels and reacting rather than playing in our faces. They sent the puck back into the neutral zone, but I had it, which let Nikki's line change for Isaac's.

Carolina changed, too, and there was Travis, the fucker, smirking at me. I could nearly hear Paxy praying that I kept my head attached to my neck. I glared at Travis and passed the puck to Isaac without looking away. The puck whizzed past Travis, out of his long reach and straight onto Isaac's tape.

Bull's-fucking-eye. That wiped that grin off Travis's lips. So did the tic-tac-toe play between Isaac and Ozzy, who put the puck into the Carolina net, tying the game.

Thank fuck.

While we were heading to the bench for fist bumps, Travis shoulder-checked me. "Hey Julie, whose dick you using as a pacifier later?"

I spun around. "Your dad's."

That didn't go over well, but Paxy hauled me down the boards before Travis reached me. "Two minutes, thirty-two seconds," he said.

Time on the clock.

A minute thirty later, Paxy and I were back on the ice, this time with a line that had Elias at center and Isaac on the wing. Coach had chucked the forward lines into the blender in an effort to get that final goal.

Travis was out as well, and I knew what was coming when I glanced back and saw him heading at me. I shot the puck behind the goal to Paxy, then I rolled out of Travis's check. He hammered himself into the board.

"Little fucker," he snarled. "Thought you liked being hit."

"Too bad you're old and slow." Then I was gone, up the ice, putting distance between me and him, then taking a pass from Elias and snapping it on goal.

The puck rang off the iron and out.

"Fuck!"

Isaac kept the rebound in at the point, cycling it to Paxy. The next instant, Travis checked Isaac hard into the boards, and my resolve to keep my cool snapped like a twig. Paxy probably sensed that, because he yelled, "Lans!" and shot the puck toward me, forcing my attention back on the game before I did something idiotic. I tossed the puck to Elias, and took back my spot at the point.

Inside, I seethed. Isaac looked none the worse for wear, though, so the hit hadn't been bad. In fact, Isaac snapped a shot on goal, but it was blocked up and out of play. A whistle and a breather.

Elias's line headed back to the bench. Paxy and I stayed out. Twenty-seven seconds left.

"Still can't hit the net, Julie?"

I wanted to punch that smug smile off Travis's face. He knew it, too. Knew which buttons to push. So did I, though. "How many goals you got this season? Zero? That why they call you Cants?"

He came straight at me, fury in his eyes. The linesmen intercepted him first, though. "Hey, hey, you want a penalty?" the ref barked. "'Cause that's how you're gonna get a penalty."

Travis settled down, but the glare he gave me could've melted the ice we were skating on.

Nikki slid past and *that* look I knew—one that meant a certain set play from the faceoff. Hopefully, we could score here and not go into overtime.

We won the faceoff and hammered away at their goalie, but somehow—somehow—the puck stayed out.

Unlucky bounces. Good saves. A combo from hell. The counter ticked down and the horn sounded.

Fuuuuuck.

Overtime was more of the same. We had possession the majority the time, got tons of chances, but couldn't put a puck into the back of the damn net.

If nothing else, we'd salvage a point from this. Five out of six on the road? Not bad at all. But I fucking wanted this win. *Needed* it. But now we were going to a shootout, so it was all on the goalies and the shooters.

I was shooting third for our team.

No one scored the first two rounds. Fuck my life. I hopped over the boards and sent up a prayer.

*Please let me score this one.* I'd been good. Hadn't taken a penalty. Hadn't slugged Travis.

I took the puck on my stick and headed toward the goalie, who tracked my every move as boos sounded around me. Pump fake, backhand shot up and over the shoulder.

I shouted. The red lights went on. Our fans in the audience screamed. Our bench was a riot.

The rest of the arena was silent.

I got fist bumps before taking a seat.

The next skater out for Carolina was Travis Canterbury. I couldn't watch, but I couldn't not watch. Davy was good—and had stoned the other two skaters—but Travis could be such an intimidating fuck, and I *had* taunted him about not scoring yet this season.

Oh God. If he scored, this was on *me*.

Davy looked huge. Way on top of the crease and he followed Travis's every move. The shot whizzed high glove side and Davy—

—snatched that fucker's puck right out of the air.

I was over the boards an instant later and jumping into Davy's arms. Then the whole team was piling on us like we'd won the cup.

Felt like that.

Isaac found me in the press of teammates. "You're fucking beautiful! You won the game!"

I'd won the game. In Carolina. I'd beaten Travis without using my fists. "Câlisse." The relief that washed through me almost had me crumpling to my knees. I leaned some of my weight on Isaac.

He took it, but gave me an alarmed look. "Nisha!" he called.

Suddenly Nikki was on my other side. "Hey, Jules. You okay?"

"Yeah, yeah. Just really fucking tired." I laughed, found my feet and gave Nikki a shove. "I won the game."

"A king." He grinned back. "You want that puck?"

That sobered me fast. "Yeah, I do."

He nodded. "Already told Tavish."

I punched him in the arm. "You fuck."

"Game meant a lot to you, huh?" Isaac brushed my arm with his.

Oh that look from Nikki was something else. "We don't win against Carolina that much, and winning here?" I gave Isaac my best smile. "Something special."

Isaac studied me, though he was smiling, same as everyone else giving me a bump or smack.

That same woozy wash ran through me, and I leaned over, putting my stick on my knees. "God, I need food. Then a nap. Then a good night's sleep. And another nap."

Nikki laughed, and we skated toward the bench and the tunnel to the visitor's locker room. "Be glad we're not at home, eh?"

"Oh God," I groaned. "They gave me first star, didn't they?"

They had. I craned my head up and saw it on the screen. When I looked away, I caught sight of a lone player down on the home bench.

"That motherfucker," I murmured.

"Julien," Nikki said, sharply. "Ignore him."

Yeah, best plan. I let Isaac and Nikki pull me off the ice and into the locker room.

Getting out of there was a blur. I packed my shit, showered, and ate, then I passed out the second my ass hit the bus seat. Isaac woke me as we pulled into the hotel. "I'm going to make a wild guess that you're not up for the bar tonight."

"I'll be lucky if I can make it to my room." After we exited the bus, I slung an arm around his shoulder like a drunk man. "Please go have fun for me?"

"Sure. How much sleep did you get last night?" He steered me toward the door.

"Two hours? Three? I don't know." That dream had taken more out of me than I'd thought. Being here. Not throttling Travis.

Isaac blew out a breath. "Fuck, dude."

I shrugged, and waved a hand as we took the elevator up to our floor. "It's Carolina."

"Biggest rivalry," he said, his voice quiet.

Right then, I knew Nikki had been correct. I needed to tell Isaac about Travis. "Not just that." I tried to find the words to explain, but my brain kept repeating "that motherfucker" and God, I didn't want to tell him how I'd fucked up my rookie year. And the year after. How I'd very nearly fucked over the entire team.

We made it to my room, and I kicked off my shoes before collapsing face first onto the bed. "Câlisse."

"You're like a cat," Isaac muttered. "How about taking your suit off, first?"

"Cats don't wear suits." I rolled and sat up, then stripped off my jacket and tie before starting in on the buttons of my shirt.

"Oh my God." Isaac snatched both from the floor and marched to the closet. "This is not a five hundred dollar suit."

I tossed the shirt toward him, then shimmied out of the pants. Those followed the shirt. "Dry cleaner will fix it." Then I fell back on the bed.

After some rattling of hangers and an exasperated sigh, Isaac nudged me. "Maybe you should get under the covers before passing out?"

"Too much work." I opened my eyes to find one very hot

hockey player in a suit with his hands on his hips and an incredulous look on his face. "What?"

"I'm trying to decide if I should threaten you with punishment or just tuck you in."

Warmth bloomed in my chest and I worked the sheets free from the bed. "Tuck me in. Go have fun in the bar. Punish me later."

That cocky smile returned. "You want it all."

"Always," I said.

Isaac helped me under the covers, then palmed my cheek before leaning down to kiss me. "Do you have an alarm set?"

I closed my eyes and groaned. "I don't even know where my phone is."

He patted my cheek. "I do."

A moment later, he shoved the damn thing into my hand and I set an alarm that would get me up and out in time for breakfast. "Not beating you there tomorrow."

Isaac's eyes danced, and he kissed me again. "We'll talk about punishment later." Despite how bone weary I was, I still shivered, and he got the wickedest of smiles. "Good night, Julien."

"Bonne nuit." I closed my eyes and was gone, sleep eating me whole.

# Chapter 15

## Isaac

I closed Julien's door as quietly as I could. Not that there was any danger of waking him; my phone had shrieked obnoxiously to announce I'd received a text while I'd still been next to his bed, and he hadn't even stirred. I'd bitten back a curse and berated myself for not turning my phone's volume back down; I always left it kind of loud after a game because my parents would often call if they'd watched, and I couldn't always hear it in the locker room. I usually remembered to turn it back down. Not this time. Oops.

Now that I was out of Julien's room, I read the text.

*You coming?*

Nisha. Probably down at the bar with everyone else. And yeah, I was coming.

But in the empty hallway outside Julien's room, I paused. Something was off, and I didn't like it. Julien had been... different tonight. On the ice. Off it. Before the game. After. He'd been so weird, I wasn't even surprised he'd been unusually subdued despite scoring the game-winning goal against our rival. Which he had been—he'd celebrated, but he'd treated that hard-won victory like he'd just gotten a call that the results of some ominous test had come back negative. He'd almost collapsed against me, and as soon as he hadn't had to hold himself up anymore, he'd all but passed out.

*Jesus. What if we'd lost tonight?*

I rolled my shoulders as I started walking away from his room toward the elevators. There was a lot I didn't know about Julien, and I accepted that. He'd tell me more as he was comfortable. That was fine.

But I wondered if he knew how many cards he'd shown tonight. Or how many of our teammates had tipped his hand for him.

As I rode the elevator down to the lobby to join the guys at the bar, bits and pieces of tonight flashed through my mind like a post-game recap, and every frame involved Julien. Hockey moved fast, and my attention was hardly on him the entire time, but I had to be aware of him like I was aware of anyone else on the ice with me. And when I was on the bench, I watched intently. Plus there were replays, replays, and more replays. I didn't catch everything, but I saw a *lot*.

Three separate times tonight—and those were just the times I'd been watching—a particular Carolina player had gotten close to Julien. They both did a lot of chirping with everyone, and they could be scrappy as fuck anyway, but with each other, it was entirely different. Every single time Julien laid eyes on that player, he'd... Well, I often likened him to a cat, and in those moments, I'd been genuinely surprised he didn't hiss at the guy.

That same player had checked me later on. I hadn't even realized it was him in the moment. Not until I'd recovered my balance, moved on, and noticed that Julien looked like he was ready to break his stick over someone's head. Curiosity had pulled me to the iPads after my shift, and I'd watched it all play out: the player checking me, Julien's temper visibly snapping, and Paxy pulling his focus back to the puck before anything got out of control. Julien only started calming down after he'd skated past me at one point and we'd exchanged "you good?/I'm good" nods. Then he'd been fine, at least until the next time the two of them struck sparks off each other.

"One of these days," Ozzy had muttered to Benson while we'd been sitting on the bench late in the third period, "Landry is going to beat the shit out of him."

Benson had responded with a grunt, then gestured at the object of Julien's frustration with his water bottle. "Good. Fucking punk is asking for it."

I had to agree, and I wondered a few times if it would be worth the penalty to drop gloves with the guy. Just for the chance to take a shot at his smug face.

*Fuck with him one more time, Canterbury. I dare you.*

Oh, he did, and it was tempting, but one look at Julien had calmed me right back down. As satisfying as it would've been to knock a second tooth out of Canterbury's hockey smile, I knew Julien. The instant Canterbury laid a hand on me, Julien would lose his shit, and he'd probably earn himself more than some time in the box.

So for Julien's sake—and for the sake of not handing Carolina a power play—I'd kept my gloves on and my fists out of Canterbury's face.

The elevator doors opened, and I shuffled out into the mostly empty lobby. I really didn't feel like socializing tonight, but if I went up to my room, I'd spend the entire evening poring over all the replays as if I couldn't already see them in my head. I'd be the one barely functioning tomorrow because I'd stayed up too late trying to parse whatever the fuck had been happening between my boyfriend and that dickhead who needed to be relieved of a few more teeth.

As if I didn't know.

Okay, I didn't *know*, but I had my suspicions. I couldn't

think of any other explanation, and every time another theory fell apart, my heart sank a little deeper.

*That asshole? Really?*

For tonight, I'd try to relax with my teammates and get it all out of my head until I had a chance to talk with Julien. We'd be home tomorrow. We'd have time. Between now and then, I needed to chill the hell out.

The bar was noisy as always, though the guys were fairly subdued tonight. It had been a long day and a hell of a game, and we had an earlyish flight tomorrow. Everyone was definitely in the mood to wind down rather than party, and that was fine by me.

I got an ice water at the bar, then found Elias and Nisha sitting in some armchairs by the fireplace, and they gestured me over. I took a seat in an empty chair beside Elias. Given how crowded the bar was, I got the feeling they'd saved the seat for me.

*Elias Karlsson and Nikolai Sidorov are saving seats for me in the bar*, the little fanboy voice in the back of my mind exclaimed. *Holy shit.*

I chuckled to myself behind my water glass. Someday that novelty would wear off, but not tonight.

Elias leaned closer. "How is he?"

I didn't even have to ask who he meant. "He's beat." I gestured vaguely toward the elevators with my glass. "Pretty much passed out as soon as he got into his room."

Elias scowled, but he nodded as he picked up his drink. "Just as well. He needs to sleep."

So I wasn't the only one who noticed. Not that Julien was exactly subtle about it when he was sleep-deprived.

"What about Larry?" I asked. "Any word on him?"

Nisha tilted his beer bottle in the same direction I had. "Probably asleep too. Coach said he's good." He paused. "Good as can be expected."

"Should've been a fucking penalty," Elias grumbled.

Nisha huffed a humorless laugh. "If those assholes got penalties for playing dirty, they'd have to move their bench into the box."

"I'd pay to see that," I said.

That got an actual chuckle out of Elias, and Nisha and I joined in. We didn't talk any more about the game. We drank a little. We shot the shit with our other teammates. We got more updates on Larry (he had a wicked headache and his neck hurt, and he'd be on concussion protocol for a while, but there was nothing alarming).

At one point, my phone buzzed. I thought it might be my parents or Darian, but to my surprise, it was Chad Weyland, an old friend who played for Carolina.

*Hey*, he'd written. *Sorry we couldn't meet up. Had to take off right after the game. Maybe next time.*

I frowned at the text. We'd been good friends for a long time. We'd gone to some of the same hockey camps in high school, and we'd played against each other in college. We were both rookies this year and had spent a lot of the summer and the pre-season texting about how excited we were to be pros and how different this world was from college hockey. Over and over, we'd promised to grab a beer when our teams played each other, which they would a few times this season.

But his texts had mostly stopped when the season had started. I'd reached out yesterday about tonight's game, saying I was excited to see him and wanted to take him up on his promise of a beer, but there'd been no response. And tonight, he hadn't been on the ice—healthy scratch, apparently.

Well, damn. The off season, maybe. I'd get in touch then. Or next time we played Carolina. For now...

*No worries. When you guys play in Pittsburgh, beers are on me. BTW how are things?*

He responded with a thumbs up. Nothing more.

I put my phone aside. Was there a full moon or something tonight? Jesus fuck.

The evening started to wind down. As guys steadily filtered out to call it a night, Elias, Nisha, and I continued to lounge in the mostly empty bar. I was tired as hell, but the Seattle-Vegas game on TV had caught our attention, and we'd all decided to hang back and watch the end of this bloodbath. It might've been recorded—West Coast or not, it was pretty fucking late—but whatever. We had to see how it ended. Or, well, how badly Seattle got stomped.

"Oh my God." Nisha rolled his eyes. "How have they *not* pulled that goalie?"

Elias made a disgusted sound. "The backup can't be any worse than this. Jesus."

I nodded, rolling a sip of water around in my mouth. I was kind of half-watching. Paying enough attention to notice that Seattle's netminder was on another planet and that one of Vegas's defenseman couldn't stop turning over the puck, but my own thoughts held most of my focus. Tonight's game—ours, not theirs—didn't sit right with me. The way Julien had been definitely didn't sit right.

I surreptitiously slid my gaze toward my two teammates. They were kicked back, watching the game and sipping their drinks. Nisha seemed lightly buzzed. Elias was relaxed, though I was pretty sure he was still sober. There was no one else here except for the bartender, who was well out of earshot. Perfect time to feel them out a little, especially since they probably weren't expecting it.

The thing was, some of the guys still seemed to brush me off as a naïve kid who didn't have two brain cells to rub together. Even Elias and Nisha, despite getting to know me more recently, still thought I was a clueless kid sometimes. They were kind of right—I admittedly *was* naïve about anything that wasn't hockey.

But I wasn't stupid.

Letting someone think I was could work to my advantage, though. Made it easier to read people. Catch them off guard. Get a bead on what they really thought before they had a chance to pull a mask into place.

I casually sipped my drink. "What's up with Julien and Canterbury?"

Nisha nearly spat out his beer.

Elias froze. Too late, he tried to play stupid. "Canterbury?" He shook his head. "What about them?"

I tilted my head and cocked a brow, hoping it conveyed *Really?*

"Oh, Jesus," Nisha muttered into his drink. "They've barely started dating and he's already turning into Jules."

Elias didn't laugh. He glanced at Nisha, and something unspoken passed between them. Nisha's expression shifted from stoic to plaintive to resigned, and he finally made a *go on* gesture to Elias. Our captain didn't look pleased, but he faced me. I wondered if they knew how much they'd already told me, though they were raising more questions than they were answering.

Elias took a deep breath. "It isn't our place. Julien—he should be the one to tell you."

"But there *is* something there." I flicked my eyes between them. "It wasn't my imagination."

Both my teammates looked pained. Ashamed, even, as if they hadn't meant to tell me as much as they had. And maybe it wasn't fair of me to be asking them to. Julien had a right to be the one to tell me, or to decide if I knew at all.

I exhaled. "I don't want details. I know it's not your place. I..." I swallowed. "After the way tonight went, and after what Nisha said to me the other day..."

Elias shot Nisha a look, and Nisha put up his hands. "What? What did I say?"

"When you told me to be careful with Julien." I absently swirled my mostly empty water glass. "Since you apparently didn't mean he might hurt me, I assumed you meant you wanted *me* to be careful not to hurt *him*."

The way they both winced said it all.

I wanted to ask, *It was him, wasn't it?* Because who else *could* it be? But I wouldn't make them say it. If anyone said it out loud, it needed to be Julien, even though I was pretty sure now that I knew the answer. If Travis Canterbury hadn't hurt Julien in the past, then God help us all if Julien ever crossed paths with the person who did.

So yeah. I had my answer. Confirmation of what I already knew, really.

I leaned forward to put my glass on the table. "Like I said, I don't want details. I was just worried." I met Nisha's gaze. "And I *won't* hurt him."

Nisha nodded slowly. "I know. You're a good man. That asshole?" He waved his free hand. "He is…"

"*Not* a good man," Elias said with unexpected venom. He drained his drink and put the glass down next to mine. Then he looked at me, his expression more serious than I'd ever seen it, and when it came to Elias, that said a lot. "Listen to me, Isaac. Julien doesn't like to talk about these things. Sometimes I don't think he even lets himself think about them. But I know him." He gestured at Nisha. "*We* know him." He put a firm hand on my arm. "He thinks the world of you. He doesn't want to screw up this thing between you. But his past…" Elias grimaced, then squeezed my arm. "Give him time to show it to you. Just don't give up on him."

An unexpected lump rose in my throat. Give up on him? Fuck no. And from what Elias was saying and Nisha's solemn expression, there was a lot more going on here than even I'd realized.

*What the fuck did he do to you, Julien?*

But all I said was, "Don't worry. I won't."

---

*My place. ASAP. Bring an overnight bag. Wear the gray suit.*

My heart thundered as "Read" appeared under the text I'd sent to Julien.

It thundered even faster when the icon appeared to show that he was typing.

*Which gray suit?*

I laughed into the silence of my car, which was still idling in the training center parking lot. It would never stop blowing my mind that I could give Julien Landry an order, and his response would either be immediate obedience or a request for clarification so he could obey. That was seriously heady.

And yeah, which gray suit? Because he had plenty, and yes, I may have had photos of several of them saved in my phone, but it felt a *little* too fanboyish to dig one of those up and send it. Instead, I told him, *Surprise me.* I followed that with the grinning devil emoji for the hell of it.

He responded with a saluting emoji. Smartass.

Last night was still bugging me, but I tried to put it out of my mind for now. I wanted us to spend some time together in the present before we started digging into the past, and I was also trying to be mindful of what Elias had told me. That Julien wanted to get this right and would open up to me in due time. I could be patient. All I wanted was for Julien to be happy, and after last night's bullshit with Canterbury, I wanted to focus on *making* him happy. Today would be all about feeling good and enjoying the here and now.

And maybe pissing off my neighbors and splintering some furniture.

I squirmed in the driver's seat. *Are we there yet?*

Movement outside caught my eye, and I looked up to see Julien and Elias crossing the parking lot. Of course, Julien still had on the dark blue suit he'd worn on the plane. He was hot as hell in that one, but like me, he probably wanted to run home, grab a shower, and change clothes after spending half the morning in the air. Hence my request for a different suit.

As they passed near my car, I revved the engine. Both of them looked. Elias chuckled and rolled his eyes. Julien almost stumbled, which I thought served him right for the "I might spend the day in bed" comment that had almost put me on my ass another time. Then he grinned at me, tugged at the lapel of his jacket, and winked.

I couldn't wait to see which suit he picked out.

He didn't keep me waiting long, either. I'd just finished putting away the coffee I'd had delivered from a shop he liked in the Strip District, and I was entering an order for groceries when my doorbell rang.

And oh dear God, Julien had worn exactly the suit I'd had in mind. He probably had a million gray suits, but this one was dark, ever so slightly metallic, and with the faintest hint of blue, almost like graphite. He'd paired it with a black turtleneck, which...fuck.

In the doorway, I looked him up and down, not even trying to hide that I was leering at him.

He was grinning, but his forehead creased with subtle concern. "Is this the one you wanted?"

"Uh-huh." I motioned for him to step inside, watching him as he did because *oh my God*. "Exactly what I had in mind."

The concern vanished and the grin turned wicked. "So I guessed right?"

I toed the door shut behind us as he set his bag down. Then I slid my hands over his hips. "I'm pretty sure you of all people know which suit makes you look the sexiest."

He laughed, which made my spine tingle. I was such a sucker for that smile, and especially after last night, it looked so, *so* good on him. I wanted more.

I pulled him in close, wrapping my arms around him. "You have anywhere to be tonight?"

"Besides a reservation for two in your bed?"

I chuckled. "Yes. Besides that."

"Nowhere else." He swept his tongue across his lips. "What about you?"

"I'm on the same reservation, so I'm not going anywhere." I lifted my chin and he came down to meet me in a kiss. Oh, that was good. Definitely what I needed right now. From the way he melted against me and slid his hands up my back, he needed it too, and I happily gave it to him. This was definitely going to be about the two of us and the here and now. Nothing that existed in the past or outside my apartment mattered.

I drew back and ran my fingers through his long hair, which was still slightly damp, bringing to mind an image of him in the shower. "I, um... I ordered some of that coffee you like. For tomorrow."

Julien's eyebrows flicked up in surprise. "Which kind?"

"The Bar Italia. From La Prima." My face burned, because of course it did. "It was what you had at your place, so I assumed..."

He blinked. "You noticed the brand of coffee I drink?" He didn't sound weirded out. Just genuinely surprised.

"I notice a lot of things." I combed my fingers through his hair again, just because I could. "And I figured if I'm going to keep you here all night, I should at least have coffee around that you like in the morning."

He stared at me, and I wondered if maybe that was a stupid thing to do. We were both used to drinking whatever coffee a hotel had available, and I'd seen him come in with cups from gas stations and fast food places more than once. He was hardly picky about coffee. So maybe this was—

Julien kissed me softly. Lips barely leaving mine, he murmured, "Thank you."

He sounded like he meant it, too.

Relieved, I pulled him in closer, and the kiss lingered for a long moment. It was gentle and slow and nothing like the way we usually made out in foyers, but it was hot and sexy in its own way. We'd get to the bruising kisses and rough sex soon enough. First, I wanted to indulge in kissing him like this. When I'd just been crushing on him, I'd noticed he had the most beautiful lips, and now I loved the way they moved with mine. I loved how his tongue teased and explored, and I loved the vibration of his soft, almost inaudible moans.

I broke the kiss, wondering how it was possible to be so out of breath from something so subdued. "Curious about something..."

Worry flashed across his expression, and I instantly regretted the words because he probably thought I was going to ask about last night. Right now of all times.

"Do you ever enjoy fucking like this?" I asked. "Slow, and...?"

The worry vanished. "If the person I'm with wants to."

"But do *you* enjoy it?"

Julien held my gaze. After a moment, an asymmetrical grin tugged at his kiss-swollen lips. "I haven't been with many people who make it enjoyable. But I have a feeling you would."

"Yeah?"

"Oui."

"I can't decide if that's a challenge, or..."

He laughed, once again giving me a rush because fuck, seriously, I could *not* get enough of that gorgeous smile.

"So if I said I wanted to take it slow and easy tonight..." I slid my hands up his chest. "You'd be game?"

"Isaac. You should know by now." He trailed his fingertips down my cheek and looked right in my eyes. "*Anything* you want."

Oh God, he meant it. I knew he did. I still couldn't quite get my head around how sexy it was to have this man willing—all but begging—to do anything and everything I wanted in the bedroom.

I closed my fingers around his lapels and tugged him in so I could kiss him again. "I do want to. A nice, slow fuck until you can't stand it anymore and you're begging me to let you come."

I had half a heartbeat to think that sounded like cheesy porno dialogue, but the shuddering breath from Julien's lips and the way his knees seemed to wobble told me I'd hit what I was aiming for.

"That would drive you wild, wouldn't it?" I brushed a kiss across his mouth. "Just feeling every...single...stroke...until I give you permission to get off?"

Whatever he said, it sounded both French and profane. Then he growled, "Yes. It would."

"Yeah?"

He licked his lips and nodded. His voice was shaky and his accent thick as he whispered, "Anything you want, Isaac." I loved how he could make it sound like he was simultaneously offering me what I wanted and begging me to take it before he lost his mind.

"I do want that." I gripped his lapels tighter and shoved him up against the wall, and he gasped as I said, "But not tonight."

Then I kissed him exactly the way I knew he liked it—hard, deep, messy, demanding—and he whimpered as he took it all. He grabbed my ass and pulled me against him, driving groans from both of us as our cocks rubbed together through our clothes.

"Not slow tonight," I panted between kisses. "We're going to go upstairs..." I paused to kiss him again, hard. "And I'm going to fuck you until you can't move."

Julien didn't say a word.

His strangled whimper said it all.

# Chapter 16

## Julien

I was going to die on these stairs.

Isaac, with his hand on my ass, urged me up the spiral staircase that led to his bedroom loft. Gripping the railing, I tried not to trip as I hustled up the treads. The stairs were a stunning visual focus, but fucking impossible to navigate with pants tight from a raging hard-on and with my brain running in multiple directions at once.

I'd picked the correct suit. Isaac wanted to make love to me—not just fuck me. Take his time and make *love* to me. He'd bought one of my favorite coffee blends because he wanted me to stay the night and also stay here in the morning.

I wasn't used to that. I either left or my hookup did. No one wanted me around after the deed was done, and frankly, most times I didn't want to be there either.

But with Isaac? I never wanted to leave. Or have him leave.

Then there'd been that moment I'd thought he'd ask about yesterday, and the absolute panic from that. I needed to talk to him about Travis, but I had no idea how to, or when.

Right now? Now Isaac was going to fuck me until I

couldn't walk. Or think. Or both. Hopefully both. God, I wanted my brain to stop already.

I tripped over the last step and nearly face planted onto the hardwood floor.

Isaac caught me. "Hey."

"Sorry." I was breathless, a complete wreck. "Your stairs are a nightmare."

The expected laugh didn't come. Instead, Isaac turned me so we were face to face. "Julien, look at me."

Too much in my head, but I couldn't not obey, so my gaze met his.

Deep brown eyes I wanted to get lost in. I took a breath, then another, and the chaos in my mind settled a little.

Concern flickered in Isaac, but also resolve. He cupped my cheek and brushed his thumb over my lower lip. "I want you here with me. Focused on one thing, and one thing alone: how you're going to obey me."

I gulped in air at the snap of my brain onto his words. *Please.*

"Yes?" He raised an eyebrow.

"Oui," I whispered. All the noise in my head quieted. "Whatever you want."

When the corner of his lips turned upward, I nearly fell to my knees, but he hadn't asked for that, so I waited, his hand still on my cheek, and his thumb still brushing over my bottom lip.

"Good. Very good."

Those words said in a similar manner by a different man would've caused terror, but hope blossomed in my chest, along with such a deep need that I trembled where I stood.

Isaac patted my cheek. "Come with me and stand by the foot of the bed."

I did exactly that, moving as if I were in a dream.

Isaac crossed over to a small armchair near the towering

windows that looked down upon the Monongahela River and downtown Pittsburgh, unbuttoning his shirt sleeve as he went. When he faced me, he rolled that fucker up, exposing his forearm. Then he did the same with the other sleeve. God *damn*.

Isaac was built, especially in his legs and ass, but every bit of him was toned and tight, including those mouthwatering arms. I couldn't help staring. Couldn't help raising my gaze to his equally mouthwatering grin.

Then he sat in the chair and crossed one leg over the other.

Nikki had named me King all those years ago, but it was Isaac who claimed that title in this space.

I must have whimpered, because Isaac huffed a laugh. "God, look at you," he said. Then he did, examining me up and down like he would a work of art. Or his next meal. Or maybe both.

I'd never felt more exposed or glorious as in that moment.

He nodded, as if to himself. "Take off all your clothes, Julien. Slowly. Carefully. Hang up your suit in the closet like it's worth the money you spent on it. Fold the other things and put them on the shelf in there." He waved his hand toward the closet.

I froze for a moment, and he raised an eyebrow again, and fuck, the things that did to me.

Some deep part of me sang out in joy, and I shifted from foot to foot. "Where should I put my shoes?"

Isaac flicked his gaze down to my feet. "Shelf," he said, then pinned me with that sharp look again. "They're stunning."

I'd picked out a pair of dark gray hand-tooled Italian leather shoes. Not a pair I wore often, but they worked with this suit.

This suit. This order. Fuck, this was *punishment*.

*Someone* had done his reading. Someone had also figured

out that this would frustrate the *hell* out of me. Usually, I undressed quickly, taking no bother about my clothes until later. Last night had been a perfect example of that.

Obviously, Isaac had been more than a little annoyed, and I was about to reap that reward, as it were.

I gave him what he asked for, slipping my shoes off and placing them on the empty shelf in his closet. My jacket followed, that going neatly onto a hanger.

Fuck, this was hard—to not toss the clothes aside, to be careful and methodical while Isaac sat imperiously and watched as he fondled himself through his jeans.

Sexy as hell. Made it even harder to not rip everything off and throw myself at his feet.

I carefully unbuttoned and unzipped my pants, stepping out of each leg. Those followed the jacket onto the hanger, and I took the time to make sure the pressed fold remained sharp.

"So you *can* take care of your things." Wry amusement there. He squeezed the bulge in his pants.

Dirty as hell, too.

"I can, yes."

His smile and hooded eyes nearly put me on my knees, where I wanted to be. "Turtleneck," he said. "And everything else."

I fucking *loved* this. My body and mind sang with frustration, but beyond that lay a deep calm that welled up from my soul.

By the time I was naked, I was rock hard from the way Isaac tracked my every move as he worked his hand over his cloth-covered cock.

"Come here." His voice felt like my own desire, rough and sharp.

*Finally.* I needed him on me. Inside me.

He nodded at the space between his legs where a pillow

had been thrown at some point. My knees hit the pillow. He snaked a hand into my hair, tugged me to him, and took my mouth in a kiss that left no question of who was in charge.

Wasn't me. Not at all.

He yanked my hair, and a glorious shower of pain had me groaning and squirming in pleasure. My only thought was Isaac.

Isaac. Isaac. Isaac. His hands in my hair. On my skin. Gripping, pulling, pinching. He undid his jeans and took out his cock.

My moan was plaintive and wanton.

"You want this?" He stroked his dick, a hand still tight in my hair, keeping my scalp on fire.

"Yeah." I licked my lips and stared back at him. "Make me choke on it."

His eyes widened, but there was fire there. "Then fucking suck my dick, Julien. All of it."

I was hungry to obey, and oh did he make me do it, fucking me as rough as I wanted, pounding into my mouth while grasping my hair until tears streamed from my eyes. I choked on his dick, with a few glorious moments of not being able to breathe, but never once worrying we'd go too far.

Yes, Isaac had control, but I could've ended the blowjob in an instant.

I wanted it to go on forever. The pain and submission blotted out the scrambled mess of my mind. All that mattered was the cock in my mouth and Isaac's pleasure. His moans and curses.

"Fuck! Take it all. Hold it there, like that. God *damn*, Julien."

Perfect. Utterly perfect. Every stroke, every press of his hand on the back of my head. Every tug of my hair.

By the time Isaac pulled me off his cock, tears were

streaming down my face and I ached for more. "Don't stop," I begged. "Please don't stop."

He stood, yanked me up by my hair, and kissed me hard. "I'm not even close to being done with you."

When my bare back hit the cold glass of the window, I yelped and squirmed. His thigh pressed against my balls and he wrapped a hand around my cock, pumping me until I was close to coming. Couldn't help grinding against him. "Isaac. Please, please!" My voice was raw.

"Not yet," he said, then took my mouth in a bruising kiss. When he relented, his teeth brushed against my throat. "Tell me what you want."

"Fuck me. Use me. Make me stop thinking," I babbled against him. "Make me stop—"

Isaac hauled me off the window and threw me against the bed, then caught my hair again, and I moaned deep and long. I loved this. I had height on Isaac, but he used his strength to put me where he wanted me. The floor. The bed. Against the wall. Over furniture. We grappled and kissed and rutted until I was breathless and moaning.

My back hit Isaac's mattress, and he crawled up my body. "Will you hang up your clothes from now on?"

"Depends," I murmured.

He lowered all his weight onto me, our cocks sliding together deliciously. "On what?"

"What gets you doing this to me again."

That got me a chuckle. "Hang them up, Julien." Then he bit my shoulder, hard. Twice. Then once more.

I moaned and arched into him, trying to find purchase on his arms as pleasure rocked my brain.

He wriggled free and sat up. "Stay there."

Given that he was reaching for his nightstand, I did exactly as told. I loved our extended bouts of—I guess foreplay, if being tossed around counted as that—but I also wanted to be railed so badly right now.

Watching Isaac put a condom on and lube up shouldn't have been sexy—but it was. I already had my legs spread wide when he crawled back between them.

His grin was lopsided. "I still can't believe you want me." Before I could reply, he circled my hole with lubed fingers, and words vanished from my head. My gasp morphed into a deep moan when he pushed inside me. His voice turned deep and sharp. "That you let me do this to you." Then he finger-fucked me until I couldn't breathe, let alone beg him to make me come.

I did protest when he slipped his fingers free. "Isaac..."

He loomed up over me. "You still talk too much."

"Want me to shut up, you have to—"

Isaac slid his dick into my ass, then rammed it home. After that, he didn't give me any time or space for words. It was all I could do to moan or cry or even breathe through the pleasure of being filled up and fucked mercilessly by Isaac. He had my hair and my mouth as he slammed into me, shaking me down to my bones. I'd been teetering on the edge of orgasm most of the night, between the damn suit, the face fucking, the window and everything else, that it didn't take long for oblivion to rush toward me.

I tried to tell him, and maybe he understood, because he took my dick in his hand and jacked me off, and I was gone into a haze of pain-spotted pleasure.

"Oh fuck," Isaac moaned, then pounded me like he wanted to wring every last drop of bliss he could from my flesh and bones.

Everything vanished, and I think I touched the edge of heaven, screaming and crying all the way.

Sometime later—I wasn't sure when he'd pulled out of me

or tugged a comforter over our bodies—I realized Isaac was combing his fingers through my hair.

"Hey, Julien."

"Oui." That came out as a croak. God, I was a wreck—but a happy one for a change. "Hey, hi."

That smile. "You're so fucking gorgeous, did you know that?"

I grinned up at him. "Oui."

That got me one of my favorite Isaac expressions—he squeezed his eyes shut and laughed in a *what the fuck?* manner. His eyes were shining when he gazed down at me again. "Humble, too."

"Non. Not very, at all."

"I hadn't noticed." The kiss he planted on my lips was sweet and tender. Such a contrast from earlier.

Too much to take in. I wrapped my arms around Isaac and pulled him close, burying my face against his shoulder. My heart did things it hadn't done in years. Hope dug claws into my soul. My mind, free from its normal chaos, housed thoughts that made sense. This. I needed *this*.

Isaac hugged me back, murmuring something into my ear I couldn't make out.

"Quoi?"

He pulled back, his brow wrinkled in confusion. "What?"

I couldn't help laughing. "Sorry, sorry, that's what I was asking."

I'd never tire of the happy crinkles around his eyes. "My French is *really* bad, you know." The crinkles turned thoughtful. "I should download one of those apps."

That had me sitting up in bed. "You don't have to learn French for me." Hardly anyone on the team knew French. Elias, because that man picked up languages like other people picked up socks. Also Lucas Cote, who was from Montréal. The other Canadian players had a passing knowledge of simple phrases, and both Nikki and Paxy had picked up some of my more creative curses. But that was it.

"But if I wanted to?" Honest curiosity.

God. I was in love with this man. *Fuck.* The thought hit me hard as my heart tumbled in my chest. I scooted back and leaned against his headboard, then ran a hand through my hair, teasing out a few of the tangles. "I mean—you can. I wouldn't mind or anything. But you don't have to."

"Would you talk to me in French?" His cocky smile was back.

Two could play that game. "Oui."

That got the desired snort, and he snuggled up next to me, his hand smoothing over my abs. "At least the basic stuff. Would come in handy when we go to Montréal."

We'd play up there sometime after Christmas. I tapped my fingers on the part of the comforter covering my thigh. "My family goes to games when we play there. Most people from Saguenay only speak French, but my brother and sister and their kids are pretty fluent in English. My parents aren't, though."

Isaac stirred against me, and was silent for a long moment. "You want me to meet your parents?"

Did I? I nodded slowly and whispered, "Oui."

Isaac splayed his hand across my chest. "Oh." Then he cupped my cheek and turned my face to him. "Guess I better download that app, huh?"

There was joy in Isaac, and my heart somersaulted again, so I kissed him, much like I'd put away my suit. Slowly and carefully. I must've gotten it right because he looked a little dazed when I pulled back.

He licked his lips. "We're getting serious, aren't we?"

"Yeah." I looked away, my fingers dancing out a rhythm on the bed as a thought flickered through me. We spent pretty much all our free time together now. When I met

Isaac's gaze again, I spoke it out loud. "Do you want to tell the team?"

That dazed look morphed into shock, then a tiny smile bloomed on those beautiful lips. "Oui?"

I shoved him. Not hard, but enough to make him laugh. "God, you are..." Perfect. Wonderful. "Something else," I finished, breathless.

Sometimes I thought Isaac might actually be able to read my mind, especially when his eyes danced like that and he smiled that secretive little grin. "All right," he said. "When?"

That was a good question. Before a game was not the best time. Nor was after. At a practice? Coach would kill us for distracting the entire team when we should be focused. Then it hit me. "Oh. I'm hosting Thanksgiving this year."

Isaac stared at me. "You're Canadian."

I raised an eyebrow. "And Nikki's Russian and Elias is Swedish. We take turns hosting. Big houses. Letters on our sweaters."

"But none of you actually celebrate Thanksgiving!"

I shoved him again. "I do. In October, when it *should* be celebrated."

He couldn't stop laughing, and a moment later, I joined him. We ended up curled into each other's arms, still leaning against his headboard.

Isaac brushed my lips with his. "So we're *dating* dating, huh?"

I didn't say "oui" this time. All I had to do was grin, and I got that perfect laugh.

When he sobered, he nodded. "Okay. Thanksgiving." He paused, then added, "Do you need help with cooking?"

"No, no." I waved a hand. "With something that big, we have it catered."

"So no burning the turkey?" There was a wicked turn to his smile.

I sat up. "Do I look like someone who can't cook a turkey?" I wasn't at Paxy's level in terms of cooking, but I could hold my own.

"I mean..." He shrugged and tucked his hands behind his head, flexing those arms of his. "You're Canadian. Do they even have turkeys up there?"

I rolled my eyes. "Do they even have turkeys where *you're* from? Isn't it all salmon over there?" I couldn't keep the laughter from my voice. "But yes, I can cook. You?"

"Mmmhmm." He craned his neck to check the clock on his nightstand. "In fact, I should be getting a grocery delivery soon."

My stomach rumbled at his words. He snorted and I placed a hand over my belly, huffing in amusement. "Guess we should get moving, then."

Isaac sat up and threw his legs over the edge of the mattress. "You want coffee?"

I followed his lead and climbed out of bed. "How late are we staying up?"

He shot me a look that nearly had me on my knees again. "How's your stamina?"

Despite wanting to fall at Isaac's feet, I crossed my arms and tossed my hair out of my face. "Better than yours."

"Want to bet on that?"

I lifted an eyebrow. "Do you? I may be older, but which of us spends twenty-eight minutes on the ice every other day or so?"

Isaac chuckled in a particularly evil way, grabbed a pair of gray sweatpants from his dresser and headed into his bathroom. Only then did I notice his jeans and button-down crumpled on the floor.

By the time Isaac came back, I'd picked them up, folded them neatly, and placed them on the foot of his bed.

That got me an interesting look, then a nod of approval,

and every bit of me flared with joy. "I should get my bag," I stammered.

"And I should get the coffee started." He winked at me. "Come on."

My overnight bag was where I'd left it by the door, so I hauled it back up those treacherous stairs, got out a pair of sweatpants and cleaned myself up. Returning to the main floor, I found Isaac in his kitchen, pouring beans into a rather nice espresso machine. I whistled low. "Fancy."

He glanced over his shoulder. "Only the best for a king."

Damn. Too much time with Nikki. I coughed a laugh. "Don't you start with that." I pulled out one of the stools by the kitchen island, sat, then winced. "Ow, fuck."

Isaac gave me one of his low sexy chuckles. "Sore, are we?"

I mimicked his "Sore, are we?" then waved a hand. "Testament to your prowess."

That got me a snort.

"No." I folded my arms onto the island. "I mean it, Isaac. You're an amazing lover."

He must've finished with the coffee machine, because there was a loud moment of grinding, then a low rumble. He turned around, a blush touching his cheeks. "You're inspiring."

That had me looking down at my hands. I traced the veins of color in the white marble countertop. "Thank you." Flashes of yesterday crept into my mind, as did Nikki's admonishment. "Isaac," I said, slowly, "There's some things I should tell you, so you know."

He pulled out the other stool and sat. "Yeah?" He placed his hand on mine, stilling my fingers.

"Yesterday's game—I said it was more than just a rivalry." I met his gaze. "It's still a rivalry. Carolina's knocked us out of the playoffs three times. But for me—it's personal."

He gave my hand a gentle squeeze. "I had a feeling."

My bark of a laugh was bitter. "I was the idiot who dated Travis Canterbury. We never told anyone, and it ended badly."

Not even a hint of shock on Isaac's face. Someone had either told him, or he'd put one and one together. Probably the latter. Isaac was smart. Perceptive. While I'd managed to keep from fighting Travis last night, I'm sure our interactions were—noticeable.

"He's the last person I dated. After him I—didn't want to get that close to anyone." I shrugged lightly and held his hand tighter. "Until I got to know you."

He took that in, his eyes searching my face. "And you're okay with the team knowing about us?"

I nodded, the reason falling like a sudden rain shower in my head. "I was his dirty little secret," I whispered. "That was —horrible. So much shame and anger. I don't want to do that to you. I don't want to be like him." I turned my hand and clasped his fingers. "Maybe what we have can go somewhere, but if we start it with a lie or hiding, I—" My voice cracked.

Isaac twined his fingers in mine. "You're not like him."

I fought back the roil in my brain and belly. "God, I hope I'm not."

Just then, the espresso machine spat out a small cup of very rich-smelling coffee, and we both turned to watch.

"Americano?" Isaac look sideways at me "Or do they call it something different in Canada?"

That fixed the cracks in my heart, so I bumped my shoulder into his and chuckled. "Yes, an Americano. Do you have creamer?"

He did. We had to let go of each other, but were rewarded with a very nice cup of coffee each afterward.

He sipped and hummed appreciatively. "This *is* good."

"One of my favorites." I turned the mug between my palms. "They have some limited edition blends that top this one, but this they always have." I lifted my gaze. "I can drink any coffee, really, but I prefer the best when I can get it."

Isaac looked into his own cup and there was that blush again, but then his brow creased. "Can I ask you something? About Travis?"

Rock straight into my stomach, but I nodded.

"He's not out, is he?"

I shook my head. "Not that I've heard." In moments of weakness, I'd checked his Instagram. "Model girlfriends, I think." Like so many of the guys in the league who dated women. "I work hard to avoid that asshole."

"Except when you can't."

Yup. "Makes the games even more chippy, and I can't tell anyone why."

Isaac opened his mouth—then snapped it closed. After a moment, he spoke. "You don't want to out him."

"I despise that man," I said. "But I vowed not to be the kind of asshole he is, so no. I can't out him."

Isaac brushed a hand through my hair, then leaned in to kiss me. "From what I've seen, you're not like that guy at all." He sat back. "Way better player."

This time I was the one to lean in and steal a kiss. That turned into something much longer and interesting—right up until Isaac's phone buzzed.

He groaned. "Grocery delivery."

I pecked him on the lips. "Let's go see what you bought, chef."

He laughed, rose, and headed for the door and I followed, happy to go wherever Isaac led.

# Chapter 17

## Isaac

The games leading up to Thanksgiving were a roller coaster. An easy win followed by a crushing loss followed by an absolute battle that ended in a two-one loss after a shootout. After that, a hard-won victory. Morale was high that night, only to take a steady dive over a three-game losing streak that saw two players—Paxy and Manning—benched with injuries. Manning was going to be out for a while thanks to a torn ACL. Probably the rest of the season.

At least Paxy wasn't down for long; he'd aggravated an old injury in his hip and just needed to rest it for a few days. Julien had looked relieved as hell when Paxy had joined us for this morning's skate. He'd done all right with his temporary defensive partner, but he and Paxy were magic together.

We'd needed that magic tonight, too. Holy hell. We'd played at home against Long Island, and after their embarrassing loss two nights ago, they'd been out for blood and redemption. They'd almost gotten the latter, too—their goalie was a brick wall, and despite all of our best efforts, they'd absolutely hammered Davy with pucks all night. He'd been a brick wall too, though. In the end, we denied Long Island their redemption thanks to a single goal scored by Nisha on an assist from Paxy during a power play.

So, no redemption, but they did get some blood.

In particular, *my* blood.

"It doesn't look that bad." Julien peered at the stitches above my lip as we ate after the game.

"Now you'll have scar!" Nisha declared with a grin, pointing at me with his fork. "Like real hockey player."

I rolled my eyes and poked at the sort of numb, sort of tender corner of my mouth. "Great."

Julien laughed, sitting back in his seat across from mine at the table. "Eh. It builds character." He picked up some chicken on his fork. "And it'll only be visible when you stop shaving during the playoffs."

That actually lifted my spirits a bit. It was still way too early to know if we were going to the playoffs, but the possibility made my heart flutter.

He must have seen it too, because he smiled one of those knowing smiles that didn't do a damn thing to stop that fluttering. "See?" He winked. "You'll be fine."

"Can he even *grow* a beard?" Elias asked.

"Fuck you," I grumbled.

The guys laughed, and we continued eating. That was a struggle for me thanks to the stitches. They were still partially numb, which was probably a good thing, but it didn't really help me put food in my mouth. It reminded me of that feeling after I'd been to the dentist, complete with some teeth being sore. They weren't loose or anything, though. I'd be going to the dentist this week just to make sure there wasn't any damage, but the team doc wasn't too worried.

I managed to gingerly chew a bite of halibut, which was the softest protein they had on offer tonight. I was a bit of a snob about fish, having grown up in the Pacific Northwest, but this was good. Everything the team was served was good.

And tonight, it had the added bonus of not aggravating my sore mouth.

"Funny," I said after a while. "I always thought the first time I'd bleed during a pro game, it would be from a fight."

"It *was* a fight," Elias said.

Julien's brow quirked. I eyed our captain.

Elias glanced between us. Then he shrugged as he deadpanned, "Your face lost a fight with someone's stick."

Julien and Nisha burst out laughing. Elias's mouth barely twitched.

"Ass," I muttered, but I couldn't help chuckling. Elias finally let himself laugh, and the four of us continued eating and bantering. As much as it sucked, getting a high stick to the face, it *had* given us the four-minute power play that had given Nisha the opportunity to score that one precious goal. We'd won, breaking our short but demoralizing losing streak, and even my spirits couldn't be dampened tonight.

We finished our meal, and everyone eventually started filtering out for the evening. That was when reality sank in and those good spirits started to wane in favor of uneasiness. My sewn-up face hadn't cost us the game, but it did make my evening plans...complicated.

I watched Julien putting on his overcoat, and I just stopped myself from chewing my lip. That would've been a *bad* idea. But I almost couldn't help it, because damn, I had some nerves that I'd never experienced before.

For weeks now, we'd wound up sleeping together after every home game. We couldn't really do it at away games—not until we'd come out to the team—but when we were in Pittsburgh, it was his place or mine. There'd been one night when he'd been absolutely wrecked after spending twenty-nine minutes on the ice during a brutal battle of a game, and we hadn't done more than jerk each other off in my shower before collapsing in bed, but post-game orgasms were a foregone conclusion.

Which meant tonight…

I swallowed hard as Julien exchanged a few bantery barbs with Paxy before heading my way. He was in such a good mood tonight, joking with the team and in the kind of high spirits that came after breaking a losing streak. Knowing him, he was looking forward to capping off the night with a rowdy fuck that left his legs shaking.

I was not looking forward to disappointing him.

Oblivious to me tying myself in knots, he met my gaze. "Ready to go?"

"Yeah. Yeah, sure." I wasn't, but this wasn't a conversation we were having in here with our teammates and maybe a few hot mics still hanging around. So, I fell into step with him, and we headed out to the parking garage.

"How are you feeling?" He gestured at his lip. "Still numb?"

"It's wearing off." I pushed my hands into my pockets. "It'll probably feel great in the morning."

He grimaced sympathetically, not offering anything to suggest I was wrong. Awesome. Something to look forward to. Better than a concussion, though, so I'd take it. Poor Larry would probably still be benched by the time I got my stitches out. Perspective and all that.

And we were almost to the parking garage. Crap. I couldn't put this off anymore.

Taking a deep breath, I slowed to a stop.

So did Julien. He studied me, concern written all over his face.

I broke eye contact, and I wondered if it was my imagination that my lip started throbbing harder as heat rushed into my face.

"Isaac?" More concern.

I pushed back a surge of embarrassment and held his gaze. "Look, about tonight..."

Deep crevices formed between his eyebrows. "Yeah...?"

"I, um..." I couldn't handle his scrutiny anymore and dropped my gaze as I reached up to scratch my neck. "Are we still going to your place?"

He studied me, clearly not following. "You...don't want to?"

"I do, but I mean, I can't... There's no way I'm..." Fuck, why couldn't I talk? I looked at him again.

His eyes flicked to my lip, and understanding seemed to dawn, followed immediately by what I thought was horror. He stiffened like I'd kicked him. "Do you think I'd expect you to want to be physical? With...?" He gestured at his lip again.

It was amazing how hard it was to be this nervous and uncomfortable and *not* bite my lip or purse them. "But if we're going to your place, then we're—"

"Isaac." Julien shook his head. "I knew as soon as I saw you go down that you weren't going to want sex tonight."

"Really?"

He laughed dryly. "I've been high-sticked in the face before. It's, um, not much of an aphrodisiac."

I managed to chuckle, more heat rushing into my cheeks. "No, it really isn't." I hesitated, then pathetically admitted, "It fucking hurts."

"I know it does. If you'd rather call it a night, I'll understand, but if you're up for the drive, I'd love it if you stayed with me."

"Even if I can't..."

"Oh, Isaac." He sighed, and I wondered if he was fighting the urge to reach for me. We were alone for now, but that could change in a hurry. "Listen, I know we fuck a lot, but it's not something we have to do all the time. You're not always going to want sex and neither will I. That would be true even if we *didn't* do something physically demanding for a living." He looked right in my eyes, and his voice softened even more as he said, "That doesn't mean I don't want to see you. Or spend the night with you."

"Oh. Wow."

Julien gave me a lopsided grin. "If you hadn't noticed, I'm not just in this for sex. If I was, I wouldn't have suggested telling the team about us on Thursday."

My heart somersaulted, both from the comment and from the reminder about Thursday. Oh God. *This* Thursday. That was coming up *fast*.

I laughed as I avoided his gaze. "Well, now I feel like an idiot."

"Don't." He gave my shoulder a perfectly platonic pat, and we continued toward our cars. "You've never done this before. We're both still figuring it out."

"True." I glanced at him. "So, your place?"

That smile *almost* made me reconsider taking sex off the table tonight. Almost.

I did feel like an idiot for doubting him, too. Though we'd fooled around at every available opportunity since we'd started, it wasn't like he'd given me any reason to believe sex was the price of admission to be around him. No reason except simply existing as a man who was way too gorgeous and way too amazing to notice me, never mind want me. But all along, he'd been someone I enjoyed talking to and who seemed to enjoy talking to me whether we were on the ice, on the plane, or in bed. Wherever we were, whatever we were doing (or not doing), he'd become a friend as well as a lover.

Still, the reassurance was unexpectedly, well, reassuring. It was getting harder and harder for my inexperience and insecurities to creep in and tell me Julien wasn't actually interested in *me*.

He *was* interested in me. He wanted me. He *liked* me, and

that didn't ebb and flow with my ability or desire to put out the way team morale did with wins and losses. When sex wasn't an option, he still smiled at me. He still gave me that conspiratorial wink before getting into his car. He still glanced in his rearview to make sure I was behind him.

And tonight, in the ridiculously comfortable bed in his familiar bedroom, he still held me just as tight while we drifted off together.

*Holy shit,* I thought before sleep closed in. *Julien Landry likes me.*

---

FROM WHERE HE sat on a barstool, Coach peered at us over Julien's kitchen island. His eyes flicked to me. Then to Julien. Then back to me.

His expression betrayed nothing, which probably meant we were about two seconds away from his pissed-off coach voice echoing off the high ceilings.

Thanksgiving guests would be arriving soon—within the next hour—but for the moment, the house was empty except for the three of us. Silent, too, though Julien's words were still ringing in my ears a full thirty seconds after he'd spoken them.

"Rivera and I—we're dating."

I held my breath, concentrating on *not* biting my tender lip. Julien was anything but still, tapping his fingers on the counter and toeing the edge of the tile beneath the island. If my heart was pounding like this, I could only imagine what his was doing, and I wished I could reach for him and at least try to settle him down.

Which…hell, why not? I wouldn't be telling Coach anything he didn't already know.

So, I put a hand on Julien's forearm. His fingers stilled. So did his foot. After a moment, he closed his eyes and exhaled, the breath ragged and giving away how nervous he really was. No wonder he'd barely slept last night. Not that I had either, and it hadn't been entirely because of him tossing and turning.

I shifted my gaze back to Coach, and I realized he'd fixed his attention on my hand. Which was still on Julien's arm. I didn't let go, though. Coach knew. The contact was calming Julien. Coach was going to yell at us either way, so—

"Do I look stupid to the two of you?" Coach asked in that long-suffering, why-do-you-boys-do-this-to-me voice I'd heard during a few intermissions.

I blinked. Beside me, Julien tensed.

"Stupid?" I asked. "What?"

With a heavy sigh, Coach sat back, folding his arms loosely across his chest. "I'm not sure you're aware, kid, but the league pays me an extraordinary amount of money to do the equivalent of herding cats. Part of that entails being absolutely aware of what's going on with every single one of those cats. Like if two of them aren't getting along." He inclined his head. "Or if two of them are getting along *very* well."

Ah, that familiar heat in my face. I was in good company, though—Julien was blushing too.

Coach's expression hardened. "Listen, because I'm only going to say this once. I don't give two flying fucks what you boys are doing, as long as it stays off my ice and doesn't affect my team. You two get into a spat, or you split up, or..." He flailed his hand. "I don't give a shit, and I don't want to see it. You sort it out on your own time." He jabbed a finger emphatically into the counter and eyed both of us. "As long as you're on my ice, you're Landry and Rivera, and you're teammates working toward the same goal, which is a winning team. Am I clear?"

We both nodded and said, "Yeah, Coach."

"All right." He relaxed a bit and exhaled. "And I suppose

you had me get here early so you could tell me before you come out to the team over Thanksgiving dinner."

Julien laughed. "Something like that."

Coach grunted, rolling his eyes. "Well, better than in the locker room."

"That was kind of the idea," Julien said. "Tell everyone when we don't need to focus on hockey and when there aren't any reporters around."

"Reporters?"

I nodded. "We're, um... We figured we'd start with the team, and then go public... I don't know. Eventually."

"Good luck with that," Coach muttered. "Once it's out..." He grimaced.

I glanced at Julien, and when he met my gaze, he shrugged as if to say, *Eh, I'm not worried.* Okay. If he wasn't worried, then neither was I. Well, not much. I was kind of worried. I still wasn't used to people knowing who I was, never mind caring who I dated. The first time my name had trended on Twitter had almost broken my brain (and thank God it was for a goal and not because I'd royally fucked up). What kind of shit would they say about us? It wasn't like we were the only queer guys in the league, but I hadn't heard about any players dating teammates, and that might—

Julien's hand materialized on the small of my back, and my breathing immediately slowed. I hadn't even realized it had sped up or that I'd been quietly panicking over us coming out publicly, but he must've caught on. Though it was usually me calming him down with a touch, that could work both ways sometimes, and right now, I was grateful for it.

"Breathe," he said.

I nodded. And I breathed.

Coach watched us both as if he couldn't quite believe what he was seeing. Then he shook his head. "Whatever makes you boys happy. Just keep it off my ice." He gestured toward the fridge. "Gimme a beer, Landry."

Julien laughed, sounding relieved, and he fished a beer out of the fridge, uncapped it, and pushed it across the island. Coach lifted it in a mock toast, then took a deep pull, probably mentally cursing us and all his other "cats" for aging him prematurely.

Not long after that conversation, people started arriving. The whole team wouldn't be here—quite a few of the guys had gone straight from last night's game to the airport so they could join their families today—but there was no shortage of guests, either. Nisha and Elias were among the first to arrive, carpooling with Larry. Larry was cleared to drive, but he was still having some headaches, so Elias had apparently insisted, and no one said no when the captain went mother hen on them. After those three, there was a steady trickle of people until Julien's enormous house was packed and loud.

Several people brought wives and kids, and I kind of fell a little harder for Julien when I realized he had a room full of games and toys to keep them all entertained. For his nieces and nephews, he insisted, but convenient when teammates brought kids over. Uh-huh. I was on to him. The way he smiled as all the little ones lit up at the sight of that play room—yeah, it might've been primarily for his nieces and nephews, but he was a sucker for kids, and it was *fucking adorable*.

The adults dispersed throughout the house. Some watched football in the living room. Others socialized in the dining room where the caterers had set up a few gigantic platters of hors d'oeuvres and munchies. Parents rotated in and out of the playroom so there was always supervision, but everyone still had a chance to eat and relax.

Unsurprisingly, quite a few of us ended up in Julien's basement. After all, you could take the hockey player off the ice, but...

"Crisse, could you guys not *try* to hit the I-beams?" Julien grimaced and wiggled his finger in his ear. "Fucking hell." My ears were ringing too. Jesus, that was loud.

"Hey, it's not our fault you have all this tempting metal hanging around." Ozzy reached up and tapped the I-beam with his stick, which fortunately didn't clang quite as loud as when someone beaned it with a puck. "You could cover it with pool noodles or something."

"Cover you with pool noodles," Julien muttered into his water glass.

"He might be on to something," I said to Julien with complete innocence. Gesturing at the exposed metal, I added, "Cover it with foam or something until some of these guys can actually control the puck."

That prompted a chorus of "*Oooh*" and "Rookie's got *jokes*," and Ozzy smacked me across the shin with his stick as we all laughed. Julien shot me a wicked look that almost made me forget all about hockey or being surrounded by our teammates.

Paxy passed the puck to me across the concrete floor, and I caught it on my stick. "Talking a big game, Rookie." He jerked his chin toward the opposite wall. "Let's see you hit it."

I shrugged, adjusted my grip on my stick, and fired the puck at the series of "goals" that had been set up. They were mostly impossibly small boxes made out of PVC and duct tape, and they were definitely a pain in the dick to hit. Especially the ones up high on the wall, which was what Ozzy had been aiming for when he'd hit the I-beam instead.

My puck went right in, hitting the plywood backstop with a satisfying thunk before ricocheting back out and rolling across the floor onto Nisha's stick.

"What the hell?" Benson shook his head and flailed his hand at me, then the wall of fuckery. "How is he so good at hitting all that bullshit?"

I shrugged. "Practice?"

"Practice?" Ozzy snorted. "How much time have you been spending in Landry's basement?"

Julien choked on his water. I froze, then glared at Nisha. He shook his head, staring wide-eyed back at me as if to say, *I didn't tell anyone!*

"What?" Ozzy watched us, wide-eyed. "What did I say?"

The basement was suddenly dead silent. The sounds of voices and football carried from upstairs, but down here, no one moved or said a word. I realized a moment too late that if we'd just played it cool and fired back something snarky, no one would've thought anything of it. But...a moment too late.

And much like in the kitchen with Coach, it occurred to me that we weren't trying to keep this a secret anymore. We'd had every intention of making it not a secret today. Now was as good a time as any, right?

I looked at Julien. He looked at me. I shrugged.

Julien took a breath as he put his glass aside. "Uh, well—"

"Wait, wait, wait." Ozzy gestured at both of us. "Are you two...?"

"Lans and Rivs are fucking?" Jackal asked.

"Hey!" Paxy smacked him with his stick. "There's kids in the house. They're *dating*." He turned to us. "Right?"

Julien looked completely baffled by the way this conversation was going, but after a couple of beats, he shook himself and nodded. "Yes. We haven't come out publicly, but..." He wrapped his arm around my shoulders. "We're dating."

The basement was instantly full of voices talking over one another. I was relieved (though not overly surprised) that no one seemed upset or put off by us being together. Homophobes didn't last long in the league anymore, and Coach sure as shit didn't put up with it.

I was definitely surprised by some of the things they were saying, though.

"Dude. Larry's not going to believe this." Davy was typing something on his phone.

Sanders had also started typing, shaking his head and laughing as he did.

"Ha!" Paxy slapped Benson's back. "Pay up, mofo!"

"Oh, come on." Benson rolled his eyes as he pulled out his wallet. "That was a lucky guess."

"Lucky guess? Pfft." Paxy poked him with his stick. "Just because you're the only one who didn't know."

"Wait, what?" Julien stared at Paxy. "You knew?"

Paxy shot him a look that said nothing if not *you dumbass*. "Really, Lans? Really?"

Julien still stared.

"Oh, for God's sake." Paxy shook his head. "I'm your defense partner. I *know* you. And I've known about"—he waved at the two of us—"for a while, because I have *eyeballs* that are attached to a *brain*."

"That's debatable sometimes," Elias said.

Nisha huffed a laugh. "Sometimes?"

Paxy flipped them off, and they laughed and fist-bumped. He started to say something, but right then, the basement door opened and someone came thundering down the stairs.

"Are you guys lying?" Ortiz leaned on the railing, phone in hand. "Are they—" His gaze landed on me and Julien, and his eyes turned huge. Then he shouted over his shoulder, "Yeah, they're fucking!" He started back up the stairs. "No, I don't mean right *now*. Jesus, dude." The door shut again.

Oh God. The look on Julien's face...

I laughed and put my arm around his waist. "I'd say they all took it pretty well."

He shifted that look to me, but as soon as our eyes met, his expression softened to a smile. "Yeah. They did." He pulled me in closer, and right there in the basement with several of our teammates, he pressed a kiss to my forehead.

Naturally, that prompted a chorus of, "Awww," and Paxy yelled, "Get a room!"

Julien gave him the finger. Paxy responded with the same, coupled with a big grin.

Julien muttered something in French, then let me go. "I should go get a handle on the rumors they're probably all starting upstairs."

"Yeah, good idea. I'm right behind you."

Or, well, I was.

Before I'd reached the stairs, Paxy stopped me with a hand on my arm. To my surprise, his expression was one of complete sincerity.

"Listen, in all seriousness, I've known for a while." He nodded in the direction Julien had gone. "I don't know when it started, but I know he's been different because of you."

I couldn't say if it was because I was so used to him being a smartass or what, but the words left me speechless.

"You're good for him, Rivs." He squeezed my arm. "It shows."

"I..." I swallowed, then finally managed to find my voice. "Thanks. He's been good for me too."

The smile was surprisingly sweet and devoid of his usual snark. "Yeah. I figured." And then the snark returned. "Just go easy on him before games, yeah?" He winked. "I need him to be able to skate."

Before I could respond, he jogged up the stairs after Julien, leaving me standing there like a dumbass.

Was this real?

"Hey, Rivs?" Sanders called to me, looking up from thumbing through his wallet. "How long has this been going on?"

"Uh..." I thought for a moment. "Since...um..."

"Was it before the Florida game, or after?" Jackal asked.

"Before," I said.

Sanders hissed a curse, pulled another twenty out of his wallet, and shoved it at Jackal.

So much for flying below the radar. Someone probably had a spreadsheet somewhere of everyone's bets, odds, everything. And Julien and I hadn't had a clue.

Chuckling to myself, I left them to continue figuring out their payouts, and I headed upstairs to help Julien wrangle the rumor mill.

# Chapter 18

## Julien

We had the Friday after American Thanksgiving off. No game, no practice. Such a rarity. Saturday, we'd be back at the practice rink and we had an afternoon home game on Sunday, so after a lazy morning in bed with Isaac, I hauled myself into the basement for a workout. While backbreaking sex with Isaac was quite a physical feat, I couldn't fuck my way into game condition, even if I wanted to.

Isaac joined me for most of my sequence, but after two rounds of sprints on the bike, proclaimed that he desperately needed a shower and some coffee. Couldn't help chuckling. Even Nikki, competitive to a fault, tended not to finish a workout with me.

When I came into the kitchen after my shower, Isaac sat at the island in a pair of black sweatpants and one of my old Griffins T-shirts, tapping away on his laptop.

"Wearing my number already?" A fresh cup of coffee with the perfect amount of creamer sat on the counter in front of the chair next to him. "Is this for me?"

"Yes to both questions." He looked up, and his smile took my breath away.

I still couldn't believe we were together. Dating. Out to our coach and team. I slid into the seat next to him, claimed a kiss, then a sip of coffee. I had to be the luckiest man alive. "Thank you for the coffee."

"Well, it's your coffee. I just made it for you." Before I could reply, he turned his laptop toward me. "Are either of these hotels good?"

Both the places were downtown. Both high-end. "They're fine. The league uses this one." I pointed to the one on the right, then at the other. "And the baseball league puts their players up in this one. But why are you looking at hotels?"

"My parents are visiting for Christmas. They want to see me play in the league, since they couldn't make it out for my debut." He studied the laptop screen. "Neither of these are close to the rink. I know they'll want to watch practice, too." His brown eyes were full of worry when he turned to me. "Do you know if that's okay?"

Was that okay? I chuckled. "Perfectly fine. That's what my family does, since practice is open to the public." I paused. "Do you want to meet them? Everyone's coming down for Christmas."

There was that dazed expression again. Did I look like that when my heart flipped in my chest, and heat spread out to my fingertips? How deep would this go? I was in love with Isaac, but I had no idea how to tell him. Didn't know if this was too fast or too slow. My only other experience with love had been —twisted. Warped by Travis's actions.

Isaac's eyes, his smile, didn't lie, and he was fucking *adorable* when he was shy. "All of them?"

I nodded. "My parents, my siblings, and all the kids." Then I was the one who got lost in thought.

That must have changed my expression, because concern returned to Isaac's. "What's wrong?"

"Nothing." The thought that bounced around my head

was a good one, but I didn't know if Isaac would agree. "You know, I planned to tell my family about you before they came down. I figured that would be easier than springing it on them while they're here."

He nodded warily. "Uh, sure?"

I drummed my fingers on the top of the island, unsure of Isaac's answer, but I plowed ahead anyway. "I was just thinking that even with my family here, I have a spare bedroom. Your parents could stay here rather than at a hotel." Hotels were awful, even expensive ones. Sure, I stayed at them a lot, but they pecked at my nerves. I didn't want to subject anyone to that if there was another option.

Maybe I grew an extra head or something, because Isaac stared at me like he no longer understood what sat before him. "You want our families to meet."

"Yes?" I said carefully. "They're going to anyway, or do you want to keep us a secret from them?"

Since we'd come out to the team, that was going to be impossible. Coach was right—keeping it out of the public eye would be hard, but from our own families? I couldn't do that. Hell, my sister had already been peppering me with leading questions because she sensed something was up. I was too upbeat. Laughed too easy. I'd tried to pass it off as being happy with the season so far, and the way I was playing, but I knew she wasn't buying what I was selling.

"Isaac..." I collected my coffee, sat back in my chair, and tried not to look as despondent as I felt.

"Oh God, no!" He touched my shoulder, then my cheek, as if to reassure me, his face full of horror. "I didn't mean we shouldn't tell them! I absolutely want our families to meet, and I planned to tell my parents that we're dating. I just—" He grasped my hand and looked around the kitchen, as if searching for the right words. "You offering this is a *lot*. This is your home. You don't know anything about my parents."

I needed Isaac in my arms, so I tugged him toward me until he slipped off his chair and I was able to bury my face against his chest. "I know one thing about your parents," I said, muttering against the T-shirt, then I looked up into his beautiful face. "They raised you."

The cascade of expressions was amazing to behold. Then Isaac leaned down and kissed me, sweetly and lovingly. A far cry from our usual devouring, scorching kisses, but this left me as breathless.

"You have such a big heart."

"Eh." I shrugged. "I have a big house."

Sometimes it was hard to be alone here. Sometimes I needed the space. I absolutely lived for the times when I could fill it with the people I loved. Family. Teammates. Here Isaac was, standing before me, that quirky smile on his lips as he studied me. He could be both. Maybe was both. Tabarnak. That was a *thought*.

Isaac's smile widened.

"What?"

He laughed and sank back onto his chair. "You're amazing. That's all." He sobered a little. "I'll call my parents later, but I think they'll say yes to staying here."

I hoped so. And I hoped my family would take as quickly to Isaac as I had.

---

MY FAMILY ARRIVED three days before Christmas, *all* of them. Six adults and five kids. Three carloads of Landrys. Well, my sister's wife's last name was Roy, but while visiting me? She was a Landry through and through, as were her two kids.

Rather than go to the house, they drove straight from the airport to the practice arena, so there were eleven people in the stands wearing my jersey and screaming their heads off when I stepped out on the ice to practice.

Same thing, every single year. I laughed and waved to my family as I skated past, then bumped shoulders with Isaac, who'd followed me out onto the ice. "Still want to meet them?"

He was laughing, but also had a bit of an awed expression. "Yes, but you didn't say they were all like *you*."

"They're not! I'm the sedate one."

That got me a smack on the back of my helmet from Nikki. "Liar." Then he skated toward my family and banged himself off the glass, much to the delight of the kids. Lots of calls of "Mononcle Nikki" from the nieces and nephews.

Coach gave me a *look*. I returned that with an innocent shrug, and crossed over to him. "I don't encourage them! You know that."

This time he chuckled. "Eh, they're not any worse than the youth hockey teams."

Elias joined us and snorted at Coach. "You love it when they come into town. Best cheering squad in the league."

Coach gave a rare smile, then blew the whistle to get things started. Then he worked us hard for an hour. Little skirmish drills. Small area work, then both power play and penalty kill practice. Felt good, though. Team spirit was high, and everyone was cheering for every goal, spurred on in part by the loud section all wearing my name.

At the end of practice, Isaac joined me and gestured at my family. "So you know, my parents came in at some point."

I spun around on the ice and nearly tripped over my own skates. "Oh, shit."

Sure enough, another couple had joined my family, and they could only be Isaac's parents. He looked like a combination of the two: his father's hair and jawline, but his mother's nose and mischievous eyes, especially the way they glinted when she laughed at something my sister was saying. "Oh my God, what is Marie telling them?"

I tried skating over, but Nikki threw his arm over my shoulder and steered me toward the locker room. "Come on, King. You stink. Shower for you."

We ate as well, then had a short team meeting. My parents knew the drill and where to wait until the staff fetched them. The biggest issue was that the rest of the team loved my family, too, and some of them were taking off to visit their own families once tomorrow's game was over, so when mine entered, complete chaos reigned.

When I'd suggested our families stay together, I hadn't considered that I would meet Isaac's parents for the first time in the team locker room, nor had I anticipated that it would be twelve-year-old Josephine who'd run into the room shouting "Mononcle Julien, Mononcle Julien!" while dragging Isaac's mom behind her. She let go of Mrs. Rivera, then threw herself around me.

"Ooomph. Josie!" I laughed, and tried not to blush furiously when Isaac's mom smiled at me. I looked down at my niece—but not so far as the last time I'd seen her. "T'as tellement grandi!" She'd shot up by several inches.

"In English!" she demanded. "Mom says I need to practice." Before I could even answer, she'd grabbed Mrs. Rivera's hand again. "This is Isaac's mom."

I was face to face with Mrs. Rivera, with my family and teammates all around me. "Hi," I stammered. "I'm Julien."

That had to be the worst hello ever and my cheeks were an inferno. Then a familiar touch at the small of my back had me straightening and swallowing.

"Hi Mom. How was your trip?"

I didn't hear her answer because a small army of Landry children went swarming past me and straight to Nikki, all of them shouting out his name. Then they caught sight of all my other teammates, and the noise ticked up to an ear-numbing level.

"Oh God, I'm so sorry," I said to Isaac and his mother when we could all hear again. "We're a handful."

She chuckled. "You don't have to apologize for having a wonderful family."

Isaac slid his hand up to my shoulder. "Mom, Dad, this is my boyfriend, Julien."

Shit, Isaac's father was there, too. Of course I knew that, but somehow looking into his eyes made this all real. My loud, obnoxious family, our teammates, and Isaac's parents. I stuck out my hand and tried the whole introduction thing again. "Hello, nice to meet you."

That turned out a little better. Both of Isaac's parents, Crystal and Jay, were delighted to meet me. Their trip had gone well. They shared some tidbits about life in Astoria and people Isaac knew. All the while, my brain was in overdrive. I had no idea where *my* parents were. Or Marie. Or my brother. But Isaac's steady hand on my shoulder kept me in place when all I wanted to do was stride around the locker room. Or run away.

I bumped Isaac with my hip. "I should find the rest of my family."

Another arm slid around my back, and my sister, Marie, was at my side. "We're fine. Maman and Papa are talking with Elias. Mathieu is speaking with Coach Lavoy." Then she looked around me to Isaac. "I'm Marie. You're dating my baby brother." She gave me the tightest squeeze.

"Ooof, Marie! Arrête."

She poked me. "English, Julien."

This was a *disaster*. I croaked a laugh. "My sister, Marie."

Something in Isaac's mom's eyes sparkled. "We met. You have the sweetest family!"

"The stories I heard about your boyfriend." I recognized

Marie's sly grin, because it was my own. *Shit*. She turned to Isaac's mom. "You should tell him about the player Isaac had a crush on in college."

Next to me, Isaac tensed. "Oh no, Mom!" Horror spread like wildfire over his face.

"Oh, him! I don't remember his name. Began with a J, I think. Long dark hair. Pretty face. I think he was a defenseman, like you."

The absolute *blush* on Isaac's cheeks.

"Oh really?" Now I was grinning as widely as my sister. "French Canadian, as well?"

Isaac's grip tightened on my shoulder and his mother nodded. "Julien," he gritted out.

"That's it! His name was Julien, just like yours!"

"Mom!" Isaac practically exploded. "It was Julien Landry. *This* is Julien Landry!"

Mrs. Rivera blinked a few times, then took a closer look at me. "Well, you *are* a very handsome young man."

"Oh my God, Mom." Isaac buried his face in his hands, then pushed back his hair. "Really?"

"You had a crush on me?" My cheeks hurt from grinning, and the look Isaac gave me was part plaintive *please stop*, part *you-are-so-going-to-pay-for-this*. Maybe this whole meet-the-parents thing wasn't so bad after all.

Marie gave me a shove. "Three-quarters of hockey fandom has a crush on you."

"Three-quarters of hockey fandom isn't dating me," I snapped, then stared into Isaac's eyes. "Only Isaac is."

Now *that* was a look I knew well. I was, indeed, going to pay for this, but in a manner we both enjoyed. Too bad my house would be bursting at the seams with our families for the next five days.

"Oh." That from Marie, and it was a serious exclamation, no teasing behind it. When I met her gaze, she was studying me. "Julien."

Oh *hell*. She saw it. Saw what I hadn't told Isaac because I wasn't sure if this went beyond a crush for him. Maybe? I had no idea. Didn't want to put any pressure on him. This was as new to him as it was to me.

Thank God Marie just smiled and gave me a small nod. I suspected she'd corner me later and ask what she clearly already knew.

More shouting erupted from the far side of the room, and I looked over to find Nikki playing floor hockey with my two nephews and one of my nieces. No idea where the sticks and balls came from. Knowing Nikki, he'd probably brought them for exactly this moment.

He loved my siblings' kids, and they loved him. But boy, the racket they were making... When my niece scored on him, he celebrated more loudly than she did.

Following that outburst, Coach entered the room with Mathieu right behind him. "Landry," Coach barked above all the noise, and somehow the whole room fell silent.

"Coach?" I hazarded.

That rare smile broke out on his face again. "Time for you and Rivera to take your families home. Staff wants to get out of here." Amusement there.

Groans of disappointment from the kids. "Hey!" One of my two nephews ran up to Coach. "Can we skate on the rink? Pleeeeeease?"

Mathieu gave an exasperated sigh. "Brian, non. Not tonight. Maybe some other time."

Coach lifted his gaze to me, then chuckled. "God help the next coach in the league that ends up with a Landry on their team." Then he looked down at Mathieu's son. "Christmas Eve, *if* your parents let you."

"*If* you're good," Mathieu followed up, quickly.

Cheers all around from the kids. They'd be good. They

usually were. Rambunctious and full of energy, yes. They were Landrys, after all. We didn't stop moving until we were dead tired. Even then, we might keep ourselves spun up. "Right," I said. "We really should go."

Getting out of the facility took time. I left Marie, Mathieu, and their spouses to corral the kids. With Isaac and his folks in tow, I went hunting for my parents and found them in the lounge with Elias.

"Maman. Papa." *Finally*.

"We decided to wait out the chaos," Elias said, and both my parents laughed.

"The kids," my mom said, "They're so..." She mimicked something exploding all over the room.

"Just like we were, eh?" I gave them both hugs. Then I took Isaac's hand. "C'est mon chum, Isaac." I turned to Isaac. "Isaac, these are my mom and dad."

He still had color on his cheeks, but he offered his hand, and said, "Hi, it's really nice to meet you."

Maman pulled him into a big hug and Papa patted him on the shoulder.

"You make Julien happy," Maman said.

Now heat was in my cheeks. "We need to head out. They want to close up." I repeated that in French.

Elias rose from his seat. "Guess I should go, too." He shook my father's hand, and kissed my mom on both cheeks.

She grasped Elias's hands. "You come to dinner on Christmas. It's not good to be alone."

Elias's gaze flitted to Isaac, then settled on me. "You have a houseful the year—I don't know if I'll fit."

Concern, then shame zipped through me. Nikki had invited himself, as usual. With everything going on, I hadn't had a chance to invite Elias yet. I figured he'd come with Nikki, as always. That was a mistake.

"I— Please come." I blurted out. "Elias, you're my family, too."

Papa patted me on the shoulder and I saw approval in his eyes.

Elias's smile was small, but I read the sheer amount of relief in the drop of his shoulders and way he looked down.

Wow, *fuck*. This was *bad*. I turned to Isaac. "I need a minute."

He knew enough about the dynamic between me and Elias to understand. "Sure," he said. "I'm riding with my folks so they can find your house in the woods." He nodded to Elias.

Papa also sussed out that I needed a moment with Elias, so he led my mother toward the locker room and the rest of the family.

When we were alone, I leaned on one of the lounge chairs. "Oh my God, Elias. I'm so sorry."

The smile was gone, and he let me see all the hurt in his eyes. Elias had given me so much over the years, even a room in his old townhouse that hellish second year so I wouldn't be alone.

"Ah fuck. I'm a fool. I didn't get a chance, and I thought—"

"You thought because Nisha decided to go that I'd be tagging along as well." Bitterness there.

I couldn't deny it, so I just waved a hand, ending the gesture with a slap to my thigh. I was such a thoughtless, selfish friend sometimes. "I'm sorry, Elias."

"I know you are." He gripped my shoulder and gave me a shake so I'd look into those fiery blue eyes. "Nisha and I are *not* the same person, Julien. I'm not some kind of add-on to him."

"Elias," I said helplessly. "I don't think of you like that, I promise!"

He studied me for a long moment, and his grip tightened. "You and Nisha have always had the stronger connection."

I blinked at him. Oh shit. *Shit*. Elias was—*jealous* of me and Nikki? "That's not... I'm not sure that's true."

Elias snorted and let go. "Oh, I know it is."

God, I had no idea how to navigate this mess. "Please come to Christmas at my house. It wouldn't be the same without you, and the kids love seeing you." I paused and added. "I do too, you know."

His smile was the gold of dawn on frost, still bitter and biting, but with a hint of the warmth to come. "Of course." Then he nodded at the door. "We should go."

---

Getting everyone settled into the house and their rooms took time. So much time. Isaac's parents fussed that their room was too big. The kids fought, as they did every year, over who got to sleep up in the loft in the back bedroom, so we had to work out a sleeping schedule to make sure everyone got their turn up there. I was summarily banished from my own kitchen by Mathieu and his wife, Zoe, who proceeded to cook up an excellent meal for all of us.

Then again, they'd had me order a ton of food for the week. More would arrive tomorrow. "There are restaurants, you know," I said.

"There are five children full of the energy of your family," Zoe said. "You want to manage them in a restaurant?" She had a knowing grin.

She also had a good point, so I gratefully ate the meal she and my brother made.

Isaac's mom and the kids helped with cleanup. My mom, sister and her wife settled into the living room, Isaac and I stole off to my office for a quick moment alone, and both our dads vanished into the basement. The telltale clinks of pucks off I-beams filtered up through the floor.

"Really?" Isaac looked exasperated.

I pulled him into a hug. "Hey, it's bonding. That's a good thing, right?"

"My dad's a horrible shot." He leaned into me. "He's great at baseball and golf, but hockey definitely doesn't run in my family."

It ran in mine, though I was the first to make it into the big league. "Mine's a sniper. Maybe he can teach your dad a few things." I kissed his temple, and that seemed to settle him. "Your parents are fine. My family is a whirlwind."

Isaac chuckled. "They love you."

That they did, and I was grateful for that. In the darkest days of my first two years in the league, it had been my family's love that had kept me anchored here. Their love, and Nikki and Elias's friendships and care.

Elias. *Fuck*. I leaned my ass against my desk. "I should tell you what happened with Elias." I recounted the conversation, then rubbed my forehead. "I completely fucked up there and nearly alienated one of my best friends." I gestured helplessly. "I don't know what to do."

Isaac unwound one of my arms from where I'd crossed it over my chest, twined our fingers, then settled next to me against the desk. "Well, you apologized and made amends. And now you know to ask Elias specifically, rather than assuming he and Nisha are a pair."

I nodded, and with my free hand tapped on my thigh. "I don't understand why he thinks I have a stronger connection with Nikki than he does. We're all close, but he and Nikki are so much closer—" I blew out a breath. "Elias—he's *jealous* of me." Despite the one night Nikki and I spent together, we'd only ever been friends. As for that night—I was grateful for it.

That one time with Nikki taught me that I hadn't been completely broken by Travis.

Elias and I had never spoken about it, but I had no doubt he knew about that night. I'd always assumed Nikki had explained things... Shit.

Isaac's fingers twitched in my hand, and he was quiet for a long puzzling moment. "When I first got here, I wondered if you and Nisha were an item, so I can kind of see where he's coming from."

I let out an exasperated croak. "But Elias knows—and you know now—that there's nothing between us!"

Both of Isaac's eyebrows shot up. "You two are incredibly tight. He's your best friend, your family even." He waved toward the rest of the house. "Your niblings see him as an uncle. That's not *nothing*, Julien!"

He had a point. "I always felt like the third wheel. I never considered that Elias might feel that way, too." I scuffed my toe against the hardwood floor. "I guess they're not a 'thing'."

That got a snort from Isaac. "Or they are—or Elias wants them to be."

Okay, that was also a possibility. Nikki was an open book. Elias? More like one of those ancient tomes that had been locked away in a forbidden archive. Every so often, as had happened earlier, he let people see in.

Isaac squeezed my hand. "Sounds like most of the issue is between Elias and Nisha."

I nodded, brought our entwined fingers to my lips, and pressed a kiss to Isaac's knuckles. "Thank you for listening."

He rotated around so he stood between my legs, cupped the back of my neck, and kissed me.

God, yes. I slid my hands to his amazing ass and squeezed. When he came up for air, we were both panting. I leaned my forehead against his. "This house has too many people in it." I was never quiet during sex, and I wasn't about to let my parents hear me screaming in pleasure. Or the kids. My siblings, eh, they could handle it.

Isaac laughed. "I'm sure we can figure something out."

"Not tonight, though. I'm exhausted and we have a game tomorrow."

He tugged me off the desk. "Then let's go wind the house down. If we can. Should only take a couple of hours."

I snorted. Isaac already had my family figured out. Perhaps because he had *me* figured out.

---

IN RETROSPECT, winning a scrappy, snippy game against Cleveland on the twenty-third wasn't nearly as hard or as treacherous as family skating at the practice rink on Christmas Eve. But if nothing else, I'd started making amends with Elias. After the game, I'd pulled him aside to ask if he'd be at the skate.

"I have no one in town," he'd said while putting on a pair of leather driving gloves.

I cocked my head. "Lea wants to ask you some questions about being a center." She was fifteen, the eldest of the pack, and well on her way to becoming quite the young hockey star. "And you know the other kids will want to play, too."

He met my gaze finally, surprise with a tiny bit of delight peeping through. "Really?" He paused. "All right. I'll come then."

Now that we were all here, I might have made a huge mistake. Elias was in goal. Without pads. Without a helmet. Against four of the five Landry children and Nikki.

"Please don't get a concussion!" I called out. "Coach will make me bag skate at practice for the rest of the season if you do." Hell, he might do that anyway, if word got out.

As if this all wouldn't end up on someone's Instagram story.

Elias laughed. Loudly. It echoed across the rink to where the youngest of the team's kids and their parents were puttering around the ice.

Hell. I pulled out my phone, snapped a photo, typed, *This is not my fault!* across it, and posted.

Isaac was over near the penalty box with Louis, practicing jumps. He was good, too. Certainly wouldn't win any figure skating awards, especially since hockey skates weren't designed for the moves he was trying. Louis's jumps were far more polished.

Kid had taken a different on-ice path. Good for him. He, like Josephine, was twelve and had the whole world in front of him. I remembered that age, the freedom and the dreams. Somehow, they'd gotten me here. A strange wash of elation and melancholy rolled through me, and I skated backward around center ice, eying our logo. So many years. All the ups and downs.

The mistakes and triumphs.

Isaac made another jump, and landed well. Louis cheered.

Over by the makeshift game, Nikki yelled and raised his arms. Elias was on his side laughing, and Lea was celebrating a goal as if it had just won the cup.

I wrapped my arms around myself. Everything. Everything in the world had made this moment possible. I'd go through all of it again, if it meant having this family, this team, these people in my life.

And Isaac. Oh God, I was absolutely hopeless for Isaac. Marie must have noticed me staring, because she skated over, wrapped an arm around me and laid her head on my shoulder. "T'es en amour."

"Oui."

She gave me a squeeze. "Ça te fait du bien."

Maybe, hopefully. Isaac laughed at something Louis said, and his gaze snagged on mine, his smile wide and eyes sparkling.

"Oui," I said to my sister.

Truth was, I was in the best, happiest place in my life.

# Chapter 19

## Isaac

I made it until about three in the afternoon on Christmas Day before I had to slip outside and catch my breath.

Don't get me wrong—I adored Julien's family, and it was a blast having them here along with my parents, Elias, and Nisha. It was just a lot. Julien had described his family as bilingual chaos, and he hadn't been joking. The house was loud, with voices in both French and English, with kids running around, playing with their new Christmas presents while the adults socialized, shot pucks around the basement, ate, drank, and cooked.

Julien and his siblings effortlessly translated between the two languages so everyone could keep up, though translator apps helped in a pinch. God only knew what our moms had been talking about as they'd sat on the couch, passing a phone back and forth and giggling. I wasn't sure I wanted to know.

Nisha spent part of lunch explaining to my dad with a completely straight face that he'd been a classically trained opera singer before turning to hockey. According to him, he'd had a brief but storied career that would one day be chronicled in an Oscar-worthy biopic full of intrigue and drama. Unfortunately, a falling stage light had ended his career, but the head injury had left him with Acquired Savant Syndrome, which gave him exceptional talent as a hockey player.

He even pointed at a few scars on his face and the side of his neck as he'd grimly—but not graphically—explained how lucky he'd been that the broken glass hadn't killed him.

"I started playing hockey as soon as I was out of the hospital," he proudly declared. "The stitches weren't even out yet, and the league was already offering me contract."

I had to give him credit—he was good at selling bullshit. My dad, not one to be gullible, actually looked like he might be starting to reluctantly buy it right up until Elias beaned Nisha in the head with a dinner roll and said, "Do I need to find the video where you told a reporter those scars are from sledding face-first into a tree when you were seven?"

Nisha huffed indignantly and muttered something in Russian, to which Elias responded in the same language.

"What did they say?" my mom asked.

"Never mind, never mind," Julien said quickly. I had no idea what they'd said, but he was probably right that it didn't need to be repeated.

"You never know," I offered. "I could totally believe he used to be an opera singer."

My three teammates eyed me incredulously.

I shrugged. "I mean, he did have a pretty impressive falsetto that time Paxy doused him with cold water in the shower."

That earned *me* a dinner roll to the head and had everyone in stitches, including Julien who was practically wheezing as he translated for his parents.

The whole thing, from Christmas Eve through Christmas morning and into this afternoon, was warm and loving and festive, but by mid-afternoon, my ears were ringing and my head was swimming. It reminded me a little of my first concussion, when everything had suddenly been too loud and vibrant, but it had all stopped making sense. I wondered how in the world Julien was coping, given how he often slipped away from the team to collect his thoughts during post-game evenings in bars.

Then I caught sight of him helping one of his nephews—Brian, I think? I was still learning names—put together a Lego set, and he'd seemed all right. Laughing and joking with his nephew as they pawed through the piles of colorful plastic, he seemed as at ease as he ever was. Kind of ironic, since he was the one who usually got overwhelmed, but this was probably even more familiar chaos than the team. This was his family. Of course he was at ease.

I needed a minute, though.

Under the pretense of making a phone call, I slipped out the kitchen door onto the back deck. It was brisk out here, being December in Pittsburgh, and it felt good. I liked the cold. Reminded me of stepping out onto the ice. That first breath of the chill air of the arena before exertion had me sweating under my gear.

I rested my hands on the railing and gazed out at the rolling lawn and the thick forest encircling Julien's house. It was so quiet and peaceful out here. My apartment wasn't exactly in a noisy part of town, but living in the city meant a certain amount of noise. Here, it was just... quiet. I'd loved that about this place from the first night I'd spent with Julien, but today it was even more welcome. Aside from the cold breeze, it was absolutely still out here. That was what I needed—stillness.

The only thing that might've made it better was some water nearby. A crashing surf. A lazily flowing river. Something. But this would do. It pulled my focus and soothed my nerves, and I suspected Julien would probably need some of the same before too long; family or not, he was bound to hit his limit sooner or later. I'd keep an eye on him.

In the meantime, I took out my phone, scrolled to one of my FaceTime contacts, and sent the call.

"Hey, Puckster!" Darian smiled at me from the screen. "Merry Christmas!"

"Merry Christmas. How are you doing?"

"I'm good. Hiding from the family until dinnertime." They grimaced. "Needed a break, oh my God."

I laughed quietly. "Yeah. Same."

"You?" They snorted. "Bro, your family is chill as shit."

"Yeah, they are. But it's not just them this year."

"Spending Christmas with your hockey buddies?"

"Uh... Well..." I muffled a cough. "You could say that."

Interest sparked in my friend's expression. "Is that right?"

The warmth in my face had chased away the bite of the afternoon. "Uh-huh. My, um... My parents and I are staying at..." I tilted the phone slightly, showing them the house behind me.

"Oh my God, that place is massive!" They pulled their phone closer, making their eyes huge on the screen. "Is that like some millionaire AirBnB thing?"

I coughed a laugh. "No. No. It's, um... It's my boyfriend's house."

Darian's eyes were even bigger, and it wasn't the perspective that was doing it. "No shit?"

"No shit."

"So, your parents have met him *and* they're staying with him?" They whistled. "This sounds serious, dudebro. I was going to ask how things are going with him, but apparently they're going good."

"They are, yeah. They're..." I couldn't help smiling like a dork. "They're really good. I keep thinking it can't actually be that serious for him, but this"—I gestured at the house—"was his idea. So maybe it is?"

"Maybe it is, he says." They rolled their eyes. "Oh my God. Clearly this man is into you if he's putting your parents up for Christmas. Have you met his family? Oh, wait, you said you needed a break because—wow, Isaac. So when are you shacking up?"

I laughed, shaking my head. "Let's not start forwarding my mail quite yet, okay?"

"Okay, okay, fine." They cocked a brow. "Do I at least get a name? A picture? You're killing me over here."

"Uh..." Well, we'd told our team and our families. Shouldn't my best friend be in the loop too? I grinned.

Before I could speak, though, Darian smirked. "Wait, he's rich? Don't tell me you landed one of your hot teammates."

"Um." I cleared my throat. "About that..."

Their eyes went huge again. "Which one? Did—Jesus H. Christ, Isaac, don't tell me you scored *Julien Landry*."

Laughing, my blush no doubt visible from the ISS, I nodded. "Yes. Yes, I did."

"For real?" Darian stared at me for so long, I legit thought one of our phones had frozen. Then they said, "No. Stop. You're lying."

"Nope. And he is..." I couldn't help sighing happily. "Oh, man, he's pretty as hell on TV, but in person, he is so sweet, and funny, and..."

"Hot?" they supplied.

I nodded. "*God*, yes. But I mean, he's also..."

"Oh, Lord." Darian touched their chest. "You are falling for this man, Isaac."

Scoffing, I shook my head. "I think the 'I'm falling for him' ship sailed a *long* time ago."

"Aww, that's so cute!"

I couldn't even feel the cold air anymore, my face was so

hot, but I was also smiling because...yeah. I'd absolutely fallen for Julien, and I knew it. There was no question. I wasn't quite ready to tell him that, and with as skittish as he could be about things, he probably wasn't ready to hear it, but it would keep.

"I'm so happy for you, hon," Darian said.

"Thanks." I shook myself and met their gaze on the screen. "And we're still sort of keeping it on the DL, so..."

An eyebrow flicked up. "What's my silence worth to you?"

I huffed. "First-class ticket to Pittsburgh and a glass-side seat?"

Darian's eyes went wide again. "I was joking, but holy shit, yeah, I'll take you up on that."

"You better. I haven't seen you in person in ages."

"Pay up, and I'm there."

We continued chatting for another ten or fifteen minutes, and they caught me up on everything in their life, how their family was doing, and the latest gossip about that one diner in town that we'd long ago decided *had* to be a front for the mafia. Eventually, we ended the call, with me reiterating my promise to buy them a plane ticket and a glass-side seat. I'd given up trying to convince them they should sit in one of the VIP suites—they wanted to be down near the action where they could actually see the sweat and blood flying. I couldn't blame them.

As I was pocketing my phone, the kitchen door opened behind me. I figured it was Julien, finally needing an escape from the noise, but to my surprise, it was Elias.

"Oh, hey," I said. "Taking a break?"

"*Yes.*" Elias glanced back at the house and exhaled. "I always forget how..." He gestured as if he were trying to find the word. "...*busy* Julien's family gets."

I laughed. "Yeah. They're, uh... They're something else. Great people, though."

He smiled. "They are."

I watched him, and the conversation I'd had with Julien the other night played over in my head. About how he'd upset Elias over the invitations to Christmas. I didn't want to overstep, but there'd been some tension there today. Not outright hostility. Nothing anyone else had probably noticed at all. Just...friction that didn't usually exist between the two of them. A couple of musicians *slightly* out of tune.

Clearing my throat, I leaned against the railing. "It is pretty chaotic when they're around, isn't it?"

"It is." He was still smiling as he watched the festivities through the French doors. "But he loves it."

"He does." I studied Elias. "I'm amazed he can concentrate on anything when they're around."

The smile warmed a little, turning fond. "It's a wonder Julien concentrates on a lot of things. Bring the Landry tornado into town..." He nodded as he trailed off.

"Yeah." I chuckled softly. "He literally almost forgot his stick for the family skate, and we were all the way out to the parking lot before he realized he didn't have his keys."

"His keys? Shit. I hope the staff hadn't already locked up. They'd never let him hear the end of it if they had to let him back in."

"I said he forgot. I didn't say I did."

"Good." Elias turned that fond smile on me. "You really are good for him, Rivs. No wonder he's less stressed this year—he's got you keeping up on the things he forgets."

"I do what I can. He's so happy when they're here, but even the normal things slip his mind, you know? Even the things he'd never forget, like his stick or his keys."

"Yeah." Our captain laughed quietly, watching Julien and the others through the glass again. "His mind is something else when he's trying to keep up with—" The halt was abrupt, but the change in his expression was a slow erosion from fondness to an epiphany to an even deeper epiphany. Then something like regret.

I didn't ask. I was pretty sure I didn't need to. He'd put the pieces together. Julien hadn't overlooked him or taken his presence for granted. He hadn't assumed Elias and Nisha were joined at the hip. He'd been overwhelmed and overstimulated, and Elias had known for far longer than I had what that could do to Julien's mind. To his memory.

After a moment, Elias turned to me, looking vaguely sheepish. "It's getting cold out here. We should go back in and see if they need help with dinner."

"Yeah. Good idea."

I followed him back inside. It was still noisy and full of activity, but the chaos wasn't nearly as overwhelming this time. The break had definitely helped.

As soon as I'd set foot in the house, Lea called out, "Isaac! There you are!" She waved me over. "Come down to the basement! We're going to beat Mononcle Nikki and Mononcle Julien!"

"Ha!" Nisha puffed out his chest. "You can try!"

Lea turned a look on him that was so defiant, no one could ever doubt that she and Julien shared DNA. "*You* can try, old man."

Julien, who'd been pouring himself some water in the kitchen, barked a laugh. "She chirps like a pro, doesn't she, Nikki?"

Nisha muttered something, rolled his eyes, and headed for the basement.

Lea looked at me again. "Please, Mononcle Isaac?"

Oh. Wow. I'd already become an honorary uncle. Holy shit.

"Uh." I cleared my throat. "Sure. Just let me grab a drink." I swiped the glass Julien had finished filling and held it up like a trophy. "On my way!"

The indignant look he shot me had me cackling all the way down the stairs.

---

"You're never going to hear the end of that, you know." I glanced at Julien as I unbuttoned my shirt. "She's, what, fourteen? And she beat two professional hockey players?"

"Fifteen." He laughed, and despite the loss he and Nisha had taken, he was beaming with pride. "She's got a gift. It's in her genes."

I rolled my eyes. "Or it's in the hours of practice she does."

He pursed his lips, then shrugged before he pulled off his own shirt. "Maybe. But the genes help."

"Uh-huh. And Nisha's blood alcohol content probably helped too, but that kid's aim was…" I whistled. "She's *good*."

"Oui. She's going to go places with skates on, that's for sure." Julien tossed his shirt in the hamper, and when he faced me again, his expression was more serious. "I'm glad Elias joined us too."

"Yeah?" Our captain had come down, beer bottle in hand, and added his heckling to the chirping going on between both sides.

Julien nodded. "I thought he was still mad. About the…" He rolled his hand as some color bloomed in his cheeks. "But when we were all down there, it felt, I don't know…normal again?"

My heart fluttered. Oh, thank God. "I figured you guys would get back to normal before too long. He has to understand you didn't do anything malicious, you know?"

"I know. But I don't want him to believe I'd neglect him either."

I hooked a finger in Julien's belt and pulled him toward me. "He knows you better than that."

Julien hesitated, but he slowly relaxed, resting his hands on my sides as his features softened. "It was probably in my head more than anything. But I feel better after today."

"Good." I pushed myself up to kiss him. As I came back down, I said, "Today was a lot of fun, too. I'm really glad we did this."

That smile would never in a million years fail to make me warm all over. "Me too." He carded his fingers through my hair. "I could go for a shower before bed."

"Same. Mind if I join you?"

His smile was tired but sweet. "Like I'd ever say no."

"Ooh, even in the locker room? I mean, now that we're out, and—"

"Oh my God." He rolled his eyes, took my hand, and tugged me toward the bathroom. I just chuckled.

We stripped off the rest of our clothes and stepped into his enormous shower. I'd thought I'd hit the jackpot because of the shower at my place, but Julien's? Good Lord. We could probably fit the entire team in here if everyone got cozy. With the two of us, it seemed like renting out a whole ice rink because you wanted to build a snowman in the corner. Overkill much? But the water was hot and the pressure was high, and it beat on both our backs from twin heads while we —predictably—spent most of the time making out. We got clean and all, but we couldn't be in here and keep our hands off each other. No way.

"Too bad we can't do this in the locker room," Julien said between long, lazy kisses. "Imagine how relaxed we'd be on the ice?"

I laughed. "Yeah. We'd be so relaxed we'd lie down on the bench and take a nap."

He chuckled too, and then we were off and kissing again. We were both hard, both sliding wet hands all over each other's bodies—it was impossible not to be turned on when I was wrapped up in him like this.

"I love having our families here," he murmured, "but I won't lie—I can't wait until it's just us again."

"Oh yeah?" I grinned against his lips. "Why's that?"

He squeezed my ass, pulling me close as if I couldn't already feel his hard-on. "So we don't have to be quiet anymore." He brushed his lips across mine and growled, "I miss fucking."

"I miss it too." I dragged my nails down his back, drawing a gasp out of him. "I guess we'll have to be quiet."

He tensed. Then he lifted his head and met my gaze. "I'm never quiet during sex."

"No." I teased his nipple with my thumbnail. "But you could be, if properly motivated."

His eyebrows climbed. "Isaac..."

"I can't wait anymore." I swept my tongue across my lips. "I want you. Tonight. All we have to do is be quiet."

He bit his lip, and the noise of the shower almost drowned out his soft whimper.

"See?" I whispered. "You can be quiet."

"*Isaac...*"

"It'll be worth your while." I leaned in and kissed under his jaw. "You know it will be."

Julien groaned, kneading my ass with his strong hands. "I can't... You turn me on so much, I'll—*fuck*." He gasped as I bit his collarbone.

Meeting his gaze again, I grinned. "Oh, baby. You can. And you will."

The helpless sound he made was beyond sexy. In a voice that was plaintive with a hint of resignation, he said, "There's gags in the bedroom."

"Nah." I trailed my thumb along the edge of his jaw. "We won't need those."

"You want me to be quiet, don't you?"

"Mmhmm. And you will be. Because I told you to."

Julien closed his eyes and pushed out a breath. "You're evil."

"Are you saying no?" If he was, then I'd back off, but something told me he wasn't.

He looked at me, desire smoldering right alongside his frustration. "I am absolutely *not* saying no." He gestured toward the bathroom door. "I'm just saying that if anyone hears anything, *you're* explaining it at the breakfast table. Not me."

I met him with a challenging grin. "You sure that's a good idea?"

Oh, the horror on his face.

"Just stay quiet." I lifted myself up and kissed him again. "Then you won't have to worry about exactly how I explain the noise to our parents."

He grumbled something in French, then slid a hand up into my hair and kissed me deeply. I pulled him close, letting him lead for a moment before I took over and pushed him up against the wall. As soon as his shoulders hit the stone tiles, he gasped and his back arched.

"Stay quiet," I teased before claiming another kiss. He whimpered again, relaxing (sort of) against the cold wall. I drew back and looked in his eyes. "We should get out and dry off before we finish in here." I gestured around us. "Since everything echoes."

Julien bit his lip. Then he shut off the shower, and we both stepped out.

Excitement zinged through me as we dried off. The prospect of sex with Julien always had me climbing the walls with anticipation, but this was going to be different. I'd found a new way to tease him and make him obey me, and though he put on a show of aggravation, I was pretty sure he was even more turned on by it than I was. Trust Julien Landry to step up to a challenge.

Little did he know I had every intention of making it even more interesting.

He always took a few minutes longer to dry off than I did since he had long hair and he *hated* having a damp pillow. While he continued with that, I hung up my towel and headed for the door.

Hand on the doorknob, I paused. "Oh, there's one more thing."

Julien froze, alarm written all over his face behind the strings of wet hair.

I grinned. "*You're* on top tonight."

Then I left the bathroom, suppressing a chuckle at the strangled sound he made. I climbed into bed, lay back against the pillows, and slowly stroked myself as I waited for him.

I was admittedly nervous. I occasionally used toys when I jerked off, so it wasn't like I wasn't used to being penetrated, but I'd only bottomed for someone else twice. Both times, I'd been disappointed, feeling less like the guy was into me and my pleasure, and more like I was a hole for him to come in. Both guys had been more responsive when I was on top. More into what I was doing and into doing things for me. When they'd fucked me, they'd seemed to close off to everything except thrusting into my ass and getting off, as if my pleasure and orgasm were afterthoughts.

Me and Julien—we were way too into each other when we had sex. Completely focused on each other and nothing else. I'd learned early on that I could command his full attention, enough to quiet the noise in his world and in his head, and we'd both reveled in it. I didn't imagine that would change if we switched positions. Julien was way too good to be a disappointing top.

It wasn't long before the bathroom door opened, and he

emerged with his hair wetter than it usually would be and his eyes full of fire.

"You"—he pointed sharply at me as he crossed the room—"are an evil man."

"Am I, though?" I nodded toward his very erect cock. "Because you look pretty turned on to me."

Julien growled something I didn't catch, and then he was over me, hips between my thighs as we started making out all over again. I very nearly forgot we couldn't be loud; if not for Julien being unusually quiet, I probably would have forgotten myself. But he remembered, so I did too, and the room was silent except for the wet sounds of kissing, the soft slide of hands moving over skin, and the bed accommodating our shifting weight. I loved it when Julien was vocal, but this was sexy in its own right. I wasn't sure if I was just hyperaware of him vibrating with need, or if he was trembling more than usual because he was both aroused out of his mind and trying *so*, so hard to obey.

"See, baby?" I whispered. "You can be quiet."

He growled against my lips. "We're barely doing anything yet. When we—oh, fuck..." He inhaled sharply as I started stroking him between us. "Isaac..."

"Fuck me," I breathed.

He shuddered, his cock stiffening in my hand. "Please tell me you're serious."

"About bottoming for you?"

The affirmative was more of a whimper than words, but I understood.

"I wouldn't suggest it if I didn't want it." I gave him a slow, appreciative stroke. "Probably can't take it as hard as you take me."

"Mmph. No wonder you wanted to do it when we have to be quiet."

I laughed. "That crossed my mind, yes."

He groaned softly, then kissed me in a way that was anything but soft. It was deep and demanding as he rocked his hips and fucked into my hand. "Oh God…"

"Don't come yet," I said in a harsh whisper. "You're not coming until you're balls-deep in me."

He grunted and jerked, and for a second, I thought he'd come after all. But then he pushed himself up and sat back on his heels. "Turn over," he panted. "On your hands and knees. If I'm going to top you, you're going to be damn ready for me."

"Oh yeah?"

"Uh-huh."

"Lube?"

"In a minute."

Huh. Well, he had more experience than me, so I'd follow his lead. I did as I was told and turned onto my hands and knees. The mattress shifted slightly behind me, and then—

Oh. Oh, *that* was why he didn't need lube quite yet. Holy *fuck*. His tongue was just… Wow. I let my head fall forward, and I closed my eyes as I tried to remember how to breathe and also stay quiet as he worked utter magic on my ass.

My arms shook under me. The room spun around me, and that was before he started teasing my cock and balls with his fingertips, and I… Jesus fuck, how did he do that?

*Stay quiet, Isaac. Come on. Stay quiet. You can do this.*

I pressed my lips together. Had we been alone in the house, there would've been curses pouring off my tongue right now. He wasn't going to make me come—not like this—but he had me brushing up against that edge, close enough to make me think release was almost within my grasp, and—

*Not a sound. You can do this.*

"Julien," I ground out as quietly as I could. "Oh my God, Julien. Fuck me."

He ran his tongue around my hole once more, and I

almost murmured a prayer of thanks as his weight shifted. He was sitting up. "You liked that?" He sounded like he was grinning. Like he knew damn well that I did.

"No one's…" I struggled to catch my breath. "No one's ever…"

He stilled. "You've never been rimmed?"

"Uh, you know I don't have a lot of experience, right?"

"Well, yeah, but you said you've bottomed before. Didn't they…?"

I shook my head.

Julien was quiet for a moment. Then he made an annoyed sound, and I imagined he was rolling his eyes, but a second later he trailed light fingertips down my spine. "Well. It's their loss." He brushed a kiss across the back of my neck, and his words came out as a purr. "Because they missed out on licking someone so responsive."

I shivered, kneading the edge of the mattress. "I need… I need to learn to do that for you."

"Mmm, you're welcome to practice as often as you like." He kissed my neck again. "But I'm pretty sure you want to get dicked down first, eh?"

"Now that you mention it…"

He huffed a laugh, dropped another kiss just below my hairline, and then leaned away. The condom wrapper tore, giving me the same rush of *"oh boy, here we go"* I'd had the last two times I'd done this. Except…not the same. There'd been fear those times. Fear of pain. Fear of not being able to get off or get him off. Fear of embarrassment or any number of things since sex was such a huge unknown for me.

That fear was gone this time. I trusted Julien and I trusted myself. And if I'd had any doubts left that he'd top me with the same attentiveness and enthusiasm as he bottomed, those had vanished while he'd been driving me wild with his tongue.

"Hey." He slid his palm up my back. "You all right?"

"Yeah." I twisted around to glance at him. "Just...nervous, I guess?" That wasn't a lie. I wasn't afraid of Julien at all, but I *was* nervous.

"I'll go slow." He paused, then added a bratty, "Kind of have to, since we can't make noise."

I snorted. "Shut up and put your dick in me."

He laughed loud enough it probably could have been heard elsewhere in the house, then immediately clapped a hand over his mouth. I had to do the same as we both stifled more laughter.

"Goddammit," he muttered, which didn't help.

That had me giggling all over again, and he was shaking with amusement of his own. In bed. While we were having sex.

*"This isn't porn,"* Darian had told me. *"It's real life. If you can't laugh when someone's dick slides out at the wrong time or someone gets cum up their nose, then what even is the point?"*

Okay, so that wasn't precisely what we were laughing at right now, but I understood their words on a more profound level now. We could crack up in bed. One of us could say something to make the other laugh, and it made it all fun and playful instead of weird and awkward.

Because I couldn't possibly fall any harder for Julien.

The click of the lube bottle scattered my thoughts, and so did his fingers, slick and gentle, stretching me open for him. I had enough clarity to wonder if he liked doing a ton of prep or if the other guys I'd been with hadn't put in as much effort as they could have, but I didn't have enough clarity to care all that much because oh, *fuck*...

"Julien," I moaned as quietly as I could.

"Something wrong?" he taunted. "Hmm, I could just do this. Tease you all—"

"You know you'll pay for it once I can make you scream again."

His hand stopped moving.

"That's what I thought."

He huffed a melodramatically petulant sigh, and I managed a brief laugh before he withdrew his fingers and scrambled my brain all over again. The head of his cock against my ass made my thoughts go completely blank.

"Oh, fuck," he breathed as he pressed in. "Isaac..."

I couldn't speak. All I could do was tremble and sort of breathe as he eased himself in. I had no idea if he was being careful or if he was teasing me, only that he was taking his sweet time and it felt *amazing*. I couldn't help rocking my hips to complement him, and he peppered the air with whispered curses in at least two languages. Once he was moving easily, sliding in all the way on each stroke, he kept up that pace, holding my hips in his strong hands as he slowly, gently fucked me.

Slurred French whispers rolled off his tongue, and then he breathlessly murmured, "I didn't think your ass could get any sexier."

"Yeah?"

"Oui." He ran his palms up and down my back. "You have the hottest ass I've ever seen, and now you've got my dick in it." He pushed out a ragged breath. "Écœurant."

I didn't completely understand what he was saying, but I got the idea. I'd watched myself fucking his ass enough times, I knew exactly how much of a turn-on it was.

The even bigger turn-on? Watching his face while I drove him wild.

*Damn. I can't see his face right now.*

"Wait."

He stopped moving, and concern laced his voice. "What? Are you all right?"

"I'm good." I looked over my shoulder. "But I want you on your back."

"On my..." He paused, then groaned. "Isaac..."

"On. Your back."

Whatever those French words were, they were definitely curses. If they hadn't been before, they were now.

Julien obeyed, though. He pulled out, making us both gasp, and then lay on his back beside me. As I climbed on top, he bit his lip and swore.

"Guide me down," I ordered.

Without hesitation, he steadied himself and did as told, gently nudging my hips down until his cock started to slide back in. Then he let go, and he arched under me as I took him deeper. "Fuck..."

"Uh-huh." I grinned down at him. "That's the plan."

He gazed up at me with desperate, feral eyes.

I picked up a little speed, riding his cock *just* fast enough to coax the faintest, rhythmic creaks from the mattress. Goddamn, this was hot. His dick felt amazing, and the view was spectacular. His skin was ruddy, his damp hair splayed out on the pillow, the grooves between his muscles extra pronounced as he tried like hell to stay in control. Whenever I topped him, his expressions were a mix of bliss and pain. This time, there was plenty of bliss, and something like pain, but it was more like deep concentration. The intense focus of someone standing on a tightrope, resisting the pull of gravity through sheer willpower.

"That's it," I whispered. "You can stay quiet."

He squeezed his eyes shut and slid his hands up my thighs as he mumbled what I thought was my name.

"You can." I closed my hands around his wrist and pinned it above his head. "And you will."

He glanced at his arm, then looked up at me, a million emotions in his expression. No fear. Not real *I'm-in-danger-fear*, anyway. Roller-coaster fear. Suspense scene in a movie fear. The uncertainty of dangling over a precipice with the knowledge that came with safety nets and piano wires.

Or maybe that was what I was feeling.

"You good?" I asked breathlessly.

Julien swallowed. Then he nodded. "Oui. Yeah. I'm..." He closed his eyes again and shivered, pushing his cock up into me. "God, Isaac, I want you to make me scream."

"Oh, I will." I leaned down and kissed him. "But tonight, you're going to be quiet." I pinned his other arm, my hand encircling just below the *Now* tattoo. "For me."

He bit back a moan.

"Will you do that for me?" I rolled my hips, keeping up a steady rhythm on his steel-hard cock. "Will you stay quiet for me?"

"I..." His features tightened, a flush creeping down his face and neck, his eyes those of a man who was this close to not caring who heard him cry out. But he swallowed again and licked his lips. "Yes. For you."

The words and the determination behind them gave me a rush, and I leaned down to drop a kiss on his swollen lips. The muscles in his forearms twitched and tensed in my tight grips, and his hips fell into a rhythm with mine, rolling together and driving him into me just hard enough to make my head spin without giving us away to the rest of the world.

"Isaac," he pleaded. "I can't... I can't stay quiet."

"You can." I tightened my grasp on his wrists. "And you will."

"*Isaac...*" Ooh, the desperation in his voice was so delicious.

"Can you come like this?" I asked.

He pressed his lips together and shivered hard. Then he nodded. "Yes. I'm... God, Isaac, I'm going to."

Another rush. Fuck, yes. This man who usually needed

rough, near-violent sex to even enjoy it was on the edge now, ready to lose it despite us staying slow and quiet.

"Don't make a sound," I whispered. "I want you to come, Julien."

"Oh God," he moaned, arching under me as his arms strained against my hold.

"Not a sound." I rode him as fast as I dared, as fast as the bed would allow us while still remaining discreet, and I watched in an absolute daze as the man I'd fallen for started to come unraveled. His orgasms sometimes seemed to crash into him out of nowhere, but this time, it was a slow, steady build—a spark traveling a long fuse on its way to release as Julien writhed and squirmed and swore.

"Isaac..." My name came out as a ragged breath. "Fuck, Isaac..."

"Don't make a sound, Julien."

He stifled a whimper. Arched again. Tensed all over.

And right when I knew the spark was about to touch dynamite, I whispered, "Come in me."

With a gasp, Julien wrenched his arm free, clapped his hand over his mouth, and *just* muffled a cry as his hips bucked and jerked, his orgasm powerful and silent—for me and no one else. *Perfect*.

Then he sighed and collapsed back on the bed. "Oh my God."

"Told you." I bent to kiss him. "You can stay quiet with proper motivation."

He grumbled something as he wrapped his arms around me, and before I could ask him to repeat it, he kissed me. It was long, lazy, and breathless, and his whole body trembled as he held me. I couldn't believe I'd done this to him. Talk about heady as hell.

Julien loosened his embrace, and as he sank back to the pillow, he panted, "Let me finish you. Let me suck you off."

Oh, that sounded hot, but I wasn't done teasing him. "You just want something in your mouth."

He looked up with eyes full of bratty hunger. "Oui, but you won't have anything in your mouth, so *you'll* have to stay quiet."

"Game on," I growled.

He eyed me, then chuckled. "Let me get rid of the condom. Then my mouth is all yours."

# Chapter 20

## Julien

I wrapped the condom in tissues and threw it into the bathroom trash, all the while avoiding looking at myself in the mirror. I had an idea of what I looked like, but seeing myself would only make me think—and I desperately didn't want to think right now.

I was wobbly, inside and out. The sight of my cock in Isaac's ass, then the view of him riding me as he held me down—my God. Replaying that ignited everything in me all over again. My legs felt as if I'd skated a whole sixty-minute game, and my mind—there was so much rambling around in there, bumping off thoughts and emotions.

At some point, I needed to sort all that out. But not now. Now? I had a cock to suck and a lover to make scream.

Isaac was lounging in the middle of my bed, as if he owned every bit of space in the bedroom. Maybe he did. I loved him in control, adored that he pushed me, and tested my strength, both physical and mental. Making love like that—God. I hadn't realized that was possible.

"So, are you going to stand there all night and stare at me, or come suck me off?" Teasing lay in Isaac's voice.

I loved that, too. No condescension, just humor and kindness.

"You're beautiful," I said as I crossed the room. "I must be the luckiest person alive to have you in my bed." I crawled up the mattress until I loomed over Isaac, then stole a kiss from his lips that were ever so slightly parted in surprise.

"Me?" he murmured, then tucked some of my hair behind my ear. "You're the gorgeous one."

"But look at this..." I ran my hands down his chest, teasing his nipples. He arched under my touch. "And this." My fingers danced over his abs. "And these thighs." They were massive and perfect, and I settled between them. "And this dick can turn me inside out." With that, I took him in my mouth, circling my tongue around the head.

"Oh, fuck, Julien." So quiet. Almost a whisper. His hand threaded into my hair, then tightened. "That's right. Suck it. Take it all."

I wasn't sure how he managed to growl so low and quiet at the same time, but his voice slid over me like pain and pleasure, and I went down with every bit of skill I'd mastered over the years, opening my throat and repeatedly taking him deep.

He whimpered, and beneath my hands, those impressive thighs flexed. "Yeah, like that. Keep going."

My pulse, pounding in my ears, was louder than the slick and wet sounds, or the quiet groans and curses. I knew he was close when he stopped making any sound, and his body trembled beneath me, so I flicked my gaze up, and locked eyes with him.

Unfair, really. Isaac gasped, and much like I had, clapped his hand over his mouth to stifle his yell, fell back against the mattress, and came down my throat.

I drank every last drop with gusto. When I pulled off, Isaac tugged me up by my hair, kissed me hard, and yanked even harder.

I fucking melted, because I always did for him. The pain and pleasure. The roughness and the tenderness. The control I needed to lose—and gain. Isaac somehow understood me, cared about me, not just himself or his pleasure.

I wasn't a doll or a hole or a conquest—I was—me. He saw *me*.

"Thank you," I whispered against his lips. "Thank you for this. For everything." There were tears in my eyes and I didn't even know why.

Isaac brushed them away. "Anytime," he said. "Always."

Then he held me until I stopped trembling. Neither of us was asleep, but for a change, I'd relaxed into the quietness of the house, listening to Isaac's heartbeat juxtaposed with my breathing. Thoughts trickled in and out of my skull, but nothing stuck. Pure bliss, this quiet. This stillness. So hard to find for me.

Eventually, Isaac smoothed a hand down my back. "Need to get up."

I gave a little groan in protest, but rolled off him and followed him into the bathroom to clean up and brush my teeth. The Julien who stared back at me in the mirror looked tired, but utterly satisfied. Even more so when Isaac wrapped his arms around me.

"I know you'll say it's nothing, but thank you, too. For all of this. Opening your house to my parents. Sharing your family with us. This has been the best Christmas I've had in years."

"And you got your ass fucked," I murmured.

He smacked me hard on the chest, and I flinched away from the sting, laughing. He didn't let me get too far though.

"I'm trying to be romantic here!"

God, romance. I was terrible at that, even as much as I was hopelessly in love with Isaac. I drew him into a kiss. "Someday,

I'll wine and dine you. Roses. Good food. Candlelight. All that."

He chuckled. "Have to be off-season. Can you imagine trying for a night on the town now?"

Our upcoming schedule was a killer in the run up to the playoffs. The only break was a weekend in February for the All-Star game. As we headed back to bed, one of those meandering thoughts in my mess of a brain bounced forward. "Vegas," I blurted out.

He halted at the edge of the bed, confusion written into his sleepy face. "Vegas?"

"The All-Star weekend. Come with me as my plus one." I crawled in bed.

Isaac followed, sliding under the covers. He gently brushed my hair from my face, and stared into my eyes. "How's that going to work? We're not out publicly."

There was that. I gave him a shrug and a smile. "So maybe I'll invite the rookie to see the show?"

"Uh huh." Then he kissed me, and my mind went back to being pleasantly free of thoughts.

Isaac took his time exploring my mouth and nibbling at my lips. "Oh my God," he said when he came up for air. "You're purring."

I could only laugh at that. "Am I?" I didn't purr. Maybe moaned a bit? Who knows. I hadn't been paying attention to anything other than his lips on mine and our bodies pressed together.

He slapped me on the chest again—gently this time—then relaxed. "Do you think they'd let you do that? Take the rookie to the All-Star game?"

"Absolutely." I had no idea, but I'd make it happen.

"All right," he murmured. "I've always wanted to go."

"It's settled then." I rolled as much as I needed to flick the nightstand light off. "Vegas."

Then we curled into each other and fell asleep.

---

FALLING asleep had never been an issue with me. Hockey wore out my body like nothing else—except maybe Christmas with my nieces and nephews and a stellar round of sex with my boyfriend. I was gone as soon as I'd hit the pillow after turning out the light.

Now, however, I found myself suddenly awake in the middle of the night, vague unease in my chest and wisps of an unpleasant dream fading in my mind. The house was quiet, other than the gentle breathing of Isaac next to me. Blue-gray light filtered in from the doors to the deck, and the ceiling had an almost ghostly surrealness to it.

I hated when my brain did this. So hard to get back to sleep. Disquiet seeped into my bones, that nebulous feeling I'd forgotten something important, and my heart kicked up a notch.

If I'd been alone, I'd have tossed the covers off and paced the room. Maybe gone downstairs to the kitchen. But Isaac was here and our families were asleep in the house—I was safe. I wasn't alone. There was nothing to worry about right now. I *knew* this.

Breathe in. Hold. Breathe out. Repeat. And again. A few more times, and my pulse settled, but I was awake, and all the thoughts I'd pushed aside started to roam around in my head. Ghosts in a graveyard, I called them, since Travis had delighted in calling me empty-headed.

Ah, fuck. *Travis*. I didn't want to think about him, but sometimes it was hard not to, especially with Isaac. The kind of relationship we had, the friendship, the sex—especially the sex—was so different from what I'd done with Travis.

Or, rather, what Travis had done to me. I had no illusions

anymore that I'd had any control in that relationship. Back then, I'd fooled myself into thinking it had been mutual, but in retrospect, no. Not at nineteen, not as a rookie trying to break into the league. Not while being fucked by my idol. That "relationship" had been a mess. Travis hadn't done anything illegal, aside from the beer on my birthday; we'd both been adults.

*Yeah, right*, a voice in my head murmured. *Do you want to take a closer look at that?*

Non. No. Some graves in my empty head needed to be left undisturbed.

Next to me, Isaac stirred and pressed closer, and I let out a long exhale.

Isaac said I wasn't like Travis. Intellectually, I knew I wasn't. Isaac and I—we were both in control here. Yes, he was a rookie, but at twenty-two, he wasn't the kid I'd been. Only five years lay between us.

And I wasn't the one fucking his mouth. Even me topping him tonight—that had been all Isaac—not me. Physically, sure, but I'd been the submissive in that picture, getting off on obedience the same way I got off on being thrown around.

*Submissive masochist*, the books and websites said. I gave a mental shrug. Made sense, to a certain degree. After Isaac had confessed to doing research, I'd done the same, also buying the books we'd picked out, and there in the pages I found bits and pieces of myself.

I'd figured out in my last year of major juniors that I liked hard, pounding sex, especially if I was the one on the receiving end of it. Gender didn't really matter when it came to partners, nor how we had sex—but the more physical and rougher, the better.

Loved it, still. Even if Travis had taken advantage of that.
Fucker.
Isaac wasn't taking advantage of me—not at all. I knew I

could say no. He knew he could say no—he *had* said no, in fact, though I would never have pressured him for sex, especially after an injury.

We were out as dating to our families and friends—to our whole damn team. Other than Elias and Nikki—and the asshole himself—no one knew I'd even dated Travis.

Different. Everything was different. I closed my eyes. That day Isaac had ordered me to his apartment, then put me on my knees to suck him off with barely a word—that had been one of the hottest fucks anyone had ever given me.

Surpassed only by tonight—sex that hadn't been rough or fast. Isaac had ridden my dick and kept me quiet only with an order and my desire to obey him. I'd come harder than I had in a long time. I shivered and instinctively turned toward Isaac. Someday, he'd make good on his threat to fuck me nice and slowly—to make love to me. No doubt I'd be a crying mess by the end.

Hell, tonight I'd been in tears, and Isaac had done nothing more than brush those aside as if it were a perfectly normal thing to well up after really intense sex, as if it were okay for me to have *feelings*. What a concept.

Wow, *fuck*. I blinked into the dim light. I needed to put that asshole Travis and his bullshit behind me. Move on with my life—maybe a life with Isaac.

*That* was a thought, one that sent a buzz rippling through my body, and cleared out the ghosts of my thoughts like a sunrise over a cemetery. My head wasn't actually empty, I knew this. And right now? My life was so full I could only be grateful and thankful Isaac had stepped out into the cold so many nights ago.

Maybe, maybe we gave each other things we both needed. I was utterly in love with Isaac, and I was starting to think he might be in love with me too.

I clung to that thought, closed my eyes, and listened to Isaac's slow, deep breaths until I stumbled back into sleep.

---

THE NEXT TIME I WOKE, it was to morning light and shrieks of laughter in the hallway, then the pounding of feet on the stairs. Joy settled into my heart.

Next to me, Isaac grunted. "Kids are up."

"We should get up, too. Practice today."

That got me a longer groan. "Ugh, fuck, I forgot." He rolled toward me and winced.

I couldn't help smiling. "Sore ass?"

He snorted. "Not as sore as yours will be next time."

Couldn't help the laugh either. "Something to look forward to, then." I leaned in and stole a lingering kiss, then brushed a thumb over his cheek. "Was last night fine, though?"

He took my hand and kissed my knuckles. "Of course it was. You were perfect."

"I..." God, my head was a mess again. "This—what we're doing. Our families. The team and Coach. I don't want to pressure you into—"

His fingers landed on my lips. "Julien." There was a sharpness there, but from worry. "Where's this coming from?"

*My past.* I swallowed that answer, though. "My brain." That was true, too. "I don't want to screw this up."

This time, he was the one who stole a kiss. "I promise I'll tell you if something's wrong, if you promise to do the same."

Seemed like an even trade. He still held my hand, and placed it against his heart. I couldn't see the ink on the inside of my wrist, but I knew the single English word written there, in thin flowing script, almost hidden in the rest of my sleeve.

*Now.*

*Now. Now. Now.* A constant reminder to live in the present, not the past. "I promise."

Just then, loud banging on my door echoed through the room. "Mononcle Julien! Mononcle Isaac! Get up! Mom's making pancakes!" Brian's voice cut through the silence. Then he pounded on the door again.

I rolled to my back, then shouted, "Câline de bine, we're up!"

"They're up!" Brian shouted. Then his footsteps thudded down the hall and the stairs.

The bed vibrated slightly from Isaac stuck in a fit of laughter. "You really are all cut from the same cloth."

I grabbed my pillow and thumped him on the chest. "Do you want pancakes or not?"

Still laughing, he tossed the pillow back, then crawled out of bed. "Of course."

A few minutes later, we were both dressed in sweats and T-shirts and in the kitchen. Zoe had made pancakes, and the rest of our combined families had also made a pile of eggs, some bacon, and a huge fruit salad.

I stole a grape out of the bowl. "I didn't know I had strawberries."

"Oh, I went out this morning," Isaac's mom said. "That nice tall blond friend of yours recommended a place in the little village nearby."

"His name's Elias, Mom. He's the team captain."

Isaac would never not look cute when absolutely embarrassed by his parents. I wrapped my arm around his waist. "Elias's also a food snob. That market is *good*." I paused. "Thank you, Crystal."

She waved my thanks away, and I found where Isaac got his blush from.

Somehow we managed to eat with the chaos that is my family, get ourselves put together, and make it to the rink in time for practice. Mind you, they'd pushed back the start time to 1PM, but it was still a close call.

Practice went remarkably well, considering it was the day after Christmas. Our families—well, mostly my family—caused a whirlwind of activity in the stands and noise like a hockey game, even though we were only working on line rushes and board battles.

This time, we met our families back at the house—after the on ice portion, Coach had us reviewing video. The game tomorrow wouldn't be easy—they never were after the holidays—but we were facing LA. We didn't see them that often, and the western conference style was just different enough to throw off our expectations.

We were in contention for a playoff spot—the top five teams in our division leaping over each other every week. We were in the mix, and every damn point counted. Had all year so far. This was no different.

After the video session, while Isaac chatted with Ozzy about a play, I managed to catch our Media VP. "Hey, Kelly, who do I talk to about taking someone with me to the All-Star weekend?"

She gave me a sly smile. "Like a certain rookie, so he can see what it's like?"

"Uh." My face heated.

"Come on, Julien, you should know by now that I know everything that goes on with this team. I kind of have to."

"We're not out to the public," I stammered. "I mean, dating-wise. I think everyone knows I'm out." Oh God, why was I rambling? "But yes, I want to take Isaac."

"Already done. Turns out, they're doing a little media meet-and-greet for rising stars, so having Rivera go with you is perfect." She paused. "I know you value your privacy, but Julien, people *will* notice soon. You're going to need a strategy for coming out, or for when you two are outed."

I didn't even want to think about that. "We'll figure something out."

She nodded. "Let me know if you need help."

She was the pro, after all. "Thanks, Kels."

So much to consider. The looming future. The lurking past. Shit. By the time we got back to the house, I'd hit that wall where everything was getting to be too much. I loved my family, but I ached for quiet. A moment of stillness. I parked in my garage and sat, my fingers gripping the wheel. That wouldn't be happening anytime soon.

Isaac slid his hand onto my thigh. "Hey, what do you need?"

"A glass of water, my back porch, and ten minutes alone." I gave him a weak smile. "Won't happen."

"Yes it will," he said. "Come on."

I'm not sure how Isaac managed it, but somehow I walked through the whirlwind of my family, got my water, and stepped out into the cold evening. My hair was still damp from my shower at the rink, so I pulled up the hood on my sweatshirt and leaned against the railing.

Nothing but trees, the waxing moon, and patches of snow on the ground. The temperature was low enough that I could see my breath, and the woods beyond my house were blessedly silent.

I closed my eyes and tried to let my head settle, tried to ignore the ghosts of thoughts.

*You're not good enough for him. You're not good enough for anyone.*

*Fuck off*, I thought. I absolutely was.

*Are you sure? You take and take from others.*

I grimaced into the night, then let my gaze drift up to where the stars hung above the tree line. Inside my house was proof that the voice inside my head was lying. And yet—

I still listened.

Fuck. I sighed, set down my glass, and pushed back against the rail, stretching my arms out, then hung my head between them. *You're a mess, Landry.* Travis's voice in my head again. Why now? I didn't understand.

Right then, the patio door opened. I straightened, and kept staring out at the trees.

"Julien." Mathieu settled next to me, leaning on the railing and taking in the expanse of woods beyond the grass.

"Matty." My voice sounded tiny, and young.

We looked a little alike, my brother and me, but his face was longer, less delicate. He also had the same kind smile as our father. "Je l'aime."

I chuckled. "Moi aussi." More than liked. I was head over heels in love with Isaac.

He turned and studied me.

"What?"

"Nothing." He was grinning, though. "Just thinking that even Elias and Nikki were overwhelmed the first time they met all of us, and your Isaac isn't." The grin fell into something more serious. "He takes care of you. Like Zoe and Audry."

My siblings' spouses. I toyed with my glass. "He does." In ways I would never discuss with them. Which was fine. There were things I didn't want to know about my siblings, either. I gnawed my lip. "What if I fuck up, Matty?"

He pulled me into a hug. "You won't. You're smart and you're a Landry."

Yeah, I was a Landry—Julien Landry. That was the problem.

Mathieu stepped back and gave my shoulder a squeeze. "Don't overthink things. He loves you just as much as you love him."

Then he headed back into the house, leaving me alone with my water, the night, and a head full of ghosts.

"God, I hope so," I said to the breeze.

The ghosts, like the woods, were blessedly silent as well.

I took another few minutes to soak in the quiet, then turned my wrist to see the faint trace of my ink in the moonlight before plunging back into my life.

Now, not then. Isaac was now. My family was now. Joy was here.

Tomorrow would bring another game. Those were the things that mattered.

# Chapter 21

## Isaac

I made good on my promise to Darian, and a couple of days into the new year, I flew them into Pittsburgh. Yes, first class, and yes, with a glass-side ticket for the game.

"Team colors?" I said with a grin as I hugged them on the curb outside baggage claim. "That's awesome."

They drew back and playfully twirled their hair, which was its usual dyed-black but with gold highlights this time. "I wanted to be festive!"

I chuckled. "You'll need a jersey to match."

"Pfft." They hoisted their backpack onto their shoulder. "You say that like I didn't buy a Rivera jersey the instant they went on sale."

My jaw fell open. "Are you serious? Dude, those are like three hundred—I could've bought you one!"

"It was worth it. Now let's get going. I'm tired of airports."

"Eh, I don't blame you. Come on." I took the handle on their rolling suitcase and we loaded everything into the back of my car.

"Fancy ride," they commented, giving the car an appreciative look. "This job definitely agrees with you."

I couldn't help grinning as we both slid into the seats. "It's, um... It's been pretty great, that's for sure."

"It's been pretty great." They rolled their eyes. "Says the man driving a Porsche Cayenne."

I chuckled and pulled away from the curb.

"So." They shifted in the passenger seat. "Your man really doesn't mind putting me up?"

"Nah. He insisted. Which... I mean, at least you'll have a bedroom at his place." Some of that familiar heat rose in my cheeks. "I bought a pretty small apartment, but he's got a bunch of extra rooms, so..."

"And you don't think he offered as an excuse to have you there while I'm in town?" Their voice was playful and knowing. I couldn't argue with them, either.

"Oh, I'm pretty sure he did. But he also isn't about to let one of my out-of-town guests sleep on a couch or cough up for a hotel when he's got room, so we all win, you know?"

"Mmhmm, it sounds like it." Darian paused. "He really sounds like a sweetheart. I mean, yeah, yeah, we all know he's gorgeous and amazing at hockey, but ever since you two started dating... Hon, I've never seen you this happy."

I smiled as I watched the road. "I've never *been* this happy. I keep thinking something's going to happen or he's going to suddenly decide he isn't into me, but..." I shook my head. "It's just been so good."

"My God. Isaac, you're legit glowing." They sounded awestruck. "I'm serious—I can't wait to meet the man who's made you..." They waved a hand at me. "Like this."

"You won't have to wait long." I glanced at them. "I mean, it'll probably be after the game tonight. He had something else going on today—a charity thing, I think—so he took off after practice this morning."

"Well, I'll have to meet him sometime. Since I'm, you know, crashing at his house." They paused again, and I felt the pointed look they were aiming at me. "I'm not going to have to listen to the two of you, am I? Like, after lights out?"

A laugh burst out of me, and I shook my head. "No, no." Beat. "The drugstore sells earplugs, so—"

Darian howled. "Oh my God. Dude, I swear on all that's good and unholy, if I can hear you guys playing Hide the Salami, I *will* join in with a full running commentary."

I glanced at them. "You wouldn't."

"Try me."

We exchanged another glance. Then we both laughed, and I kept driving.

But I did make a mental note to keep Julien as quiet as possible while Darian was in the house.

---

IT TOOK mere seconds to find Darian in the crowd during warm-ups. Partly because I'd bought the ticket and knew exactly what seat they were in, and partly because, in addition to their black-and-gold hair, they'd brought a sign. A *big* sign. One that read, in giant *glittery* letters surrounded by glittery red hearts, *OMG RIVERA I'M YOUR BIGGEST FAN!*

I rolled my eyes as I skated toward them, and I tapped my stick on the glass as I shook my head. Everyone around them laughed and snapped photos, and Darian grinned. With another eye-roll, I skated away to continue warming up with the team. I'd expected as much from my best friend. We'd both trolled each other incessantly ever since we'd become best friends in second grade, and I wouldn't have expected any less tonight. I mean, I was the one who'd tiptoed into the background of their sophomore homecoming dance photos in a Scream mask after slipping the photographer twenty bucks not to say anything. I was pretty sure Darian's mom *still* hadn't forgiven me for that.

At one point, as I was firing pucks at the net, Julien was casually gathering the pucks that had gone behind it. I glanced over, and I found Darian standing behind Julien, gesturing wildly at him and fanning themselves.

"Oh, dear God," I muttered to myself, but I couldn't help laughing.

And it was just my luck that Julien picked that moment to look up at me. He furrowed his brow, evidently puzzled, and oh, fuck me, he turned around.

Darian—along with some of the other fans around them who'd joined in—waved frantically at him.

Julien stared, and I had about two seconds to be mortified before he shook his head and laughed. Then he scooped a puck onto his stick and sent it up the glass. As they often did, it caught on the net, but after a few tries, it went up and over, landing right in my best friend's outstretched hand. They glanced around, probably to see if there were any kids in the vicinity, but there weren't, so they triumphantly waved the puck at me.

I chuckled, then went about finding another puck to shoot at the goal.

When someone skated up beside me, I sensed without even looking that it was Julien. "If we ever let them meet my family..."

"Oh God." I met his gaze, and the mixture of amusement and incredulity in his cracked me up. "I, uh, did tell you before you agreed to let them stay at the house that they're..."

"Energetic?"

"Just a bit."

"Uh-huh." But he was smiling. Then his brow furrowed. "That sign—please tell me they didn't use glitter in the house?"

"What?" I looked innocently up at him. "What's wrong with glitter?"

The horror on his face...

"I'm kidding." I tapped my stick against his skate. "They brought it with them. I didn't even see it until now."

Julien made a face, but he couldn't quite hide the smile. As we continued warming up, I skated past Darian one more time to wag a finger at them, which made them grin even bigger. At least I knew they had the good graces not to try to distract me during a game. Warm-ups were one thing. Once the timer started for real, everyone was all business.

And tonight, apparently business was going to be fast and fierce. We were playing Boston, and I don't know who lit a fire under their asses after the sluggish game we'd had on their ice a few weeks ago, but holy shit. Nobody scored during the first period. There weren't even that many shots on either goal— no one was letting anyone get near a crease long enough for any meaningful attempts.

It was Benson and Ortiz who finally broke the standoff eight long minutes into the second period. One of Boston's forwards got sloppy on a pass, and Ortiz snatched the puck and *flew* up the ice. Boston's defensemen closed in around him, but Benson found some open ice, Ortiz sent him the puck, and there was *finally* a goal on the board. Benson's first of the season, too.

After a grind like that, a team could either get demoralized and fall apart, or they could get pissed off and determined to even up the score. Boston was pissed off. The game turned a lot more physical. Lots of checks. A few scuffles that didn't quite turn into fights, but had the crowd frothing at their collective mouth the way they did on nights when everyone knew a fight was coming. When you could just *feel* it in the air that, at some moment, *somebody* was throwing gloves.

That moment came with eight minutes left in the third period, and the gloves that came off were mine.

I'd taken a couple of checks that had my temper flaring. One defenseman had gone to the box for tripping me. My fuse was already getting short.

And then one of their forwards had gone in trying to score, and he'd sent Larry sprawling. Larry, who'd already been out with a concussion once this season.

Motherfuckers could check me and trip me all they wanted, but you don't mess with the netminder. You just don't.

Everything around me disappeared except for that smug, mustached jackhole, and we went at it, fists flying in between yanking at each other's jerseys. Someone grabbed my shoulder. I didn't know if it was a ref or another player, and I was too pissed off to care.

We slammed into the boards. I was distantly aware of people pounding on the glass and shouting, but mostly I was focused on decking that son of a bitch and trying to stay upright while he was trying to drag me down.

My helmet was suddenly gone. Then his elbow smacked my cheekbone, stunning me for a second, and the ice shifted under us. As we tumbled, I regained my senses, and I managed to land on top of him. I got in one more blow before strong arms hauled me off him and onto my skates. The ref had me in a bear hug, and I kept right on shouting past him, not really knowing or caring what I was saying anymore.

It felt like minutes, but it was really all of about twenty, maybe thirty seconds before we were pried apart. As the ref guided me toward the penalty box, I was still pissed, but I made myself calm down. I had to. I'd already quite possibly given Boston a power play; I needed to have my head in the game when my two minutes was up.

As it turned out, they didn't get a power play. We both

went to the box for five, and though I was definitely still fired up, I was too busy dabbing blood off my nose and lip to pay attention to him talking shit through the divider.

*Whatever, dude. Just keep your hands off our fucking goalie.*

I was still bleeding after they let me out of the box, so I went into the locker room to get checked out. The trainer and the doc confirmed that aside from a few tender spots and the nosebleed (which had stopped), I was fine, and by that point, the game had ended with a win for us.

Larry fist-bumped me and told me the other guy deserved it. Nisha slapped my shoulder and said I should've busted the guy's jaw, which earned him a side-eye and a sigh from Elias. And Julien…

He didn't say a word, but I knew him. Once the initial concern had passed—once he was sure I was uninjured—there was pride in his eyes. Amusement. And oh, good God, something we did *not* need to discuss in the locker room.

*What was that about making sure my friend doesn't hear us tonight? Fuuuck.*

---

"I CAN'T BELIEVE I got to see you fight!" Darian exclaimed as I led them down one of the back hallways after the game. "And right where I was sitting, too!"

"Was it? Oh, yeah, I guess it was right by you, wasn't it?" I laughed. "Well, good." With a slap to their back, I added, "You got my money's worth on that ticket."

"Damn right I did." They eyed me. "How bad did he fuck you up, anyway?"

I scoffed. "Pfft. I fucked *him* up, thank you very much."

"Uh-huh. So what was that all over your face?" They gestured at their nose. "Transmission fluid?"

"Something like that." We reached the end of the hall, and

I took them into the room where my teammates were eating. We didn't usually bring people back here, but I'd cleared it with my coach and teammates, and there wouldn't be anyone changing in this room.

"Holy shit." Darian stared at the row of chafing dishes as I handed them a plate. "Is this—do they feed you like this after every game?"

"And practice. And before games." I nudged them forward. "Help yourself—they make a ton."

"Fuck, dude." They picked up some tongs and reached for one of the remaining lobster tails. "I'm in the wrong line of work."

Once we'd filled our plates, I led him across the room, heart pounding with excitement and nerves and God knew what else as we approached a table with two seats remaining.

I took a breath and put my plate down. "So, um." I cleared my throat. "This is my friend Darian." I introduced Nisha, Elias, and, of course, Julien. Darian shook hands with everyone before taking a seat across from me, beside Nisha. They looked from one face to the next, and their usual snark and sass was MIA. Probably because they were completely starstruck.

"So you've known this guy many years?" Nisha asked. "You must have stories."

"Uh..." Darian stammered, but then recovered, and their grin almost drew a groan out of me. "A few, yeah!"

"Darian," I warned.

"What?" They spread their palms before picking up their utensils to eat. "I'm sure they have stories too, right?"

My teammates laughed. Especially my boyfriend. I glared at him, and he responded with exactly the kind of innocence I'd expect from Darian.

"Oh, God." I closed my eyes and exhaled. "Why did I introduce the two of you?"

More laughter from all four of them. Fuck my life. And yes, everyone had stories. Darian told the one about the homecoming photos. Elias didn't believe them, but Darian had the pictures on Facebook and showed everyone.

The captain shook his head as he handed back the phone. "I can't believe the photographer let you do that."

"Hey." I shrugged. "Twenty bucks is twenty bucks."

In unison, Darian and Julien muttered, "That's what she said."

Nisha smacked his hand on the table and laughed. Elias chuckled too. I wanted to groan, but what could I say? I had a type when it came to friends.

The five of us continued talking trash and sharing hilarious stories, and not just about me or Darian. Julien told Darian about how Nisha had almost convinced my father of his opera singer roots, which gobsmacked Darian since they knew how difficult it was to persuade my dad of anything.

"Holy crap." They shook their head. "All the bullshit we tried to sell your dad when we were kids, and he buys *that*."

"To be fair," Elias said, sounding amused but also startlingly fond, "no one spins a tale like Nisha."

Nisha laughed. "Like when I convinced your mother that you'd be allowed to play for both the US and Sweden at the Olympics?"

Elias's fondness and amusement vanished—mostly—in favor of annoyance. He muttered something in Russian, and Nisha responded in kind, grinning like an idiot.

"What'd they say?" Darian asked.

"Never mind," Julien and I both said before Nisha could translate.

The banter continued like that all through dinner, with Darian sliding effortlessly in with the teammates who'd become my friends and boyfriend. It had only been a few months since Nikolai Sidorov, Elias Karlsson, and Julien

Landry had been living legends. Men who I barely considered myself worthy of sharing the same ice. Now they were Nisha, Elias, and Julien, and we were sharing a meal with my childhood best friend, everyone on level ground and like we'd all known each other longer than those three had.

I wondered if any of this would ever feel normal.

Then I realized...it did. It had for a long time.

This was my life now. These were my people.

In ways I'd never imagined before...

I'd made it.

---

IT WAS late as hell by the time Darian, Julien, and I made it back to Julien's place, and even later when we all called it a night. Dinner had gone on for ages, and the three of us had ended up talking in the kitchen until God knew how late. Clearly I'd had no reason to be worried about Darian and Julien getting along—I could barely get a word in edgewise with those two.

"So wait," Darian said at one point as they leaned against the kitchen island. "If you make the All-Stars, you get sent to Vegas to play hockey and, like, do Vegas?"

"There isn't much *time* to do Vegas." Julien shrugged. "But yes."

"Still. Even if you just get to grab dinner at one of the swanky-ass places..." They lifted their water glass in a mock toast. "When is that, anyway?"

"First week of February."

Darian's eyebrows jumped and they grinned me. "Ooh, you get to spend your birthday in Vegas? Nice, bro."

Julien turned to me. "That's your—oh, it is, isn't it?"

I nodded. "Yeah. The fourth."

His soft little smile made my knees weak. "The skills

competition is that night, but we'll do something earlier in the day."

"Eh." I shrugged. "You should be focusing on—"

"We'll do something earlier in the day." He wrapped an arm around my shoulders and pressed a kiss to my temple. "Don't argue with me."

I elbowed him. "Brat."

He laughed and bumped me with his hip.

"Oh my God." Darian was grinning like a dork. "You two are adorable."

I blushed, of course. Julien just laughed and kissed my temple again.

The three of us kept chatting for a while, but we all started winding down fast, so we finally said goodnight. By the time Julien closed the bedroom door, it was a wonder no one had passed out from sheer exhaustion. Especially him, given how social interaction could wear him down.

But after he'd closed that door, he turned to me. And oh, hell, there was something in his eyes that said sleep wasn't in the cards for *either* of us any time soon.

"Your friend is great," he said, "but I have been *dying* to get you alone since the third period."

"Have you?"

"Uh-huh." Hooking a finger in his already loosened tie, he crossed the room, smoldering eyes fixed right on me. "How's your face?"

"My..." I hesitated. He'd caught me so off guard, I'd actually forgotten about the dull throb in my cheekbone. "It's... I'm a little sore." I swallowed. "But I'm good."

"Are you?" He slowly drew down the knot of his tie until it slipped apart. "Because you took a few solid hits out there." There was concern in his expression—he really was making sure I was all right—but something else gleamed *much* hotter.

"Nah." I shrugged. "He got in a few, but he was more interested in trying to get my jersey off."

Julien breathed an almost soundless laugh and stepped closer, his presence pushing me right back against the bedroom wall. "I can't blame him." He looked me up and down. "I wanted to get your jersey off right then too."

Oh. Fuck. So I hadn't imagined that look in the locker room.

"Yeah?" I swept my tongue across my lips, catching a vaguely tender spot. "What about now?"

There it was—that feral hunger that he admirably kept in check when we were around other people.

We weren't around other people now.

Julien stepped closer and pressed me into the wall, our noses inches apart. "What can I say?" His voice was a low, husky growl. "Watching you fight is hot as hell." He grinned. "You're sexy when you're angry."

I wanted to scoff and say he was crazy, but hadn't I ogled angry Julien Landry for years? I couldn't imagine I was anywhere near the ballpark of how hot he was when he was pissed, but with the way he was looking at me right then...oh, fuck. Maybe in his eyes, I was.

"I could pass out in bed right now," he said in that growl. "But I watched the replay too many times. *Way* too turned on to sleep."

He watched... Holy fuck.

"Yeah?" I slid my hands up his chest. "What do—"

"Fuck me," he demanded. "Right now."

"Right—"

"Against the wall." His lips grazed mine. "On the floor. I don't care. Just..." He ducked his head and kissed my throat, both of us groaning as his teeth grazed my skin. I wanted that hunger on my mouth, but he must have known as well as I did that kissing wasn't in the cards right now. Damn it. I loved his kiss. What he was doing to my neck, though...oh God. Soft lips. Rough stubble. Hot breath. *Fuck*. Maybe we couldn't kiss like we usually could tonight, but that didn't mean we couldn't do anything.

And fatigue be damned, I suddenly wanted to do *everything*.

"Get me a condom," I ordered. "And the lube."

Surprise and hunger both flashed in his eyes, and then he did as he was told, leaving me panting and trembling against the wall. Oh yeah, I could do this. Especially if I fucked him from behind so we *couldn't* kiss. As much as I loved making out with him while we screwed, it wasn't happening tonight, and I could make this work. Definitely.

As Julien pulled a condom and lube from the nightstand, Darian's voice suddenly echoed in my mind:

*"Dude, I swear on all that's good and unholy,"* they'd said, *"if I can hear you guys playing Hide the Salami, I will join in with a full running commentary."*

Right. Darian was here. And though they were a few doors down the hall, and they'd probably passed out after a long day of traveling, I knew they'd make good on that promise if they heard us.

Julien returned with the supplies and offered them to me.

As I took them, I said, "We're going to have to be quiet again."

"I figured." He bit his lip. "I'll try."

"Try?" I quirked a brow. "Oh, I think you'll be quiet." I reached up and grabbed a handful of his hair. "Because when I tell you to be quiet..."

He closed his eyes and sucked in a breath, shuddering in my grasp.

"Can you be quiet?" I asked.

"Oui. Yes." He looked at me again. "*Please*, Isaac."

I was so tempted to shove him up against this wall and

fuck him into oblivion, but the lust and need in his eyes—I wasn't about to miss that. Not a second of it.

So instead, I manhandled him around, guided him into the bathroom, and bent him over the counter roughly enough to drive a grunt out of him. "Get those pants off."

He didn't need to be told twice. Resting on one forearm, he undid his pants with the other while I fumbled with my own. By the time I'd rolled on the condom, we were the very picture of heat-of-the-moment hunger. Rumpled, half-buttoned shirts. Pants around our ankles. Ties hanging around our shoulders.

"Isaac." He fidgeted, rocking back against me like he was searching for my cock. "Please."

I pressed a couple of lubed fingers against his ass, and he closed his eyes and let his forehead rest on his arm as groaned French rolled off his tongue.

Then, "Fuck me. Now. Please."

I teased him with the slow strokes that I knew drove him out of his mind. Keeping my voice to a low purr that wouldn't carry to the guest room, I said, "You're really this turned on from watching me fight?"

Breathing hard, Julien met my gaze in the mirror through the strands of mussed hair that had fallen over his face, and oh, wow, yes, he really was that turned on from watching me fight. "What do you think?"

I was out of witty comments, so I slipped my fingers free. "Don't move."

That was a tall order when it came to Julien. Moving was as constant as breathing for him. But he knew what I meant. Fidget, rock, clench and unclench his hands, swear—but don't *move*.

I put some more lube on my cock. Our height difference made this angle a challenge, but when I nudged his knees apart, that brought him down enough to even us out. I guided myself in, and Jesus Christ, I was never going to get tired of the way he responded when I slid into him. Sometimes a cry of pleasure. Sometimes a low groan. Sometimes just a shudder. Always responsive, though, and it was addictive.

"Hard," he pleaded, kneading at the marble counter as if he might find some purchase. "Isaac..."

"Gotta stay quiet," I said through my teeth. "If I fuck you hard, we'll both—"

"Please." He met my eyes in the mirror again, his expression gone completely feral with hunger, and I was genuinely surprised I didn't come from that alone. "Hard. Need it... God, Isaac..."

"You going to be quiet?"

Through strands of unruly hair, his reflection met me with a challenging look. "Think you can make me?"

Fuck, it was like he knew exactly where all my buttons were.

I grabbed his hair and hauled him upright, and by some miracle, he muffled the startled cry. Then I let go and clapped my hand over his mouth instead, and we both groaned as he tightened around my dick.

"Not a sound," I growled, and thrust into him, keeping my other hand on his hip to steady us both. He whimpered against my hand, and his breath came in hot, harsh rushes through his nose, but he was quiet enough. No one would hear him. No one but me. Because this was all for me—his need, his surrender.

I buried my face in his hair, trying like hell to keep myself silent. I didn't even care that I was brushing up against the tender spots on my mouth and cheekbone. The pain barely registered over the need for friction and to drive more near-silent groans from my trembling boyfriend. On the ice, I'd fought like a man possessed, barely aware of anything but fury. Right now, everything was crystal clear—every stroke I took inside him, every tickle of his hair against my nose, the heat of his skin, the sting in my lip. It was all high-def and overwhelming and—

And then I opened my eyes again.

Oh. *Fuck.*

Julien was the very picture of arousal and abandon. Skin flushed. Eyes squeezed shut. Hair as disheveled as his clothes. Cock fully hard. My hand still firmly over his mouth.

*All for me. Oh God, this is all for me.*

"Look at us, Julien," I whispered in his ear. "Open your eyes and look at us."

His eyelids fluttered. Then his gaze seemed to sharpen, and we locked eyes in the mirror. I kissed the side of his neck, and he shivered hard enough he had to brace one hand on the counter.

"You are so fucking sexy." I snaked my hand from his hip to the front of his partly unbuttoned shirt. "Goddamn, Julien..."

He moaned against my other hand as he rocked his hips with mine.

I grabbed a handful of his shirt just for something to hold on to, and I thrust into him for all I was worth. The counter creaked, but at this point, I didn't give a damn. If Darian made good on their promise to heckle us—fine. I needed to be as deep as Julien could take me. Needed to fuck him as hard as he could handle. Needed to watch us both come unraveled.

Julien was getting there fast, too. I could feel it.

"Get yourself off," I ordered.

His whole body jerked as if my words alone had done the job. Then, one hand still braced on the counter for support, he started stroking himself, and I swore he almost melted right there in my arms. My hand muffled a helpless whimper as his shudder almost knocked us both off our feet, and when he squeezed his eyes shut, hot tears slid down to my thumb and forefinger.

"Oh yeah," I purred shakily in his ear. "That's it. Show me how much you like it."

His lips moved against my palm, but the words didn't make it past my hand. I got the message, though. It was impossible to miss in the way his knees were threatening to buckle and his ass was clenched hard around my cock. I buried my face against his neck again to stifle a groan, and then sank my teeth into his shoulder.

Instantly, Julien's entire body jerked, and he dragged me right over that precipice with him. Without thinking, I let go of his mouth and grabbed his hip for support, and a string of mumbled French half-sobs tumbled off his lips as we both slumped over the counter. He held himself up on shaking arms. I pressed my forehead against the back of his neck. For the longest time, we stood there, breathing together while the counter kept us from collapsing to the floor.

Then the long evening started to close in. The game. The fight. The socializing. The sex. I was...holy fuck, I was exhausted.

Which meant Julien must have been absolutely dead on his feet.

Still holding on to him, I carefully pulled out. "You good?"

Murmuring what sounded like an affirmative, he turned around and leaned unsteadily against the counter, eyes still wet and hair tumbling over his face. "Fuck, Isaac..."

I grinned, wrapping my arms around him. "So, what you're saying is... Next time I get into a fight, I need to get you alone as soon as possible?"

He huffed a tired laugh as he rested a hand on my waist. "Oui."

"But maybe not where we'll get caught, right?"

The next laugh was still heavy with fatigue, but there was a spark of mischief in his eyes. "I don't know. Could be fun."

I rolled my eyes and kissed his forehead. "Come on. Let's get a shower and get some sleep. I'm about to collapse."

"Me too." He gently cupped my face, avoiding the sore places, and...oh, that smile was everything. Playful. Sweet. Horny. Tired. "Worth it, though."

Yeah. It definitely was.

# Chapter 22

## Julien

The flight to Montréal didn't take long, and we'd be landing mid-morning, so I didn't bother with my usual gin and tonic, especially since I'd be seeing my family that afternoon. I gritted my teeth and pushed back on my anxiety during takeoff. Isaac casually uncurled my fingers from the death grip I had on the armrest and laced his between mine.

God, the warmth in his eyes. The seriousness. No recrimination for my obvious fear, just determination to be here for me while I literally rode it out. It helped, having that physical connection, the reminder that I wasn't alone, that no one thought me weak.

Travis had delighted in my fear. Hell, he probably still did. At least now I didn't have to sit next to him during bad turbulence and listen when he leaned over to tell me exactly how I was going to die when the plane crashed.

That year and that man could go fuck themselves. I forced myself to take a few deep breaths and gave Isaac's hand a squeeze. Nikki tapped my shoe with his and nodded. Elias raised a questioning brow.

"I'm fine," I murmured to them all. "I think."

Elias chuckled at that.

The *fuck-this-shit* feeling lightened when we leveled out, but it never went away. I think that's why Elias and Nikki started playing cards with me that second year—to keep me distracted and engaged while the metal tube we were stuck in made its way through the air.

I blew out another breath, and loosened my grip on Isaac.

Elias must've noticed me relaxing, because he smiled. "Lans likes to be in control."

Oh, I had *earned* that dubious look from Isaac, in so many pleasurable ways.

"In situations like this. I can't see where we're going. Can't do anything if things go wrong."

"You don't know how to fly," Nikki said.

"Exactly," I said. "Plus we're stuck in these seats for hours." That was the worst part. Not being able to move around. "I hate it," I admitted.

"Hadn't noticed," Isaac said.

I kicked him—gently—and everyone laughed.

In the end, the flight wasn't *that* bad. We got in a round of Spades, had some snacks, and then we were on the ground.

By lunchtime, I'd shaken off the last of my stress—with a little help from time spent making out with my roommate. The team travel coordinator had paired me and Isaac in the same room without so much as a comment. Benson, Isaac's previous roommate, would've had their room to himself if he and Isaac were still paired up, so it made sense to drop the pretense that we weren't sleeping together. Telling the team had made everything easier.

I'd miscalculated slightly, though, about telling our families, because every head in the hotel lobby turned when Rose and Brian both shrieked, broke free from Mathieu and Zoe, screamed "Mononcle Isaac!" and threw themselves at him, nearly taking his legs out as they wrapped their arms around him.

Isaac laughed, oblivious for the moment at how everyone was staring at him. "Hey, bonjour," he said. "Comment ça va?"

The kids laughed, delighted, and answered, talking over each other.

I stared at Isaac. "T'apprends le français?"

"Oui." He laughed. "Un peu. I have an app."

"Oh, an *app*," I said. "I see." Somehow, he'd managed to get in lessons without me noticing. Sneaky. Not impossible—but sneaky. His accent was—well. I could understand him, and so could the kids. Josie joined her siblings, who were tugging Isaac down and trying to get him to say more words because the way he said them was strange. To say the least.

The whole damn lobby was watching us. Mathieu shrugged in an annoyingly arrogant manner that I recognized, since I had the same damn shrug. "Les enfants l'aiment bien."

The kids had good taste. But there was very little reason my family should suddenly be taking to our rookie forward. "I may have not thought this through," I murmured to Mathieu.

He merely chuckled.

My sister and parents weren't even here yet. Oh God, we were *fucked*. There was no way we could hide our relationship from every person watching us.

Suddenly, Nikki's voice boomed across the lobby. "Hey, hey, Landrys!" He strode forward in a dark blue suit, Elias at his side in a gray double-breasted suit. I had invited both—individually—to join my family and Isaac for lunch.

The two younger of the three shrieked again, and wrapped themselves around Nikki and Elias. "Mononcle Nikki! Mononcle Elias!"

One part relief and one part worry flooded through me.

We were still the center of attention, but now Isaac was just like Nikki and Elias, and not very obviously my lover.

Except I wanted everyone to know. *Everyone.* I wanted to shout from the rooftops that I loved Isaac Rivera, his charming smile, his sparkling brown eyes, and his commanding presence. He wasn't just a fantastic hockey player—he was perfect.

And I was *his*.

We needed to have a conversation, and soon.

No time at the moment, though. My parents arrived with Marie and her family, and the absolute force that was my family all in one place descended upon the poor hotel. They were, unsurprisingly, used to it. The team stayed here every time we played Montréal, but that didn't stop me from feeling bad about it.

"We should head to the restaurant." I repeated that in French, and somehow we managed to get everyone moving in the same direction. Luckily, there was a very good place nearby that could accommodate a party of ten adults and five children. I always called months in advance to book a private room.

Lunch was absolutely amazing, as always. My mother sat next to Isaac, and they chatted in a combination of French and English for the better part of the meal, to the sheer delight of my mother. She looked around Isaac to me. "C'est une perle."

Oh *shit*. "Oui, Maman. Je sais."

Marie bumped my shoulder with hers and laughed.

Isaac had the look of someone desperately trying to parse words. He gave up, and his plaintive look was endearing. "What?"

Because I loved when Isaac descended into utter astonishment coupled with an embarrassed fluster, I told him. "She told me you're a keeper. I told her I knew."

There it was, complete with the chin dip and smile and the crinkles around his eyes. "Oh."

I was so damn in love with him. I had no idea I could feel like this for anyone, and for it to be *him*, this kind, thoughtful, passionate person—that blew my mind.

He met my gaze and grinned. "I'd like that, too."

Oui. Completely gone for Isaac.

In the relative privacy of our gathering, I could hold Isaac's hand on either his or my thigh. Smile at him the way my sister and brother smiled at their spouses. Physical affection wasn't anything new to me—Nikki tended to sling his arm around Elias and me, as well as some of the other guys, but half the time when I looked at Isaac, I wanted to pull him close and kiss him. On the cheek. On the forehead. Just—let him know how much I cared.

Around my family and friends, once the wait staff was out of sight, I could. Those short bursts only whet my need for more. Every day, it would be harder to hide, I realized.

A couple hours later, we said goodbye to my family, left a sizable tip, and headed out.

Marie gave me a long hug. "Prends soin de toi."

"Always."

She rolled her eyes, because she knew me.

When she hugged Isaac, she murmured something into his ear, and he laughed. "I'll do my best."

Mathieu's daughter Rose latched onto Isaac's leg. "S'te plaît, Mononcle Isaac, viens nous visiter à Saguenay?"

"I..." He crouched down to her level. "You want me to come to Saguenay? Is that right?"

"Oui! This summer! Please?"

The other kids reiterated this in both English and French.

Isaac looked up at me, stunned. Desire in his face—he wanted to say yes, but there was concern, as well.

"I try to make it up for a week or two every summer. You're welcome to join me," I said.

That had the kids begging even more, with cries of "please" and "s'te plaît" overlapping each other. Even the older ones were joining in now.

God, my heart.

Isaac laughed and held up his hands. "All right, all right. I'll work things out with your mononcle."

Oh, the cries of excitement. My parents looked as happy as the kids, as did my siblings.

On the walk back to the hotel, Nikki threw his arm over Isaac's shoulder. "You passed the family test."

Isaac's eyes went wide. "Has anyone else?"

Elias snorted. "No. Lans doesn't date." He paused, and his expression softened into a grin. "Well, he does now." Unexpectedly, Elias mirrored Nikki, and wrapped an arm around my shoulder. "I'm happy for you both, you know. But the way you two look at each other? Someone's going to figure out that you're an item."

"Yeah, I know." I glanced at Elias, taking in both his smile and the worry he couldn't keep from his eyes. "I'd say fuck it and let's get caught, but Coach said not to be a distraction."

Isaac grunted. "I'm not really looking to be the center of a media frenzy."

There was that. No matter how we played this, the media would be on us like hounds. At least if we had a plan, we could mitigate some of that. "Let's talk to Kelly after this road trip."

"We can help cover for you," Nikki said.

"Oh God, no!" I said.

Elias laughed, and pulled me tight against him as we entered the hotel. "Never ask Nisha for help, Lans! You know that."

"He's not asking!" Nikki said, pulling Isaac along with

him toward the room where we'd be having our team meeting. "I'm telling him."

"Elias, please help."

He unhooked his arm, then pushed me into the room. "You're on your own, Lans. Nisha is his own keeper."

"Fuck you both," I grumbled.

Isaac, for his part, laughed. "I think you're both *very* helpful."

"Oh, screw you, too."

Oh hell, I hadn't expected that smoldering look or his smile. The one that said, *Yes. And you'll be your knees for it.*

Nikki must have caught the edge of Isaac's stare because he slapped me on the back. Hard.

"God, you're all impossible," I grumbled.

Coach's voice boomed from across the room. "Well, now that our esteemed leadership group is here, let's get started."

I checked my watch. "We're not late!" We still had five minutes.

"Yes, Landry, I know." Coach pointed at the empty seats. "Sit your ass down anyway."

I sat, to the chuckles and smiles of my teammates.

Isaac sat to my left, while Nikki plopped his butt down to my right, and gripped my shoulder. "No worries, King. Everything is good."

It really was.

---

A COUPLE HOURS AFTER DINNER, the hotel bar was loud and raucous, between most of our team and some of the hotel's other guests noisily watching basketball. Multiple languages hit my ears. The amount of French was welcome, but disconcerting. After so many years living in the States, coming back home was always strange.

Both the team meeting and dinner had gone well. We'd studied film. Tomorrow we'd look over more, then practice before the game. After that, we'd jump on a plane for Ottawa. This was the last time for a couple of days that we could cut loose—so we did.

Of course we were recognized, and the table Nikki, Elias, Isaac, and I commandeered was approached multiple times, mostly for selfies with fans, but a few were looking for more than that. We rebuffed those, gently, and got back to watching basketball on the huge screen nearby. I had no loyalty to either team, but it was one of those intense back-and-forth matches where the points flew up the scoreboard. Nikki and Elias spent the evening ribbing each other, since they supported the opposing teams.

"Ah, my friend, my friend." Nikki slung an arm around Elias, and practically pulled him onto his lap. "You know nothing about basketball."

Elias pushed back. "You think you do? Five years ago, you didn't even know what a three-point shot was!"

Isaac burst out laughing. "Oh my God, really?"

"No," Nikki said, waving away Elias's comment. "Of course I know the game. I just wanted Elisha here to think I didn't. I played in school, you know!"

Elias rolled his eyes. "You did not. All hockey, all the time, you said."

"As if you were any different, and yet—tennis." Nikki didn't let Elias go, and they got into a fast discussion that I couldn't follow. My Russian wasn't nearly as good as theirs. The back-and-forth rivaled the intensity of the basketball game.

While they argued, Isaac leaned close. "Elisha?"

"Oh," I said. "Nikki does that when he wants to rile Elias up."

"So, I should never use it." Oh that smirk.

I laughed outright. "Not unless you want a six-foot-two, two-hundred-pound Swede pissed off at you." I waved a hand at the pair, who were still arguing. "It's between them."

Nikki gave Elias a little shake and Elias cracked a smile. His return shove was half-hearted. "Ah, fuck you, Nisha."

"Whatever you say, Elisha."

Elias rolled his eyes.

I took a chance and draped an arm over Isaac's shoulder for a few moments. "Do you know basketball?"

"Not a damn thing," Isaac said. "But I can tell you all about baseball."

"Ugh, I know your dad played, but baseball's almost as bad as golf. All that...sitting."

He snorted. "Not something you enjoy."

"I can be persuaded." I gave him a sly smile.

He raised an eyebrow.

Nikki howled with laughter. "You two—" he said, then stopped when Elias cuffed him.

I dropped my arm from Isaac's shoulder, because wow, that was not at all discreet.

When I looked over, Isaac was staring down into the remnants of his beer with the biggest shit-eating grin I'd ever seen on those amazing lips of his.

"Anyway." He nodded at the TV. "Your team is up, Elias."

We shot the shit like that for a while, ribbing each other until the basketball game was over. In the end, the team Elias favored won, and we were all treated to an unusually exuberant captain, much to Nikki's dismay.

As we were finishing our drinks—Isaac had switched to water at some point—a woman slid up next to me. "You're Julien Landry, right?"

She was blonde and young—college age, if I had to guess. Pretty. She wore a very flattering low-cut dress that screamed puck bunny. I didn't begrudge anyone out to fuck a hockey player—especially since I had no room to talk. There weren't any real jerks on our team, so if she ended up with someone, she'd be fine. Wouldn't be me, though.

"I am," I said, leaning back in my chair and smiling up. "Hello."

Next to me, Isaac tensed. I gave his foot a subtle tap. *Chill*.

"I, uh, was wondering if I could get a selfie with you?" She leaned down a little, and ah yes. The sexy red bra. The expression Elias was trying to maintain on the other side of the table was absolutely priceless. Nikki, however, was appreciative.

"Sure," I said. "Do you want me to stand, or..."

"No, this is fine." She crouched down, and pressed her face against mine. Nice perfume. Warm hands. She was model-sexy in the image displayed on the phone, and I gave her my very best smile.

*Snap.*

"Can I text this to you?" A breathless question. Wet lips, big doe eyes.

"No, that's okay." I kept my smile but shook my head.

There was her disappointment, on cue. "Are you sure?"

"Yeah," I said, then quietly added, "I have other plans tonight."

"Oh," she said. "Sorry."

"Not a problem."

"Do you want my selfie?" Nikki asked.

She looked over. "Oh! You're Nikolai Sidorov!"

He smacked Elias. "See, someone recognizes me.

Elias's smile turned icy. "Of course they do."

Nikki stood, and took a photo with the woman. Of course they got to talking and drifted away from the table. And of course after another few minutes, they were nowhere to be found.

Beside me, Isaac looked around the bar, then stared at me. "Uh, did that just happen?"

"Yup. Get used to it. You'll get fans like that, too. It's not all signing jerseys with Sharpies."

"Shit." He sank back in his chair. "And Nisha just—" He waved a hand.

"Yes." I swear, Elias almost snapped the arm off the lounge chair. "He does that sometimes." Then he sighed and rose. "It's late. I should head to bed." His motions spoke of dismay and fatigue.

I stood and caught him by the shoulder. "Hey, you good?" I met his gaze and searched his eyes, looking for the truth.

There was nothing but frost behind his smile. "Of course."

I didn't call out his lie. I merely gave his shoulder a squeeze and let him go.

Next to me Isaac exhaled. "Well, shit."

"Eh, it's Nikki and Elias. They'll be fine." They always were, in the end.

I settled up our tab—it was my turn anyway—and Isaac and I headed up to our room.

*Our* room. The one we were sharing. In the elevator, I eyed Isaac. "Did you really think I would pick up someone?"

"I mean—no. But—"

I crossed the elevator, grabbed him by the suit jacket and kissed him. He gave a startled gasp, then reached up and yanked my hair. Hard. Suddenly, I was the one gasping for air.

"Behave," he growled, and there was fire in his eyes.

"I *am* behaving." I nuzzled his cheek. "You're the only person I want to fuck, Isaac."

We separated as the elevator doors slid open, and I sauntered toward our room, Isaac following. Once inside, I tossed my key card on the desk and started loosening my tie.

"Julien." Isaac's voice was conversational.

"Hmm?" I turned, and his command and presence rooted me to the floor.

"Get on your knees. Now."

Soft words, spoken low and with an absoluteness that had me obeying without thought. My hands slipped from my tie and landed on my thighs. I trembled as he strode toward me.

His fingers tipped my chin up, and his gaze bore down into me. "Do you have any idea what you do to me?"

I licked my lips. "I have an idea, yeah."

His laugh rumbled through my bones. "I bet you do."

That smile alone could get me off. "Isaac..."

His fingers brushed my lips, silencing me. "You really love this, don't you? Being on your knees for me. Obeying me." Heat there, but also wonder.

"If I didn't, I wouldn't be here." I paused. "*Any*thing, Isaac. Anything you want from me."

"Pourquoi?"

I had to chuckle at his pronunciation. "Because I trust you. You're not going to hurt me." I gave a small shrug. "Well, not in ways I don't like, anyway."

His grin was full of teeth. "I do love watching you cry and moan when my cock's inside you."

God, the shudder that ran through me. I wanted that so much. My dick strained against my pants. I swallowed, my pulse thudding in my ears. "Is that what you want?"

That smile widened. "Eventually."

Oh damn. *Yes*, my soul sang. Anything at all. My expression must have been so readable, because Isaac responded with a look of hunger so intense that I whimpered.

He bent down and pulled my loosened tie from my neck. "Get up and take off your clothes."

After I stood, he handed my tie to me. I knew better than to drop my clothes on the floor like I wanted, so I headed to the closet while unbuttoning my shirt, then stripped off each item carefully, hung my suit, and set my shoes inside neatly.

The only things I tossed were my underwear and socks, and those went into a dirty laundry bag.

When I turned back to Isaac, he stood by the bed, still fully in his suit. "I brought some things from home." He held a pair of cuffs in one hand and soft rope in the other. The last time I'd seen either was when Isaac had checked out my drawer of toys.

"Oh fuck." The words tumbled from my lips and two thoughts collided. First was that he was going to tie me up and fuck me in our hotel room—that was high up on my random fantasy-with-Isaac list. The other was that he'd said *home*. Not your place, but *home*.

I didn't know what to make of that. Well, I *did*, but I didn't know that to make of *that*. My house was Isaac's home. *I* lived in the place Isaac thought of as *home*.

Isaac Rivera loved me.

"I'll take that as a yes."

"Oui." I huffed a laugh. "Oh my God, Isaac."

"Come here."

His smile was the best thing in my whole damn life. I went, how could I not? Isaac put the cuffs on my wrists, and in short order had me tied down to the bed. My legs were free, but a single order of "don't move" from him as he crawled between them in that black suit of his kept me relatively still.

I trembled and twitched. Pulled on the cuffs, but my legs stayed where he'd pushed them, even as he kissed and licked his way up my thighs to my balls. Then he sucked on those, and I nearly lost what was left of my mind. "Oh fuck, Isaac, please!"

The evil chuckle he gave almost had me coming against his cheek. I bit my lip and twisted on the mattress, too aware that hotel walls—even in expensive hotels—weren't that thick.

"This is better than I imagined." Isaac loomed over me,

the end of his tie sliding against my chest. "I don't even know where to begin."

"Anywhere," I said. "Just hurry up."

"Rude." He flicked one of my nipples, then pinched it. Hard.

I arched, as the pain flooded my already primed nerves. I think I moaned. I know by the end, after he'd abused the other one, I was panting.

Isaac slid off the bed, and stripped off his coat. He kept himself in my view as he loosened his tie and worked open his shirt, then crossed to the closet to hang everything up. I craned my neck to watch him uncover every bit of his flesh.

His ass was perfect. And his abs. And those impossible thighs. Shit, how was I this lucky? "Fuck, t'es magnifique."

He gave me one of those dazzling smiles, then grabbed lube and a box of condoms from his bag. "Mixing French and English."

"Fuck is a perfectly fine French word," I said.

"Mmmhmm." He crawled back onto the bed, tossing the condom box to one side of me. "I guess that's why you say it so often."

"I don't—"

Isaac sucked the head of my cock into his mouth.

"Oh, *fuck!*"

I shuddered as he chuckled around me, then moaned as he sucked me off in earnest. The ropes creaked against the bed frame, as I strained against them. I wanted to thread my fingers into Isaac's hair, but I was helpless to do anything but look and feel.

Isaac slid his mouth off me. "Don't break the bed." Deep amusement there.

"Easy for you to say," I gasped.

"Very," he said, reaching for the lube. "But you're going to obey me anyway, aren't you?" He teased my hole with a finger.

I thumped my head against the pillow. "Isaac..."

"Aren't you?" he purred, and pushed two fingers inside me.

I bit my lip to keep from crying out, but when he found my prostate, I couldn't keep the moan back, or the curses. But I didn't break the bed.

"Julien."

"No. Breaking. Bed." I heaved out a breath. "Got it."

"Good." He stopped torturing me. Or so I thought. With great care, Isaac rolled a condom down my dick, and those devilish eyes met mine. "I had another thought, but I need your opinion on something."

I flexed my arms and thrust into his hand as he lubed me up. "You pick the strangest times for conversations."

"Do I?" He crawled up me, then took my mouth in a demanding kiss that left me moaning, thrashing, and harder than I thought possible.

"Isaac," I moaned. "You're killing me here."

"I know." Those lips moved over mine, teasing the hint of a kiss. "I want to ride you until you come, then fuck you until I do. You think you can handle that?"

My eyes wanted to roll into the back of my head just thinking about it. The pleasure. The pain. How long I'd be suspended between both. "I love being fucked after I've come," I whispered. "Hasn't happened in a long time."

Mostly because my past partners usually came before me —and exhausted themselves in the process. Isaac seemed to have the same stamina as me when it came to sex.

Making up for lost time, indeed.

He kissed my throat. "Let's see how hard I can make you cry."

Really fucking hard, as it turned out. Isaac rode my cock like he wanted me to split him in two, even as I strained against my bonds. I had no control, and it was the most glorious thing in the world, especially when Isaac growled at me, "Harder, Julien. I want to *feel* it."

I plowed into him with everything I had, and God, the gasp he made, the way he threw back his head in pleasure, that about undid me.

I clutched at the rope tied to my cuffs. "Isaac!"

Sweat beaded on his brow, and he licked his lips. "Close?"

I couldn't form words, so I hoped my groan was acknowledgement enough. I was right on the fucking edge.

Must have been, because Isaac leaned down, found my nipples, and twisted them hard. "Now, baby."

Everything went white as pleasure and pain crashed into me, and I gave up any pretense at remaining quiet.

When I could breathe again, I blinked the tears out of my eyes, and found Isaac above me, still on me. He was biting his lip and staring down. "Look at you. Now who's magnifique?"

"Still you." My voice was hoarse. "Oh my God."

There was that chuckle that warmed my bones. "I'm not done with you yet." He lifted himself off my cock, took care of the condom, then pulled another out of the box.

My body hummed. After he slicked up, he worked on my hole again, but I shook my head. "Just fuck me."

"But—"

"Please." Tears at the corner of my eyes. "Believe me, I can take it."

I did, groaning as Isaac eased himself in. Crying out with every thrust, my nerves on fire with pleasure. This was worse —and better—than hovering on the brink of orgasm. I was out of my mind, and practically out of my body. No idea how long Isaac thrust into me, but it was perfect and hard, and I sobbed when Isaac sank his teeth into my shoulder and came inside me.

After that, I wanted to sleep forever. I also wanted to lace on my skates and go score a hundred goals. I really was the luckiest man alive. All I could do at the moment, though, was sink into the mattress and weep hot tears.

Isaac brushed my hair out of my face. "You okay?"

"Perfect." I smiled weakly at him. "Absolutely."

He ran a hand through his own hair. "I can't believe..." His expression was almost bashful. "Let me untie you."

When he did, I heaved myself up, wrapped my arms around him, then dragged him to the mattress so I could kiss him. Repeatedly.

Eventually, he pulled back. "Let's get cleaned up before we pass out?"

"Sure."

When we'd managed that and were under the covers, I pulled Isaac close and threw my leg over his. "How much crap do you think we're going to get tomorrow for the noise we made?"

He laughed and nosed into the crook of my neck. "You mean the noise *you* made?" His breath was hot against my skin. He waited until I finished my embarrassed chuckle to continue. "Depends on who's next to us."

I pulled back so I could see his face in the not very dim light of the hotel room. "Is your ass going to be fine for tomorrow? You rode me *hard*." I tried to keep the glee from my voice.

"Next time, I'll order you not to come," he whispered. "And see if you can obey."

I shivered against him. "We can try that, sure."

"Good." He kissed my shoulder. "Anyway, I'm fine. You?"

I was far more used to getting fucked that way than he was, even if he'd pretty much drained me with pleasure. "I'll be fine."

"Ready to beat your hometown team?"

I scoffed. "They're not my hometown team. Quebec City is closer to Saguenay."

"Yeah, but they're not getting a team for another two years."

The league was finally expanding again, which was both good and bad. There'd be an expansion draft, and who knew what that would bring. No use in worrying about it, though. I shrugged. "I love the city of Montréal. The Fleurs, on the other hand..."

He vibrated with laughter. "So two points?"

I kissed his temple. "Two points. And a goal from you."

"And from you?"

I gave another shrug. "Maybe an assist? We'll see."

---

No one gave us any crap at all, quite probably because it all went toward Nikki, who was nearly late for the team breakfast and sported quite the bruise on his neck. Wolf whistles sounded around the room.

I thought Elias might grind his teeth off when Nikki sat. "Had fun, did you?"

I swear, ice formed on my coffee. Isaac gave me a worried look. He wasn't the only one. Paxy bit his lip and Larry became very interested in his eggs.

Nikki sipped his coffee, his brows furrowing. "I did," he said, slowly. "She was nice. I figured, why not? It's nothing anyone else hasn't done."

Elias deflated slightly and waved a hand, but said nothing. He went back to pushing food around on his plate.

There was one person at the table who absolutely didn't hook up with anyone during the season, and that was Elias. He wasn't cold—around fans, he was sunlight and warmth, even when someone was obviously trying to get into his pants. He ignored that part. Or was oblivious—I'd never figured out which.

After a few uncomfortable moments, Nikki sighed. "I'm sorry I upset you, Elisha."

This was one of the rare times when that nickname didn't have Elias fuming. "You didn't. But tonight's important."

"All the games are important," Nikki countered.

Elias sat back and crossed his arms. "Exactly. Which is why people shouldn't be fucking around."

Nikki rolled his eyes and waved a hand at me and Isaac. "Talk to them about fucking around."

"Us?" I feigned surprise. "We would never...!"

Larry laughed. "I have no idea how you manage twenty-eight minutes every game, dude, with nights like that."

Isaac shrugged, a little arrogance in his smile. "He's got stamina."

A tater tot hit my chest. "I don't want to hear it," Elias said.

"Why are you throwing food at me? He started it!" I pointed at Isaac.

Nikki wagged a finger at me. "Oh no, my friend. You started it. I don't know how, but I'm sure you did."

I flipped Nikki off, and he laughed. So did Elias, which was good.

"See," I said to Isaac later, when we noticed Nikki and Elias shooting the shit with Ozzy, both laughing easily. "They're fine."

We headed back up to our room to pack and change before heading over to the arena for the game. "We're going to win," I repeated to Isaac. "Promise you."

And we did, five to three. Isaac scored, as I'd predicted, and so did Ozzy, Elias, and Nikki. I didn't get an assist—instead, I potted an empty net goal.

On the bus to the airport, Isaac leaned close and whispered into my ear, "I should fuck you like that more often, huh?"

None of my teammates knew why I suddenly burst out into gleeful laughter.

Well, maybe one did, because Nikki turned around and threw his hat at me, which only made me laugh harder.

Perfect. So beautifully *perfect*.

My phone buzzed with an incoming text, and I glanced at the screen.

*Empty net goal for an empty-headed player. See you at the All-Stars, Julie.*

*Fuck!* I dismissed the text and shoved my phone away.

"Hey." Isaac placed his hand on my arm. "Everything all right?" Love and concern in his voice and in his touch.

I let out a sigh, and rolled the tension from my shoulders. "Yeah. Just—" I gestured at my phone. "Spam. So annoying."

"Block the number?"

I gave a shrug. "Doesn't really help, does it?"

He chuckled, took my arm and leaned against me.

I was so in love with Isaac. I loved my team, too.

No one, not even goddamned Travis Canterbury could take that away from me.

# Chapter 23

## Isaac

Our team's charter jet had a lot of perks, but one didn't cross my mind until Julien and I headed for the All-Star game: nonstop flights.

I'd taken for granted the lack of layovers. Probably because they'd never really bothered me unless my flight was delayed or I'd stupidly thought that, yes, I could totally get across Denver or O'Hare on foot in twenty minutes.

But this time, I was flying commercial with Julien, and though our layover in Minneapolis left us plenty of time to easily make our connection, it still meant he had to endure takeoff and landing twice in the same day. I'd had hope for a while that he might be okay—as okay as he ever was in the air—after the first flight. After all, that leg of the trip was smooth and uneventful...right up until we'd landed with all the grace of a kid's toy being tossed down the stairs. By the time they called priority boarding for our connection, Julien had stopped sweating, but he absolutely looked like he was on the verge of puking.

And fuck me, but we were out in public, so even as we settled into our seats, there was only so much I could do for him. Order him a gin and tonic when the flight attendant came by. Try to gauge if talking to him would be a welcome distraction or if it would distract him from whatever he was doing inside his head to pull himself together. Watch helplessly from across the broad space between us thanks to the wide armrests in first class. I didn't think I'd ever find myself missing the confines of coach, but at least that would've put us close enough together for me to touch my foot to his or find some way to offer quiet reassurance.

His gin and tonic came, and Julien swallowed a good third of it in one gulp. Then he closed his eyes and leaned back against the seat, fresh sweat beginning to bead along his hairline. The crevices deepened between his eyebrows, and his jaw worked like he was either trying really, really hard not to get sick, or like he was trying to keep his teeth from chattering. Both, maybe.

The helplessness was killing me. This flight was longer than the previous one. Four hours and some change instead of slightly under two. And to make things even more fun, I'd surreptitiously checked the weather on my phone in the terminal. While I was no expert on air travel or weather, it looked like there was some fuckery brewing in the sky between here and Vegas, and that did not bode well for Julien's blood pressure.

There had to be something I could do. Right now, I was seriously regretting not giving in to the impulse to say fuck it, rent a car, and drive the rest of the way to Vegas. It was only like sixteen hundred miles. I could've driven until the booze was out of Julien's system, and then we could've traded off until we got there. We'd both be exhausted, but maybe he'd be a little closer to sane.

I'd talked myself out of it, though. Julien needed time to rest before the skills competition and the game. There was media shit for both of us tomorrow afternoon, and there was no way in hell we'd get there in time via car even if we drove nonstop. We had to fly.

But goddamn, as the plane started to taxi toward the runway, I had some serious regrets about not throwing the road trip card. We'd been back in Pittsburgh for two days before we'd boarded this morning, grabbing some desperately needed downtime after the Montréal-Ottawa-Toronto road trip. We could've made it if we'd left yesterday or the day before. Damn it.

The flight attendants went through their safety briefing, which seemed to make more color slip out of Julien's face. He gripped his glass so tight, it was a miracle it didn't shatter. It was like every comment they made about emergency exits, flotation devices, and leaving carry-on items aboard reminded him of the deathtrap we were in. That never seemed to bother him on the team jet.

Then again, on the team jet, he had Nisha, Elias, and me distracting him at every turn, at least until the gin seeped in far enough to calm him down. Cards. Conversation. Shit-talking. Maybe that was what he needed now.

I hesitated before reaching for him. We were in public now, even if we were in the back row of first class and no one except the people across the aisle could see us. They were focused on their newspapers anyway. And seriously, at this point, who the fuck cared if someone saw us and wondered? For all I knew, no one on this plane even recognized us. Well, aside from those girls who'd been in one of the other boarding groups and almost lost their minds when they saw Julien. Couldn't blame them.

So...fuck it.

As the pilot told the flight attendants to be seated for take-off, I reached across the wide armrest and put my hand on Julien's arm.

He sucked in a sharp breath through his nose, but he

didn't open his eyes. Beneath the sleeves of his shirt and suit jacket, the muscles of his forearm were rock hard.

Staying quiet enough that only he could hear me, I adopted the voice I usually only deployed in the bedroom. "Julien. Look at me."

He obeyed, turning a startled gaze on me.

I ran my thumb along the side of his wrist. "Breathe. I know this sucks royally, but this part will be over soon."

He swallowed hard, letting his eyes flutter closed as he nodded slowly.

"Take a drink." I squeezed his arm. "Keep breathing."

It sounded so fucking useless. There was nothing I could say to lessen his fear because neither of us had any control over the plane or the pilot or goddamned physics. All I could do was reassure him that I was here, and with as shaky as he was, that didn't seem like nearly enough.

But he did take a drink. And he did keep breathing.

The plane took off, and aside from some light turbulence on the way up, it was uneventful. Steadily, it began to level out, and the announcement that people could use electronic devices seemed to unwind some of the tension in Julien. He took a deeper swallow from his gin and tonic, and he brushed sweat from his forehead as he swore in French.

"Respire," I reminded him, and a smile actually cracked through his brittle façade. Probably some amusement over my admittedly terrible French. I'd take it.

"I'm breathing," he assured me. He turned to me, the smile faint but unmistakable. "I'm sorry. Flying with me is..." He sighed, shaking his head, and said something the foreign language app apparently hadn't gotten to yet.

"Hmm?" I asked.

"Nothing." Another shake of his head, and then he took another swallow of his drink. Pressing the glass to his forehead, he sighed. "God, *fuck* flying."

"Would it help to do something to pass the time?"

He eyed me, glass still against his forehead. "What did you have in mind? Because I'm a little too fucked up for the Mile High Club."

I snorted. "Do you honestly think we could both fit into one of those lavatories?"

He seemed to actually think about it, then shrugged as he lowered the glass to take a drink. "It's first class. You'd be surprised."

I just rolled my eyes. Okay, the gin and tonic was helping if he could make jokes. But in my mind, I could still see the ominous weather report and its menacing red and orange clouds over multiple states. There was only so much I could do to help him stay on an even keel, and my best bet was to do all of it. "What about cards?"

"You want to recruit someone else to play Spades?" he asked wryly.

"I was thinking a two-player game." I leaned down and fished a deck out of my bag, making a mental note to thank Elias for advising me to take one along.

*"You've got four flights with him,"* he'd told me as he'd pressed the weathered box into my hand. *"Trust me."*

Julien watched with interest as I unboxed the cards and started shuffling them on the armrest. "Two-player games, eh? What did you have in mind?"

"You ever played War?"

He shook his head as he set up his tray table.

Good. A game he didn't know, which meant it would take more concentration for him. Hopefully that would pull his focus away from the fact that we were at thirty-eight thousand feet, a tidbit of information our pilot had helpfully supplied. I'd never thought much of the pilots announcing our cruising altitude until I found myself sitting next to someone who was terrified of flying. Now I wished the guy would just *shut the fuck up* and *fly the damn plane* instead of reminding my boyfriend how much space there was between us and the ground.

I ran Julien through the rules of War, which were pretty straightforward. Then I split the deck, twenty-six cards apiece, and we started. He caught on fast, and he was beating me right up until we both showed sevens. That meant, well, war. We each put three cards facedown, then brought out a fourth card face-up. Both aces. Out came three more facedown cards and one face-up apiece—a four for him and a king for me.

"Oh, that's bullshit," he groused as I collected all the cards.

I laughed wickedly. "That's War."

He hmphed, then threw down a queen, which easily beat my three.

The game didn't require much in the way of skill. It was all dumb luck, really. It was also frustrating as all hell, and it definitely irritated him a few times just like it did me. But when he was rolling his eyes and cursing over losing a hand, he wasn't paying attention to the fact that we were still rocketing through the sky in a metal deathtrap.

War also took a *long* time to win. The object was to collect all of the cards, but inevitably, one person would get down to like five cards, and then there'd be a war, which they'd win, and suddenly the playing field would be level again. Another point in this game's favor under the circumstances. By the time Julien beat me, we'd been playing for over an hour. One down, three to go.

"I think we should teach this one to Nikki and Elias." He sipped his drink, which was mostly melted ice by this point. "Watching them play would be funny as hell."

I laughed as I shuffled the cards. "If we teach them War, they're going to wind up brawling on the plane."

Julien barked a laugh, which was good to hear. He was way more relaxed than he'd been earlier. Getting a little drowsy too, so he'd probably nod off before too much longer, which was also good.

*Please let this continue for the rest of the flight. He's been through enough today.*

Whoever I was talking to apparently disagreed on that, though, because...yeah, no, it didn't continue for the rest of the flight.

We were maybe three hands into our second game of War when the plane gave one of those downward jolts that made even my stomach jump into my throat. A collective gasp rippled through the cabin, and the pilot helpfully turned on the seat belt light as if to make sure we all knew we hadn't imagined that bullshit lurch. Or the subsequent lurches. And rattling. I shuddered when the plane did; I hated that feeling like the whole aircraft was going to shake itself apart.

Julien? He went *white*.

He still had a card in his hand, and he managed to grab his glass—which was mostly full of water—before it tumbled off the tray table, and he just...froze. Eyes closed. Lips pressed tightly together. The hand holding his card was shaking slightly, though I honestly couldn't be sure if that was from fear or from the turbulence itself.

"Julien." I put my hand over his wrist again. "Look at me."

God, the utter terror in his eyes was heartbreaking. I'd known people who were afraid of flying to varying degrees, but I'd never seen it run this deep in someone. He was fearless to a fault on the ice—bold to the point he took risks that could set him apart from all our peers but could also land him in the box or on the injured list—but air travel reduced him to this. To someone excruciatingly aware of his own mortality and helplessness, and that made my chest hurt. It would've been painful to see in anyone. In someone as strong and resilient as Julien...fuck.

I swallowed my own emotions and ran my thumb along

the cuff of his sleeve, barely letting it brush his skin. "You're going to make it through this. With me." It sounded so useless, damn it. What else was I supposed to say, though?

He moistened his bloodless lips. "How does this *not* scare the fuck out of you?"

Oh, now didn't *that* question offer up answers that could either soothe him or make this a hundred times worse? I could make him feel stupid. Or I could terrify him even more. Or I could...I don't know, say the wrong damn thing? Pile God only knew what emotions on top of the tangled mess he already was? Julien trusted me, and that trust meant the world to me, and I didn't want to fracture it over a badly judged answer at a time when he needed the right words.

Heart thumping (and not from the turbulence), I laced our fingers together and went with the best answer I could— the honest one.

"It does scare me," I admitted.

His eyebrows jumped as if he hadn't expected that.

Panic flared behind my ribs. Oh fuck. Had I misread the situation?

He gripped my hand as he searched my eyes. "It does?"

I nodded. "I think it scares most people to different degrees. We can't control what happens. We can't pull over on the side of the road. When the plane moves suddenly"—I gestured around us as the plane shuddered and lurched again —"it hits all those lizard brain instincts because millennia of evolution didn't take into consideration all the people who are way smarter than us who figured out how to make air travel really safe."

Julien watched me, his expression unreadable.

I genuinely had no idea if I was making the situation better or worse, but I kept going. "I've read all the stats and research and...I know up here"—I tapped my temple—"that it's safe as hell. But I'm as human as the next person, and yes, when we hit turbulence or the landing is rough, it scares me."

He kept studying me, and I wondered if he knew how hard my heart was thumping with the absolute certainty that I'd torpedoed every effort either of us had made to get him to the other end of this flight without losing his mind.

Slowly, though, the death grip he had on my hand loosened. He released a breath and eased back against the seat. I wouldn't say he'd relaxed, but some of the tension had dissipated. It was something.

"My ex..." He stared up at the seat belt light as if he needed something other than me to focus on. "Whenever we hit turbulence or something, he'd..." Julien closed his eyes and shook his head, laughing bitterly. "God, he thought it was hilarious."

Rage surged through me, knocking the panic out of the way. "He *what?* He thought it was *funny* that you're afraid of flying?"

Julien huffed another humorless laugh. "Of course he did. It was something he could use to make me squirm. During shit like this..." He gestured as I had, indicating the plane shaking around us. "He'd tell me how we were going to..." His teeth snapped shut and he swallowed like he was pushing back a lump. Or vomit. Then he croaked, "He just thought it was fucking hilarious."

"He's a *liar*," I growled with more vehemence than I'd intended, which said something.

Julien turned to me, eyes wide.

I softened my tone and squeezed his hand. "I don't know the whole story with him. I don't know if I ever will. That's... It's your call. But what I do know is that he was an asshole to you, and you deserved better." I paused, then added through my teeth, "You especially deserved better than someone who thought it was funny to be..." I finished with a sharp huff and rolled my eyes, mostly because I was sure if I continued, I'd end up shouting and drawing everyone's attention. This flight was eventful enough without the air marshal entering the chat.

Julien watched me with a mix of emotions I couldn't quite parse. Then he actually relaxed. As much as he ever did at thirty-eight thousand feet, anyway. "He was a dick."

"Yeah. He was. And I don't care what he said—being afraid of flying is nothing to be ashamed of."

The faintest of smiles broke through, and he ran this thumb along mine. Then he leaned back and closed his eyes. As the turbulence settled down, so did he, and before long, his breathing had slowed and his eyelids were fluttering the way they did when the gin and tonic knocked him out on a flight.

I indulged in a sigh of relief, and despite us still being technically in public, I didn't let go of his hand. I just prayed that we'd been through the worst, and that everything was smooth between here and Vegas.

I was starting to doze off myself when Julien murmured, "Isaac?"

I turned to him. "Hmm?"

Eyes still closed, he smiled. "Merci beaucoup."

I glanced around, making sure we weren't on anyone's radar. Then I brought his hand up and brushed my lips across his knuckles. "Bienvenue."

Julien laughed softly, probably at my pathetic French pronunciation.

I didn't mind.

---

I'D BARELY CLOSED our hotel room door behind us before Julien faceplanted on the bed in a flurry of French that was probably a mix of curses and "oh, thank God that's over."

He'd dropped his jacket on top of his suitcase, hadn't bothered taking off his shoes, and he groaned as he buried his face in one of the pillows.

I winced as I watched him. It had been a long, long day, and it was a genuine miracle he'd made it this far before he'd collapsed.

I would've loved to say the flight was uneventful after that initial bout of turbulence, but that had only been the beginning. The seat belt light had been on more often than not, and rightfully so—I was amazed none of the flight attendants turned an ankle or something, and there'd been several periods where they hadn't been up and around at all. During one of the sporadic stretches where it was apparently safe for the flight attendants to move around, Julien had ordered another gin and tonic. A double this time. Way more than a lightweight like him should be consuming, but I didn't say a word. I'd been fully prepared to let him lean his drunk ass on me on the way off the plane and out of the terminal if it came down to it; whatever it took to get him through.

By the time we landed, he'd started sobering up, mostly because the last hour or so had been too rough for the flight attendants to be up and around. Landing hadn't been too bad, thank God, but Julien had been miserable anyway. Drained. Rattled. Well on his way from drunk to hungover.

Somehow, he'd made it here and onto the bed we'd be sharing for the next few days.

On any other night, I'd have chastised him about his clothes, but tonight, I just quietly hung up his jacket, which had slid off his suitcase and onto the floor. Then I parked our suitcases across the room so neither of us would trip over them. I carefully removed his shoes and put them beside mine in the closet.

After I'd taken off my jacket, tie, and belt, I eased onto the bed next to him on my side and stroked his hair. "Hey. You okay?"

He exhaled hard and turned toward me, stubble scuffing on the pillowcase. Gazing up at me with exhausted, bloodshot eyes, he murmured, "I'm better now that we're on the ground."

"I'm sure."

He closed his eyes. "Ugh. I need a shower. I'm disgusting."

"I could use one too." I ran my fingers through his hair. "We'll take one in a bit."

He looked up at me again, questions in his expression that I couldn't quite read. I didn't know if he wanted to ask something of me, or if he was expecting me to ask something of him. We were good at reading each other—scary good—but we were both tired, he was still sobering up, and I could only imagine the jumble of thoughts in his rattled brain. I decided we could be forgiven for not having that effortless telepathy right now.

I rolled onto my back. "Come here."

His brow pinched.

I patted my chest.

He pushed himself up, slid closer, and rested his head on my shoulder. Closing my eyes, I wrapped my arms around him, and after a moment, Julien exhaled and relaxed against me. For a while, we just lay there, and I listened to his breathing and his heartbeat as his hair tickled my chin.

It was Julien who finally broke the silence. "I'm sorry."

I looked down at him, though I couldn't see his face. "For what?"

He sighed, then lifted himself up to look at me through the strands of hair that tumbled over his eyes. "Today. It was..." He shook his head and avoided my gaze. "Flying with me isn't for the faint of heart, I guess."

I brushed his hair out of his face. "Julien. Look at me."

He swallowed, but after a second, he did as he was told.

"You don't have anything to apologize for." I caressed his cheek. "I just wish I could've done more for you."

"More?" His eyebrows shot up. Then he sighed and covered my hand with his. "Non. Isaac, you did so much."

"All I did was get you a drink and play cards with you."

"And tell me that you were afraid too." He pressed a kiss to the center of my palm, and when he met my eyes again, he offered a tired smile. "It's easier when I'm not alone." The smile fell, as did his gaze. "But I asked so much by—"

"Julien." I lifted my head and kissed him softly. "It wasn't too much. Not by a long shot." Combing my fingers through his hair, I whispered, "I'd do anything for you. Keeping you sane while we're flying is a *low* fucking bar."

He watched me with wonder in his eyes. Then he cupped my face and kissed me, letting it go on a bit longer this time. Barely breaking the kiss, he murmured. "Thank you."

"You're welcome."

We shared another kiss, and then he rested his head on my chest again. I stroked his hair, letting him relax against me. He really felt like he was relaxing now, too. As if it were finally catching up to him that we were safely on the ground. That the flights were over. No more takeoff and landing. No more turbulence.

Well, not today, anyway. We were only in Vegas for the All-Star game. Then it was back to Pittsburgh and on the road with the team.

I mentally ran through the schedule for the next couple of weeks. There was a calendar on my phone, but reaching for that meant letting go of Julien, so I went with what I remembered. We'd have one day after the All-Star game to dick off in Vegas. Then there was a travel day. Practice two days after that. Game the following day.

Gazing at the ceiling, I said, "Pittsburgh is about two thousand miles from here."

Julien propped himself up on his elbow. "Hmm?"

"Two thousand miles." I looked at him. "That's... If we left the day after the All-Star game and drove back, we'd be cutting it close, but we'd make it in time for practice. Or maybe we can convince Coach to excuse us from one practice, since the game isn't until—"

"Wait. Wait." Julien shook himself. "Drive? What are you talking about?"

"If we rent a car and drive back, then you won't have to fly again. Not until we're on the road with the team, anyway."

He blinked. "Are... Isaac, you'd drive two thousand miles to avoid..."

I brought his hand up and kissed it. "I'd drive that far and more to keep you from going through what you did today."

He stared at me in disbelief.

"I mean it," I said. "I know we can't avoid flying when we're with the team, but if you want to drive back this time, say the word. I'll rent the car and talk to Coach. Whatever you need."

More disbelief. Then, slowly, his expression shifted to a sweet smile. He sat up and gestured for me to do the same. When I did, he curved a hand behind my neck and looked right in my eyes.

"I have everything I need." He drew me in and kissed me, letting it go on for a long, sweet moment. "I'll be all right flying back. But...thank you."

"Any time." I smoothed his hair. "If you change your mind, say so. The offer stands."

That smile. Jesus.

"Thank you," he whispered. Then he looked down at himself and frowned. "Ugh. I'm disgusting. Shower?"

"Yes. Definitely."

He started to get up, but hesitated, some renewed worry creasing his brow. "I, um... I don't think tonight will be..."

It took a second for the pieces to click together, and when they did, I touched his arm. "Julien. We're both exhausted. You've been through hell. Sex can wait."

The relief that crossed his face sent a flash of fury through me reminiscent of what I'd felt on the plane. I didn't ask, but I had a feeling his trepidation just then had to do with the same man who'd poked at his fear of flying.

*Fuck that guy. Jesus.*

As we both stood, I put a hand on Julien's waist. "Let's get a shower, and then get some sleep."

He grinned, almost masking the relief he shouldn't have needed to feel. "Before this trip is over, though..." He nodded to the bed. "We really should fuck on that."

"Oh, we will." I kissed him, then steered him toward the bathroom. "*If* you behave."

He almost tripped.

I laughed and followed him in to take a shower.

# Chapter 24

## Julien

By the next morning, I felt human again, rather than a bundle of anxiety loosely held together by willpower, gin, and the stunning kindness of my boyfriend. Isaac had suggested ordering room service for dinner, since I was in no shape to venture out onto the Strip. Good call. After that, he ordered me to get into bed, and I obeyed without question. I think I fell asleep as soon as I hit the pillow. Didn't wake up once.

No bad dreams. No nightmares.

Now, after a night of good sleep, I had several cups of coffee in me, and I waited with a bunch of other players from our division in the calm before the media storm.

Isaac was off at his own rookie shindig, so we'd meet up later after all the interviews and appearances were through for the morning. I ended up in a conversation with Matti Kanerva, one of the defensemen from Philadelphia, about the upcoming skills competition.

"I can't believe they're making us skate backward against each other. They should throw in a few forwards and see how they do."

I had to laugh, "They won't because they know those guys

will wipe out turning the corners, and they won't let us show them up. Superstars, you know."

He cackled. "Then there's you."

"Me?" I waved that away.

He rolled his eyes. "Have you seen your stats? You're the best in the league, Lans. Hell, I wish I could skate like you."

"I wish I could shoot like you. What do you have now? Fifteen goals? I'm stuck at nine."

"You have thirty-six assists. Forty-five points." He shrugged. "Got me beat by ten, there."

I looked down and smiled. "There is that."

"Ah, there he is, Mr. Humble." He gave me a warm smile.

"I do try," I said, and he laughed then mock punched me in the arm.

We shot the shit for a couple more minutes before he got pulled away for photographs. Soon, I was fetched and led to my own photo shoot, then to a meet-and-greet with some fans, then I got to sit behind a table and answer a bunch of questions. Was I excited to be here again? How did I think the Griffins were doing this season? What was my favorite event? Same questions every year. Did get a new one, though.

"What are your thoughts on Isaac Rivera? He's been quietly racking up points. Do you think people underestimate him?"

I had to think about the last part for a bit. "I—almost hope they do? Gives us an edge." That got me some chuckles. "No, I mean, Rivs is good. Strong on the puck. Deceptively quick release. He's smaller than some other forwards, but he can hold his own, you know? Fights hard in the corners. I think this is only the beginning for him. You'll see."

I worried a little, because he was our third center, but he was good enough to be in the top six. With Nikki and Elias, those center spots were taken, though in theory, Nikki could play wing, too.

Glad I didn't have to make those decisions.

A couple more questions were thrown my way about the season, about how Larry was doing after his concussion (fine), and about a betting scandal that had rocked the New Mexico Suns.

"I don't really have much to say about that. I don't understand gambling to begin with, so..."

"Not hitting the slots, then?"

I gave a bark of laughter. "No, no. My luck is *horrible*. I'm even bad at bingo."

"You play cards with your teammates."

"Yeah, but mostly Spades. There's some skill involved and nothing but pride on the line." I paused. "And I have enough that I can lose some once in a while. Probably good for me."

Laughs from the reporters.

They wrapped up the media portion with some more photos and some video spots, then I was finally on my own. That gave me a chance to step back, breathe and soak it all in. I was glad to be here, on the ground. In one piece.

Isaac had absolutely no idea how much he'd helped yesterday. I couldn't have gotten through that without him. Whenever it got *that* bad during a flight, Travis was there in my head. Laughing at me. Calling me weak. Telling me I was going to burn alive. That I'd never see my family again. Whenever I'd gotten upset, he'd had the gall to say he was only joking, only trying to *help* me get over my fear. Of course, he'd expected sex afterward, too.

That absolute *fucker*. God, I had been such an ignorant fool falling for his charm, his praise, his rugged good looks, and that smile. He was rotten to the core. I wondered if anyone else had been taken in by that shit, or if I'd been the only one. At nineteen, I'd had *naive* stamped across my forehead—an easy target. Travis had taken every advantage of that.

My mind lurched to the fact that he was here this weekend. Thankfully, Carolina was in a different division so I didn't have to play *with* him. With any luck, I wouldn't need to play against him, either. But somewhere, in our hotel and in this arena, that man existed, and the knowledge sizzled at the edge of my nerves.

*Fuck.* I needed some space before I crawled out of my skin.

I found Kelly, who'd also travelled to Vegas. She was coordinating the team's media and PR presence. "Hey, Kels, if you see Isaac, can you tell him I went for a walk to clear my head?"

Kelly had been around long enough to know I needed downtime from the noise and the chaos. She'd seen me get squirrely when I'd had to sit too long for interviews. As she'd said, she had to know the team inside and out. "Not a problem. Where can I tell him to find you?"

"Ice level."

She gave me a nod, and I was gone, walking with a smile and a purposeful stride. A few media folk tried to flag me down. I waved and pointed in the direction I was heading. "Be right back." The restrooms were this way, but so were the stairs. The latter had a guard on them, but my face plus my badge got me through the door, and I was heading down while loosening my tie and unbuttoning the collar of my shirt.

I liked wearing suits. Yes, I looked good in them, but I also felt good in them—confident. Sexy. Like I could take on the world. Even when my self-confidence was in shambles, there was something about putting on a suit that steadied me and chased away those demons, but I'd had enough of the tie for the moment. I needed my neck free. Needed to be able to breathe.

I exited into the relative quiet of the bowels of the arena. I'd been to Las Vegas enough to know my way around, but all arenas at ice level looked similar. Concrete. Piping. A certain hum. A chill and a dampness. From the murmur of sounds, there were other people down here, but no one right where I was, which was good. I needed quiet, needed not to be so fucking *on*.

Having Isaac here was a delight and he steadied me like no other, but we weren't out as a couple, so there was an extra level of carefulness that grated against me. At breakfast, we'd had to pretend we were just friends, not lovers. That set me on edge, especially after the intimacy of him calming me during that flight.

We were hiding, and I didn't want to anymore. Didn't think he did, either. We'd talked about speaking with Kelly, but there hadn't been any time in the schedule—and neither of us wanted the media attention to screw up the on-ice chemistry the team had going.

Though, our dating shouldn't be that much of a thing, really. There were other men in the league with queer partners; we certainly wouldn't be the first. Wouldn't even be the first to date another hockey player. Hell, Zac Peters, who played with LA, was married to Bryan Long, who was with Seattle, and they'd made it work without much fuss.

I rubbed my face and headed down a hall, looking for a space I could duck into. Yeah, I needed to talk with Isaac. Frankly, it would be better to come out ourselves, in our own way, than be forced by someone else. Or worse, blackmailed. Travis had nearly done that to me, but I'd taken away his threat to out me as gay by leaking the video of that threesome. If I was going to be out, I wanted it to be as a pansexual—since that's what I was. The couple had been kind enough—actually ecstatic—to be known as the ones who'd fucked Julien Landry.

The hall I'd ducked down led to a door with an alarm. There were rooms, but they were either locked, or obviously off-limits, so I turned around.

And stopped dead in my tracks, my heart leaping into my throat and my mind screeching to a halt. Standing halfway down the hall was the man I never wanted to see again, the man who I couldn't get out of my mind or my life.

"Hello, Julie," Travis said, and his smile was the unkind, cruel one I'd grown to fear my rookie year.

Suddenly, I was nineteen again, my heart racing and my brain trying to figure out how to placate this man—the man I'd thought I'd been in love with. Every instinct told me to flee, but there was nowhere to run. Only two exits: the alarmed door behind me and the hall past the man in front of me.

I swallowed bile, and ground out, "Travis."

His chuckle cut me like a knife. "Still can't handle the pressure of life, can you? Running away. Hiding. Big superstar like you?" He shook his head, and I remembered that look, the one that said I couldn't do anything right. "Always the scared little shit."

Rage and despair clawed inside me. Travis was wrong about me. But he was also right. I *was* scared. I couldn't make it through any of this by myself. Couldn't even survive a plane ride. "Why are you here?"

I knew this smile, too, and my stomach dropped to my feet. "To see you, of course." He drew closer and I resisted the urge to back up, to give in to the terror he wanted to see.

"Me?"

"My old friend." He was within arm's reach now. "My dear little *fuckbuddy*." Vehemence in that last word. He stopped inches away, well within my personal space.

My heart hammered like I'd bag skated three times after a hard practice, and my mind went blank, like it had when I was nineteen and scared shitless of what saying no to Travis might mean.

Non. Pas cette fois. I shook my head. "I was never your friend. You made that clear."

"Oh, Julie," he murmured. "Still so dramatic." He slid his fingers under my lapels, and my breathing stuttered when he straightened my suit, then brushed down the shoulders. "You always did have an eye for fashion, even if you were the messiest wreck in existence."

Every nerve in me vibrated in horror and fury. This fucking *asshole*. "What do you want?" I tried to sound bored, but it came out as a growl.

That laugh. *Fuck* that laugh.

I should push past him, just—go. I couldn't move. Frozen like always.

"To see what I made you into."

That—my vision dimmed and I wavered. This time, I did take a step back. "You didn't make me into anything," I snarled, and it took effort to uncurl my fist.

Not the time or the place to drop gloves. Assaulting Travis would give him everything he wanted.

The asshole fucking patted me *on the cheek*. "Everything you are—number one defenseman, league leader, alternate captain—it's all because of me. You were a *mess*, Julie. Could barely skate. Weak shot. You needed a strong hand to straighten you out." He leaned in, close enough that the scent of his aftershave filled my nostrils. Smoke and musk. "And a big cock pounding that pretty tight ass of yours to motivate you."

My nails bit into my palms, and I wanted to puke. "Touch me again and I'll break your hand." Somehow, I managed soft, even words, despite the rage boiling inside me, and the suspicion that, despite *everything*, he was right.

I don't know if it was what I'd said or my tone that made Travis step back, but satisfaction zipped through me until the next set of words dripped from his condescending mouth.

"You even have a rookie of your own, hanging on your every word." He smirked. "Wonder if he'd like some—advice —from a real hockey player?"

I stepped forward, tightening my fists. "You stay away from him. Don't you fucking go near him."

"Touchy, touchy." He raised his hands and took a step back. "So volatile."

Same thing, every time. Work to push my buttons, then act as if I was out of line to react. "God, you haven't changed."

"Neither have you. Remember that, Julie." His voice wormed into my skull.

I was about to snap something back when I heard the very last thing I wanted to hear at that moment: Isaac.

"Julien? Are you down here?"

"Ah, there's your puppy," Travis said.

"Julien?"

"Here!" I called out, hating how strangled and panicked my voice sounded. Gave too much away, but that had always been the case with Travis. He'd planted the buttons. Laid the mines. He knew what he was doing.

Isaac's footsteps quickened, then he was in the hallway. "Jul—" He came to a halt, his gaze snapping from me to Travis.

"Good to catch up," Travis said, in his perfect hockey media voice. "I'll see you around, Julie."

He nodded to Isaac, then was gone, rounding the corner into the main hallway that ran around the arena.

I sagged against the nearest wall, and spat out, "Osti de tabarnak."

Isaac hurried toward me. "Are you all right?"

"No." I uncurled my hands and peered at my palms where my fingernails had pressed into my flesh. No broken skin, but there were indentations. "I wanted to rearrange his face."

He took my hand and traced those marks with his finger. "Do you want to talk about it?"

"No," I said softly. I never wanted to talk about Travis. "He's an asshole. It was just—" I waved a hand after him.

"Same shit he used to say back then." I was a disaster. He'd made me into the player, the person I was. So hard to shake that, because at some level, it was *true*. "Can we go outside?" I met Isaac's worried gaze. "I need to see the sun. Maybe get some lunch?"

"What's your schedule say?" Isaac's smile was the opposite of Travis's. Warm. Inviting.

I was, in fact, a disaster. "Oh God, the schedule." I pushed off the wall and dug out my phone. Miraculously, I wasn't late for anything. In fact, I had the next several hours open. Tonight would be the skills competition, but until then, I was free. I thrust my phone at Isaac. "Does this say what I think it says?"

His brow crinkled as he studied the screen. Then he scrolled up and down a bit. "Do you think it says you can have lunch with me?"

"I absolutely think it says that."

He grinned and handed the phone back. "You're right."

God, I needed that smile, that humor. The weight of Travis slid off me, and I grinned back. "Lunch?"

"Do you need to change?"

"Do you like me in this suit?"

He gave me a once-over and raised an eyebrow. "This a trick question?"

An honest laugh poured out of me, and I clapped him on the shoulder. "Come on, let's get out of here."

Isaac drew me out of the depths and helped me back into the light.

## Chapter 25

### Isaac

I WAS WORRIED ABOUT JULIEN. Though he'd shaken off some of whatever had gone down, he wasn't okay and he wasn't hiding it. That exchange with Travis obviously hadn't been pleasant, and though he'd settled considerably since his ex had walked away, his hackles were still...not up, but not quite down either. It reminded me a little of how he'd be in the locker room or on the ice after one of his rare fights—the worst was over and he'd mostly shaken it off, but some of the fury still simmered around the edges. That could either bring out the pissed-off side of him that drove pucks into the back of the net, or it could throw him *just* far enough off his game to set Twitter ablaze with "Jesus fucking Christ, Landry turned over the puck *again*?"

Right now, as we walked from the ice level back toward civilization, I couldn't tell where he landed on that spectrum. Was he going to shake this off after some sunshine and food? Or was this going to fuck up his mood for the day? Kill his concentration for tonight? In fact, I had to wonder if that hadn't been part of Travis's plan.

Either way, I wasn't having it. Over my dead body was

Travis ruining Julien's mood, his day, or his game. Fuck that. Julien had been through enough at the hands of that dickhole, and he'd already been through enough on this trip thanks to the air travel debacle. He deserved to have his head in the game, and I didn't mean one of Travis's bullshit head games.

A few feet shy of the last door separating us from other people, I stopped. Julien did too, turning an inquisitive look on me.

"Hey." I touched his arm. "Tell me honestly." I nodded back in the direction we'd come from. "You don't have to tell me about it, and you don't have to be okay, but... Tell me, is there anything I should know about? Is there anything I can do?"

Though his shoulders sank a little as if the subject exhausted him, Julien shook his head. "It's... I'll be fine. We had some words, and seeing him always fucks with my head, but..." He paused. Exhaled. And then, to my surprise, a soft smile lit up his face, and he rested a hand on my waist. "I'm with you now. That makes everything a hell of a lot better."

The sincerity in his eyes was unmistakable, and I was glad I was helping, but much like on the plane, I still hated the helplessness. The inability to do more than just be here and be better than the alternative. I understood this was out of my control, but it sucked. I hated it. I wanted Julien to be happy. I wanted to pop Travis's claws out of his skin and make him forget the man ever existed.

But I couldn't. And I couldn't pry in and pull the truth out of Julien because that was a boundary of his. He wasn't ready to talk to me about Travis. Maybe he never would be. That was his decision and I would respect it, no matter how much I hated knowing there were painful wounds hidden beneath the surface. The best I could do was the equivalent of pulling out a deck of cards and talking him through the turbulence.

"Okay." I managed to keep my frustration out of my voice. "If there is anything, or if you do want to talk, say so."

Julien's smile grew a little, and the fatigue and anger in his eyes ebbed in favor of that warmth that always weakened my knees. He touched my chin and dusted a soft kiss across my lips. "I will."

That was all I could ask for.

We shared one more kiss. A second or two longer than the first, but there was too much potential to get caught in here, so we didn't let it linger. Instead, we exchanged smiles, then headed out into the crowded corridors of the arena.

"So, lunch?" He tugged at his sleeve as if he needed something to do with his hands. "There's a million restaurants on the Strip. What are you in the mood for?"

I shot him a playful look and waggled my eyebrow. "Is that a baited question?"

Julien laughed with some actual feeling, and I was pleased with the faint pink that spread across his cheeks. It would never stop being a novelty to make Julien Landry blush. With a playful bump of his shoulder against mine, he clarified, "What kind of *food*, Isaac?"

I shrugged. "Eh. I could—" The vibration of my phone in my jacket pocket cut me off. Then I heard the ringtone over the noise. "Hang on a sec." I tugged my phone out and stepped out of the flow of traffic. "Hey, Mom."

"Hey, honey! Happy Birthday!"

I chuckled. "Thanks."

"Are you doing anything special? Where are you right now, anyway?"

"Uh, I'm in Vegas." I looked up at my gorgeous boyfriend, and I couldn't help smiling. "Julien and I have some time to kill, so we're hunting down some food."

"Oh! That sounds—wait. You're in Las Vegas with Julien?

You two aren't eloping, are you? Isaac Matthew Rivera, if you elope with—"

"Mom, Mom, calm down," I laughed. "We're not eloping!"

Julien's eyes were suddenly huge, his expression so full of *what the fuck* it was comical.

"Okay," she said. "You'd better not. If you marry that man, your father and I expect an invite."

Now my face was on fire, and I had to clear my throat. "You'll get one. I promise."

"We'd better." She sounded hilariously indignant. "Do you boys have plans to celebrate your birthday? That man is spoiling you rotten, isn't he?"

With complete honesty, I said, "He always spoils me."

The confusion in his face vanished, and his smile sent a rush of warmth through me.

My mom and I kept the call short as we usually did, and as I pocketed my phone, I said, "Sorry."

"Don't apologize for taking a call from your mom." His eyebrow arched. "She thinks we're eloping?"

"Well, I mean..." I gestured around us. "We *are* in Vegas."

He laughed, rolling his eyes. "Please. As if Nikki and Elias would ever forgive us if we didn't invite them."

I chuckled, but as we stepped back into the flow of traffic, it occurred to me that he hadn't brushed off the idea of eloping or getting married at all. He'd just acknowledged there'd be hell to pay if we snubbed our friends.

Okay, I was definitely reading too much into what he'd said and what he hadn't said. But whatever.

We finally broke away from the crowd and stepped out into the crisp early afternoon. It was in the fifties today, which was a nice switch in February, and it was perfectly comfortable in our suits.

It was also crowded as hell. Every restaurant had a crowd

or a line out front. Some had twenty-, thirty-, forty-five-minute waits. Neither of us was starving by this point, so we just kept wandering.

We passed one café with a sign out front announcing free birthday drinks. Julien glanced at it, then did a double take and halted so abruptly, someone behind him almost crashed into him. Oblivious to the passerby cursing him out, Julien turned to me, eyes wide with horror. "Oh. Fuck. Today is your birthday!"

I slipped my hands into my pockets. "It is, yeah."

"Shit." He winced. "I completely—I'm sorry. I knew it was, but today's been so—"

"Julien." I shook my head. "We've both been running around all morning, and yesterday knocked you on your ass."

"But it's your birthday. We have to do something for it."

I shrugged. "Okay, we're going to lunch. We can call that—"

"Non." From the way he was looking at me, he was fighting hard not to reach for me. Had we been alone somewhere, he'd have had his hand on my face or my side, and suddenly my skin itched with the absence of his touch. "I'm not going to half-ass your birthday. We'll do lunch, but tonight, after everything is over, I'm taking you out."

"You have a lot going on tonight." I gave him a gentle nudge to start walking again. "We can do a raincheck. Honestly."

"Fuck that." He smiled in that way he did that almost made me trip over my own feet. "We're doing something for your birthday tonight. I promise. It'll be late, but..."

"A casual lunch is fine. I'd rather spend tonight in the room, depending on how much you have left after all the peopling and the skills competition."

I might have gotten a little too much satisfaction out of *him* tripping over *his* own feet.

Then I thought about what I'd said, and I sobered. "In fact, since you do have a lot of peopling today, we could go back to the hotel and do room service."

Julien glanced at me, brow pinched. "Is that what you want to do?"

Now that I thought about it...yes. Because even I was a bit peopled out, and if I was, then he had to be running on fumes. Plus the hotel did have pretty good food, and if I had to wait an hour for my food, at least I could be lounging on that super-comfortable bed instead of standing around a restaurant lobby with my thumb up my ass.

"Actually, yeah." I gestured for us to head back the other way, and as we did, I added, "I could use the quiet."

It was hard to tell over the noise of the Strip, but I was pretty sure he sighed with relief. Damn. I should've known that was what he needed. He'd insisted he wanted to go out, but after he'd been put through every possible wringer in the last twenty-four hours, I should've taken charge and said, no, we were going to back to the hotel for some downtime.

Duly noted for next time. Read the situation better. Read Julien better. Take the reins.

A couple of blocks from our hotel, a squeal of, "Oh my God, Julien Landry!" halted us both in our tracks, and we turned to see five girls who were probably around my age, maybe a little younger, hurrying toward us. They were wearing All-Star jerseys, and three of them wore Julien's.

I glanced up at Julien to gauge him. He wasn't bristling or looking like he was ready to run for the hills, so I relaxed, but I did murmur, "Say so if you want to bail."

He made a quiet sound of acknowledgment, and a second later, we were surrounded by the excited fans. He probably wouldn't speak up if he was overwhelmed, but I'd keep an eye on him. If I read that he wanted to get out of here, I could fake a phone call or insist we had to be somewhere.

So far, so good. He smiled genuinely through photos, and he signed jerseys and phone covers.

One of the girls turned to me, studied me, and then her eyes lit up. "Oh! You're Isaac Rivera!"

I felt myself blush. "Yeah. Yeah, I am."

"I didn't know you were here!" She smiled brightly. "You're not on the All-Star team, are you? Or were you—"

"No, no." I laughed softly and shook my head. "I'm just here to cheer him on."

That prompted some puzzled looks, and a pang of *oh shit* slammed into my chest. Did I tip my hand too far?

"Every rookie should come to the All-Star weekend," Julien said casually as he signed a jersey. "It's motivation."

*Good save, baby. Good save.*

One of the girls glanced at each of us, then turned a smile on me. "Well, with the way you play, you'll be an All-Star for sure."

I laughed nervously. "No pressure, right?"

They continued chatting with us and getting selfies and signatures for a few more minutes. They weren't as forward as the woman who'd come on to Julien—and ultimately Nisha—in the bar not long ago. Definitely starstruck, and there were absolutely some *oh my God he's gorgeous* gazes thrown at Julien when he wasn't looking, but they were respectful and happy to chat about hockey, the skills competition, and their thoughts about tomorrow night's game.

"The Western division is toast." The brunette wrinkled her nose. "Why in the world would they put Paulson in the net when Holloway is *right there*?"

"Because if Los Angeles sent Holloway," one of the others said, "they wouldn't have been able to send Cortes."

Her friend seemed to consider it, then shrugged. "Okay, fine. But Paulson? Really?"

"Eh, don't underestimate him," Julien said. "This hasn't

been his best season, but when he's on his game, he's a brick wall."

The conversation continued like that for a minute or two, and then they thanked us profusely for talking with them. As they left, Julien watched them chatting excitedly over the photos and autographs. His expression was hard to read. He liked interacting with fans, and nothing about the exchange had felt off to me—God knew I'd been watching for it—but something didn't seem to be sitting right with him this time.

In fact, he seemed more bothered than he had when we'd left after that encounter with Travis. Not in the same way—he wasn't angry or hurting—but he was off-balance in a way I couldn't put my finger on. He seemed...distracted. And not necessarily in a good way.

Neither of us said much on the way into to the hotel. Once we were back in the privacy of our room, I asked, "You okay? You've been a little..." I waved my hand in front of my face. "Not here. Since we talked to those fans."

"I, um..." He avoided my gaze as he shrugged off his jacket. "I guess I was just thinking. After we talked with them."

"What about?"

Without turning to me, he said, "Did you see how they were looking at us?"

I furrowed my brow. "I saw how they were looking at *you*."

He shook his head. "No, they were looking at both of us. And each other. Kind of like they were trying to..." He pursed his lips, and then he met my gaze. "Sooner or later, someone's going to figure us out."

My heart dropped. "Oh. So I guess we should... uh..." Fuck. What *was* the answer? Stay farther apart in public? Be even more careful about how we interacted? Scrutinize every word we said so no one—

"Maybe it's time to stop hiding."

I blinked. "What?"

"Our teammates know. Our families know." With a shrug and a crooked but cautious smile, he added, "Why keep hiding it?"

Lips parting, I stared at him. "You want to come out? Publicly?"

That smile. Oh my God.

"Yes," he whispered. "I do."

Oh. Wow. My heart was no longer in the pit of my stomach and instead fluttered behind my ribs. "How, um... How do you want to do this?"

His lips quirked. Then he took out his phone. "I have an idea."

He wrapped his arm around my shoulders and held out the phone with the screen in selfie mode. It was a perfectly benign shot—two teammates smiling together. He snapped it, but instead of letting me go, he said, "Let's get one more."

Like I was going to say no to a selfie with my ridiculously hot boyfriend. I kind of felt like one of the fans downstairs, but in that moment, I really didn't care.

Still holding the phone out, he turned to me. "Isaac."

Without thinking, I turned.

And Julien's lips met mine.

And the camera snapped again.

It gave me a rush, knowing there was a picture in existence —on his phone, no less—of the two of us kissing. It was nothing that would cause a scandal if it got out. Nothing inappropriate. But a photo now existed of a kiss between me and Julien.

Julien broke that kiss and lowered his phone. He looked at the photos with a gorgeous grin on his lips, and then he showed them to me. "All right if I post these?"

"Both of them?"

He nodded.

I looked at both. God, that second one was hot. My heart raced. We were really doing this. We were putting them out there for all to see. Once we did, there was no taking it back. Was I sure about that? Really, really sure?

Yes. Fuck yes, I was. I'd been dying to tell the whole world about this amazing man who had somehow become my boyfriend, and why the hell should we wait another second?

I handed back the phone. "Do it."

"Yeah?"

I grinned. "Oui."

Julien huffed a soft laugh. Then he focused on his screen. As he typed, he was grinning from ear to ear, looking ridiculously adorable. Even a little shy. "And...done." He tapped the screen emphatically and met my gaze. "We're out."

Heart pounding, I picked up my own phone. There was an Instagram notification. He'd tagged me in a post. I knew he had, but seeing the notification definitely made it real. Oh. Wow. We *were* out. That was thrilling and terrifying and kind of made me choke up because...because people knew. We didn't have to hide anymore.

Hands a little shakier than I expected, I opened the app. He'd posted both pictures, which I'd expected. The smiling teammates selfie, of course, and the second...oh Lord, that was going to be my lockscreen.

And then I read the caption:

*Bonne fête, Isaac. Mon coéquipier. Mon ami. Mon amour.*

My French was still woefully limited, but I recognized some of those words. Didn't I? Was I reading them wrong? Or was he...?

I swallowed, my heart going wild as I tapped *See Translation*. The words on the screen shifted to English.

*Happy birthday, Isaac. My teammate. My friend. My love.*

I stared up at him, and the blush on his cheeks almost made me swoon. "Julien..."

He touched my face. "Now the whole world knows. And so do you." Drawing me in, he whispered, "I love you, Isaac."

I tossed my phone aside and had to wrap my arms around his neck to keep from melting to the floor. As I pressed my lips to his, he held me tight against him, and I didn't think I'd ever been happier than I was in that moment. We weren't hiding anymore. We weren't a secret. And not only that, Julien loved me. He'd said the words out loud. Said them to the entire world.

I drew back enough to speak, and my voice was thick as I said, "I love you too."

He grinned against my lips just before he claimed another kiss, and I swore his whole body relaxed against mine. No, it was more than that. Relief came off him in waves, and I didn't think it was because we'd finally blown the lid off our secret. It was as if he'd been afraid of how *I'd* respond.

Which... Could I blame him? My God, he'd put his neck out there. Publicly. That was heady anyway, but from a man who'd been through what he had—from someone whose emotions had been someone else's plaything for so long—it had to have been terrifying, and it was exhilarating to know he felt safe enough with me to lay himself bare like that. That he was *so sure* of his feelings and of what we had, he'd done the equivalent of a center ice proposal despite the very recent reminder of someone who'd bled him dry.

He wasn't fearless. He had reasons to be afraid. He'd been burned and bitten before.

But he'd done it anyway.

For me.

"Jesus, Julien..." I whispered unsteadily. "I love you so much."

He held me even tighter and kissed me again.

From the dresser where it had landed, my phone pinged with a text. Then his did. A moment later, mine did, only it was three messages in rapid succession. Before those had finished going off, his phone rang.

Julien broke the kiss with a laugh. I couldn't help chuckling too.

"Guess people are starting to see it," he murmured, still laughing.

"Ya think?" I kissed him again, though it was hard when I couldn't keep a straight face. And I wasn't going to keep a straight face as long as our phones kept going off. "Should we shut them off?"

"Mmm, no." He held me tighter and nudged me toward the bed. "That means stopping."

"It does, but—"

One of the phones pinged again. Then his ringtone started up again. The generic one, I thought.

We both collapsed into laughter. He buried his face against my neck, his whole body vibrating.

"Okay. Okay." He drew back and brushed a few strands of hair out of his face. "Let's turn them off."

"Good idea."

We separated and quickly silenced the stupid devices. Then I turned to him and grinned as I hooked a finger in the knot of my tie. "While we're at it..." I nodded sharply at him. "Get all of that out of the way."

Julien blinked, as if caught off guard by the order. It only tripped him up for a second, though—he quickly started shedding that gorgeous suit, which he dutifully hung up before tucking his shoes neatly in the closet.

"Nicely done." I wrapped an arm around his waist after we'd both stripped, and I slid my hand up the middle of his bare chest. "Anything worthy of being on this body deserves to be taken care of."

Julien chuckled, curved a hand behind my neck, and kissed me. We stumbled toward the bed, half-kissing and half-laughing, but as we sank onto the mattress where we'd slept last night, we were all business. Breathing hard. Kissing harder. Hands sliding all over each other's skin.

I knew Julien's body like I knew my own. I knew *us*. But everything felt different this time. It was like the secrecy had been keeping an extra layer between us, and now that layer was gone. We were out, we were in love, and now every touch and every kiss seemed…more. More real? More open? I didn't know. Just… *more*.

"Isaac…" He squirmed under me as I kissed along the side of his throat.

"Hmm?" I nipped his shoulder, making him moan. Then I came up so we were looking at each other. "Tell me what you want."

He licked his swollen lips. "I want you to fuck me like you always do, but…" He grimaced. "The skills competition…"

Oh, right. He was in the backwards skating competition. Not a good time for his ass to be sore.

"I can still fuck you if you want me to. Just…not so hard you'll be hurting tonight."

He moaned with a mix of arousal and protest. "But I *like* it when you fuck me that hard."

Laughing, I shrugged. "And I *will* fuck you that hard. Later."

Julien bit his lip.

Grinning down at him, I slipped into that commanding voice that always turned him on so much. "Tell me what you want."

He shivered under me. "The same thing I always want —you."

"You have me." I kissed him lightly. "Question is, what do you want me to do? Fuck you? Suck you off?"

"Fuck me." He slid his hands up my chest. "God, Isaac. *Please* fuck me."

"Even with the skills—"

"*Yes.*"

I considered it, then grinned. "Hmm, I did tell you I was going to top you nice and slowly one of these days, didn't I?"

His eyes widened with alarm.

I grinned even bigger. "No time like the present, is there?" Before he could respond, I pushed myself up and off him. "Get me a condom and some lube."

He didn't hesitate, scrambling toward his suitcase. When he came back though, he *did* hesitate. "Um…"

"What?"

"We, uh…" His gaze was fixed on the condom in his hand. Then he met my eyes. "The league tested us both for everything under the sun before the season started. I haven't…" A hint of a blush bloomed in his cheeks, and he shook his head slowly. "I haven't touched anyone since then. No one but you."

I watched him, trying to follow where he was going. Then I glanced at the still-wrapped condom, and the piece clicked into place.

And my God…the trust. As much as he'd been burned in the past, I hadn't wanted to suggest abandoning condoms until I knew he was ready. I'd trusted him from the get-go, and I hadn't touched anyone else either, but with Julien's history, this had to be his choice. He had to initiate it.

Now, he was.

I moved closer to him, gently plucked the square from between his fingers, and tossed it on the nightstand. I'd barely turned back to him again before he wrapped his arms around me and kissed me deep and hard.

Oh yeah. It was on. And I was going to fuck him bareback? Yes, yes, *yes*.

"Turn over," I panted. "I need to… God, I want you right now."

He didn't keep me waiting. He turned onto his stomach, and after I'd teased him open with my slicked-up fingers, I guided my cock to him. No barrier this time, and...oh, hell. It was perfect. So hot and sexy and overwhelming. I hadn't even realized how much the condoms muted the sensation, and my arms shook under me as I tried to stay in control. I'd barely pressed into him and I already wanted to come.

Not yet, though. I was going to enjoy this. Every second of it. Every stroke.

And we were going to take it *slow*.

There'd been so many times where I'd taken him hard and fast, and I'd slowed down when discretion called for it, but this time... Oh, fuck. This time, we could make all the noise we wanted, but I rocked in and out as slowly as I could, core muscles quivering with the exertion of staying this slow. This controlled. Every stroke took ages.

And it was more than the need to be gentle so he wouldn't be sore tonight. I'd wanted him like this since forever. Slow, and perfect—savoring every slide of my cock in and out of his gorgeous ass, especially now that there was nothing between us. Holding him close. Moving with him. Breathing with him. All the hunger and need that we brought into bed every single time, but restrained. Reined in while I just...*felt* him. Felt us. Lost myself in the heat and the intimacy and the overwhelming certainty that I could move literal mountains if I thought that would make this man happy.

We fell into a rhythm together, his hips rolling exactly right to complement mine. He wasn't trying to drive me on or urge me to fuck him faster—just moving with me. Taking me. Gasping and cursing in both languages as I rode him slower than I ever had before.

"Isaac," he whispered. "Isaac, please..."

"I know this won't get you off," I whispered unsteadily. "I know you need...I know. But..." I sucked in a breath as a shudder ran through me, and then I brushed his hair aside and kissed the back of his neck. "God, baby, let me feel you like this. I'll...I will so make it worth your while."

He pushed out a ragged breath. "It already is."

"Are you—"

"Don't stop," he begged. "More."

Oh, I didn't want to stop, and I absolutely wanted more. Including Julien's talented mouth. I pulled out and sat back on my heels. "Turn over."

He hesitated, but then he did, rolling onto his back, and when our eyes met, my breath hitched.

Tears ran down his face. Alarm shot through me. It wasn't unusual at all for him to cry when we had sex, but that was when things were rough and painful. This was...not.

"Hey." I caught a tear with my thumb and brushed it away. "You all right?"

He nodded as he shakily swiped at his eyes. "Oui. Yeah. I'm..." He closed his eyes, squeezing another tear free.

My heart pounded. "Should I stop? We can—"

"No." He shook his head and looked up at me with wide, wet eyes. "Don't stop."

"Are you sure?"

Julien nodded again, running trembling fingers through my hair. "I don't know if I can handle it, but...please, don't stop."

I hesitated, wondering if now was one of those moments when I needed to take charge and gently insist that I didn't want to overwhelm him. If he was trying to push through, whether out of fear of upsetting me or sheer stubbornness, refusing to admit he was hanging on by his fingernails.

He cupped my cheek and gazed up at me with pleading eyes. "Isaac. Please. I want this."

I held his gaze, searching for any hesitation, but all I found was need.

Without a word, I came down between his thighs, and I guided myself to him, and he closed his eyes and whimpered as I pushed in with a long, slow stroke.

"This good?" Fuck, I was out of breath.

Eyes still shut, he nodded, arching under me. "Oui." He mumbled something else in French, and I had no idea what the words were, but his shaky, plaintive voice told me everything I needed to know.

I found a steady rhythm again, rocking in and out of him just as slowly as I had from behind. "Oh God. You feel…" I struggled to find breath, never mind words. "You feel so good, Julien."

He murmured in French. Paused. Then, as if he'd realized I didn't know the words, he said, "You feel amazing."

I looked in his eyes. He looked in mine. Jesus, he was so beautiful. So utterly gorgeous and focused on me as if no one and nothing else existed in his world. The same way no one and nothing else existed in mine.

He licked his lips, carding his fingers through my hair. "Je t'aime Isaac."

I didn't need a translator app for that, and as I came down to kiss him, I whispered, "I love you too."

Julien smiled that sweet, amazing smile that always left me in a daze, and then he drew me all the way down into that kiss. We kissed. We moved together. We held each other. This was nothing like any sex we'd had before, and I never wanted it to end.

It wasn't going to last forever, though. I wasn't going to. I was too turned on. Too hungry for him. Too close to that exhilarating precipice I'd only ever been to with Julien.

"Do you want me to come like this?" I panted. "Without a condom?"

Julien nodded, eyes full of emotion as he gazed up at me. "Yes."

Any other time, I'd have made him beg for it. And maybe some other time, I would. But today had been a roller coaster for him, and he was already beyond wrung out, and this wasn't the time for it. We could play games later. All I wanted to do now was give him anything he wanted and everything he needed.

"Touch yourself," I ordered. "I want to feel—oh, God, yeah..." I let my head fall beside his as he clenched around me. Julien gasped for breath, and he grabbed on to my hair. Not hard. Not like I'd have grabbed his. But the touch and the gentle tug at my scalp gave me goose bumps, and I squeezed my eyes shut and thrust a little harder, driving moans from both of us. I was absolutely lost in everything. Sensation. Heat. Closeness. Him. My orgasm was closing in fast, and I rode that wave toward its crest, ready to lose it, ready to come in him even if the intensity promised to break me, and—

Julien cried out in French as his body jerked under mine, and the sudden tightness around my cock and the heat of his cum against my stomach drove a roar out of me, and I thrust all the way into him as I came so hard my eyes stung.

With a ragged sigh, I slumped over him, face buried against his neck as I tried to catch my breath. We'd been so slow and subdued, and yet I was winded as if we'd broken furniture like we usually did. Shaking, too.

Julien was shaking even harder than I was. Except...

No, something was different. As my mind cleared, I realized the way he was trembling didn't match the way he usually did after we'd fucked.

Despite the unsteadiness in my arms, I pushed myself up, and my heart dropped.

He had his hand over his eyes, but he couldn't hide it—he was crying. Really crying.

"Julien?" I carefully pulled out and turned on my side next

to him, draping my arm across his stomach. "What's—are you okay?"

Hand still over his face, he nodded, but he didn't speak.

My heart thundered and my stomach twisted. What was happening? Had I done something wrong? Pushed him too far?

*Come on, baby. Talk to me.*

Little by little, he pulled himself together. Finally, he pushed out a ragged breath, lifted his hand off his face, and shakily wiped at his eyes. I had no idea what to expect when he turned to me, but I definitely didn't anticipate his soft, heartfelt smile.

"I'm okay," he whispered. "It's..." He swallowed hard and gave a little self-deprecating laugh as he found my hand and laced our fingers together. "Today has been a lot."

"It has. But...has it been too much? I don't want to overwhelm you."

"You always overwhelm me." Julien brought our hands up and kissed my knuckles. "That's one of the things I love about you." He looked in my eyes again. "This isn't too much. You're not too much. It's perfect. All of it." He sniffed sharply, then exhaled. "I think that's sinking in—how perfect this is."

I was speechless, so I did the only thing I could think to do—I pulled him close and kissed him. And then I held him, and he held me. I adored this man. I'd worried for a moment that I'd hurt him or, hell, *broken* him, but no. He'd just worn on his sleeve the same emotions that were rushing through me right then.

This *was* overwhelming.

But yes, it was perfect.

And I was the luckiest man in the world.

## Chapter 26

### Julien

I didn't deserve Isaac, didn't deserve his love. But I had him and that anyway, and it was amazing. I loved him so much it hurt.

Now everyone knew.

I tried to wrap my head around the way he'd made love to me, how he'd moved so slowly inside me. Careful, tender sex wasn't something I was used to. I'd always thought I'd needed the pain and intensity, the desperation and physicality of a hard, bone-rattling fuck to get me off.

Turns out that wasn't true. All it took was love, actual love, and a partner who cared about me. The crying had worried Isaac, but that moment had been so beautiful, so *intense*, I couldn't take it all in. Even now, if I thought about it too long, tears threatened.

That had also been the first time I'd ever had sex without a condom—turned out to be a first for both of us. It was—well, a little more messy. But also a hell of a lot more sexy.

"Should we do that again?" I asked while we cleaned ourselves up.

Isaac's cheeks were ruddy. "Yeah. I—yeah." Then he got that wicked grin of his. "And I want to ride your dick raw."

That made my head spin anew. Strange to feel like a rookie again—and for a good reason rather than because of my bastard ex, but here I was—and Isaac loved me, actually loved me.

After the low of earlier, this high was almost too much to take, especially since I'd nearly forgotten Isaac's birthday. Seriously, what kind of boyfriend does that? Apparently *I* did. Tonight needed to be special. Magical. Romantic. I had no idea how I was going to pull this off.

After we ate our room service lunch (sitting around in bathrobes, because why not?), I eyed my phone with trepidation. "I'm going to need to turn that back on."

His laugh was joyous. "Me too. Let's get it over with."

So we did, and we both took some time to sort through texts and voicemails. Isaac was smiling as he scrolled through his notifications, and that lip bite was so damn cute.

My own cheeks hurt while I responded to my siblings and Elias and Nikki. We'd been tagged in a post by the team account too.

Ooof. Kelly. I texted to apologize for not giving her a heads-up. That got me a response pretty fast.

*Not a problem. Had a plan in place if you guys were outed. But your post was perfect. Happy for you two.*

Of course Kelly had a plan. She was absolutely spectacular at her job. I almost asked her for recommendations for a restaurant that I could take Isaac to tonight, but then remembered I had a food snob as a best friend.

So, another text to Elias.

*Hey, where should I take Isaac for dinner tonight for his b-day? Someplace spectacular and romantic.*

Didn't take long for him to reply.

*It's Vegas. You can't go wrong with any of the high-end places, for either food or ambiance.*

Then he listed a few places, including the restaurant in the Eiffel Tower.

*Eiffel Tower? Really?*

*Hey, the food is good, and so's the view. You wanted romantic, right?*

There was that.

*Thanks. I owe you one.*

*I'll add it to your long tab.*

I sent him the middle finger emoji.

He replied with the same one, but added, *Tell Isaac happy birthday.*

I chuckled. "Elias says happy birthday."

There was that warm smile I loved so much. He held up his phone. "Nisha says you better take me somewhere nice."

"I plan to." Then I flipped over to Nikki's number and sent him the middle finger emoji, too.

He sent me a kiss and a peach for *kiss my ass*. Then added, *Happy for you, Jules. Have fun.*

When I looked up again, Isaac was silently laughing.

"What?"

"We're two thousand miles away from them, and you guys are still giving each other shit."

"Eh, it's what we do." I gave my best flippant shrug, and Isaac fell back on the bed in silent, happy convulsions. I set my phone aside, and joined in, holding and kissing him. I could happily do that all day.

Of course, right about then, my phone went off with an alarm to tell me to get my ass ready for tonight. I wasn't ever late, and I was especially not late for games. I certainly wouldn't be late for anything this weekend.

Plus, I had a dinner reservation to make.

When I walked into our division's locker room, the whole place broke out in applause. Matti gave a loud whoop and clapped me on the shoulder. "Keeping that a big secret, huh?"

I hoped my cheeks didn't look as hot as they felt. "I mean, our team's known for a couple months, so not that much of a secret. But we figured, why not let everyone know?"

"You better be taking that man somewhere nice tonight." That came from Taylor, one of the two guys from Buffalo who'd made the All-Stars. "A birthday in Vegas?"

"Of *course* I am. What do you take me for?" I grinned, and started pulling my gear on.

Laughter all around.

Thankfully, the spotlight on me was entirely stolen when Matti's daughter ran into the room. On her heels was a boy in a Washington Riverhawks jersey.

Kids. Gotta love them. Brought a smile out on everyone in the room.

I dressed and watched the young storm of chaos take over, even passing a ball back and forth with my stick for the kids until it was time to head out onto the ice for warmups. We skated around for a bit, and I went through my normal stretches and skating to get my legs warmed up, then did another few laps around the ice, then switched to some backward work.

Travis was out here, too, for hardest shot, but I ignored him as much as I could.

Isaac was hanging out with Kelly, and our other team media folks a few rows up from the bench. He'd lost his suit jacket somewhere along the line, and gained a Griffins baseball cap. He gave me a huge smile and a nod when he noticed me, and I waved back. Then we were corralled off the ice, and to one of the Zamboni doors.

"Hey," Matti said, as we waited in line to be introduced. "Just a heads-up: Travis Canterbury was talking shit about you."

I snapped my teeth and grunted. "He's always talking shit about me. Fucking asshole."

"Right? I mean, don't get me wrong, I hate playing against you and the Griffins, but that guy?" He shook his head. "The stories I've heard. I wanted you to know. Said you're taking advantage of a younger player."

"That's rich," I muttered, then added, "I'm only five years...well, four and a half years older." Not *eleven* years older, like Travis had been.

"Yeah, everyone just looked at him and changed the subject."

Good. "Thanks, man."

Matti gave me a slap on the shoulder, then nodded. "You're up."

I skated out to my introduction and a huge roar went up in the crowd, more than I'd gotten before at an All-Star game. Always a bit surreal to look up and see yourself on the big screen, but then the camera changed.

And there was Isaac. Holy fuck. While I knew he'd be playing fan for the better part of this weekend, I hadn't expected him to be *wearing my jersey* and standing at the glass with a bunch of the other division spouses and partners. Only my momentum kept me heading toward the bench because I was frozen for a moment. Then I blinked, scanned the crowd for him, and waved.

That got me more cheers.

When I finally made it to the bench, Taylor gave me a look. "You are totally in love with that man."

Ah shit. I hadn't realized it was that easy to see. So I gave Taylor a shrug and a smile. "Yeah."

"Good for you. You've seemed a lot calmer out there." He

nodded to the ice. "Which I hate, 'cause it means you're harder to play against."

"Eh," I said. "You guys didn't do so bad last game."

"Yeah, except for that whole overtime goal from Sidorov, off your pass."

"Sorry?"

He laughed. "You are not."

I wasn't. Sure, we'd given them a point, which wasn't great in division games, but we'd gotten two, so that was fine. "What can I say, I like winning."

"Don't we all?" He looked up at the screen. "You gonna win tonight?"

I thought about the defensemen I was up against and rocked my head side to side. I was fast, to be sure, but the fastest? Skating backward? In my loopy, happy, *in love* frame of mind? "Honestly, I think it'll be Enger. Kid has good legs." He was twenty-four, played for Boston, and was having a breakout year.

"My money's on you," Taylor said.

I gave him a look. "Not *actual* money, I hope."

"God, *no*. You could blow a tire, or trip over that pretty hair of yours." He waved a gloved hand. "I'm just saying, you're gonna be the best here."

We'd find out soon. The first event was the standard fastest skater, and a speedster from the Western division won that. Then they were announcing backward skating. Thankfully, I wasn't the first up—that was Matti.

"Good luck!" I tapped my stick against the boards.

He didn't do too badly, coming in at 16.215. The next skater eeked him out at 16.197, then I was up, to more cheers from the crowd. I didn't dare look at Isaac, or I'd lose what little focus I had.

Still, I gave it everything I had. I'd always loved skating backward, and that's probably why I ended up a defenseman, even though I wasn't the biggest guy around. So when the buzzer went off, I flew—well, at least as fast as you could wheeling backward. Felt like an eternity, but when I looked up after crossing the finish line, my time read 16.132.

Well, *shit*. First place. I grinned, and headed back to the bench. When I sat, Taylor grabbed my shoulder and gave me a shake. "Doing your man proud." He nodded up to the screen, and there was Isaac again.

Then it hit me. "Wait—are we—we're a *story*?"

Matti gave me this incredulous look. "You think?"

I stared up at the screen, which now showed Enger getting into position. He was the last skater for this portion.

In a flash, it was over, and there was his time: 16.147. Both Matti and Taylor smacked me on the shoulders and back in celebration. I stood, waved to the crowd—and Isaac—then I got interviewed about my win and what I did to prepare for the event.

*Kissed my boyfriend and posted it to Instagram, then he made love to me until I cried.* I didn't say that, though. "I mean, not much? Warmed up my legs, that's all, really. I don't know if you can prep for something like that."

Was I looking forward to the game tomorrow? "Oh yeah. It's always fun to get out there and play with some guys you don't see on your side of the ice that often. Good stuff."

Then they were setting up for the next event. Hardest shot. My only hope was that Travis flubbed it. And speak of the devil...

He came skating toward our bench. Taylor gave me a look. I rolled my eyes.

"Nice job, Julie."

I stared at Travis and shrugged. "It's just skating."

"Fast skating," Taylor said.

"Backward," Matti added.

Travis laughed and patted the boards. "Nice job with the kid, too. You're really turning into me, aren't you?"

I stopped moving. Stopped breathing. By the time I could suck in air again, Travis was gone, and my brain was screaming. I *wasn't* like Travis. I wasn't using Isaac. Fuck! We were out in public, something that *never* happened during that horrible year with Travis.

*Our secret, Julie. All this just for me. No one else.* God, I could still feel his hands on me.

"Hey man, are you okay?" Taylor's hand landed on my shoulder.

I shook off the memory and swallowed the bile. "Yeah, yeah, I'm fine."

"What the fuck was that all about?" Matti looked out to where Travis stood on the ice with the other competitors.

"He's an asshole, that's all." I took a breath, then another, then chanced a look over to where Isaac had been—only he was at the glass now a couple seats down, staring at me, his lips parted and worry written all over his face.

God, I loved him. Wished he were on the bench with me. I huffed out a laugh. So not like Travis. Not at all.

Isaac smiled back, and that warmed my soul. Though when I turned to watch the hardest shot play out, I couldn't help shivering a little.

*I'm not like Travis. I'm not.* I dropped my gaze to my glove, and tipped back my hand so I could see the word written on my wrist. *Now*.

Here and now. With Isaac. Who I loved. Who loved me in return.

*Please, don't let me be like that fucker. Please.*

AFTER THE EVENTS, I took a shower to wash away the smell of hockey equipment and the stink in my mind of Travis. He'd lost the hardest shot—hadn't even broken one hundred miles an hour. Served that shit right. Then I put my suit on—the gray one Isaac loved so much—and met him outside the locker room. He was wearing his jacket again but had my All-Star jersey draped over his arm.

I cocked my head and smiled. "Do you want me to sign that for you?"

I would never tire of the crinkles he got around his eyes when he laughed. "Can I get a signed stick, too?"

"Is that what the kids are calling it these days?" Kelly muttered.

"Oooh. She's got jokes now!" I said.

Kelly batted her eyes at me. "You owe me, Lans."

Isaac choked on a laugh. "Oh, I probably owe you, too."

"You do, but he's more fun to tease." She poked me in the lapel. "You have your schedule for tomorrow?"

I pulled out my phone and brought up my calendar to show her. "Have you ever known me to be late?"

She patted my shoulder. "All right. Go have fun, boys. Happy birthday, Rivs."

"Thanks, Kel."

It took us a bit to break free of the crowds. We signed a few items, had a few selfies, and some photos taken. Got a lot of congratulations and happy birthday wishes, then we were strolling down the Strip with our badges tucked away. Isaac took my hand. "So, where are we going?"

"Paris Hotel."

He pulled me to a stop. "You're taking me to the Eiffel Tower?" His grin was a masterpiece.

"I am." I pushed a hand through my hair and tried not to sound nervous. "Is that okay?"

"Yeah, it's fine! Just...a little on the nose?" My God, he was beaming. "I mean..." He gestured at me.

"Well, yes, but it's Las Vegas. If it's not over the top, you're not doing it right." This time, he chuckled, and I pulled him into a walk again. "Besides, you can practice your French."

"Oh my God. You're going to make me work on my birthday?"

"Oui."

Isaac's laughter was music to my ears.

# Chapter 27

## Isaac

Julien wasn't kidding—the view from the Eiffel Tower Restaurant was spectacular. Sitting at our intimate table by one of the picture windows, we had the Bellagio fountains laid out below us, framed by Caesar's Palace in the background. The fountains were amazing. I loved water anyway—it was so peaceful and soothing—and even when the show was over and the water was quiet and calm, I could stare at it all night long.

On any other evening, I would have done exactly that.

But tonight, my view would have been the same whether we were here or seated in some dark corner of an old diner.

He was gorgeous, of course. He never *wasn't* gorgeous. Dressed in that suit, long hair perfectly arranged and a little bit of scruff dusting his jaw—oh, yeah, he was sexy as hell. As we'd crossed the restaurant to our table, my hand resting comfortably on the small of his back because *oh my God, we were out*, people had noticed. Some hockey fans, yes—you could tell by the starstruck gasps—but some who just tracked him across the room like he was the most beautiful person they'd ever seen.

They didn't know the half of it.

It still felt like a fairy tale. Julien had been every facet of the man I loved today. Sweet. Playful. Vulnerable. So ridiculously romantic he left me speechless. So sexy I could barely stand it. Then he'd been that man I'd crushed on in college—the cocky defenseman who knew he was hot shit on the ice, except he'd also found me in the crowd and melted a little, switching back to the boyfriend who'd told me he loved me. He was every fantasy I'd never let myself imagine coming true, and he was also a gentle, wounded heart who I wanted to heal and protect.

Somehow, on my twenty-third birthday—the first birthday I'd celebrated as a professional hockey player—I was at a table for two with Julien Landry, and he was gazing across the table at me...like *that*.

*How did I get so lucky?*

Julien cocked his head, lips curling into a lopsided grin. "What?"

"Hmm?" Oh. Fuck. Had I been staring? Yep. Busted. I cleared my throat as that familiar warmth rose in my face. "Nothing. Nothing. Just..." Hell, why dance around it? So, I grinned back. "Just enjoying the view."

He laughed, gaze darting away from mine. "The view everyone comes up here for is..." He motioned toward the fountain.

I shrugged. "Yeah, but I think half of them have forgotten about the fountain too." I glanced around, and oh, yeah, there were a few people sneaking surreptitious glances at the beautiful man sitting across from me.

Julien brought his water glass up to his lips. "You're supposed to watch the fountain. That way it isn't weird when I'm staring at you."

Good thing I wasn't taking a drink right then. I chuckled and rolled my eyes. "I'd say you're such a romantic dork, but that would kind of be the pot calling the kettle black, wouldn't it?"

He winked. "Oui."

We both laughed and shifted our attention to the menus. We really were being romantic dorks tonight, and I loved every second of it. My mom had asked if Julien was spoiling me rotten.

*Mom, if you could only see us now.*

Hell. Maybe she could.

I cleared my throat. "You know, we've got this amazing backdrop." I tapped my knuckle on the window. "Think we should post another selfie?"

The way his smile lit up put the Bellagio fountains to shame. "Your phone or mine?"

My phone this time. Then I sent him the image, and with his blessing, I posted it to Instagram with: *"Don't worry, Mom—he's spoiling me rotten!"*

When he read the post, he gave the sweetest laugh, and he commented, *"Only the best for the man of my dreams."*

Good Lord. This man. The restaurant could have served us cardboard dinner rolls and overcooked meat, and I'd still be chalking tonight up as one of the best evenings of my life.

In the back of my mind, I did a little fist pump and mentally flipped off Travis. He'd tried to get under Julien's skin earlier. Christ, had that really been today? Yes, it had, and for a little while, he'd succeeded. But Julien had rallied, and all the tension from earlier was gone from his shoulders and his jaw. He was relaxed. He was happy. Looking at him now, no one would ever guess he had any demons, never mind that one of those demons had been tearing at him just a few hours ago.

*And there is nothing I won't do to keep you this happy.*

Dinner was, of course, amazing. No cardboard dinner rolls or overcooked meat in sight. Despite being in the desert, we split a smoked salmon appetizer that Elias had recommended, and even my Pacific Northwest salmon snobbery had to admit it was to die for. He'd also recommended a few wines, and I'd deferred to Julien since I wasn't much of a connoisseur. I couldn't have remembered or pronounced the name to save my life, but it was damn good.

We both had steaks, and fuck it, it was my birthday—we added half a Maine lobster tail apiece. Then I had the Eiffel Tower Soufflé with pistachio, which had me questioning for a few minutes if I was actually dead and this was heaven. Julien went for the crème brulée, the first bite of which drew a sound out of him that made me think highly inappropriate thoughts.

Julien paid the bill, tipping our server generously, and we headed out into the cool evening. I was mildly disappointed that dinner was over, but it was hard to feel too sad when I had Julien's arm around my shoulders as we strolled along the Strip. Though I'd worried at first about us being publicly affectionate, given that we were two guys, no one who noticed us had seemed bothered by it as we'd walked to the restaurant earlier. Now, I was feeling too good and might've had a little too much wine to really care, though I did stay as vigilant as any gay man had to with a partner in public. Such was life.

As we started past the Bellagio fountains, I noticed a lot of people were crowding against the railing.

"Think the show is about to start?" I asked.

"Probably. It runs every fifteen minutes this time of night." He paused. "Do you want to watch?"

We'd watched it a few times from our table, but...yeah. I did want to watch now that we were down here. He wouldn't mind, would he?

Before I could answer, he gently steered me into a gap in the crowd, right up to the concrete railing. Then he wrapped his arms around my waist.

"It's water," he murmured. "I don't even need to ask if you want to watch."

I twisted around slightly. "How... Wait, how did you know that?"

Julien laughed and pressed a soft kiss to my cheek. "Did you think I didn't notice?"

"Uh. Yeah. Actually." As I faced the dormant fountain, I laughed, though I wasn't sure why. "I didn't think it was that obvious."

"Maybe not to most people." He nuzzled my hair. "But I notice things about you. The fountain. The apartment overlooking the river. It's not hard to see." I had a split second to be a little embarrassed and wonder if he thought I was weird because of the way I was always drawn to water, but then he murmured, "Why do you think we walked this way?"

That was when I realized our hotel was in the opposite direction. That I'd been so blissed out and happy, I hadn't even batted an eye when he'd led me this way instead of toward our hotel.

"You know me so well."

His lips curved against my cheek.

Before either of us could say anything, the fountains came to life with bright lights, the roar of water rushing upward, and loud music coming from unseen speakers. The show had been cool from up in the Eiffel Tower, but it was so much more impressive down here. The water seemed to shoot higher. The rows of jets seemed to stretch farther. I was absolutely mesmerized, watching the water dancing in the warm light while I was wrapped in my boyfriend's arms. The whole thing brought me a sense of calm and peace I didn't think I'd ever known before. It was as if, even if it was only for a few minutes, everything in my world was perfect.

All too soon, the lights dimmed and music faded away. The water calmed to a gentle trickle and quietly lapped against the pool's edge.

Still holding me, Julien kissed the side of my neck and whispered, "Bonne fête, mon amour."

"Merci." I turned around in his arms and gazed up at him. Though the fountain lights had gone down, there was no such thing as complete darkness in this city, and there was just enough light to illuminate his face. The warmth in his eyes and his smile... God, I really was the luckiest man alive.

I touched his cheek, then lifted my chin for a kiss. There were people moving past us, the foot traffic picking up now that the show was over, but right here in this spot, the world was completely still and quiet.

Through the noise, I thought I heard a camera snap. Maybe it was pointed at us. Maybe it wasn't. If it ended up online somewhere, oh well. Let people look.

I drew back and met Julien's gaze. His eyes were full of the same serenity I felt after this evening and watching the fountain. It was just... Everything was perfect. Absolutely perfect.

*Is it too much to ask for this to last forever?*

---

THE NEXT DAY was the All-Star tournament. There were four divisions—Southern, Midlands, Western, and our division, Eastern—and the winners of the first two games would compete in a third for the overall title. The games consisted of two ten-minute periods of three-on-three play, so they'd be fairly quick.

First up, Eastern against Southern.

Sitting in the stands with some of the other spouses and partners, I was admittedly nervous about this game. Not because the Southern division had won three years in a row and was predicted to again, but because of who was on that team.

As the first lines came out for the faceoff, I gritted my teeth.

Flanked by a winger from Miami and a defenseman from Atlanta, there he was—Travis Canterbury.

Julien wasn't on the ice yet. He was on the edge of the bench, fidgeting like he always did when he was itching to play. A minute or so into the action, the shift changed, and he was halfway across the ice before the center and winger had even finished swinging their legs over the boards.

The game was intense as hell. Not that I expected a boring game when each team was comprised of the best players throughout the league, but everyone playing this round wanted it, and they wanted it bad. Southern was determined to hold on to their title. Eastern was determined to yank it away. And seriously, who wanted to get eliminated in the first round of a tournament, even if it only had two rounds?

Eastern scored first with a beautiful shot from New York's star winger, and Southern answered with *three* goals in rapid succession. East scored again, but the Southern coach challenged it. After review, it was ruled off-sides, and the point was dropped from the board. Not a disaster, but not great for morale either.

By the end of the first period, despite strong playing on both sides, Southern had a solid two-point lead. Julien looked pissed. He hated losing anyway. When Travis was on the ice? Oh, boy.

The second period brought with it fresh netminders for both sides, and that alone started to turn the tide. Washington's goalie could be an absolute sieve sometimes, but when he brought his A-game, he was a brick wall to end all brick walls.

He'd brought his A-game today.

Southern pelted him with shot after shot, but he wasn't letting anything through. Hell, one of Southern's wingers crashed into him by accident, and even *he* didn't get past the goal line.

At the other end of the ice, Atlanta's star goalie was holding his own...sort of. He made some amazing stops, but then the puck got past him, and by sheer dumb luck, hit the crossbar and bounced. No goal, but it was enough to screw with his confidence. With some goalies, that didn't take much, and with one ping of puck on metal, the netminder was off his game.

Eastern took *full* advantage.

Two goals in a row tied up the score. Then Southern cranked up the heat and managed a few shots, but none of them went in.

A pass flew over everyone's heads toward a player in a perfect position to score. Out of nowhere, Julien jumped straight up, caught the puck in midair, dropped it to the ice, and skated like hell toward the other goal. The other goal that was completely unprotected except for the rattled netminder.

My entire section was on our feet, all of us roaring, "Go! Go!"

One of the opposing players was on his heels, but he wasn't close enough. The goalie shifted right to left, trying to anticipate where Julien would shoot.

I genuinely thought Julien was going to fake like he often did, then knock it in after the netminder had reacted. Turned out, he didn't need to—apparently he saw an opening, and he chipped it in just past the goalie's left skate.

My section went *wild*. Julien pumped his stick in the air, and his teammates nearly bowled him over. Eastern had taken the lead, and if they could keep this momentum going, they could knock Southern out of the running before they'd even had a chance to defend their title.

Tina, one of the spouses, elbowed me and pointed at the screen above center ice.

I looked up, and...

Oh my God. *Really?*

The camera was fixed right on me.

Below that:

*Pittsburgh Griffins Center Isaac Rivera.*
*Julien Landry's boyfriend.*

My face had to be brighter than the goal light, but I smiled and waved, trying not to die as a collective "aww" went up all around the stadium.

One of the other spouses tapped my shoulder. "You guys are so cute."

I chuckled. "Thanks."

Right then, Julien, still beaming from his goal, skated past me and waved. I returned it.

"So cute," said a chorus of voices around me.

If there were any negative reactions to us, I sure as hell couldn't hear them. I did see one, though.

During the excitement, Southern had done a line change. Travis was on the ice now, and he was not happy. He shot daggers out his eyes at Julien, who ignored him.

Then Travis said something. Julien glared at him and fired something back that clearly didn't improve his ex's mood. I was actually kind of surprised Travis didn't snap his stick over his knee or something, but he wisely focused on the faceoff instead.

Fuck that guy.

I just silently prayed that Julien kept his head together. The game still had four minutes to go, and a lot could happen in that time. With so few men on the ice, no one could afford to lose their focus.

Julien's shift ended, so at least he had a breather. A moment later, Travis's did too, and as he skated past Eastern's bench on the way to his own, he quite clearly said something to Julien. Even from this far away, I could feel

Julien's hackles go up. The pissed-off cat energy was unmistakable.

Fortunately, another player put a hand on Julien's arm and spoke to him, and whatever he said seemed to bring Julien back down to earth. He exhaled. Then he looked at his teammate and nodded.

I exhaled. Oh, thank God.

The game went on at breakneck speed, Eastern clinging to (and trying to widen) their lead. Southern was *determined* to get that puck into our net and tie things up, and with a minute and a half to go, they succeeded. The arena was absolutely alive with energy as people cheered for their respective side, and both teams raced the clock to snatch the lead.

Twenty seconds.

Fifteen seconds.

Julien passed the puck to one of his guys.

Twelve seconds.

The player caught it on his stick. Went for the goal.

Eight seconds.

He faked.

Six seconds.

Passed.

Four seconds.

The third man on the line fired a slapshot at the net.

Two seconds.

*Goal*.

My voice was going to be raw from shouting, but I didn't care. My section cheered, and the Eastern players high-fived and hugged.

I didn't usually gloat over other teams looking defeated. I'd been there. It sucked.

But I didn't feel too bad about enjoying the absolute fury on Travis's face.

Because seriously.

Fuck that guy.

---

AFTER THE MIDLANDS-WESTERN game (which Western won), there was a show by some band I didn't care to see. It would be like half an hour long, and I needed something to drink anyway, so I slipped out of the stands and into the crowded corridor. Every concession stand had a line, but whatever. There was time.

I was just stepping into one of the lines when someone called out, "Hey, Rivs!" I looked around and quickly found the source of the voice—my old friend Chad Weyland. I'd bumped into him yesterday at the rookie shindig, but we'd been getting dragged in separate directions and hadn't had time to talk.

"Oh, hey!" I held out my hand for a half-handshake, half-hug. "How've you been, man?"

"I'm..." His smile faltered a bit as he let me go, but he shrugged it away. "It's been an adjustment, you know? The big leagues."

"Yeah, I hear that. Your team's doing great this season, though."

Smile still half-hearted, he shrugged. "Don't know how much I'm contributing to that, but..."

"Eh, I know the feeling. How are you liking living there?"

"It's not bad." The smile livened up slightly. "Charlotte's nice."

Right. Carolina. My stomach lurched. Travis Canterbury's team. Ugh. "How's um—how's that going? Your team seem like a good crew." I wasn't lying—the rest of the roster were, as far as I knew, perfectly decent guys.

Weyland slid his hands into his pockets and shrugged again. "They're good. It's just a lot of pressure, you know?"

He chuckled and gave me a playful punch to the shoulder. "Looks like *you're* getting along with one of your teammates." He was clearly trying to keep the comment light and friendly, but he sounded vaguely uncomfortable, which was odd. Weyland was straight, but I'd never known him to take issue with queer players. He'd been practically joined at the hip with his university team's backup goalie, who was out and proud.

I laughed, trying not to let on that I'd noticed his discomfort. "Yeah, that was, uh... That was unexpected. But it's been good. Julien's a great guy, and the whole team has been awesome. I'm really happy where I landed."

"Good. Good." He nodded subtly and glanced around. "Hey, I gotta run, but I wanted to say hi. We should catch up sometime."

"Definitely." I paused, then cautiously added, "Maybe when you guys are in Pittsburgh? The offer still stands for a beer."

Another half-hearted smile, and he couldn't quite look me in the eye as he said, "Yeah, maybe. We'll see." He met my gaze this time, and the smile seemed a bit more genuine. "It was good to see you, though. We'll talk soon!"

"Yeah. Talk soon."

We shook hands, and Weyland disappeared into the crowd. The exchange had left an odd taste in my mouth, but I tried to shake it off. From the time we were kids, Weyland had always been very by-the-book. In his mind "it's not against the rules, just frowned upon" meant "it's against the fucking rules." So, yeah, me dating a teammate probably sounded weird to him. Like I was playing with fire or something.

Maybe during the off season, we could reconnect, and I'd feel him out a bit more. It was hard to get a bead on someone when your only interactions were either on the ice or between moments of chaos at media events.

I felt bad for him that he was struggling so hard to adjust

to life in the big leagues. It was a big adjustment. It was hard. I'd been extremely fortunate to land not only Julien, but also Nisha and Elias, who'd taken me under their wings both on and off the ice. Especially with a dickstain like Travis on his team, I really hoped Weyland had a teammate or two who did the same for him.

The concession line crawled forward. As I waited, I caught up on some texts. Julien had sent a few, of course, though he was getting ready for the final game now. My mom and Darian had both gushed about last night's restaurant selfie. I must have had ten different texts from people who'd seen me on the screen after Julien's goal, which answered the question of whether that had been broadcast or was only visible to people in the arena. Couldn't say I minded.

I was writing out a text to Nisha—who'd been talking trash, because of course he was—when someone else appeared beside me.

A flat, unreadable voice said, "You're Isaac Rivera, aren't you?"

I looked up, and my throat constricted. As I clumsily pocketed my phone, I tried to play it cool. "I am. Why?"

Travis Canterbury, dressed in a suit instead of his game gear, looked me up and down. Then he grunted and nodded sharply. "Now that I see you up close? Yeah. I'm not surprised. You seem like his type." He smirked and stepped closer, encroaching on my space enough to set off alarm bells in my head. "I can say a lot about him, but the man's got good taste."

My skin crawled. I wanted to back away. Hell, *run* away. Instead, I stood my ground and glared up at him, not sure whether to challenge him or roll my eyes and ignore him. How much of a scene did I really want to make in a room full of camera phones?

But he didn't give me a chance to respond. "Landry—he's

using you, you know. That's all he's ever done." He inched closer, moving *well* beyond the edge of my comfort zone. "What a kid like you needs is a *real* man. You know..." He actually winked. "Someone who knows what he's doing? Because once that idiot's done with you, he's going to—"

"Oh, my God—*there* you are!" Someone I'd never seen before in my life appeared beside me and grabbed my arm. "We have to go! We're late to the media scrum!"

"The media—" *He's pulling you away from Travis—don't question it!* "Oh. Shit! That's today?"

"Yes, and they're looking for you." He gestured at my clothes. "You still have to get dressed. Come on!"

And just like that, this stranger was hauling me away from the concession line and from Travis Canterbury. The asshole called after us, but his voice was lost to the crowd and the pounding of my heart. Confused and relieved, I followed this guy through the crowd until he showed a pass to an usher and we were let into an empty hallway.

As soon as the door had shut behind us, he stopped and faced me. "I'm sorry." His shoulders dropped. "I just... I don't know. The way he looked coming out of the locker room, he was on a mission, and that's never a good thing. I followed him, and I saw the way he was looking at you, and..." Shaking his head, he looked toward the door again before meeting my gaze with apologetic but earnest eyes. "Watch out for Canterbury."

I swallowed, still completely confused. "I, um... Yeah. Yeah, I got that impression." The scene replayed in my head a couple of times, and I studied this stranger. Now that I really had a look at him, he was a hockey player. I'd seen his face before, though I couldn't put my finger on who he was or where he played. Midlands division, I thought, especially since his hair was damp like he'd showered recently. Okay, so all that explained how he'd recognized me, but now I had even *more* questions. "Do you know him or something?"

He avoided my gaze. "I saw the way he was looking at you, and…" Another shake of his head. "You're a young player. Exactly his type. You, uh… You don't want a piece of that."

He didn't give me a chance to parse his comment or ask any further—he brushed past me, stepped through the doors, and disappeared into the crowd.

For a long moment, I stood there in the empty hallway, wondering what in God's name had just happened. Travis's sleazy fuckery seemed kind of on-brand for him based on what I'd gleaned from Julien and everyone else, but some stranger showing up and intervening? That was…weird.

A knot formed in the pit of my stomach. I still didn't fully understand what had gone down between Julien and Travis. I understood precious little of it, really, and I wouldn't ask until Julien was damn good and ready to tell me. I didn't even know if I should tell him about this encounter. I didn't want to lie to him, by omission or otherwise, but how much would it freak him out? Fuck. I didn't know what to do. I might need to get some advice from Elias or Nisha before I broached this with Julien. That felt skeevy and backhanded, but what the hell else was I supposed to do?

And regardless of how little he'd told me about his past with Travis, some pieces were starting to fall together on their own. They were impossible to miss, and each time another one clicked into place, more questions arose. More horror sank deep into the pit of my stomach.

I stared at the place my nameless rescuer had been standing.

*What did he do to you?*
*And what in God's name did he do to Julien?*

# Chapter 28

## Julien

We won the All-Star championship game, which I hadn't expected, since the Western division team was stacked with future Hall of Fame players. Winning against the best two players in the world when they were playing side by side rather than against each other? We kept our heads, though. Played strong, had fun, and we got rewarded with goals and saves.

Afterward was a blur of happy chirping with the guys I'd soon be playing against, then a media scrum, then talking to and signing things for fans. At some point, Isaac materialized nearby, and I immediately felt centered and calm. Somewhere in the back of my mind, a voice whispered *you're using him*, but I shut that down. Fuck Travis. He'd been at me the entire previous game, and even after. I hated his voice, hated that it was still in my head after all these years.

I *loved* Isaac. I would do anything for him. And he loved me.

On the walk back to the hotel, he wrapped an arm around my waist. "What are you going to do with your share of the prize money?"

I hadn't thought about it, but I knew exactly what I'd spend it on the instant he asked. "I'm putting in a pool in the yard. One of those stone ones, with a big waterfall."

He pulled me to a stop and stared at me.

I continued babbling. "A hot tub, too, but that'll be right by the house. I should have put one in, ages ago."

People flowed around us. Isaac kept staring. "You're putting in a pool with a waterfall."

"Yes."

"For me?"

I couldn't help the grin forming on my lips. "Oui."

Isaac reeled me in and kissed me. Hard. Right there on the street. I was so startled, I squeaked.

He broke the kiss, grabbed my hand, and tugged me back into a stride. "Let's go. I have plans for you."

Apparently, those plans involved being slammed against the wall of our hotel room, undressed, then fucked without mercy pretty much all over the room, in as many ways as Isaac could manage. My orgasm was sharp, vicious, and perfect. I was in tears by the end, and Isaac was a picture of smugness. Then he laid me out on the bed and tenderly made love to me until I was sobbing again, for entirely different reasons.

I couldn't get enough of him. I never wanted this to end.

Once I could move and think again, we cleaned up and crawled into bed. I snuggled close, my head on Isaac's chest, and one leg thrown over his. He traced his fingers idly over the firebird on my hip. "Your ink is beautiful."

"A compliment to my artist." I paused. "I'd meant to get a griffin, for the team, but after my third year, that was more appropriate. Rising from my ashes, and all that." I shifted slightly so I could look down at the tattoo. "Took three sessions. She was shocked that I wanted such a large piece for my first tattoo, but after that third year…" I huffed out a dark laugh. Despite everything Travis had planted in my head, despite him targeting me on the ice, I'd won the award for best defenseman, putting up a goal total I still hadn't eclipsed, though I'd gotten more points every season since. "I wanted to remember it." There was the proof that I wasn't the awful, shitty player Travis had said I was. Still said I am.

Isaac's fingers danced over my skin, and his lips brushed my forehead. "You've always been private about your tattoos. Thank you for telling me that."

I tilted my head up for a kiss on the lips. "None of it's secret, per se. But honestly, people should be able to figure out some of it. Like my sleeve. I've seen so many theories, but the answer is right there." I rotated my arm slightly. "Just...look."

Isaac sat up, so I propped myself up on my other arm, and let him examine the ink that covered my shoulder to my wrist. There was a twining pattern of branches with maple and birch leaves, plus the occasional blue iris. In between, as if sheltering in the foliage, were images. Animals, birds, and the like, plus the one symbol that should've given the whole scheme away: three crowns.

Isaac furrowed his brow, tipped his head, then sat up a little straighter. "Wait..." He brushed a finger over the brown bear lumbering between the branches. "Is this...this is for Nisha."

I nodded.

"Oh, of course." He touched the crowns. "The three crowns for Sweden. That's Elias." Then he studied the rest of the arm. "Rose for your niece Rose?"

I grinned. "You've got it." All of the others were my family, and I named them for Isaac. The owl for my brother. The wildcat for my sister. A fish for my father. The sun for my mother. An eagle for Lea. A robin for Louis. A rabbit for Josephine. A shooting star for Brian.

"And you have room, too."

Blank spaces that had yet to be filled. "Plus my shoulder and back, if needed."

He continued to draw over the designs with his finger, and I closed my eyes in delight. To be touched like this—gently. Out of closeness. I craved moments like this, even more than riotous sex.

"Do you plan on having kids?"

The quiet question took me by surprise, and I blinked my eyes open. Isaac's brows were furrowed again, but that wasn't concern there—only curiosity.

"I don't know," I answered honestly. "I get such joy from my sib's kids, but the thought of raising my own...that's daunting." I huffed a deprecating laugh. "I don't do the greatest job of taking care of myself, after all."

Isaac snorted. "You don't do so badly."

"Says the man who keeps calming me down when I'm about to break apart." I cupped his cheek. "I'm not the most together of people."

"You're a hockey player." His smile was all quirk and light. He pecked me on the lips.

I laughed. "What about you?"

"Never thought about it. I guess it would depend on my partner."

Which could mean me, or could mean someone else entirely. We loved each other, yes. But was that enough to sustain this, considering how much of a burden me and my mind were?

Isaac turned my hand so my palm faced up. "What about this?" He ran his thumb over the word inked at the base of my wrist.

"That's me," I said, my voice a whisper. "Now."

His gaze met mine, and held.

"Sometimes the past consumes me. Eats me alive." That

was the closest I'd ever come to confessing how fucked up I was from Travis. "And when I peer too far into the future—" I shook my head. "I become paralyzed. I have to be here, now, or I won't survive."

For a third time, Isaac's brows furrowed, but this time he pulled me into a hug. "I wish I could show you how strong you are. How good you are."

I grunted. Sometimes I thought I was, other times—well. Other times, I was a nervous, weeping mess, so I suppose that answered that.

Right now, when I thought about the future, I saw Isaac there. I saw a crashing wave in one of those blank spaces on my arm. I knew, without a doubt, I deserved none of that. My past wouldn't allow it. Even the *now* was tainted by Travis.ABruptly, I was back at the arena, a moment I'd tried to forget fresh in my mind.

> *Travis grabbing me by the arm outside the locker room between games at the All-Stars. Slamming me against the wall. "You manipulative bastard." He leans in, breath hot on my face. "You don't love him. You're incapable of love."*
> 
> *Not being able to breathe staring into those eyes again, so close. Not again.*
> 
> *Matti pulling him off. "What the hell is wrong with you? Get the fuck out of here, you asshole."*

"Julien?" Alarm in Isaac's voice.

Shit. I rubbed my eyes. "Sorry. I think the games—and everything else—is catching up with me." My heart slammed in my chest, and I blinked back the tears that wanted to form.

*Now.*

I knew who I was. I wrapped my arms around Isaac and held on. I loved him, no matter what Travis said.

Didn't I?

After a time, he opened space between us, and I stared into those eyes. "Do you want to talk about it?"

God, no. "Not tonight." I gave him as much of a smile as I could manage. "Like I said, sometimes looking backward or forward is overwhelming. It's probably why I'm good at hockey. Have to live in the present."

He cupped my face and ghosted his thumbs over my stubble. "Thank you for sharing so much of yourself with me."

"You deserve more." Because he did.

He kissed me. "We have time. A whole bunch of nows. It'll be all right."

How did I end up with this absolute beauty of a man?

Isaac nudged my shoulder. "Let's turn off the light. Get some sleep. You're definitely crashing. I bet everything will look better in the morning."

---

MORNING CAME, and Isaac was right. I felt a hell of a lot better mentally and emotionally after a decent night's sleep. We lazed in bed, then had a leisurely brunch at one of the other places Elias had recommended. The rest of the day was spent sightseeing—the Mob Museum, the Fremont Street Experience, the outsides of the casinos.

At the Luxor, Isaac paused. "Would you mind if we went in for a little bit?"

I gazed at him, trying to understand his concern. "Why would I mind?"

"Casinos are designed to be a sensory overload." He paused. "But I kind of want to play some slots, just to say I played in Vegas, you know?"

I still didn't understand what he was getting at. "Let's go. I'll be fine."

After about ten minutes, I got what he meant. The noise. The lights. Even the smell. It pecked away at my mind. We took a few steps beyond the entrance, and suddenly I was lost. Every direction looked the same as every other, and it was all glittering, blinking, and loud.

Isaac had my hand, though, and led me through the maze. I didn't even know how he navigated, to be honest. I let out a breath when I saw the card tables and a bar—not so much because I had any interest in playing or drinking, but I could orient myself.

The whole place, especially the vague scent of cigarettes, made my nerves crawl.

"I'm only putting twenty dollars in. When that's gone, so are we."

"I'm fine," I insisted.

Isaac gave my hand a squeeze and his crooked smile let me know he saw straight through that lie.

We didn't leave when he got through his twenty. We left when he cashed out twenty-five hundred, about halfway through his twenty.

By that time, I was dazed, confused, and so happy to see the sky when we exited. "How—how did you manage to win?"

He shrugged, and looked a little wide-eyes himself. "Luck. I shouldn't have won, but sometimes people do—mostly so they'll keep playing. But whenever I do, I get the hell out of there."

I glanced back at the casino. "It's a lot."

"I know. Thank you for humoring me." He glanced up at the sky—maybe like me, to make sure it was still there. "I don't usually gamble, but hey, Vegas."

"Now we can both say we won in Vegas."

Isaac got this look that was—I didn't know how to describe it. Stunning. Sexy. Beautiful. His smile was the brightest thing on the Strip. "I won before I even set foot in this town." Then he curved a hand around my neck and pulled me down into a kiss.

Pretty sure I heard camera clicks. Didn't care—not at that moment—because Isaac's slow, soft kiss was my entire universe.

When he broke it, he gave me the biggest grin. "I'm dating the most beautiful man in the world. What more could I want?"

"Someone with personality?"

He gave me a gentle shove. "You absolute dork. You have enough for both of us. I'm the boring one."

I didn't argue, just grinned. "Not boring at all." Okay, so maybe I did argue.

Isaac just chuckled. "Come on. Let's go get creeped out by the wax museum."

---

THE FLIGHT HOME wasn't nearly as horrible as the one to Vegas. It was shorter—thank you, jet stream. Our layover went through Dallas, and was long enough that we ate a meal and I got my legs and brain back underneath me. I was still damn exhausted by the time we landed in Pittsburgh. We'd taken my SUV—I had one for when the weather turned to snow and ice.

Once we'd collected our baggage and headed toward parking, I offered the key fob to Isaac. "Would you mind?"

"Of course not. Figured you might ask." He flashed me that smile of his. No concerns in the world.

I was, predictably, a mess. "I'm sorry I'm so—" I waved a hand.

"Perfect?" he supplied.

I barked out a laugh. "Oh my God. If anyone's perfect here, it's you."

His hand found mine. "Neither of us is. But you're so good, Julien. I promise. Don't listen to what anyone else says."

I didn't gainsay him, just let him drive me home.

We unpacked, had a bite to eat, then crawled in bed. Despite my general exhaustion, this time sleep was elusive. Next to me Isaac breathed deeply and slowly—a sure sign he was out cold.

Me? My mind started to unpack all that had happened in Vegas. The games, my play, the competitions. My conversations with my peers. The time with Isaac. The fans. Our coming out as a couple. The support we'd gotten from everyone.

Travis Canterbury.

Tabarnak. Why couldn't he go away? Why couldn't he leave me alone? Why did what happened eight years ago haunt me to this day? And why was it breaking me apart when everything in my life was finally falling into place? My heart ached while my pulse thudded in my ears.

The Carolina game was next. Another meeting with that fucking asshole. There'd be one more before the season was done. If we made it to the post-season, we might end up playing an entire series with them.

God. I didn't even want to think about that. On the arm that bore my tattoos, I curled my hand into a fist.

*Now*. Everything was fine now. Isaac was here. I was home. We'd practice tomorrow. Elias and Nikki would be there.

In the gray light of my bedroom, I peered up at the wooden beams of my ceiling and fell into a simple breathing exercise Elias had taught me years ago, and some of the tension eased. Maybe it was time to get some help for this. I couldn't keep leaning on Isaac for all my issues.

So, the off-season, then. Find a therapist. Build a pool. Both things seemed like good plans. I'd deal with my brain then.

I didn't need to borrow trouble by thinking too far ahead.

# Chapter 29

## Isaac

My encounter with Travis needled at me like a bad itch. I had no idea if I should tell Julien about it, and even if I was going to, the question was when? And how? We were playing Carolina this week. Julien needed to have his head together, and I was afraid if he knew Travis had so much as looked at me —never mind talked shit about him and made a pass at me— Julien would lose his focus. But that meant keeping this to myself for another week. At what point was I hiding it from him? Lying to him? At what point was it unforgivable to tell him, or unforgiveable to keep it up my sleeve?

I'd been so worried way back in the beginning that I was going behind his back when Nisha had pulled me aside to tell me to be careful about Julien. That I'd betrayed his trust. Now... fuck me. This was a fucking minefield. I felt guilty every time Julien smiled at me without knowing I really was keeping something from him this time, and I felt even worse whenever I thought about how angry or hurt or...I don't know, upset he'd be when I did tell him.

It was screwing with my focus, too. During our first practice after the Vegas trip, Coach and Elias were both on my ass because I could *not* control the puck today. Honestly, it was a miracle I could skate.

"What was that?" Elias waved with his stick in the direction I'd sent the puck.

"I don't know, I don't know." I sighed and went after the puck in question. "Let me try it again."

He huffed with some barely-restrained annoyance, and I honestly didn't blame him. What was I *doing*?

Minutes later, Coach shot me a pointed look after a pass from Nisha went right by my stick. "Rivera, do you *want* to spend the rest of the season on the farm team?"

My blood turned cold. "No, no." I shook my head. "Sorry, Coach. Just a little..." I thought fast. "Jetlagged."

"Jetlagged." Benson smacked my shoulder as he skated by me. "If you can't practice with jetlag, the playoffs will destroy you!"

"I'll be fine," I called after him.

The glare I got from Coach told me I'd damn well better be fine. His threat to punt me down to the minors was likely empty—a means of getting my attention—but it actually helped. I did better throughout the rest of practice, though I definitely wasn't playing my best. Far from it.

Toward the end, Julien skated up to me, sweat plastering a few strands of his long hair to the sides of his face. "Coach was really getting after you, eh?"

I avoided his gaze as I took a swig of Gatorade. "I deserved it."

"Did you?"

"Yeah. Just, um... Couldn't get my shit together, I guess."

He said nothing, and when I looked up at him again, I wasn't at all surprised to see concern written all over his face.

I swallowed. "I'm fine. It's an off day, but...I'm fine."

He didn't seem convinced. "You were fine this morning." An upraised eyebrow asked, *Weren't you?*

"Yeah, I was." I laughed quietly and shrugged. "I don't know. I think I got up into my own head during the passing drills. Started overthinking things. I'll shake it off."

Some skepticism lingered, but then he nodded. "All right." He gestured toward the other end of the ice. "Paxy and I are going to run a few more drills with the boys from the farm team. I'll catch up with you after I get a shower."

I smiled for real. "Okay. Don't be too mean to them."

He flashed me a wicked grin, winked, and tapped my skate with his stick before he headed off to join Paxy and the two younger defensemen. I kind of wanted to stay out here and watch him. For all I teased him about being mean to them, he was actually an excellent mentor. He'd let them know when they fucked up, but he was patient and mellow. He balanced positive and negative reinforcement in ways some of my high school and college coaches should have. A leader like that had definitely earned the A on his sweater.

And I was going to earn a ticket to the farm team if I didn't find something to focus on besides my boyfriend or his ex. Like, say, hockey.

But that encounter in Vegas wouldn't let me go. Even as I shuffled into the locker room, got out of my gear, showered, and dressed, there was a part of my brain that was constantly tugging me back to the concession stand line and the man who'd accosted me. Not to mention the stranger who'd intervened. And the worst part—the fact that Julien didn't know, and I still didn't know if or how or when to tell him.

Maybe I needed some advice.

Julien and the other defensemen were coming into the locker room, the echoes of raucous chirping and laughing in the hallway heralding their arrival, so I still had time before he'd wonder where I was. That seemed like as good an opportunity as any...especially since the man I was looking for didn't seem busy.

I stepped up to Elias as he was buttoning his shirt after his shower. "Hey, do you have a few minutes?"

He glanced at me, expression blank, but then he must have seen something in mine, because his eyebrows rose. He didn't ask what was up or what was wrong. Instead, he nodded toward the other end of the locker room. "Let's go."

Still buttoning his shirt, he led me out into the hallway that passed by offices and conference rooms, and we stepped into one of the smaller meeting rooms. There was a table and four chairs in here, plus a flatscreen on the wall. As he closed the door behind me, he asked, "What's going on?"

I leaned against the wall and folded my arms loosely across my T-shirt. "I need some advice."

Our captain studied me intently. "Is this about whatever was fucking up your game today?"

Dropping my gaze, I nodded as that familiar heat rose in my face. "Yeah."

Elias pulled out one of the chairs with his foot, sat down, and crossed one knee over the other. He watched me, saying nothing, and waited for me to speak.

I took a deep breath, uncrossed my arms, and slid my hands into my pockets. "Something happened in Vegas. And I'm...I feel like I should tell Julien. But I also feel like I shouldn't. And I..." I closed my eyes, pressing my head back against the wall. "I don't know what to do."

The chair creaked. Elias's voice was gentler now, edged with worry, as he asked, "What happened?"

Just thinking about it all made me weirdly lightheaded, so I pulled out one of the other chairs and sat down. Pressing my elbows into the table, I rubbed the back of my neck and told Elias what had happened. I started with the obvious trash-talking from Travis to Julien on the ice, which made Elias scowl. When I told him what happened in the concession line, though, he sat straighter, and his lips parted as he stared at me.

After I'd finished, Elias kneaded his forehead and muttered something I didn't catch in what I assumed was Swedish or Russian. Then he lowered his hand and met my gaze. "I can see why your mind wasn't in it today."

I nodded. "Yeah. I... It's been bothering me ever since then. And I just...I can't keep it from Julien, but I can't tell him right before a game, either. Especially not when we're playing Carolina soon."

Elias closed his eyes and swore. "No. You can't. If Julien knows about this and then sees Travis..." Trailing off, he shook his head.

"So what do I do? Because I can't hide it from him either."

"I know." Elias wiped a hand over his face. "I... Fuck. I'm not sure."

I wasn't sure if I should feel better or worse knowing that Elias didn't see an easy solution either. Like I didn't feel quite as clueless, but I also didn't have an answer. Then again, Elias was single. Had been for a long time, according to Julien. I'd always kind of looked to him as the captain of all things—the older, wiser guy who could always be counted on to find the solution. Maybe that wasn't fair of me.

But before I could insist I'd figure it out on my own, Elias spoke. "He deserves to know." The captain leaned forward, folding his long fingers on the table and looking right in my eyes. "He also deserves to be able to focus. If he knows now, especially with the Carolina game coming up fast, it's going to wreck him. Possibly for the rest of the season."

"So I should wait until the off season." My heart sank, and my shoulders did too. "God, it's going to eat me alive, keeping it from him, but... You're probably right. If he falls apart because of it, he's going to resent the shit out of me for it."

"No. He won't." Nothing but certainty in Elias's voice. He shook his head. "He'll hate himself. He'll understand why you told him, and he'll want to skin Travis alive for it, but the way it affects his performance—he won't hold that against anyone but himself. Especially if it starts pulling the team down." He paused, and with a pained expression, he added, "That's how he is anyway, but especially where Travis is concerned."

Speaking of wanting to skin Travis alive...

I managed to unclench my jaw enough to ask, "What did that fucker *do* to Julien?"

Elias avoided my gaze as he shook his head again. "What little I know isn't for me to tell."

Frustration had my teeth grinding again, but I understood. Elias wasn't going to betray Julien's trust, and I wouldn't ask him to. If I ever found out the truth about Julien and Travis, it would come from Julien. It had to.

But damn, I wished he'd just tell me so I knew where all the landmines were.

Right then, my phone chirped. I looked at the screen, and unsurprisingly, I had a text from Julien. *Are you still here?*

Shit. He'd probably finished showering by now.

"That's Julien," I told Elias as I wrote back, *Be right there. Save me a seat?*

"We should eat." Elias nudged my shin with his foot. "I know it's tough, keeping something like this out of his sight. But it's the right decision. And when it does come out, I'll vouch for you. That you had your reasons for keeping that card close for the time being."

Okay, that was a relief. If Julien found out, or if he was pissed at me for waiting so long, Elias had my back. This was probably the best-case scenario I could hope for under the circumstances.

"All right." I nodded and got up from my chair. "We should, um... We *should* eat. Thanks for talking to me, though. This helped a lot."

We both rose, but instead of reaching for the door, Elias

touched my arm. He towered over me anyway, and his crystal-blue eyes drilled right into mine. "You're not deceiving him, Isaac. You're trying to do what's best for him and let him keep his head in the game. So much so that *your* head wasn't in the game today. That's not an easy line to walk."

"No, it isn't. I just hope I'm doing the right thing."

"You're making the best decision you can in a shitty situation." He squeezed my arm and inclined his head. "And this isn't your fault. This is on Travis. Don't carry his sins on your shoulders."

I swallowed. The words were eerily reminiscent of Julien's way back when I'd been blaming myself for a game we'd lost, and he'd assured me it wasn't my weight to carry. Elias was right, same as Julien had been back then. That game had been on us as a team and on the refs, the hockey gods, and fucking physics. This situation? It was because Travis had put Julien through the wringer, and then he'd accosted me in Vegas. All I was doing was keeping that second part out of Julien's sight so he could keep his head together for the rest of the season.

So Travis wouldn't get the satisfaction of throwing Julien off his game.

I exhaled slowly and nodded. "Thanks. I really needed to hear that."

"Good." He smiled and let go of my arm. "And this means you'll be focused on the ice now too, yes?" He smirked. "Or do I have to tell your boyfriend to keep you in line?"

I looked right at him and flipped him off.

"Oh, for fuck's sake." Elias rolled his eyes and pulled open the door. "You've been spending *way* too much time with him."

I laughed, and we headed down the hall to where our teammates were eating.

Julien had, of course, saved me a seat, and Nisha had saved

one for Elias at the same table. After we'd loaded our plates, we joined them.

"And where have *you* two been?" Nisha asked pointedly.

"Fucking over Coach's desk," I deadpanned.

Elias almost spat out a bite of meat, Julien choked on his drink, and Nisha barked a laugh so loud, half the room turned. It took some work, but I kept my expression innocent.

Julien recovered first, though he was still sputtering a bit. "Okay, but who was on top?"

I cocked a brow. "Who the fuck do you think was on top?"

He laughed and fist-bumped me. Elias groaned, and Nisha chuckled and elbowed him, earning a glare that only made him laugh harder.

Fresh guilt smacked me in the chest. It didn't feel right, joking and carrying on with the three of them—especially Julien—after the conversation I'd had with Elias. On the other hand, it did. I wasn't hiding the Vegas incident from him. I was just putting a pin in it until the timing was better. Between now and then, normal was good. Especially the kind of normal that had Julien laughing while the snark flew between the four of us.

Relaxing a bit more, I rejoined the banter and dug into my food.

The truth would come out when the time was right.

And Julien and I would be fine.

---

"YOU GONNA BE OKAY TONIGHT?" I slid my hands up the lapels of Julien's suit jacket. Blue. God, he looked so good in blue.

He smiled, wrapping his arms around me. "I'll be fine."

"Are you sure?"

"He's ancient history." Julien dipped his chin and brushed his lips across mine. "The longer I'm with you, the less I care about him."

I held his gaze. I didn't quite believe him, but...I did. Travis was a significant dot on Julien's timeline. There were times when I could tell the fucker was still living rent-free in his head. And yet, as time had gone on, it seemed like Travis had less of a hold on Julien. But Vegas had been different. And there'd been that encounter between Travis and me. There was a lot more going on than I'd realized, and I still didn't know quite what to make of any of it.

Apparently he'd taken my silent scrutiny as skepticism, because he ran his fingers through my hair and smiled. "I'll be *fine*. All I'm worried about tonight is racking up another win and then coming home with the man who's been learning French so he can talk to my family."

I chuckled, heat rushing into my face. "Learning really bad French, you mean?"

Oh Lord, I was never going to stop getting all fluttery when Julien laughed like that, was I? "You're no worse at French than I was at English when I first started learning it." Whatever response might've formed in my brain died away as Julien pressed his lips to mine. We didn't have time to fool around again, but that wasn't what this kiss was about anyway. It was soft and mellow—just a sweet, shared moment before we had to get our game faces on. We were at my place right now, but rooming together meant a lot more moments like these on the road, too, and I was seriously going to buy our travel coordinator a bottle of something expensive before the end of the season.

Julien broke the kiss as gently as he'd initiated it, and our eyes locked. Oh, yeah. He was fine tonight. He'd probably have some feelings and grind his teeth when he saw Travis, but his head was in a good place.

I combed my fingers through his damp hair. "What do you say we go keep Carolina from racking up another two points?"

His eyes lit up with that competitive fire that made him so sexy on the ice. "Let's do it."

We shared one more kiss, then headed down to the parking garage to get into his car. I still felt ballsy as hell, riding into games together or stepping out of hotel elevators with my hand on the small of Julien's back, and there was also this impulse to snatch it away or keep some distance between us when other people were around. I resisted that impulse, though. We were out. People knew.

Travis Canterbury knew.

I had to suppress a smug grin at that thought. While I wasn't interested in parading Julien around like some prize I'd won or some object I owned, there was something to be said for the utter triumph that came with knowing how much Travis undoubtedly hated me for this. That he probably looked at us and realized how far out of his reach Julien was now. Or maybe that was all in my imagination. Whatever. Travis could eat a dick.

Later, as we hit the ice for warm-ups, I did keep a cautious eye on Julien. As much as he insisted he'd be all right, I wanted to see how he did when he and Travis actually saw each other again.

And...yeah, he was fine.

He and Paxy even skated up to the red line at one point to exchange some good-natured barbs with Kaminski, a Carolina forward who'd played for Pittsburgh three or four seasons ago. Travis skated by, shooting daggers out his eyes at Julien, but Julien didn't even seem to notice. He was too busy laughing at something Kaminski had said.

I smiled to myself as I chased another puck toward our goal. Julien undoubtedly still had a mountain of feelings where Travis was concerned. There was history and bad blood, and none of that evaporated overnight.

But he was going to be okay.

I continued my own warm-ups. From the other end of the ice, I could see Chad Weyland warming up with his teammates. I wanted to wave hello or something, but he was too focused on the ice, the puck—hell, his own skates. He wasn't skating as loose and comfortable as he always had in high school and college either. I'd always envied how absolutely effortless his skating was, but he was wound up tonight.

Maybe that was why he hadn't responded to my text about meeting up after the game. I'd tried twice now—this game and last. Maybe he didn't want to see me. Maybe he was just overwhelmed.

I winced as I pulled my focus away from my old friend and found a puck to shoot. The big leagues were a ton of pressure, and being in the big leagues on a team favored to win the cup had to be killing him. For the millionth time since Vegas, I hoped he'd found someone to mentor him.

I glanced toward Carolina's end of the ice, and I caught a glimpse of Travis doing some stretches.

*I hope Weyland finds a mentor, but not you, fuckface.*

Warm-ups ended a few minutes later, and we all returned to the dressing room. Coach gave us the usual pep talk, reminding us multiple times that Carolina was a tough team, that they'd take advantage if our heads weren't in the game, blah, blah, blah. I mean, he was right, but like...no shit.

Julien still seemed relaxed and unbothered as he retaped his stick. He was talking shit with Nisha and Paxy, and whenever we caught each other's eye, he smiled.

I wanted to win every time we played, but I really hoped we win tonight. Decisively. I hoped Julien scored a goal, too. I could already imagine him grinning all the way home.

A win was possible tonight, but holy shit, they were definitely going to make us work for it. As soon as the puck dropped, it was on. They won the first faceoff and immediately made a run for our goal. Paxy pretty much said, "I don't think so," slammed their left winger into the boards, and sent the puck to Elias, who sped toward the other end of the ice at breakneck speed. He shot. The netminder flung it away, and Julien caught the rebound and passed it to Paxy, who fired it right into the goalie's glove.

We did a shift change, and I quickly consulted with my wingers and the defensemen about a play I had in mind. I'd been studying Carolina's videos incessantly leading up to this game, and I was pretty sure I'd sussed out a weakness. If we could pull this off, we'd be gold.

I skated to the circle for the faceoff, and oh, wouldn't you know it? So did Travis.

Travis.

Just glancing at him made my hackles go up, but I focused on the ref and the puck. All that anger over his past with Julien was getting channeled into my determination to wipe the floor with Carolina tonight.

Travis muttered something to me, but I ignored it. The ref dropped the puck. I couldn't say if Travis was slower than me, or if he was distracted by his own snark, but it worked in my favor either way: I won the faceoff and sent the puck to Julien. He shot it to Ozzy, who sent it between a Carolina forward's skates to Paxy, who faked like he was going to pass to Benson, who was wide open with no traffic between him and the goal. Predictably, Carolina players fell all over themselves to block the pass or resulting shot. Instead, Paxy passed it to me. By this point, I'd come around behind the goal, and though Weyland made a valiant attempt to snatch the puck, it landed on my tape and I sent it under the goalie's pads and into the back of the net.

I pumped my fist in the air, and a second later, my teammates were crushing me with hugs and shouting over the roar of the hometown crowd.

"Fucking genius!" Paxy smacked the back of my helmet with his glove. "Nicely done!"

I grinned. When I met Julien's gaze...oh God, was there anything better than scoring a goal and being met with the pride in his expression?

Carolina wasn't giving up after a single goal in the first two minutes of the game, though, and they answered with one of their own in short order. Near the end of the first period, the score was tied at two apiece, but we squeaked one in during the last thirty seconds.

Coach was happy with us. We were happy with our performance. I was quietly happy that Julien was all business tonight. He and Paxy were on fire defensively, and they both went aggressively on the offensive when the need arose. In fact, that third goal was Paxy's with an assist from Julien. Shorthanded, too—Nisha was in the box for holding, which was bullshit, but whatever.

Carolina's coach must have had some words with his team and lit a fire under their collective ass, because they were out for blood in the second. Even after Elias won the faceoff, it didn't take them long to steal the puck, and Larry was definitely getting a star tonight for that save alone. I watched the replay three times on the bench and still couldn't figure out how he didn't dislocate a few limbs.

The action was intense. The puck was all over the place. I fucking loved games like this, where the adrenaline was pumping and the other team made us work hard. Those were the most rewarding victories. Now if we could just stay ahead of them for another thirty minutes, we'd have that victory.

Elias's line came to the bench and mine hit the ice. I snatched the puck away from one of their forwards and looked around, then passed it to Paxy, who sent it to Julien, and then there was a battle for the puck in the corner behind our net.

I swept a glance around, taking stock of where everyone was, looking for open ice, and when I found it, I headed for it.

But in the same instant I spun around to anticipate a pass from Julien, all hell broke loose.

One second, Julien and the other player were battling for the puck.

The next, Julien threw down his stick, dropped his gloves, and launched himself at the other player.

Someone from Carolina grabbed my arm before I even realized I was heading for the fight. I tried to wrench free, but he wasn't letting go, and by that point, the refs were trying to break up the fight.

Trying.

Julien had a hold of the other guy's jersey, and he swung his fist hard, sending the man toppling and his helmet flying. As the two of them went down and the refs followed, trying like hell to pull them apart while Julien kept right on throwing punches, I caught a glimpse of the other player's number.

Forty-seven.

Travis fucking Canterbury.

"Oh, no," I murmured, my voice undoubtedly drowned out by the mix of cheers and boos from the crowd.

In a matter of seconds, the officials had them pried apart. The guy holding my arm loosened his grasp, and I skated across the ice to see what the hell was going on.

Julien was upright. Helmet gone. Hair a mess. Jersey askew. Blood running from his nose and along his upper lip. A linesman was holding him back, shouting in his face, but Julien didn't even seem to hear him.

My blood turned cold. I'd watched videos of his fights a million times. In the aftermath, he was usually either smug as fuck or in full-on pissed-off cat mode. He'd shout over the official's shoulder all the way to the penalty box, and if the other guy ended up in the box too, they'd spend the entire two or five minutes snarling at each other through the divider.

This time, Julien was...

Jesus, I couldn't even describe him. He was shaking. His expression was... Fuck, I didn't know if he was about to rip someone's still-beating heart from their chest, or if he was about to break down crying right then and there. Quite possibly both. Like he was angry beyond anything that belonged on the ice, and that anger hadn't finished boiling over, but had absolutely broken something in him.

The linesman pushed his stick into his hand and started leading him across the ice toward our bench. Julien didn't resist. He wouldn't look at anyone. Not the linesman. Not Travis. Not me. No one.

I wanted to skate after him. Talk to him. Comfort him. Find out what the fuck had just happened.

Before I could make a move, though, someone grabbed my arm again. This time, it wasn't a Carolina player.

"Stay focused." Paxy's uncharacteristically shaky voice was nearly swallowed by the crowd. "He'll be fine. And he needs *us* to be fine."

A million protests surged to the tip of my tongue, but I also knew he was right. He wasn't being dismissive of Julien. From the creases in his forehead, he was rattled too, clearly as worried and shaken as I was. But we still had a job to do. We had to keep playing until the bitter end. If we fell apart because of this, the guilt would be too much for Julien, and in that moment, I had no idea how much more he could take.

So, exhaling slowly through my nose, I nodded.

Paxy let go of my arm and returned the nod.

I glanced around and found Travis. He was on his feet now, wiping blood off his face. He was a little unsteady on his skates, and one of his teammates was helping him toward the bench. Maybe for stitches. Maybe for concussion protocol. I wasn't sure. He actually looked a bit shaken, as if Julien had beaten the holy hell out of him.

I looked toward our bench just in time to see Julien step into the tunnel, long, sweaty hair and the word *Landry* across slumped shoulders vanishing like a mirage between puzzled trainers and teammates. I hadn't been able to hear the refs over the crowd, but he'd undoubtedly been ejected.

And the game was going on. We were heading to the circle for another faceoff. Somehow, I still had to play hockey. Ideally, the level of hockey that could beat this team that was favored to win the cup.

But all I could think was...

*Seriously—what the fuck just happened?*

# Chapter 30

## Julien

Blood and bile. All I could taste was blood and bile. My head rang with the pounding of my heart, the screaming of my mind, and Travis's laughter and the words he threw at me.

*"I got you, you little fuck. I finally got you."*

Tears blurred my vision, rage pounded my chest, and I screamed, slashing my stick at the nearest wall. Once, twice—the blade snapped off—three times—the shaft shattered. I threw what was left at the floor, wrenched the fight strap free and ripped my sweater over my head. That ended up by the locker room door. One of the athletic trainers was inside, holding up a towel. "Your nose and lip..."

"Don't touch me," I snarled, and he backed away fast.

Done. Off the team. Out of the league. I didn't belong here. I never belonged here.

I tore off my gear, chucking it with all my strength. I didn't care where it landed. Wasn't wearing it again,

*"Love fucking the rook? So did I."*

I stumbled to my locker and sat, frantically clawing at the laces of my skates. Had to get them off. Had to get everything off.

I'd used Isaac. Made him fuck me. Told him that I loved him.

I wasn't even capable of love.

*"Have him doing whatever you ask. Familiar? That kid is you."*

God.

I'd become Travis. Taking and taking and taking everything I wanted. Giving nothing in return. Isaac would do anything for me. I'd used him like Travis had used me.

My stomach roiled, and it took everything I had to keep its contents inside. I heaved a sob and stumbled toward the shower, stripping off my base layer as I went.

"Julien!" I don't know who called my name. Didn't matter.

"Leave me alone!" I hit the shower, but no amount of scrubbing would wash away what I'd done.

Screwed over the team. Cost them the game. Maybe the playoffs. Just like before.

*"I made you. You're me."*

I braced my hands against the tile wall and let the water scald me. If I could crawl out of my skin, I would have.

Needed to get out of here.

Not sure how I managed it, but I got myself dressed—in the team sweats I didn't deserve to touch, grabbed my cell phone, wallet, and keys, then stumbled into Coach's office and closed the door. My phone dinged with the tone I used for my family. Had to blink the tears out of my eyes to see what was on the screen. Texts. The most recent from Marie read: *Ça va?*

No, I was very far from being okay. With shaking hands, I typed a lie and a truth.

*Ça va. Je t'explite plus tard.*

There was no explaining what I'd done. Still, I repeated that with my brother and my parents. Eventually, I'd have to tell them

I was out of the league. That I wasn't the person they thought I was. I'd lost the one thing that'd kept me going all these years—hockey—because I'd used the man I'd sworn I loved.

I scrubbed at my tears with my palm, then pressed my forehead into the edge of Coach's desk. Everything hurt. My head, my lungs. Every organ in my body. I couldn't stop shaking, even when I wrapped my arms around myself.

The horn that sounded the end of the period filtered through the walls of the office, and a few moments later, Coach slipped into the room and shut the door. "Landry?"

Whatever he saw when I looked up made his eyes widen and his lips part. He moved to his chair, then lowered himself into it. "Oh, son. What happened?"

"I fucked up." The words felt thick in my throat.

Silence for a moment. "What did he say to you?"

The truth. The stark ugly truth, and I'd wanted to kill him for it. "Doesn't matter," I whispered. My teeth chattered. Match penalty. Exactly what I deserved.

"Julien, look at me." His words were soft and kind.

Took me a moment, but I forced myself to meet his eyes.

I deserved nothing that I saw there. Not the kindness, not the concern, so I looked away, back at the carpet.

"Son, I don't know what's going on between you and Canterbury, but it's going to be okay."

"No. It's not."

"Julien..."

"No!" That came out as a strangled bark, and I sucked in air until I was sure I wasn't going to start sobbing. "Can I...go? I want to go home."

"Let me find someone to drive..."

"No." I took in a breath, sat up, and met his gaze. "I can drive."

He stared at me, his expression unreadable, then it softened into something I didn't want to see: affection. "Son, I know things look bleak now, but we have your back."

I swallowed, and didn't say anything. The tears I held back threatened to spill.

*I don't deserve your kindness. Your love. If you knew...*

"Do you want to see Rivera? Sidorov? Karlsson?"

Yes. I wanted to see them, especially Isaac, but I couldn't ever see him again. I shook my head. "Not like this."

"All right." He paused for a moment, then pulled open a desk drawer, pushed aside something, and pulled out a business card. He slid it across the table. "Take this. If you need someone to talk to who isn't us."

I took the card without looking at it. I could guess what was on it. "Okay."

He rose. "Take care of yourself, Landry. Please?"

More tears. I just nodded.

Once he'd left, I waited a bit, then slipped out of the office. I didn't see anyone but a guard on my way to the parking garage. This time of night, with the arena still full of people, it took no time to get to the HOV lane and onto the highway. A few times, I let out a sob, but I managed to grit my teeth and hold myself together for the drive, somehow.

Rote memory, I guess.

My house felt wrong. I felt wrong. My skin didn't fit. I didn't belong here either—not in this place that held too many happy memories, tainted now with the realization that every move I'd made had been self-centered. Egotistical. I'd neatly trapped Isaac into falling for me from the moment I'd sent that text with my address.

I was only going to hurt him in the end.

"You're such a fuckup, Julien." I spoke to the silence. Tears pricked, then fell. "You deserve everything that's about to happen to you."

Then I climbed the stairs, stripped off the team logo, threw everything in my hamper, and crawled into my bed.

Only then did I let go and let myself feel the pain from the remnants of my heart. The sobs came out hard and loud, echoing in the emptiness of the room.

No waterfall. No Isaac. No card games with Nikki and Elias. I'd have to sell the house. How was I going to explain all this to my family?

I'd used all those people. My family. My friends. Isaac.

Travis had been right all along. I was nothing. No talent, no soul. No brains. That had finally caught up with me, and I cracked apart in the worst way. Given Travis everything he'd wanted from me: every inch of suffering he could drag from me.

One mistake as a rookie—opening that door rather than slamming it in his face. He'd taken me under his wing and made me exactly like him.

Here I was again, my life in shambles. Except this time, no one was going to pull me out. Hell, even the minors wouldn't want me now.

At some point, the tears ran out. The silence of my house was shattered by a burst of Russian music. Nikki. *Fuck*. I found my phone in the hamper, in the pocket of my sweats and stared at the message.

*Did you make it home safely?*

I bit my lip. Far in the back of my mind, a quiet voice whispered, *He cares. They all care.*

I shook my head. They might, but they didn't know what I'd done. Didn't know how right Travis was.

I typed out a reply, though. I owed him that.

*I'm home.*

Another lie. This wasn't home anymore. I'm not sure where home was, but it was no longer this house. Too much Isaac here. Too much joy.

Julien Landry was a fraud. A monster. A user.

Everything I touched turned rotten. This place needed to be someone else's.

I flipped through my contacts until I found my agent, then sent him a text.

*Get me out of Pittsburgh. Trade or retire. Don't care.*

The response came back almost immediately.

*No. I don't know what's going on with you, J. But I'm not doing a damn thing for at least a week. Because you do care. You can thank me later.*

*I mean it.*

*So do I. Call me in a week. We'll talk. Not before then.*

"Fuck!" I tossed my phone onto the floor and curled back into a ball. Fuck everyone. All of them.

But most of all, fuck me.

I ignored Isaac's phone call and texts. Didn't get out of bed. He needed to stay away from me.

I closed my eyes and bit back more tears. Eventually the texts stopped.

## Chapter 31

### Isaac

I had never cared less about winning than I did that night. We were up by one near the end of the third, with Carolina battling to squeak in a buzzer beater to put us into overtime, and the only reason I fought so hard to keep them from scoring was to make sure we *didn't* go into overtime. I needed this game to be over so I could get to the locker room and find out what the hell was going on with my boyfriend.

During the second intermission, he'd been MIA. Coach had disappeared for a few minutes, and he'd looked grim when he'd returned, but he hadn't told us anything. He'd given us the usual pep talk and told us everything we needed to unfuck in the third period in order to hold on to our lead. Then he'd paused, surreptitiously glanced toward Julien's spot on the bench, and flatly told us not to let anything from the second period cost us our momentum.

*Okay, Coach, but what happened? Where's Julien? What's going on?*

The question had been in everyone's eyes, a lot of which kept flicking toward me as if I had some magic insight into why Julien had lost his shit. Yeah, sure, I knew him better than anyone in this room, but I probably had even more questions than they did.

None of which were answered before we had to return to the ice.

In the waning minute of the third period, we were in our defensive zone, and I joined Larry, Paxy, and Jackal in protecting our net. No way in hell was the puck getting in. No overtime tonight. Not on my watch.

One of their forwards made a shot. It rebounded, and Paxy caught it before a Carolina player could.

"Rivs!" He took off toward the other end of the ice.

I followed, heart pounding. In the neutral zone, he passed me the puck, and I shot it toward Carolina's goal...which was empty since they'd pulled their goalie.

It went in, and instead of celebrating, I was overcome with relief. No overtime. We were up by two now, with only nine seconds left to play.

Paxy threw his arms around me, which was probably all that kept me from dropping right there on the ice. He smacked my helmet. "Nice one, Rivs!"

"Thanks." I smiled as our teammates joined in, and I kept it in place as I skated by the bench for fist bumps, but goddammit, I needed to get into the locker room.

The puck dropped one more time. I won the faceoff by the skin of my teeth, and I passed to one of my wingers, who passed it to Paxy. We didn't make a run for the goal—which was no longer empty—just kept the puck moving and under our control while those last few seconds wound down.

The buzzer went off. Our hometown crowd went wild, and though I was usually one of the stragglers, I was one of the first off the ice. I hurried down the tunnel toward the locker room, stomach somersaulting the whole way.

*Julien. Where was Julien? How was Julien?*

*Would someone please tell me something already?*

I hadn't even finished stripping off my jersey before Coach barked, "Rivera. Sidorov. Karlsson." He pointed sharply toward the hallway. "Get dressed, and then get in my office."

Oh. Shit.

I exchanged glances with Elias and Nisha. They looked about as worried and confused as I did.

All three of us made short work of showering and dressing. Elias shoved a bottle of electrolytes into each of our hands and grabbed one for himself, and then we filed into Coach's office.

"Close the door." Coach sat behind his desk, expression taut.

Nisha did as ordered. He and Elias took Coach's guest chairs. I was too restless to sit, so I just leaned against the door.

"Where's Landry?" Elias's tone was laced with more worry than I'd ever heard from him. No, that wasn't it. That was straight up *fear*.

My knees shook. I held on to the bottle in my hand, but I was afraid to take a drink because my stomach wasn't having it.

Coach sighed. "By now, he's home."

"Home?" Elias asked. "Did someone take him? Tell me he didn't drive himself."

Our coach turned exhausted eyes on Elias. "Do you think anyone could have stopped him?"

Nisha swore and took out his phone. Over his shoulder, I could see him texting Julien: *Did you make it home safely?*

My head swam. So Julien had left on his own, and he'd driven, and... I met Coach's gaze. "What the hell happened?"

"That's what I was hoping the three of you could tell me." Coach folded his hands on the desk and looked from one of us to the next. "No one on the team knows Landry better than you boys. Now I need someone to tell me about him and Canterbury. Because there's some history there, and I was content to leave it between them, but after tonight, I need to know."

Elias and Nisha exchanged looks, but they both dropped their gazes.

Right then, Nisha's phone went off. On the screen, two words from Julien: *I'm home.*

My knees almost gave out. I leaned against the door and closed my eyes, letting the flurry of emotions crash over me. Relief that Julien had at least made it home and was coherent enough to respond to a text. Guilt that I hadn't been the one to send the text checking on him. Renewed worry over everything that had happened. Dread over everything I was probably going to find out in this meeting.

"Someone tell me something," Coach growled. "My best defenseman is facing a suspension and God knows what over a completely unprovoked and out-of-character attack on another player." He thumped the desk with his knuckle. "Tell me *something*, boys. I *need* to know what I'm up against here."

Nisha spoke quietly in Russian. Elias glared at him. He looked up at me with conflicted eyes, and I wondered for a moment if he was going to tell me to leave the room. But then he sighed and gestured for Nisha to continue.

Sitting up straighter, his tone and voice unusually and unnervingly serious, Nisha said, "They dated. And it was..." He grimaced as if the subject physically hurt him. "It was a bad relationship."

"Toxic," Elias supplied, venom dripping off the word. He gestured at Nisha. "We didn't know until it was over. They kept it quiet the whole time they were together. When we found out, we..."

"We tried to help him past it." Nisha sounded exhausted and unsteady. "I thought we did. But Travis... He knows his way under Landry's skin."

"But they've played against each other for years without issue," Coach said.

"Eh." Elias wobbled his hand in the air. "I wouldn't say without issue."

"Meaning?"

"Meaning that the chirping between them has always been different than it is with others. Crueler."

"The chirping from Canterbury," Nisha clarified. "Landry takes swipes in return, but he avoids Canterbury as much as he can."

"So what changed this season?" Coach asked. "Because the last time we played Carolina, they were volatile too. You all lose your minds when we play them, but Landry..." He exhaled. "Why is this all coming to a head *now*?"

Silence fell in the room. Elias tapped his fingers on the armrest.

Then Nisha looked up at me, his brow pinched. I thought he was urging me to say something, but when Coach and Elias looked my way too, I realized what was going on. No one had to say a word.

*I* was what had changed this season. And Travis Canterbury *knew*.

Coach rubbed his eyes. Dropping his hand to his lap, he asked, "This relationship between Landry and Canterbury—when exactly did it happen?"

Elias exhaled, slouching a bit, and he quietly admitted, "It was Landry's rookie season."

I didn't even register a reaction from Coach because my stomach fell into my feet. Julien's *rookie* season? Oh hell. That was... I knew they'd dated, but I hadn't stopped to run the numbers. I hadn't realized it was when Julien was a rookie.

"Wasn't..." I cleared my throat. "Wasn't Julien *nineteen* that year?"

"Barely," Elias whispered. "And Canterbury is quite a bit older."

Ice formed along my spine, and the words of a stranger in Vegas echoed in my mind:

*"You're a young player. Exactly his type. You, uh... You don't want a piece of that."*

Nervous words from a player who couldn't have been much older than me...

Who'd pulled me away from Travis...

Who'd seen a look in Travis's eyes and followed him because he'd had a bad feeling...

Holy shit. I pressed back harder against the door. Travis was a fucking predator. And there was a good chance Julien hadn't been his only victim.

But how much could I talk about that with Coach, Elias, and Nisha without showing more cards than Julien wanted to? We were already discussing more than he'd want us to. I desperately wanted to tug at this thread and find out how many people Travis had left in his wake, but the man had already taken enough power and control from Julien. Their relationship was probably already going to wind up publicized in ways Julien didn't want.

As much as anything about this situation could be, this part needed to be on Julien's terms.

I shifted my weight. "So what happens now?"

Coach sighed. "What happens now is that there will be a hearing. If I had to guess, Landry will be suspended for a game or two. Beyond that..." He waved a hand. "It's hard to say. He's never been suspended before. Hasn't had disciplinary issues at this level. So..."

Okay, so Julien's career would probably weather this. But what about him?

I folded my arms to steady them. "Did you talk to him

before he left? Is he... How was he?" The worry came through in my voice and I didn't try to hide it. "Is he all right?"

Coach's wince was answer enough. "He's not in a good place, kid. Whatever happened out there, he didn't leave it on the ice, that's for sure."

"Fuck," I breathed. "I need to call him. Check on him."

Coach nodded. "Let me know how he's doing, will you?"

"I will." I started to go, but Elias caught my hand. He looked up at me like he was going to say something, but then he released a breath and let go of my hand. What did it mean when even our captain—one of Julien's closest friends—didn't have the words?

I left Coach's office and took a moment to pull myself together in the hallway. Then I walked until I found a meeting room where I could have some privacy, and I stepped inside and closed the door.

With unsteady hands, I found Julien's contact and sent the call.

It rang.

And rang.

And rang.

His voicemail clicked on. "This is Julien, and this call can probably be a text. If it really can't, leave a message." He repeated it in French. Then there was a beep.

"Hey, it's me. I just wanted to check on you. Make sure you're all right. I'm worried about you." I had to swallow the lump trying to rise in my throat. "Give me a call or text me, okay? Just tell me you're good? I love you."

The last three words almost broke me, and I ended the call before I covered my face with my hand. I loved him so much it hurt, and it was killing me not to know what was going on in his head right now. What had driven him to beat that motherfucker into the ice.

I didn't know how he was. But it occurred to me that I did know *where* he was.

I was starving after the game. I couldn't afford not to eat after burning that many calories.

But I left anyway, and... Fuck. I'd driven in with Julien.

Fortunately, my apartment wasn't far. I was too smoked from the game to walk—especially since I hadn't eaten anything—and the Uber driver didn't ask any questions. Once I was out of her car, I went straight to mine and drove like a bat out of hell out to Sewickley Heights. Down those familiar roads. Through those familiar neighborhoods. To that one familiar driveway.

There was a light on in the house, illuminating an upstairs window, and the floodlights came on when I pulled up, but everything seemed eerily dark and still as I got out of my car. With my heart in my throat and blood pounding in my ears, I walked up to his front door.

I knocked.

I waited.

I rang the doorbell.

I waited some more.

I rang it again.

"Come on, Julien," I muttered into the silence. "Please. Just let me in."

But he didn't. No sounds came from the house. No lights came on. Eventually, the floodlights went down, leaving me surrounded by silent darkness.

I knocked a few more times because I didn't know what else to do.

Still no answer.

Closing my eyes, I exhaled into the cold night, my heart sinking even deeper into the pit of my stomach. Okay. Message received. Julien clearly wanted to be alone.

*But are you okay to* be *alone?*

*What am I supposed to do in this situation?*

I took out my phone, and my eyes blurred as I wrote out a text: *I'm heading back to my place. Please call me or text me. Something. If you need space, then it's yours, but let me know you're okay. I love you.*

And then...I left.

I made it out of his driveway and maybe half a mile down the road before I couldn't focus on the road anymore. Too many emotions were crashing over me. I pulled over, set the brake, and...

And I fucking lost it.

I'd held it together for the rest of the game because my team needed me. I'd held it together during that meeting with Coach because I'd wanted to do right by Julien. And now I couldn't anymore. I wasn't professional right now. I wasn't strong right now. I was scared, and I was worried, and I was freaking the hell out because the man I loved was on the other side of figurative and literal walls, and I just...I *hurt*.

And I didn't know what to do.

# Chapter 32

## Julien

The doorbell startled me awake, and my heart hammered in my chest. For one glorious moment, I didn't know where I was—then I did, and I nearly threw up.

Travis. Isaac. The game. The rage I'd felt. Blood in my mouth. Travis's laughter. The way his hands had gripped my hips. The text I'd sent in the airplane that had lured Isaac in.

Didn't help when the bell rang again. Nor when Isaac pounded on the door—or when he texted.

I stumbled to the bathroom and tried to heave up the contents of my stomach—except there wasn't anything there at all, so I slumped down to the marble floor and closed my eyes, focusing on the cold against my cheek. Against my side. After a time, Isaac must have left because silence descended again.

I managed to grab a glass of water and crawl back in bed. Only a few days ago, Isaac had assured me everything would be better in the morning.

This time, I knew he'd be wrong.

# Chapter 33

## Isaac

I didn't hear from Julien the next day. I knew he was alive because he had his hearing with the league to address what happened with Travis. Coach didn't say much about it other than to let us all know Julien was suspended for one game. Privately, he told me that Julien hadn't fought it, and had in fact been surprised it was only one game. He thought he deserved more. With no history of disciplinary issues, though, and with his apparently obvious contrition, a single-game suspension was deemed sufficient.

Fans and other players were torn on the issue. Some thought it wasn't nearly enough. People were calling for Julien to be ousted from the league entirely. Personally, I thought that was rich coming from people who adored Sebastian Angelo (a New York player who'd been suspended three times this season alone, including for breaking a Seattle forward's nose) and Chris Nader (who'd slew-footed a *linesman*, for fuck's sake).

It was common practice for disciplined players to give statements. Some did press conferences. Some just issued apologies and whatnot via social media.

Julien...did not.

His social media was silent. No one could reach him via phone or text. I was worried out of my mind. Hurt, too, but I tried to tell myself this wasn't him shutting me out. It wasn't about me at all—it was about him, and now wasn't the time for me to pile on him by demanding he reassure me.

But holy shit, I was worried.

Darian could usually talk me down when I worked myself up, but even they were freaked out. They'd seen the whole thing on live TV, and they'd been blowing up my phone ever since, wondering if Julien was okay, what was happening, what was going to happen. I didn't know. No one knew. I was helpless and clueless and so fucking *worried*.

And I got a hell of a lot *more* worried when Julien didn't show up to practice after his suspension was over.

Okay, maybe Coach had told him to sit that one out? That didn't make sense, but...maybe?

Except even Coach had seemed surprised and concerned when Julien hadn't shown up. I'd seen him and Paxy having a hushed conversation, with Paxy looking grim and shaking his head. Kelly had come out to the bench during practice, cell phone plastered to her ear, and she too had shaken her head when Coach had approached. By the end of practice, all three had asked me if I'd heard anything, and my answer had left them looking as unsettled as I felt.

Something was wrong.

I hadn't seen Julien in the flesh since he'd left the ice the other night. A camera in the tunnel had captured him utterly destroying his stick before he'd disappeared into the locker room, and...that was it. He'd vanished. A two-word reply to Nisha's text, and then nothing. When I'd gone by his house, nothing. My calls and texts went unanswered. The last couple of texts hadn't even been read. There were suddenly rumors about him being traded or retiring, and those had apparently been prompted by a conversation he'd had with his agent.

Now that he'd missed a practice and *no one* knew where he was, I'd rocketed past worried and into scared shitless. Like, *two seconds away from calling the cops for a wellness check* scared shitless.

What the fuck was happening?

More rumors flew. Teammates kept earnestly asking me for updates, but I had none. Every time someone walked past his locker, they'd give it a look full of worry and unease. Julien's name was on everyone's lips right now, but no one knew a thing.

Something had to give. I needed to see him and make sure he was all right. I mean, I knew he was far from all right, but could I at least confirm that he was alive?

I didn't know what else to do, so I grabbed Elias in the locker room. "Have you heard from Julien?"

Our captain frowned, and he shook his head. "No. Coach has, at least the other night, but..." Another shake of his head.

I swallowed. "He won't return my calls. He didn't answer the door when I went by. I'm... Look, I'm not gonna lie—I'm scared. I *need* to check on him. But what am I supposed to do? Break his door down?"

"Don't need to do that." Nisha appeared beside me, his expression unusually serious. "I have a key."

Elias pressed his lips together, and then he sighed and nodded. "Me too. I've been thinking about..."

I kind of wanted to have some feelings about why the two of them had keys to Julien's house and I didn't, but this wasn't the time. "Let's go, then."

They both stared at me.

"Let's?" Elias asked.

"Yes." I stared defiantly right back at both of them. "Whatever is going on, I suspect he needs all of us. And even if he doesn't..." My defiance wavered, and so did my voice. "I might need the backup." I wasn't afraid of Julien, but I had no idea what I'd be walking into.

They exchanged glances. Hell, they had a whole conversation with just their eyes, a couple of shrugs, an exasperated sigh from Elias, and then resigned nods from both of them. It made me ache for that connection I had with Julien. Ever since the Carolina game, I'd felt untethered without the man I'd been so close to on and off the ice. I wanted that closeness back. And even if I couldn't have it anymore—even if, for some reason I couldn't fathom right now, he was done with me after this—I needed Julien to be okay.

"All right." Elias turned to me. "Let's go."

My pulse kicked into overdrive. We left the training center and trooped out to the parking lot. They rode together in Elias's car while I followed in mine, and my hands were so sweaty, it was a miracle I kept hold of the wheel as we made the drive to Julien's house. Sewickley Heights seemed so much farther away today than it actually was. Like we were driving clear out to Ohio or something.

Finally, though, Elias turned into Julien's familiar driveway. Then I did. With my heart in my throat and my palms slick on the wheel, I followed him down the winding drive, and we both parked in front of the garage. In silence, we all got out and went up to the porch.

Elias rang the doorbell. Again. Then he knocked. When it was clear no one was going to answer, he took out his keys. He hesitated, staring at the silver key between his fingers as if he were weighing whether or not he really wanted to go through with this. I half expected Nisha to elbow him out of the way and kick the damn door down, but he just patiently watched Elias, brow creased with worry.

Finally, Elias muttered something in one language or another and put the key into the lock.

The house was eerily silent. Our footsteps on the hardwood floor echoed off the high ceilings as we filed inside, and no sounds came from anywhere else in the house. My heart thundered in my ears as I toed off my shoes.

Nothing in the house seemed disturbed. The TV remote was in its usual place on the coffee table. That blanket he liked to drape over himself while we watched movies was still folded neatly on the back of the couch. The kitchen looked like something straight out of a home magazine—pristine and untouched, though there were a couple of empty bottles of Gatorade on the counter. That had to be a good sign, right? But how long had they been there?

I tamped down every imaginable worst-case scenario. What if he was here, but...not? What if he was—

No. No, I would not consider that. I refused. Julien was probably not in a good mental state, but he was alive.

Somewhere.

My gaze drifted to the stairs. Then I turned to Elias and Nisha. "I'm going to check his bedroom."

They both nodded grimly. I wondered what was going through their minds right now. I wasn't so sure I wanted to know.

With my heart in my throat, I took the stairs I'd climbed a million times before. The house's second level was as silent as the first, and I had to swallow a wave of nausea as I headed for Julien's bedroom.

The door was ajar. I nudged it slightly, and a barrage of emotions crashed into me when I saw him.

He was in bed with his back to me, his dark hair a mess on the pillow and the covers wrapped tightly around him. Breathing? *Please be breathing.*

I slipped into the room, and when the door hinges squeaked, he tensed ever so slightly. A wave of relief almost knocked me off my feet, but I also winced. He was alive, but how was he going to respond to me? Oh, fuck. What was about to happen?

Without turning over, he muttered something in French. Wait. No. That wasn't French. Too sharp. And had he said "Nikki?"

I inched closer to the bed. "No. It's me."

Julien whipped around, the covers slipping enough to reveal he was shirtless, and he stared up at me with a mix of shock, horror, and a million other emotions I couldn't read on his unshaven face. "Isaac."

"Hey. I, um..." My face burned. I wasn't sure why. "I was worried about you."

He blinked a few times. Then he sat against the headboard, drawing his knees up and hugging them to his chest as he avoided my gaze. "You shouldn't be here." He was clearly trying to sound disinterested and dismissive, but there was something else in his voice. Something that said his own words hurt him.

Hoping like hell I wasn't reading the situation all wrong, I came closer. "I'm here because you are."

His shoulders sagged and he ran a hand through his tousled hair, but he didn't speak.

Right then, my phone pinged. I was tempted to ignore it, but I checked in case it was Elias or Nisha.

It was Elias: *Is he up there?*

I thumbed back. *Yeah. He's awake. Hang on.*

Julien eyed my phone. Then me. Suspicion crept into his expression along with some wariness.

"Elias." I pocketed my phone. "He and Nisha are here too. They let me in."

"Let..." He nodded slowly, as if he'd made the connection. In a resigned voice, he asked, "So they're on their way up?"

"No. I was just letting them know I found you."

He laughed bitterly. "I wasn't missing."

I inclined my head.

He watched me. Then he looked away, chewing his lip

"I haven't seen or heard from you since the other night," I said softly. "I still don't even know what happened, but mostly...I'm worried about you. I needed to make sure you were okay."

*And we both know you're not. You're alive, but you are not okay, and fuck me, but I have no idea what to do.*

Julien exhaled. "You shouldn't be here."

The words stung, but I tried not to let it show. This was Julien hurting and vulnerable and feeling God knew what, like I'd never seen before, and he might've been lashing out. Shutting me and everyone else out. Trying to isolate himself.

Or...maybe he really didn't want me to be here. Maybe I'd overstepped a boundary at a time when he needed them to be respected.

I steeled myself. "Do you want me to leave?"

"You should."

"That wasn't what I asked."

He pinched the bridge of his nose and sighed.

I took a deep breath and tried unsuccessfully to keep my voice even. "Look me in the eye, Julien, and tell me you want me to leave."

He lifted his gaze, and I held my breath, terrified he was about to do exactly that. But the longer he looked at me, the more the cracks started to show. When he finally spoke, all that came out was a shaky whisper: "You need to go because I don't deserve you."

"That's not up to you." I sat decisively on the edge of the bed, still holding his gaze. "I'm here because I love you. And no, you don't deserve me."

He flinched, breaking eye contact.

I put a hand on his sheet-covered knee. "You deserve someone who doesn't second guess himself at every turn and just knows intuitively what you need, when you need it. You deserve someone who can always be or give you what you need." Fuck, my voice wasn't going to hold. "The best I can do is be everything I can for you, and give you everything I can, and—" My voice cracked, but I made myself go on. "I'm going to fuck that up sometimes. I know I will. But I can try my absolute best to be what you need, and all I can do is hope to God that's enough."

Julien sighed and leaned back against the headboard. He stared at the ceiling, and my heart ached as his eyes welled up. When he spoke, his voice was shakier than mine. "All I've done is take from you, Isaac."

"What? No, you haven't. Jesus, you've—"

"I have." He wiped at his eyes. "I knew from the start I'd be bad for you, and I let myself fall for you anyway, and... goddammit. I'm no better than *fucking Travis*."

I stared at him, utterly speechless for a few heartbeats. He was comparing himself to *that* waste of protective gear? Travis didn't deserve to be in the same sentence as Julien, for God's sake.

I shook myself. I cleared my throat, and though I was still scared I was going to fuck this up, I slipped into that voice that always got his attention. "Julien. Look at me."

He did, eyes full of surprise. Pain. Shame.

I put my hand on his. "I don't know what happened between the two of you. In the past, at the game...whenever. But can you really look me in the eye and tell me that Travis Canterbury would ever respond like this"—I gestured at him—"if he knew how much he hurt you?"

Julien furrowed his brow. "What do you mean?"

"You're trying to compare yourself to him, but I've seen the way he looks at you and tries to get under your skin. He hurt you, he knows it, and he still holds that over your head." I squeezed Julien's hand. "You get it in your head somehow that you're *anything* like him, and suddenly you're pulling back from me and comparing yourself to him. You're trying to protect me from you. That alone tells me you are *nothing* like him."

He stared down at our hands, and it killed me not to be able to reach up and brush away the tear sliding over his sharp cheekbone. He took a breath. "I thought he loved me. I was young. A rookie. And the whole time, he was using me. Making me think he was giving when he was really taking and taking." He looked at me, fresh tears in his eyes. "That's all I've done with you, Isaac. I just...I fucking take. I'm needy. I—"

"You're not taking anything I don't willingly give." I swallowed my emotions, which took work. "And you're giving so much more than you realize. I mean, I've wondered a few times if *I've* been taking too much because being with you is..." I laughed softly, squeezing his arm. "You've taken everything I ever imagined a relationship would be, and just blown it out of the goddamned water."

He watched me, disbelief written all over his unshaven face.

I slid closer to him, and this time I did brush away that tear. "Baby, come on. You won a bunch of money at the All-Star game, and your first thought was to put in a water feature because you know I love things like that. Someone like Travis..." I rolled my eyes and huffed with irritation. "He's the kind of guy who'd realize his boyfriend loved water, so he'd have his own swimming pool filled with concrete just to be a dick."

Julien blinked.

"You're nothing like him," I insisted. "I mean it. Whatever he's made you believe—about yourself, about relationships—he's wrong. I don't even have to know what he said or what he did to be absolutely certain of that, because I can *see* how much he's hurt you. Like what happened at the game the other night?" I shook my head. "I have no idea what the fuck that was, but I know you, and I know that *wasn't* you."

"It doesn't matter if it was me or not." He wiped a hand over his face and sighed. "I failed the team. I fucking blew it. I can't even face them again because they probably all hate me. I cost them the goddamned game by—"

"No, you didn't. And no, they don't."

He watched me skeptically.

"We won that game, Julien." I ran my thumb alongside his. "Everyone was confused and had no idea what happened, but we all agreed we had to keep it together. We didn't want you blaming yourself if we fell apart, so we didn't."

Some color bloomed in Julien's otherwise pale face. "I shouldn't have put any of you in that position."

"*Travis* shouldn't have put *you* in that position." I paused. "Look at me." When he did, I softly said, "No one's angry at you. Everyone keeps asking me when you're coming back and if you're okay."

His eyebrows rose.

"They're *worried* about you." I laced our fingers together. "We all are. The only reason I didn't come here again sooner was I was trying to respect your space, but I finally..." I shook my head as a lump rose in my throat. "I was scared, Julien. Really fucking scared."

He held my gaze, and understanding seemed to slowly dawn, as if he was starting to realize where my mind might have gone when he'd vanished into the ether like that. "I'm so sorry. I wasn't...I didn't mean to scare you like that."

"I know. I figured you were in a bad place. And you obviously are." I brought up our clasped hands and held them to my chest. "I want to help you through that."

Julien winced. "See? I'm taking again. That's *all* I do is take from you. Just like—"

"*Not* like him," I said sharply, and instantly felt guilty

when he jumped. Speaking softly now, I went on, "Julien. You're a good man. You're an amazing boyfriend." I gestured toward the door as I lowered our hands between us. "Two of your best friends are waiting downstairs because they care about you and want to make sure you're all right. We're all here for you right now because you're going through hell. And if one of us were going through something—hell, if *anyone* on the team were going through something—can you tell me honestly you wouldn't be the first to kick in a door and make sure we were all right?"

He chewed his lip.

"You open your home to us," I went on. "Our families. Our friends. Nobody on the team spends a holiday alone on your watch. You say that you take, take, take, but you don't even realize how much you *give*. Like how often you check in with me or with the guys to make sure we're all right. Or what about when Nisha left with that girl and Elias was off? Or when you fell all over yourself to apologize to Elias for Christmas? Or when we didn't even really know each other yet and you talked me down because I was blaming myself after we lost one night, even though we both know *you* were upset about it too?" I paused, then cautiously said, "I have a question."

His forehead creased, but he didn't speak.

I was flying blind here, venturing into territory I knew nothing about, but...I had a feeling. So, I went with it. "Remember when I took that high stick to the mouth, and I was afraid you'd want sex that night?"

Julien bristled, shifting on the mattress. "I remember."

I met his gaze. "How would Travis have handled that?"

He tensed all over, fingers twitching between mine.

"You don't have to answer," I said quickly. "You don't have to tell me anything about him. But think about it, and tell me truthfully if you and he are really the same."

Closing his eyes, he pressed back against the headboard

again. "I should tell you. You deserve to know." He stared up at the ceiling, and almost more to himself, he whispered, "So do Elias and Nikki."

"They don't know?"

"Not the whole story, no. No one does."

"No one—" I blinked. I'd thought Elias and Nisha were holding back in our conversation with Coach, but maybe not? "You've been carrying that alone for all this time?"

His face colored, and he didn't look at me as he nodded.

"Jesus. Julien." I slid closer to draw him into a hug.

He resisted. "I...haven't showered in..."

"I don't care." I wrapped my arms around him and held him tightly against me. I was determined to stay strong and keep myself together for him. He didn't need me breaking right now, but if he wanted to break, I wanted him to know he could lean on me.

"I'm so sorry," he whispered into my neck. "The other night... I..."

I stroked his hair. "Nothing to be sorry about. I'm just glad you're okay."

He sighed heavily and relaxed against me. Closing my eyes, I held him, basking in the relief that even though he *wasn't* okay yet, he was hopefully on his way there. At the very least, he knew he wasn't alone, no matter how much he stubbornly tried to be. People loved him and cared about him whether he believed he deserved it or not, and we weren't going anywhere. None of us.

I kissed his cheek and drew back to look at him. It wasn't unusual to see a few days' worth of scruff on his jaw, but he was so pale. Maybe even a little gaunt.

I caressed his face. "When was the last time you ate?"

Julien sheepishly avoided my eyes. "It's... I don't know. I've been staying hydrated. Sort of." He winced. "Probably not enough. And food... It's been a while."

"Okay." I tipped up his chin. "I'm going to have Elias order us all some pizza. Then we're going to take a shower."

"We?" His brow pinched. "Isaac, there's no way I can—"

"Baby." I shook my head. "I would never expect you to. I'm just making sure you don't collapse." *And there's no way in hell I'm letting you out of my sight.*

"I won't collapse." The faintest ghost of a smile curled the corners of his mouth. "But I won't say no to having you with me."

I tried not to let it show what a relief that was. If he wanted privacy, I'd give it to him, of course, but I'd be a nervous wreck the whole time I didn't have eyes on him.

Unsurprisingly, Julien was a little unsteady on his feet. Someone who burned as many calories as he did on a regular basis had no business going this long without food, even if he hadn't been doing much during that time.

I texted Elias, *Getting him into the shower. Order us some pizzas from that place you like?*

He replied quickly with, *Will do. Is he all right?*

I glanced at Julien, who was standing in his boxer briefs at the bathroom counter, eyeing his reflection as if he were looking at a stranger. To Elias, I said, *He's rough but ok. Shower & food will do him good.*

Then I put my phone aside and joined Julien in the bathroom.

His gaze was still fixed on himself. "Crisse, I look like hell."

"You look like you've been *through* hell." I wrapped an arm around his waist and kissed his shoulder. "We've got you, though."

Our eyes met in the mirror, and a weak smile cracked through his miserable expression. "You're something else, mon amour."

I smiled back, then patted his chest. "Come on. Shower."

He got the water started. As I stripped off my clothes and left them piled on the counter, he eyed them contemplatively.

"No." I touched his hip. "You're not folding or hanging up anything of mine. Not this time. I'm taking care of you."

He met my eyes with a startlingly sweet and vulnerable expression. "You always do."

"And I always will." I pushed myself up and kissed him softly. "In. You need to eat."

He didn't protest, and I followed him into his huge shower. He could scrub off a game's funk in no time, but he moved slowly today. Lethargically. It hurt to see; I wasn't used to him being broken like this. Sometimes he lifted the veil enough to let his wounds show, and sometimes he could be heartbreakingly vulnerable—I'd seen him scared, I'd seen him cry—but I wasn't used to seeing him like this. I'd heard of people being so exhausted or worn down that a strong wind could topple them, and that was Julien today.

Because of Travis Canterbury.

Rage boiled up in me, burning hotter than the shower beating on my back. I'd caught a glimpse of today's games, and Carolina was playing. Travis was back in the lineup, too. He had some satisfying bruises, not to mention stitches in his lip and above his eye, so he looked like hell. But he was playing again. He was probably getting ready for the game right now, relaxing between the morning skate and warm-ups, carrying on as normal while Julien could barely stand enough to shower.

It wasn't fucking fair. Travis had caused way too much pain and had way too few consequences for it.

But I wasn't doing Julien any good, seething about his ex. I was here for Julien. This was about him. It was about *now*.

Unaware of my racing thoughts, Julien tilted his head back to rinse some shampoo out of his hair, and for a moment, all I saw was the man he didn't think he deserved to be. My boyfriend. The gorgeous hockey player who'd cemented himself a place in the sport's history books. The friend who opened his home and his heart to anyone who needed it.

He was still every bit that man. He wasn't irreparably broken. He'd just taken a knee, and I hoped he understood how many people were ready and willing to rally around him and get him back on his feet.

As he wiped some water out of his eyes, I put my hands on his waist. He met my gaze, a few wet strands hanging over his face. I meant to say something, but one look at his expression, and the words died away. Now I could see both sides of him—the man I'd known all this time, and also the one who'd quietly hurting, keeping years' worth of pain and trauma under the surface until it had finally broken free.

Forget words.

I wrapped my arms around his neck and pulled him in close. He let himself be reeled in, pressing his face into my neck, and we just stood like that for a long time, silent except for the shower rushing all around us. In my arms, he felt both solid and brittle. Strong and broken. I hurt for him, and I was relieved to be holding him, and I wished like hell there was something I could do so there could actually be some *justice* in this whole fucked-up situation.

But...now.

Right now, we were here, and he was upright, and we were holding each other. Right now, food was on its way, and Julien had support he'd clearly thought was gone.

I pressed a kiss to his cheek and held him closer. He still had a lot to sort out and deal with. There was still a lot in his world that wasn't right, and God knew if it ever would be.

But now, he knew he was loved no matter what.

That seemed like a damn good start to me.

# Chapter 34

## Julien

The sweats Isaac pulled out for me to wear were ones with the team name and logo, and I dutifully donned them. Brushing my fingers over the griffin, I swallowed the aching lump in my throat. Isaac was *here*. My two best friends were here. The team was behind me, and they weren't going to let me go. All my bones, all my muscles hurt. I was so tired of being in this kind of soul-rending pain. And maybe, maybe, there was a way out of this.

The man I loved had come to help me find it.

"Come on." Isaac held his hand out. "Let's get you some coffee and some food."

I grasped his hand and let him guide me out of my room and down to the kitchen, and yes, the scent of freshly brewed coffee filled my nostrils. Elias, probably. He never let Nikki touch the coffeemaker.

For the first time in days, my stomach didn't rebel at the thought of putting something other than water or sports drinks into it, even though I dreaded what was coming. I didn't want to tell them what had led to those few seconds on the ice, how Travis had wrenched my soul open my rookie year and kept picking away at me all these years later.

But as I looked at Isaac and felt the warmth of his fingers around mine, I was strangely calm. Maybe I needed to share this burden. I certainly had needed to hear what Isaac had said to me, his eyes brimming with emotion—that *he* didn't think he was good enough for *me*—but that I was worth fighting for.

Maybe I was.

When I entered my kitchen and saw my two best friends, I knew without a doubt they believed that too. Nikki was sitting at the island, turning a mug of coffee in his hands. Elias was pacing. Both, like Isaac, were wearing team hoodies. Both froze when they saw me, and their expressions were the same, full of relief, worry, and love. Nikki stood so fast, his chair tumbled over. Elias took three long strides to cover the distance between us, then wrapped his arms around me.

I nearly started crying again.

His hug was almost physically crushing. Mentally, it absolutely was. I buried my face against his shoulder to keep the tears inside, and clung to him. "I'm sorry."

He stroked my hair, and murmured something in Swedish, before following up in English. "I have a feeling you're not to blame in this."

Maybe. Maybe not. "I'm still sorry."

"Jules." Nikki looked as hollowed out as I felt. "We should have come sooner."

When Elias let me go, Nikki enveloped me. His hug was gentler, but longer.

"Isaac tried. I heard. But I couldn't…" There were the pesky tears. "Fuck." I pressed my face against his chest.

My Russian was piss-poor next to Elias's, but I still understood the gist of the words Nikki muttered. Basically, "Baby, it's going to be okay."

I snorted, despite myself, and he drew back to give me a little shake. "It will."

"Whatever you say, Nikki." That came out as dry as dust.

Isaac righted the chair Nikki had toppled over. "Sit. I'll get you coffee."

After Nikki let me go, I planted my ass on the chair and leaned on the counter. "I should tell you what happened, but to do that, I need to tell you *everything* that happened, and I— It's a lot."

Elias and Nikki gave each other looks I recognized. Same ones as when shit was about to get bad.

Isaac slid a steaming mug of coffee in front of me, with the perfect amount of creamer in it. God, no matter how much he said otherwise, I didn't deserve him.

"Maybe you should wait until you've eaten?" He rubbed my back.

I frowned at the mug, wrapped my fingers around the handle, and pulled it closer. I loved Isaac so much. Loved Nikki and Elias too. "Probably, but I want to start anyway."

Elias grunted and turned, heading to where the little amount of hard alcohol in my house resided. He took out the bottle of gin and four rocks glasses, but also rooted around for the whiskey he'd bought for me, then always drank. "Nisha?"

"Yes, please."

Elias showed the bottle to Isaac. "Care to join us?"

Isaac considered, then shook his head. "Not now. Maybe later."

That got Isaac a grunt and a nod. Elias poured two glasses of whiskey, handed one to Nikki, then took a seat.

"I'm not getting a drink?" I flicked fingers at the bottle of gin Elias had left on the counter.

Elias nodded to my coffee. "You have one. You can have the other after you eat."

Probably for the best. I sipped the coffee and let the

warmth and the sharp dark taste ground me. "Canterbury was one of my idols when I was young. His stats aren't great now, but when he was in his mid-twenties?" I blew out a breath. "He was a power forward. Sniper. Could dance around the defense. I wanted to skate like him."

"You skate far better than him." Elias's words were sharp and angry.

I took another swallow of coffee. Maybe. So many people said I was one of the best skaters in the league. "When Pittsburgh drafted me, I was ecstatic. I didn't know much about the team, but I did know Canterbury had signed a three-year deal with the Griffins as a free agent. I was finally going to meet my idol, see him skate in person on the same team I might be on. Sure, he was thirty, but he still had good wheels and a great shot."

Elias nodded. "He came in our second year here. Third line minutes, but racked up points anyway."

Nikki made a face, then sipped his whiskey. "He didn't like me."

I met Nikki's gaze. "You're not his type." I knew that much. Nikki and Travis were the same height, nearly the same build, too. "Too tall."

"Me too, I think," Elias said. He cocked his head, then pulled out another chair. "Isaac, sit before you pace a hole into the floor."

Isaac let out a sigh, sank into the chair, then reached across the island to grasp my hand. "I need to tell you something about Travis, but after, okay?"

I had no idea what Isaac could tell me about— "Wait, did he hit on you?"

Isaac's pained expression told me everything. Elias's hands landed on my shoulders and kept me in my seat. "Julien. He's not here."

Right, right. I let out a breath, sank back down, then took

another swig of coffee. "My rookie year, training camp was—overwhelming. I had no idea what I was doing. Everything was so much faster than in major juniors, and the players..." I let out a sharp laugh. "Older than me. I was eighteen when camp started, and I kept out of the way as much as possible. Stayed quiet—I didn't want to bother anyone. Too afraid they'd realize they'd made a mistake and ship me back home. Travis—he was kind to me."

Hard to imagine now, after everything I'd been through, but those first days, he'd set me at ease. Made me smile. "He took time to show me the ropes. Told me when meals were. Showed me around the facility. Gave me a ride over to the local shopping center so I could get some things. He even knew a smattering of French."

Nikki scowled, sipped his whiskey, and said nothing.

"He wasn't an asshole up front. He was—witty and kind. Told me I was doing okay, which..." I let out a hollow laugh and gave Isaac a shrug. "Elias and Nikki know. I wasn't good that year. I'm still surprised they didn't send me to the farm team."

"You were *young*, that's all," Nikki said. "Hell, we all were." His waving hand encompassed both Elias and me.

Elias nodded slowly. "You were *inconsistent*, not horrible. You could skate and your instincts were on par with the older guys when you didn't overthink." Then he huffed. "Which—as Nikki said—pretty much described all of us back then. But you were always the best skater. Especially backward."

That had been a point of pride—the skating. Also the quality that Travis had praised, at least at first.

"I turned nineteen about halfway through training camp, a couple of days before we hit the road for some exhibition games."

"I remember," Elias said. "There was cake in the lounge

and we had to coax you into having a piece because you didn't want to cause trouble."

"I was shy back then. Naïve and nervous." Didn't want to stand out. Didn't want everyone to notice how fidgety I was, how bad my English was—any number of things. The overwhelmed rook who couldn't sleep through the night because every sound in the hotel was wrong and woke me up.

I expected Isaac to chuckle or express disbelief, but he nodded, then reached over to take my hand. "Sensitive heart."

Everything about Isaac made me melt, but especially that smile. The way he could read me, see past all the barriers and walls. He saw *me*.

In that instant, I knew Isaac was right. I wasn't like Travis—not one bit. I had more in common with my nineteen-year-old self, whose cheeks had burned bright when I'd glimpsed 'Happy Birthday, Julien' written on that sheet cake.

"Travis said he got me the cake," I murmured. "I wonder if that was a lie."

The face Nikki made—part disgust, part snarl. "Nothing but lies ever came from that mouth."

"Sometimes he didn't lie." I hated that one simple fact. The truths Travis speared me with hurt a hell of a lot more than the lies—and made the lies hard to see.

"Julien—" Isaac squeezed my hand. "He *lies*."

"No!" My voice rose in panic, and I had to catch a breath. "You have to understand—not *everything* he said was a lie. Just —a lot of it." I pulled away from Isaac and hunched over my mug. "He lied about caring for me, I know that. But I *am* a mess. Everywhere at once—all of that."

Isaac reached over and reclaimed my hand. "You're not a mess. You're a hockey player—and you're you."

Elias leaned back in his seat and took a sip of whiskey. "You can manipulate people with the truth, you know. Especially when twisted around lies."

My every interaction with Travis since that year shifted into bright focus. The taunts, the threats. All the crap Travis has spewed at me had always been crafted to cut and hurt. To undermine what I knew and believed.

"Shit." I really needed that gin. But Elias was right—after food.

I forged ahead with my story. "The night of my birthday, Travis showed up at my hotel to celebrate. With a twelve-pack of beer."

"That fuck!" Nikki ground out the words.

That night loomed so large in my head now, but at the time, I'd been flattered that this player who I'd admired so much wanted to talk to me about my game. "I didn't think anything of it. You can drink at eighteen in Quebec. I'd had beer before, so it wasn't anything shocking." I shook my head. "In retrospect, I was a fool."

"You were nineteen," Elias said, quietly.

I stared down into my coffee, took a sip, then continued. "It started out fine. We drank and chatted about the week, how I'd done. The systems. I asked about his first game in the league. My spoken English was rocky—I needed practice—but I understood him just fine, and I managed to keep up. At least for the first couple cans of beer."

More coffee, and I rocked my neck back and forth in an effort to release some of the building tension. "The room was small, so we ended up sitting on the bed, against the headboard. He started asking more personal questions. If I was seeing anyone. That sort of thing."

*"You have a girlfriend? Boyfriend?"*
*I laughed. "No."*
*"You have a preference?"*
*I shook my head. "No. Any gender. Just need to like them."*

*"Do you like me, Julie?"*

I squeezed my eyes shut, and let out a breath. "I was so surprised when he kissed me that I think I whimpered, or gasped, or something. I guess he took that as permission, and before I could think to say anything, he was getting into it and I—didn't stop him."

Elias had his head in his hands. Isaac's grip was almost painful, and his face deathly pale. Nikki sat perfectly still, staring into his whiskey.

"He fucked me. At least twice that night. It's—hazy exactly what happened. But I didn't try to stop him."

Nikki flattened a hand against the marble top. "Could you have? How much did you drink?"

I shook my head and whispered, "I don't remember." The tears came back, and slid down my cheeks. I pushed them away with the heel of my hand. "I was pretty sick the next morning. Thank God we had off that day from camp."

I'd spent the morning in the bathroom, next to the toilet, utterly hungover, sick to my stomach, and aching from sex.

"I felt—ashamed. Like I'd done something wrong." I lifted my gaze and met Isaac's. "I figured I must have done *something* to lead him on. Convinced myself that I'd meant for that night to happen. Hoped it wouldn't ruin the friendship."

I let out a hollow laugh. "Friendship."

My lover and my friends stared at me. Finally Isaac cleared his throat. "I think I'll take that drink now, Elias."

It was Nikki who rose, poured Isaac two fingers of whiskey, then slid the glass in front of him. Then he straightened to his full height. "I'm going to kill him."

Elias laughed softly in a way that made my blood run cold. "Get in line." No warmth at all there.

Isaac took a large swallow of whiskey.

"No one is killing anyone. I tried that the other night, and it didn't go so well."

They didn't say anything. I guess there wasn't much to say.

"Next practice, Travis was all smiles and praise. He managed to get me alone for a moment, and told me how much that night had meant to him, how beautiful I was, and that he'd love to see me again." Fucking tears. I wiped them off my face. "I believed him. So we started dating. Sex after that was—better. Kinder, I guess. At least for a while. He was nice, too. Even sweet, sometimes. He told me we had to keep our relationship a secret, or we'd both get thrown out of the league." The coffee in the mug had gone cold, but I drank the rest of it anyway. "That's how it started."

Elias scrubbed his face with his hands. "My God, Julien. If I'd known..."

"If *we'd* known," Nikki added.

"You weren't supposed to. Even after it ended. No one was supposed to know."

Isaac stirred, his face still pale, and his movements had weight to them. "What changed?"

Before I could answer, Elias's phone chimed. He peered at it, then rose. "Pizza is nearly here."

Good. I needed a break. "I'll take that gin and tonic, please."

Nikki eyed me. "Eat two slices, and I'll make you one."

I ate three before Nikki placed the drink in front of me. Best damn pizza I'd ever tasted. I wanted more, but took a pause, and sipped the drink Nikki had made. It was cold, full of juniper and that tang on my tongue that I liked. The alcohol threatened to go straight to my head. Typical Nikki drink—he had a heavy hand. But I was grateful for the spirits.

I hadn't even thought to touch alcohol during my stint in bed.

"Travis wasn't that bad for the first few months," I murmured, without preamble.

I took another swallow of my drink and told my friends all that I hadn't. The way Travis had praised me, for my play, my looks, my intelligence in the days that followed my birthday. When I'd scored during the exhibition game against Cleveland, he'd been effusive and charming—and I'd fallen for that.

He told me he thought about me all the time—wanted to be with me, but if the team caught us, bad things would happen. He'd stolen kisses anyway. "He was actually a good kisser. That was the worst thing—I liked that. The attention, the affection. Made me feel like I might make it in the league. Like I was good enough."

Elias hissed something that I didn't catch, and Nikki gave him a look. So did Isaac and I, for that matter, but he shook his head, so I forged on.

"By about two weeks into the regular season, I was going over to his house to practice my shot, or work out in his home gym, or study games with him—and we were fucking regularly. I'd decided since we'd already had sex, we might as well again, and maybe I'd enjoy it more." I scowled into my drink. "I did, too. For the most part."

Travis wasn't what I'd call a thoughtful lover, but he did make sure I got off because he loved hearing my cries. There were many times when I went home feeling hollow, but wrote it off as tiredness. After I'd mentioned that, Nikki sputtered out, "You never stayed at his house?"

My laugh was sharp and bitter even to my ears. "Oh no. He fucked me senseless, told me to get dressed, then sent me on my way after telling me how hot my ass was that night."

Isaac closed his eyes. "How is it that you didn't punch him in the face before now?"

"I didn't want to be around him at all," I said. "I knew I'd lose it. I tried to keep away from him, so I wouldn't."

Isaac rubbed my back. "You have a lot more self-control than you think."

I snorted, but didn't gainsay him. Despite the pizza starting to cool, I snagged another slice. My stomach had been roiled the past couple of days, but now that my body had food again, it wanted more. A few bites and another sip gin and tonic, and I was ready to continue. "Everything changed after that eight to one loss in Toronto." He'd been so angry after that game. I'd tried to console him, but he'd turned on me. "He blamed the loss on me."

Elias nearly choked on his whiskey, sputtering, then rasping out, "On you? You were on the third D pair. Hell, you weren't even out for five of those goals!"

"But I was for three. He said if I'd done my job, I'd have blocked those shots and given us a chance to win."

"That's such bullshit," Isaac murmured. "I don't even know which game you mean, but I know it's bullshit."

"Of course it was, but I was too much of a fool to recognize what he was doing."

Nikki spit out some Russian I didn't understand. "You weren't a fool," he growled. "You were a *kid*."

Tears pricked at my eyes. "I was *me*, Nikki. Still am."

Isaac found my hand and squeezed it. "Nisha's right. You're not a fool. You're kind and honest. It's not a fault."

Fuck. The tears were going to come back. I blinked hard and took a large swallow of my drink. I told them how Travis had yelled at me for blowing the game, then cold-shouldered me for days while I scrambled to apologize. Then we fucked until I couldn't move—and the whole cycle started again. The showering of affection and attention. The kindness. The sex. The way my spirits would lift—until the next time Travis got upset about something—anything.

He told me I was a mess. I was a horrible player. Couldn't

shoot, couldn't skate, could barely fuck. Too thin, too small, too weak. Too anxious, too fidgety. Too clingy.

"Too everything," I murmured. "I didn't know how to keep him happy. I tried so hard. Worked extra at practices. Fought on the ice to defend and score. Tried to be everything he wanted me to be." I shook my head. "By the time the season ended, I was grateful for every smile and tiny bit of praise and terrified of every frown, every critical word."

Isaac seemed to chew on something—wasn't pizza. Probably was a thought. Or maybe bile. He met my gaze. "Did you tell them about what he did to you on the plane?"

That had me flatten my hands against island, and I shook my head.

Isaac cocked his toward Nikki and Elias.

Yeah, they probably should know. "You remember that flight to California?"

They both paled. Oh yes, they remembered. Elias met Isaac's questioning look. "It was bad—things hit the ceiling. Bags fell out of the overhead. An attendant broke his arm because he didn't get to his seat in time."

"Travis sat there while I had a panic attack and told me in graphic detail how I was going to die. Burn up when we hit the ground. He laughed when I started crying. Called me an absolute baby at being so overwrought by a *joke*." I spit out the last word. "Every flight after that, we hit a rough patch? Same shit."

Nikki cradled his head in his hands, and I swear he looked like *he* might cry.

I rubbed my eyes. There were things I might never tell anyone about that year. Isaac had guessed some of them. Travis insisting I blow him after a game where I'd gotten a split lip in a fight. I'd done it because the alterative was being berated for a week or two. That might have happened anyway, but if I gave Travis what he wanted, it might not.

"I went back home during the off season. My siblings knew something wasn't right. Marie tried to pry it out of me, but I never told her."

Isaac swirled his drink. "Only Nisha and Elias know?"

"And you."

Elias cringed. So did Nikki for that matter. "Well," he said. "Coach knows now. That you two dated. We...told him."

No anger came. Instead, relief washed over me like a cool rain, and that was confusing. "That's okay." I looked from Elias to Nikki. "He knew something was wrong. Gave me the business card of a psychologist."

Nikki nodded, but didn't say the obvious: that seeing a professional about all this was probably a very, *very* good idea.

I focused on Isaac. "Travis contacted me on and off that summer. Texts. Phone calls. Facetime. Always on his terms. Sometimes it was good, sometimes he'd berate me. He...posted photos of all the models he was banging in Florida, then would tell me how much he missed me. That he couldn't wait until training camp." I shook my head. "A week and a half before camp, he was traded to Carolina, and that was it."

Isaac blinked. "What do you mean 'that was it'?"

"He stopped texting. Stopped calling. A few days afterward, when I tried to call, his number had been disconnected. He blocked me on his socials."

"You've got to be fucking kidding me," Elias murmured.

"I..." I heaved a sigh and finished off my gin and tonic. "I thought he was mad at me. That somehow I'd caused the trade. I nearly didn't go to camp, but that would have made my family ask too many questions, so I did." I paused. "I shoved everything down, and focused on trying to be the best hockey player I could. I thought maybe...maybe if I got better, he'd..." My voice cracked.

Without a word, Nikki rose, took my glass and refilled it. "Only a little gin this time."

True to his word, there was more tonic and lime than gin. "Anyway. That year was—" I let out a hollow laugh. "It was a disaster, I'm still not sure why I wasn't sent down to the minors."

Elias raised an eyebrow, and I managed a chuckle. "Fine, I do know why I wasn't." Tapping my fingers against my glass, I gave Isaac a shrug. "Elias and Nikki saved my ass."

"Eh." Nikki waved a hand. "You saved your own ass in the end. We helped."

I filled Isaac in on how inconsistent I'd been. One game playing strong, the next, as if I barely understood the game. "I settled in eventually, when Coach—not this one, the previous one—chewed my ass off. At least until the Carolina game."

"Ah, shit," Isaac said. He took my hand again.

Shit, indeed. "That one I actually did make us lose."

"No," Elias said. "We all had a part in it."

I snorted. "I took nine minutes of penalties."

Nikki shrugged. "We killed off most of them."

"Most." I sipped my drink.

Elias's brow furrowed. "What happened that night?"

"Exactly what happened on the ice." I'd been out of my head. Distraught. Undisciplined. I wasn't trying to trip up players, or hit them high, or any of that. I'd been *shattered*. "What I never told you was that Travis texted me the day before."

Nikki barked out a curse in Russian and stood. I thought he'd go for the whiskey again, but he got a glass of water instead.

"He wanted to meet for dinner. Talk. Gave me a time and place."

I'd gone. Taken my seat and waited. And waited. And waited.

"He stood you up," Isaac murmured.

"Oh no, he showed up. With his girlfriend on his arm. Took a seat at the table next to mine."

I'd been so fucking embarrassed and distraught and angry. Part of me wanted to storm out, but I didn't want to give him that satisfaction, so I'd flagged the waiter, ordered my dinner, then sat there and ate it, all while Travis had wined and dined and made out with his gorgeous model girlfriend. The meal had cost a small fortune and had lain in my stomach like a rock, but I paid the check and walked out with my head high.

"I thought I'd won." Oh, how foolish I'd been. There was never any winning against Travis Canterbury, only surviving. "He called me to tell me I was a pathetic mooning lapdog not fit to be in the league, and the only thing I'd ever been to him was a hole to fuck." I spit the words out.

Elias dropped his head into his hands. "Julien..."

I shook and seethed. "I hate him so much. I wish he'd leave me alone."

Isaac shifted his chair closer. Wrapped an arm around me. "Do you see that you're nothing like him?"

No, I didn't. I did and I *didn't*.

"Wait, what?" Elias raised his head and pinned me with his stare. "You think you're like *Travis*?"

"I—"

"Julien!" Utter disbelief and horror in Elias's voice.

"I'm arrogant and self-centered. I still can't take care of myself, and Isaac—"

Isaac cut me off. "Baby, if you were anything like that waste of ice time, none of us would be here right now."

I knew they were right. *Knew* it. But I couldn't keep that voice out of my head. "That's what made me snap at the game. He said I was like him. That he'd made me into him. I was fucking a rookie like he had, and the thought that I did that to Isaac—" I couldn't keep the sob or the tears back this time.

Pushing the glass out of the way, I folded my arms on the island, buried my head, and cried.

Isaac drew warm circles on my back, and murmured, "Baby, it's okay. I'm good. I love you." He paused. "And I know you love me."

My soul felt flayed. Ragged and thin.

"He also admitted it," Nikki said. "What he did to you. Maybe not directly, but by saying that..."

Shit. *Shit*. Yes, that too. I trembled, then nodded. "I—lost control. Eight years." I shook my head, then wiped the tears from my eyes. "I'd been putting up with his shit for eight years. The fucker, he—" I exhaled. Because I still couldn't say it. "I don't think I'll ever forgive him."

"You don't have to." Isaac pushed back the hair that had fallen into my eyes. His were brimming with tears. "You don't owe him anything. Not consideration. Not kindness. Not forgiveness. Nothing."

That was the most freeing thing anyone had ever said to me. I wrapped my arms around Isaac, and held on.

A few moments later, another warm hand landed on my back. Nikki's. My eyes were watery, but I could see well enough to catch Elias's hand and hold it tight. "Thank you for being here." I kissed Isaac's forehead, then glanced at Elias and tried to tip my head back to see Nikki. "Again, in some cases."

Nikki squeezed my shoulder.

"So how did you all get so tight?" Isaac's breath was warm against my neck.

"Maybe they can tell that part." I was so worn out from talking—and I knew I wasn't finished telling this story today.

Elias's grip tightened before he let go of my hand. "Okay." He rocked his head from side to side, as if deciding where to start. "It's because of that game—the Carolina one. Afterward, Julien disappeared. No one knew where he'd gone. He'd been in the locker room with us, then he wasn't. Coach—the old one—was spitting teeth. Said if he wasn't on the bus in twenty, we were leaving him. I told him we'd find him."

Nikki picked up. "Jules was one of us, the younger guys. We couldn't leave him. Coach said he'd leave us too if we weren't on the bus."

"I was hiding in a broom closet. Figured I'd catch a flight to Pittsburgh, pack my stuff, and head back to Saguenay."

Elias rolled his eyes. "We opened every non-locked door in the bowels of that arena. Found him with about eight minutes to spare. I think the threat of Coach leaving us behind too got him moving."

"It did." I didn't want them punished for my decisions, so I went with them.

Elias told Isaac how Nikki'd sat next to me on the bus, how he'd commandeered the club seats on the plane so we could all sit together. "Julien barely spoke through the whole thing. Nisha got out a deck of cards and we made him play Rummy with us until we landed."

I nodded. "I could hardly see the cards. I was—barely holding my shit together. But it helped."

"When we finally got back to the facility, Julien starts wheeling his luggage across the parking lot. I had no idea what he was doing, so I went after him. So did Nisha."

"I was heading back to the hotel."

Nikki snorted. "And that's how we found out he was still living in a damn hotel room. A month and a half after training camp."

Isaac stared at me. "Hotels aren't your favorite."

That was a kind way to let me know he'd noticed how much I didn't like hotels. Even the expensive ones we frequented. "They aren't. But I was so convinced I'd be sent to the minors or dismissed entirely, I didn't want to get a place, then have to break a lease."

Elias nodded. "Pretty much what he said to us back then. So we marched over there, helped him pack, had him check out, and he came to live with me that season. I had a three-bedroom townhouse nearby. Plenty of room for another person, and Nisha was literally two doors down, so it worked out well."

"Probably saved my career." I sipped my gin and tonic, which at this point was mostly watered down tonic. "Elias's place was quiet. Orderly. We got into a routine—all of us. Nikki even got us extra practice time at the rink. Worked with the trainers to get me into a good workout routine. All the shit Travis had half-assed to get me in bed, they—" I waved at Elias and Nikki, and my voice choked up. "They did to make me a better hockey player."

Nikki's hands tightened on my shoulders. "Made us better players, too."

I huffed out a laugh at that.

"And after Travis, you didn't date anyone until me?" Isaac's question was innocent enough, but the look Elias threw me wasn't at all. Which, of course had Isaac searching me for an explanation.

Shit. This was not the way I wanted to talk about this. On the other hand, it was part of the whole story.

"I really didn't," I murmured.

Elias scrunched his face. Nikki patted my back, then reclaimed his seat, suddenly becoming very interested in his water glass.

Isaac was too observant not to notice. "Okay. What?"

So I sighed and shrugged. "I didn't think I could have sex with anyone after that. Not without it fucking with my head. Nikki said I should get on Grindr or Tinder and find someone to hook up with, but I— God, I wasn't even sure I could function in bed. That I wouldn't break down, you know? I didn't want to subject anyone to that."

I saw the pieces click together in Isaac's mind, and his gaze shifted to Nikki. "You hooked up."

I nodded. "Only once. But it was good, and it helped, and gave me the courage to have sex with other people again."

"It felt like you two dated," Elias said. He finally finished his whiskey, downing the remnants in one go.

There was that hint of jealousy again. I still didn't understand it. "To be fair, it felt like all of us were dating, to some extent. But no, we didn't date." I turned my attention to Nikki. "I love both of you—but there's nothing romantic there."

Nikki shrugged. "I'm glad it helped."

It had. I ran my hand through my hair, and teased out a knot. "And that's all of it, I think."

Silence fell in the kitchen.

"Did he keep texting you?" Isaac's quiet question slipped through the air.

I nodded. "Still does, once in a while. I never answer. I probably should have blocked his new number or changed mine, but I'm sure he'd find a way around both, so I never bothered. Just—little digs. Usually when I least expect them."

"Fucker," Nikki muttered into his water.

I stared into the remnants of my drink, then turned to Isaac. "You said you had something to tell me about Travis?"

His brows pinched. "I don't think you're the only one he's done this to. At the All-Stars, between games, I ran into him while I was in line to get food. He—" Isaac shook his head. "At first, I thought he was angry, but then I think he tried to come on to me. Before I could say anything, I was yanked out of line by someone posing as a PR assistant. I'd never seen the guy before. We ended up in a hallway, and he told me to stay away from Travis—that he liked young players like me, and that he was bad news."

My heart skittered to a stop, then thrummed hard against my chest.

"I think he was a player. From the Midlands division. I recognized him a little—but I don't know everyone in the league."

Elias already had his phone out, and he pulled up the photos of all the players from the Midlands that had been at the All-Stars. He shoved the phone at Isaac. "Which one?"

Isaac blinked, then studied the photos. "Vince Alexander, I think."

I knew the name, but only vaguely. "He's a forward, plays for—Texas? Minnesota?"

Elias had reclaimed his phone. "Minnesota this year. Houston last." He looked up, and around the island. "He started out in Carolina."

I squeezed my eyes shut. "Câlisse." I didn't know what to feel. Travis had fucked over someone else, too. *How many*, I wondered. Was he fucking some rookie *right now*? Was this my fault? "I have to say what happened."

"You don't," Isaac said.

"I do. I can—I could have stopped—"

"Don't," Nikki said, suddenly and vehemently. "You're not to blame for anything he does. Only he is. He chose to prey on you. Maybe others. Not your fault."

I swallowed. Nikki was right. Isaac was right, too. "I *want* to say what happened. I'm *tired* of carrying this around. It's time." I shrugged. "Besides, you know the media will be all over me until I explain what happened."

Once more, they were all silent. I chewed on my lip. "I need to tell my family first." The weight of it all crashed down on me. "And Coach and probably Kelly. The team. Fuck." That was...a lot. A lot of hard conversations. I glanced over at the clock on the microwave: 3:57 PM.

"Team can be tomorrow," Nikki said.

Elias nodded, then glanced at Nikki, and they seemed to have an entire conversation with just that look. Then he focused on me. "If you're okay with it, we can fill Coach and Kelly in, in general terms. Take that off your shoulders."

I pushed my glass around on the island as I considered their offer, then nodded. "I trust both of you. Thank you."

Isaac touched my arm. "Do you want me to stay?"

The thought of Isaac leaving now nearly tore me in two. "Please, unless your car—" My mind whirled back to the night of the game. Isaac's car had been at his house. I'd driven him to the game. Then left. "Oh shit, your *car*. I left you at the arena!" I was out of my chair in an instant, panic choking me.

"Julien!" Isaac was there, his hands on either side of my face. "Look at me."

Such command in his voice. I couldn't not meet his gaze. "I'm fine. I'm *here*, right now. It's a five-minute ride to my house from the arena. I took an Uber." He dropped his hands, then took mine and turned it palm up.

Exposing my tattoo. *Now*.

I closed my eyes and fell into his arms. "Sorry."

He held me. "It's okay, baby. Honest."

"I should give you keys."

He huffed at that. "Yeah. I should give you mine, too. Didn't think about it, since we were always together."

There was a chuckle. Elias, I think. "We should head out," he said. "We need to catch up with Coach and Kelly, after all."

Isaac and I untangled and we both gave Nikki and Elias hugs before seeing them to the door. "Thank you both, again, for everything."

"C'est rien," Elias said. "You'd do the same for us."

I would, except... "You two would never fuck up as much as I did."

Nikki shrugged. "You never know." That had Elias rolling his eyes.

I watched as they headed to their car, closed the front door, then wrapped my arms around Isaac again. "Thank you for coming to take care of me. To be here for me."

"Anytime," Isaac said against my chest. "Every time." He pulled back. "You'd be there for me."

His dark hair was getting longer. Curlier. I pushed it off his forehead and kissed him there. "I need to text my sister. She'll get the family set up for a call." I paused. "I should probably also text my agent."

Isaac nudged me toward the stairs. "I'll clean up the kitchen."

As I headed up to collect my phone, everything felt strange. When I reached my bedroom, I realized that what was in my heart—my aching, exhausted heart—was hope.

I clung to that with everything I had.

---

BY THE TIME I finished up the video conference with my siblings and my parents, I was ready to collapse. Good thing I was on my couch. I slid the laptop onto the coffee table and slumped against Isaac. He pulled me into his arms and held me.

Texting my agent had been fairly simple. He'd called me back, and we'd chatted briefly about the situation. "I'm so sorry, Julien. Anything you need from me, I'll be here. We'll make sure the league does right by you."

My family, though? God. Everyone had cried, especially my mom. So had I, for that matter. Yes, I went through it, but I also couldn't imagine being a parent and finding out years later that your teen child had been sexually assaulted and mentally abused.

Both Marie and Mathieu had looked like they wanted to kill someone. Marie had wanted to fly out here tonight. Isaac had gently dissuaded her after I switched to English long enough to say that Isaac was with me, that I wasn't alone.

She didn't argue with Isaac—just told him to take good care of me.

"With everything I have," Isaac had responded. "I'm not perfect, but I'm going to do everything I can to make sure he's safe. Loved."

She'd nodded at that.

I promised them that I'd come back to Saguenay for a chunk of time during the off season, then they'd let me go.

Isaac rubbed my arms. "Do you want dinner?"

I nodded because I was hungry. "I should do some cardio."

He gave me a look. "You've been through a wringer."

"I've been lying in bed for days. I need to move my body a little. Tomorrow's going to suck enough as it is." Hopefully, all the years of skating wouldn't fail me, and I wouldn't take a header as soon as I stepped out on the ice.

He gave me a light shrug. "See what twenty on the bike does? I'll order burgers."

I did exactly that. Afterward, I shot a dozen pucks at the net. Felt both good and absolutely awful. There was no way around sucking tomorrow. Hopefully, I could get my conditioning back up quickly. We had a game in two days.

I set my stick against the wall with great care. I *wanted* to play. I wanted to be a Griffin.

I was *back*. I still had a long climb ahead of me, and I couldn't say I was fine—everyone was right, I needed to talk to a professional—but my head was clear and there was nothing Travis could do to me anymore.

And tomorrow, I'd finally tell the world what he'd done.

# Chapter 35

## Isaac

It was barely eight o'clock, and Julien was out cold beside me on his couch.

I didn't blame him. The last few hours had left *me* wrung out, so I could only imagine what they'd done to him.

I was sitting up, my arm around his shoulders, and he leaned against me, arm across my stomach and head under my chin as he breathed slowly and evenly. I was exhausted, but I couldn't relax enough to go to sleep. There was too much whirring around inside my head. Too much to process.

Leaning my head back against the couch, I stared up at the ceiling as I absently stroked Julien's hair.

Holy shit. Everything he'd been through. Everything that asshole had done to him. I'd known for a long time that Travis had worked him over, but I hadn't known how young Julien had been. I definitely hadn't imagined just how badly he'd been abused. Even Elias and Nisha had been blindsided by it all, and they'd been there for some of it. At least for the immediate aftermath. No one had known. No one but Julien and Travis. Good God. Eight years was a long, long time to carry that abuse alone.

He wasn't alone now, though, and he wouldn't be alone going forward. He had his family, his friends, and the team behind him. Elias had texted while we'd eaten dinner to tell us they'd spoken to Coach and Kelly. Everyone wanted to get ahead of this and address it before Julien played again, so there'd be a press conference tomorrow. Coach had also said practice would be closed to both fans and media to give Julien some breathing room while he got his skates under him again. It was an unusual move, but I was grateful for it. Julien seemed to be too. I didn't think he could handle a practice with cameras peering at him the whole time. Especially not when he'd have to face those cameras afterward.

Coach and Kelly both texted Julien with some encouragement and that they were glad he was doing better. That helped, I thought. I was also beyond grateful Elias and Nisha had handled all of that; I wasn't sure Julien could have taken much more.

I was glad he'd had Elias and Nisha back then, too. The fact that Julien and Nisha had slept together—I honestly wasn't surprised, the more I thought about it. Some part of me had thought I should be jealous when they confirmed it, but I wasn't. If anything, I was relieved. I was grateful that someone who truly cared for Julien had been there to help him put the pieces back together. I had no idea what Nisha was like in bed, but I knew to my core that he was a good, kind man, and that Julien had been safe in his arms that night. Safer than he'd been before.

Thank God for Nisha. Thank God for Elias.

I exhaled into the stillness. It was a struggle, fitting all this in my head. Imagining that someone existed who could—and *would*—break someone the way Travis had broken Julien. Deliberately. Sadistically. Who did that? What the fuck was wrong with Travis? And...I mean, no one deserved that treatment, but the thought of someone hurting Julien like that...

My throat tightened, and I held my sleeping boyfriend closer as all the emotions I'd been holding back threatened to crack through. Ever since I'd found him this afternoon, I'd fought hard to keep myself together. This wasn't a time for Julien to try to take care of me or to worry about what I was feeling. He needed me to be strong for him, and my God, it had been hard, but I'd made myself stay strong all through that conversation in the kitchen and while he'd talked to his family. It had been kind of a blessing that I couldn't understand much of what he and his family had been saying, but there'd been a lot of tears and emotions that couldn't be muted by a language barrier.

Through it all, I'd forced back my own feelings so I wouldn't pile more on Julien.

Now...

Now I wasn't so sure that dam was going to hold. There was just so fucking much. Realizing how deep Travis's abuse ran. The pain in Julien's eyes and his voice. How even Elias and Nisha had looked close to tears more than once.

With my free hand, I wiped at my eyes.

I couldn't break. Not now. Julien was asleep, but he was still here, and I didn't want him waking up to me losing it.

This also wasn't over yet. Tomorrow would be more hell for him. He needed to know he could lean on me without worrying about if I could handle it.

Maybe I needed a few minutes alone. A break. If I could keep it together until we went upstairs to bed, Julien would probably be out cold the second he hit the pillow, and I could slip off for a shower and let that hide any emotions I couldn't hold back anymore.

I closed my eyes and exhaled slowly. That was all I needed to do. Hold out until we went to bed. Then cry and curse into the shower until I was sturdy enough to be what he needed. I could make it that long. Right?

Maybe.

Fuck.

I wiped my eyes again.

*Don't do it. Not now. Not while he's sitting right here.*

He was dead asleep, but if I broke down, I could easily wake him up. Not gonna happen.

I took some slow, deep breaths, careful not to jostle him in the process, and I ran my fingers through his hair. He sighed in his sleep and stirred against me. I was almost surprised he didn't start purring.

The thought made me laugh, and I pressed a kiss to the top of his head. All the times I'd compared him to a cat, and now he was curled against me, sleeping more soundly than he probably had in days, and I could imagine him actually purring.

So sweet. Such a gentle, loving man.

And so...fucking...*wounded*.

It wasn't fair that he'd been through that. Or that he'd lost so many years to believing all the poison Travis had dripped in his ear. Everyone who knew Julien could see how amazing he was on every level, but one man—one absolute trash fire of a human being—had completely distorted Julien's ability to see the beautiful, kind, funny person who was plainly obvious to the rest of us.

So much for not letting the dam break.

I tried to at least stay still, but that only made it worse. When I sucked in a breath to pull myself together, it was ragged and shaky, and...fuck me, but Julien stirred.

He started to sit up, and I quickly wiped at my eyes and cleared my throat. When he met my gaze through tousled hair, his eyes were sleepy. "Hey."

I choked back as much of this emotional surge as I could, and I forced a smile as I casually "rubbed" my eye. "Hey. You're awake."

"And you're crying."

Fuck. I cleared my throat again. "I'm..." What, Isaac? Good? Okay? Because Julien wasn't stupid.

He sat up all the way and twisted toward me, resting a hand on my leg. "What's going on?"

I sighed and slid my hand over the top of his. "I'm good. I really am. Just, um..." I took a deep breath and met his eyes, knowing damn well mine were welling up again. "Processing everything, I guess?"

Concern was etched all over his expression. "Processing—everything from today?"

"Yeah." I broke eye contact again. "I'm sorry. This isn't about me, and I don't want to pile on you. I was—"

"Isaac." He closed his hand around mine and brought it up to kiss my knuckles. "You're involved. I threw a lot at you today." He sighed. "I saw it hurt you like it hurt Nikki and Elias."

"It was hard to hear," I admitted. "But you don't need to be comforting me right now."

"You're my boyfriend. I love you. If you're hurting, I'm going to comfort you."

I met his gaze. "You shouldn't have to."

He watched me for a moment, then whispered, "Come here," and wrapped his arms around me.

As much as I didn't want to lean on him right now, I sighed into his embrace and relaxed against him. This was one place I always wanted to be—wrapped up in Julien's strong arms.

He stroked my hair like I'd been stroking his. "Listen to me, Isaac. You're not someone who can hear everything you did today and not feel anything. And me disappearing like I did—leaving you in the dark for days—that's going to affect you too." He exhaled. "It's going to hurt you. There's no reason we can't support each other at the same time."

I closed my eyes as I held him tight against me. "Still. I don't want this to be about me. This is about what *you've* been through."

"But you're a part of it." He drew back and caressed my cheek. "I won't tell you this isn't hell, but there's no one else I'd want to go through it with. Having you here..." He shook his head. "Everything you've done for me, everything you've been for me—I'm a lot stronger going into this than I would have been without you. But I know that's taxing for you. It's hard. I can see it." He touched his forehead to mine. "What kind of man would I be if I didn't hold you up like you've been holding me up?"

I curved a hand behind his neck. "You're something else. You know that?"

He laughed softly, which made my heart flutter. "You've mentioned that a time or two, I think."

I chuckled, then drew him in for a kiss. It felt good. Better than anything had since the Carolina game. Like normal was still a ways off, but we'd get there. Our relationship was fine, and everything we'd had before that night would be waiting for us after the emotional meat grinder of this whole debacle had finished with him. With us.

"Je t'aime, Julien," I whispered.

He grinned against my lips. "I love you, too." He looked in my eyes, and the fatigue of the past few days was unmistakable.

"We should get some sleep," I said. "Maybe someplace more comfortable than the couch."

"It's early, isn't it?"

"It is. But we're both exhausted." I started to get up. "Come on. We can just lie in bed until we fall asleep."

He rose too, sighing with the motion. "I wish I could promise you more once we're there. I don't know when I'll—"

"Julien." I shook my head and cupped his face. "We'll get back to that. Don't worry about it right now."

His brow pinched.

"I mean it." I took his hand. "Let's get some sleep tonight. Then we'll deal with tomorrow. Everything else—it'll keep."

He looked skeptical for a moment, but then his expression softened. As we headed for the stairs, he squeezed my hand. "You're amazing, Isaac. Don't ever let anyone tell you otherwise."

I smiled, pretending not to notice the ache in my chest because, despite how obvious it was that he was beyond amazing, someone had told *him* otherwise.

That wasn't happening again.

Not on my watch.

---

THE NEXT MORNING, I drove us to the training center. Julien was awake and focused, and he'd eaten like he had his usual appetite back, but there was still a lot happening today. One less thing for him to concentrate on seemed prudent.

As the training center came into view and I started nosing off the freeway, he shifted in the passenger seat and blew out a breath.

I touched his leg. "You good?"

"Yeah. I'm... Yeah." He pressed his elbow under the window and brushed his hair back out of his face. "Do you think Kelly would be upset if I brought a gin and tonic in with me for the media scrum?"

"Probably, yeah." I squeezed his thigh. "But I'll make you one when we get home."

Julien covered my hand with his. He didn't say anything, though. When I pulled into the training center parking lot a moment later, he took a deep breath. Then another.

"It's going to be okay." I glanced at him. "It really is."

Exhaling through his nose, he nodded. He probably didn't

believe me, and in his shoes, I might not have either. It was always hard to believe something like that was going to work out fine until it actually did, and I didn't envy him, having to face down all those reporters and pull open his wounds all over again.

Shit. Maybe a gin and tonic *wouldn't* be too much to ask.

I parked in the back lot that was reserved for players and staff. After I'd shut off the engine, I looked at him. "You ready?"

Gaze fixed on the complex looming above us, Julien nodded. "As ready as I'll ever be."

I didn't say anything. I waited to open my door until he'd opened his, and I didn't get out until he did. I was following his lead here. No rushing him. No pushing him.

We'd gone all of three steps when someone called out, "Lans?"

We both turned to see Ortiz and Benson coming in from their cars. Beside me, Julien stiffened, which I expected; he was still convinced the rest of the team was going to cold-shoulder him.

"Jesus, man." Ortiz jogged closer and threw an arm around Julien. "It's good to see you!"

"It..." Julien blinked. "It is?"

"Are you kidding?" Ortiz playfully punched his arm. "You lit Canterbury's world up and then disappeared." His expression turned unusually serious. "We've all been worried about you."

"Seriously," Benson said as he caught up with Ortiz. He clapped Julien's shoulder. "Paxy's going to be happy to see you, that's for damn sure."

Julien winced, avoiding all our gazes.

"He will," I said gently. "He's been asking about you like crazy." Paxy had texted me four times last night alone, wanting to check on Julien. Wanting to help.

"I shouldn't have worried him like that. I shouldn't have done that to any of you."

"Nah, don't be like that." Ortiz gave Julien's arm a firm squeeze. "We're just glad you're okay."

Julien met his eyes, and slowly, a little smile started to come to life. It even turned a bit smug, and he shrugged. "I had to make sure you guys could play without me."

Benson and Ortiz both groaned and rolled their eyes.

"This guy." Ortiz shook his head as he started toward the complex door. "Fucking Lans."

Julien laughed softly. I put a hand on his back and we followed them inside.

We didn't even get into the locker room before word got out.

"You guys!" Benson called out. "Look who's back!"

Julien stepped through the door with me on his heels right as every head turned, and he skidded to a halt.

"Oh, holy shit." Paxy dropped the stick he'd been taping and strode across the room. Throwing his arms around Julien, he said, "I have been so fucking worried about you, man." He didn't sound at all like he was mad—just relieved to the core to see him. Julien hugged him back. The rest of the team greeted him too. Some with handshakes. Some claps on the shoulder. Plenty of hugs. More when Elias and Nisha came in.

By the end of it, Julien looked dazed. It reminded me a little of when we'd come out to the team, and not only had they accepted it, they'd all pretty much figured it out already. They *knew* him, they cared about him, and they'd all been worried about him the past few days. It seemed obvious to me that they'd feel that way, but after everything Julien had laid out on the table yesterday, I understood why it was so shocking to him. The kid who'd shied away from having a piece of his own birthday cake because he didn't want anyone making a fuss over him, the victim of a predator who still saw him as a plaything—

no, Julien was not a man who was going to take for granted that the people around him would worry if he disappeared.

I hoped he was a little closer to understanding now that they would. That they did.

*People love you, Julien. And you deserve that.*

We did still have to practice, so everyone continued putting on their gear. Julien stepped out with Coach and Kelly, probably to get on the same page about everything, and I joined the team on the ice.

I'd been skating for a while to loosen up when Paxy appeared beside me and touched my arm. "I'm pretty sure you're the reason he's on his feet again." He tapped my skate with his stick. "Whatever it is you do for him—keep doing it."

"I can't take all the credit." I nodded toward Elias and Nisha. "It was a team effort."

Paxy glanced at them. "I'm not surprised." He looked right in my eyes. "They've always been good for him, but you..." He trailed off, shaking his head. "Just...keep doing whatever it is you do."

"That's the plan. Trust me."

He nodded sharply. "Good. You're good for—"

"Hey, hey, what's going on here?" Julien skated up beside us and sprayed us with snow. "Paxy, get your own."

"Get my—oh, shut the fuck up, Lans." Paxy backhanded Julien in the chest. Julien laughed and whacked him in the shin with his stick.

"That's enough, you two," Coach called out. Paxy and Julien both turned innocent looks on him (which weren't convincing *at all*), and Coach rolled his eyes. "If you idiots are finished, can we start practice, please?"

I chuckled as I followed Paxy and Julien over to join the team. This lightness with Julien—the playfulness with me and his defense partner—didn't mean everything was over. It didn't mean everything else he had to face today would be easy. But at least it gave me some hope that he was finding his footing again.

He had his head together for practice, too. He wasn't at the top of his game—a few sloppy passes and some shots that resulted in frustrated shouts of "Fuck!" as soon as the puck left his blade—but if anyone had been watching from the stands, they would've just seen a player having an off day. And to be fair, Julien on an off day was better than some professionals on their great days.

By the time Coach had him and the rest of the power play unit up, Julien seemed more focused, and he even got a couple of shots past Larry and into the net. He was all smiles on the way off the ice, thank God.

That, unfortunately, didn't last.

Because after he'd showered, dressed, and eaten, there was one more thing on his agenda today.

Outside the room where the press waited, Julien wavered on his feet. He'd lost some color, and I wondered if everything he'd eaten might make another appearance.

I put my hands on his shoulders. "Julien. Look at me."

He did, eyes full of a flurry of emotions, including bone-deep fear.

"Breathe," I whispered. "Everyone has your back. And I'll be there."

He swallowed. "You're coming in too?"

"Do you want me to?"

"Yes," he said quickly. "Please." The vulnerability in his voice and expression were heartbreaking. Fuck *anyone* who'd ever made him feel alone. Or like he *deserved* to be alone.

I cupped both sides of his neck, pushed myself up, and kissed him softly. "I'll be there. The whole time. Afterward, too. I'm not going anywhere, Julien. I promise."

Closing his eyes, he released a long, ragged breath. "Merci, mon amour."

"Bienvenue."

He actually laughed at that. Softly. Near soundlessly. But I'd take it.

"You've got this." I kissed him again before letting him go.

Julien nodded. Then he pulled in another deep breath. He looked at the door separating us from the waiting press, and he rolled his shoulders. Tilted his head to one side, then the other. Probably steeling himself. Steadying himself.

Then he took my hand.

And with the other, he pushed open the door.

## Chapter 36

### Julien

*Fuck*. My stomach dropped to my feet when I stepped into the room. It was packed with reporters and people with video cameras, not just the usual local folks. A table had been set up with a mic, and around that sat a pile of phones and recorders. Isaac's hand was strong in my own, and I kissed his knuckles before letting go. This part, I had to do alone. His being in the room warmed my heart, though, and I knew the team had my back, from the owners and lawyers right down to Coach, the training staff, my teammates, and everyone else. Not everyone knew the details of what had happened—I hadn't told the team yet—but the front office did. They knew what I'd reveal when asked about that fight.

Travis had made me think I was alone all these years. Like so many things he told me, this one was a lie. I was loved. Respected. Cherished, even. Yeah, I'd fucked up during the game, but I wasn't the one who had something to hide.

As I slipped behind the table and took my seat, I ran a hand through my hair, making sure it was mostly in place. I normally would have worn a baseball cap, but Kelly suggested that I be slightly more put together than my usual fresh-from-the-ice look. So here I was in a team hoodie, my hair loose around my shoulders.

I hadn't checked the news or social media to see what kind of stir my suspension caused, but from the chatter of the guys, there'd been more than a little banter out there among fans. I guess that's what happened when you tried to beat the crap out of another player with no warning.

There was fighting—and then there was what I had done. The league had every right to suspend me. But I'd sat for a game, and now it was time to tell my story.

I swallowed and looked around the room, picking out the familiar faces in the crowd. Some of the local reporters had been around the team longer than I had, and were almost an extension of the team. Friendly faces. I suspected they, too, had my back. Our team reporter was there, and she gave me a nod and encouraging smile.

I wondered if she knew the situation, since Kelly and Coach did. Wouldn't surprise me.

I adjusted the mic, my hands shaking from my nerves. Then I uncapped a bottle of water, gave Kelly a nod, and waited for the first question.

Didn't have to wait long.

"Hi Julien. Thanks for doing this. Can you tell us what happened between you and Travis Canterbury? What caused that fight?"

I brushed my fingers against the mic stand and inhaled, my stomach tied into knots. I'd rehearsed my answers to the obvious questions since last night, but reaching for those took so much out of me. "It wasn't a fight," I said, softly. "It was a reaction, and one that shouldn't have happened there. That kind of anger doesn't belong on the ice." I lifted my eyes to meet the reporter's. "I just want to say that first."

"But what was behind it?"

I huffed out a painful breath and rubbed my fingers over

the textured base of the stand, looking for something to soothe the sudden pain in my lungs. This was the moment I'd break the silence Travis had instilled in me with shame, fear, and dire warnings.

"Canterbury implied my relationship with Isaac Rivera was the same as his relationship with me my rookie year."

There were murmurs and shifting among the reporters. Shocked faces.

I pressed on. "He insinuated that I was no better than he had been, preying on a naïve rookie." I swallowed hard. "Given what I went through, the thought that I'd done to Isaac what he'd done to me—" My voice cracked, and I had to blink back the sudden welling of tears. I managed to find the water bottle and took a shaky drink to quell the pounding of my pulse. "I lost my mind. And I regret that, immensely."

"Wait," someone different said. "Are you saying that you had a romantic relationship with Travis Canterbury your rookie year?"

I found the reporter in the scrum and met his gaze. "It wasn't romantic. I thought it was at the time, but—" I shook my head. "It was sexual, though, and lasted the entire season."

"You *are* dating a rookie." A new voice.

I nodded. "That's true. But Isaac is twenty-two...well, twenty-three now..."

Isaac's voice rang out over the room. "Julien gave me the option to say no. Many times. I went to him." He got his cocky little smile. "I kissed him first."

That kiss had been perfect and wanted and so different from what Travis had done.

Silence in the room, likely because no one wanted to ask the obvious question, the one that came from what Isaac had said. I'd given Isaac the space to say no.

Travis, on the other hand...

I told them, without anyone asking. "Travis came to my

hotel room during training camp, on the evening of my nineteenth birthday, with a twelve-pack of beer."

"Holy crap," someone said. "He got you *drunk*?"

That was more of an outburst than a question, but I nodded. "Then f— had sex with me." I knew I shouldn't curse, but it was damn hard not to. My hands shook so badly that I didn't reach for the water bottle. I hugged myself, trying to keep the tears at bay, far too aware of the cameras on me. I could barely hear the low level muttering in the room over the echo of my blood in my ears.

Evidently, someone did some math. "He was thirty. Your rookie year, he was thirty years old."

I nodded "That was not a good year for me. I—kept seeing him after that night because I thought I must have wanted it, must have done something to make *him* think I wanted that. I honestly don't remember much of what happened, and I was terrified of anyone finding out. Of everyone on the team. The coaches, the fans.

"Half the time Travis told me he adored me, the other half that I was a complete disaster who wasn't even fit to play in the minors. He had me convinced that my success was only because of him. All of the team failures were on my shoulders because I lacked any ability to play hockey." I stared at the mic stand, because I didn't dare look into the crowd. "It was—difficult to play through."

God, I was going to lose it. I hugged myself tighter. "I'm *not* like him," I hissed through chattering teeth. Fuck protocol. "I don't mess with people's heads. He'd been telling me the same shit for *eight years*. I wouldn't be anything if he hadn't stooped low enough to fuck a foolish, empty-headed weakling like me. He won't leave me alone. On the ice. Off of it."

I swiped at my face with the sleeve of my sweatshirt. "When he said I treated Isaac like that, I couldn't take it anymore. But I should never have punched him. Not on the ice. Not like that. I let my teammates down. Our fans."

My throat cracked. I grabbed the water bottle even though I still couldn't stop trembling.

I hated this—hated exposing myself. Letting everyone see that Travis was right about some things. Because right now? I was a *mess*.

"Are there any more questions," Kelly asked.

"I have one." A woman raised her hand. "You said this started your rookie year. When did it end?"

I didn't recognize the reporter. "Depends on how you define end. The relationship part—if you want to call it that—ended when he was traded to Carolina. But the verbal abuse—the mind games. Those have continued to this day."

The murmurs of the reporters were infuriating. There weren't any more questions, just a flurry of whispers. "He goes after me," I gritted out. "Every time the teams meet. Texts me shit randomly. Once threatened to out me as gay." I croaked a laugh, and looked at the reporters. "Joke's on him. I'm pansexual."

"Do you—" A woman reporter cleared her throat and tried again. "Do you still have the texts?"

I blinked at her. Oh *shit*. I nodded. "I do." I'd upgraded phones several times, but had the same number with the same provider and hadn't switched manufacturers. My text messages went back *years*. I had texts from when I played in major juniors. "I—never delete stuff. Bad habit, I guess."

"Depends on your perspective," she said.

Wasn't that the truth.

This time when Kelly asked if there were any more questions, no one spoke, so I rose and made my way to Isaac and the door. Once we were through it, I collapsed into his arms.

"Baby, you did good." He hugged me tightly and rubbed my back.

"Shit, Lans." I'd never heard Kelly curse before, and she'd had a pretty good idea of what I was going to say during the press conference, too. She pushed her hair back, tucking strands behind her ears. "I'm not asking you to go out there for the rest of the season."

The relief at that was like a cool wave. I had no desire to face the media again for a good long while.

"Come on," Isaac said. "Let's go somewhere more comfortable."

That turned out to be the players' lounge. When we stepped inside, I realized the entire team had stuck around after practice. Given the wan faces and wide eyes, they'd watched my press conference. A quick glance at one of the smaller TVs confirmed that. There was the table I'd been sitting at, and some reporters still milling around.

I wet my lips and faced my team. "I didn't want to tell you before practice." I waved a hand in the direction of the ice. "We needed the work. Didn't want to be the one to bring this team down again."

"Fucking hell, Lans," Paxy said. "You're the goddamn strongest person I know." He held out his arms, and I accepted the hug. "You've never brought us down. You and Sido and Karly—you guys keep us going."

The whole team joined in on a somber version of the pile of hugs at the end of a game.

When it was over, Isaac handed me a bottle of water, and I fell down on a couch.

Elias cleared his throat and glanced around the room. "I guess this is as good a time as any to say this: If anyone has any issues with another player or a coach or staff member—you can come to me. Or Sido."

"Or me," I said. "You can come to me."

Elias nodded. "We'll help you."

"They've been helping me for years."

Ozzy shook his head. "That fucking asshole. Hell, *I* want to punch him in the face."

"I think a lot of people do." Benson peered down at his phone. "It's out on social media."

I rubbed my forehead, and closed my eyes. "Great. Just—great."

"Hey," Nikki said. "We've got you, King. We'll keep you safe."

Loud murmurs of agreement. My lips curled into a smile, even as the fucking tears threatened again.

"Thanks guys. I hope our fans are understanding."

Isaac weaved his fingers between mine, and took a seat next to me. "Oh, they will be. You'll see."

I pulled him to me and held him, listening to the murmurs of my teammates.

*Please, please let Isaac be right.*

---

WE WENT BACK to my place—I felt a little pang of guilt at that. We tried to even out whose house we spent time in, but mine was closer to the practice rink, and we'd be back there tomorrow.

Isaac shook his head when I mentioned my concern to him. "I like your house. And you're more settled here."

Ugh. There was the messy part of me, again. "I'm settled wherever you are."

He chuckled at that, and kissed me on the cheek. "I'm more settled here."

I didn't know if that was true. I did wish I had a stream in the backyard—or a pond or something that would bring Isaac peace here and now. "Come with me to Saguenay this summer. We can rent a place on Lac Saint-Jean, and there'll be water right outside every day."

The look Isaac gave me melted my heart. "I'd love that." He nudged me toward the couch. "Go sit. I'll get us something to drink."

I sat. My laptop was still on the coffee table from when I'd spoken with my family. Curiosity got the best of me and I opened it. Rather than going to social media, I checked the sports news sites I followed.

There wasn't just one article about that news conference —there were *many*. I rubbed my face. Tabarnak.

I clicked one at random, and scanned the article. The meat of it, of course, was me accusing Canterbury of sexual assault. Seeing those words made my stomach curdle and my bones hurt. I scrolled past that until my gaze snagged on a tweet embedded in the article. Not from Travis, but from another name I recognized, but hadn't seen in a long time: Miller Fredrick.

Fredrick had been drafted fifth overall in his draft year and had been expected to become a star player in the league. He'd fizzled out in his mid-twenties. Everyone wondered what had happened. He'd gone from burning it up in juniors to erratic play once he hit the league. Ended up in the minors. He played somewhere over in Europe now.

His tweet brought everything sharply and painfully into focus.

*100% believe & support Landry. Canterbury did the same to me. So sorry, Julien. #StandWithLans*

I slid the laptop back onto the coffee table, covered my mouth and curled up into a ball. I didn't cry—I think I'd finally sobbed myself out—but I shook and shook and my heart tried to drill itself through my ribs.

I wasn't the first. Intellectually, I thought I might not be. Isaac had said as much, because of the run-in he'd had at the

All-Stars, but there it was. Proof that I wasn't alone. It wasn't only me.

Travis was an absolute *monster*.

"Julien?" Isaac's voice sounded from behind me. "Oh shit, what is it?" He quickly placed two glasses down on the table, sat next to me, and pulled me into his arms.

I gestured at the laptop. "Ricker. There's a tweet." That's all I could get out.

Isaac grabbed the laptop and read. "God, I was...nine when he was drafted. Travis must have been..."

"Twenty-five," I whispered. "He was with LA at the time. I forgot they drafted Fredrick. He was so good that first year, but fell apart his second." A lot like I had, minus being good my first year. "Where's my phone?"

Isaac smoothed his hand over my hair. "Do you need it now?"

"Yeah," I said softly. "I do."

He nodded, rose, and headed to the coat closet.

Oh of course. Once I had my phone back, I pulled up Twitter, ignored all the notifications, and went to my direct messages. Ignored all the new ones there, too. Then I DMed Fredrick.

*Are you okay?*

I didn't expect a reply for a while, but I got one almost immediately.

*Yeah. r u?*

I nodded to myself. *Yeah. Got good people around me.*

*Me too. Thanks for saying something. Sorry man.*

*You ever need to talk...*

He sent me a thumbs-up.

I turned the screen off and slid it onto the coffee table. "This is the storm."

Isaac wrapped his arms around me. "I think you should stay off the internet."

I choked out a laugh. "Yeah, probably. But—I'm glad I saw that. I hate that it's not just me, but—I—none of this is our fault."

"It's not."

Something in my belly ignited and burned deep. "I'm going to bury that fucker, Isaac. He's not going to play another game of hockey ever again."

"I believe you," Isaac said. "I believe all of you."

# Chapter 37

## Isaac

Ignoring the internet and the media was easier said than done. I could barely resist looking at it myself, mostly because I was curious and nervous about the aftermath. Plus we were both getting bombarded with supportive messages from friends and family, and it was just so easy to finish responding to one and then sliiide over to another app to see what was happening.

By early evening, no one in Travis's camp had issued any kind of statement or response. Chances were, there was a lot of talk going on behind closed doors. I wondered how his teammates were reacting to the accusations. If they were rallying around him the way the Griffins were rallying around Julien, or if they were as disgusted by him as everyone else seemed to be. Maybe someone was scheduling a hearing with Travis. Or a press conference. It was impossible to say because the silence coming from Carolina right now was deafening.

The league commissioner had issued the usual statement about how they were looking into the situation, reaching out to all parties involved, and would have no comment until they had all the information.

Those were the only corners of the hockey world that were silent, though. The *StandWithLans* hashtag had blown up on every social media platform. Players past and present had posted supportive video messages to Julien. So had fans. Several organizations that worked with survivors of abuse and sexual assault reached out to him publicly and privately, asking if he needed help.

Naturally, not everyone was supportive. In addition to the odd troll under *StandWithLans*, another hashtag, *LyingLandry*, had gotten some traction. Julien muted it on all his platforms as soon as he saw it, but I scrolled through some of the tweets just to get a bead on what people were saying. It was about half homophobic crap and half people accusing Julien of throwing Travis under the bus for his own actions.

That hashtag was bombarded with Julien's supporters, though, and by the time we'd eaten dinner and settled back on the couch, those voices had mostly been drowned out.

Julien put his phone facedown on the coffee table and ran a hand through his hair. "Jesus fuck."

"It's a lot." I put a hand on his leg. "How are you holding up?"

He swallowed hard, then looked at me, and a faint smile appeared on his lips. "I'm...okay. I don't like being at the center of a shitstorm, but it's a weight off my shoulders. A big one." His gaze drifted to his phone, and more to himself than me, he murmured, "A bigger one than even I realized."

"I'm so sorry you carried it alone for so long."

He shrugged tightly. "It can't be changed."

"Neither can whatever's coming to Travis."

Closing his eyes, Julien released a long breath, and some tension in his neck and shoulders eased. I could only imagine the relief. Not only of getting rid of that weight, but of knowing that Travis would finally have to face the music. There was no escape for that asshole now. Even if the league and his team decided they couldn't (more like wouldn't) do anything, the stink of this was going to stay with Travis. He'd never get away from it. That had to be liberating for Julien.

And I hoped like hell there were professional consequences for the bastard. Coach and Kelly both thought there would be, but they'd warned us that the powers that be *could* find ways to pussyfoot around it. There was no proof. It was Julien's word against Travis's. It happened a long time ago. There were any number of ways they could insist their hands were tied and there was nothing they could do.

But then Miller Frederick had tweeted that Travis did the same to him.

A couple of hours ago, news broke that a third player—one who didn't want to be identified—had come forward with a similar story.

*Still think they're going to sweep it under the rug?* I'd texted Kelly after John Doe's statement.

She'd replied, *Some of the good old boys might try, but with three players and all the outcry from fans, especially now that there's a push to boycott the league if Travis is allowed to play? Nah. He's done.*

God, I hoped so.

And that was before Matti Kanerva and two other players from Julien's All-Star team issued a joint statement that they'd witnessed Travis harassing Julien in Vegas. Kanerva even mentioned breaking up an altercation between them that had briefly turned physical. That had given me chills, but I didn't ask Julien about it. He'd opened up enough wounds in the last few days without recounting that particular story. I did DM Kanerva, though, to thank him for the support and for intervening.

After a while, Julien's phone pinged. He'd silenced all notifications and texts except his family, teammates, and team staff, so I wasn't surprised when he picked it up. I suspected it was one of his family members checking in as they'd been doing throughout the day.

I had to smile at that. He'd been convinced he was all alone in this, but the support pouring in from his family alone was heartwarming. I still didn't know what his sister had texted him earlier that had made him tear up, only that he'd been smiling in between wiping his eyes and texting her back.

Beside me, Julien sucked in air, then muttered something in French.

I straightened. "What?"

He slid closer to me and turned the screen so we could both see it. "Kelly sent me this. Another player came forward."

He tapped a link and a video started. It was a press conference not unlike the one he'd done this morning (Christ, had that really been today?) but with Minnesota's logo on the backdrop.

And at the microphone, hugging himself in a suit and pulling in a deep, nervous breath, was Vince Alexander. The same player who'd yanked me away from Travis at the All-Star game.

"I wasn't going to make a statement yet," he said, "but there's no way I can play tonight until I do this. And I respect the player who doesn't want to be identified." He looked right at one of the cameras. "Whoever you are, I get it. If you need to reach out in confidence to someone who's been there?" He tapped his chest. "Hit me up."

"Holy shit," I whispered.

Julien nodded beside me, staring wide-eyed at the screen.

Alexander's voice was steady but precarious in that way that said he was fighting *hard* to keep it that steady. "I might as well just repeat everything Julien Landry said. The details are a little different, but the story is the same. Canterbury was traded to Carolina when I started my rookie season there. I was twenty, not nineteen. It was a bottle of Jack, not a twelve-pack of beer. But the rest..." He shrugged tightly. "I've got texts too. And there's..." His voice caught, and he stared down at the mic for a moment before he found his breath, inhaled deeply, and set his shoulders back as he faced the reporters again. Voice decidedly less steady now, he went on, "There are photos. I have them, because Canterbury sent them to me and said he'd leak them—that he'd send them to my family—if I didn't toe the line."

A reporter spoke up, "Vince, did you believe that was a credible threat?"

"I was a kid," Alexander gritted out. "I have no idea if he'd have done it, but I didn't want to find out if he would. That wasn't how I wanted my family to find out I was gay." He gestured around, eyes welling up. "*This* wasn't how I wanted them to find out either, but I couldn't stay silent anymore. Not after Landry put his neck out there like that."

Julien breathed a string of French profanity and hung his head.

I gently took his phone and paused the video. With the phone safely back on the coffee table, I turned to Julien and wrapped my arms around him.

He leaned against me, trembling. He'd crumbled after each of the other players had made their statements, and I wasn't surprised he was doing it again. I could only imagine the absolute barrage of emotions that hit him every time there was some new development. Every time there was another victim. On a good day, there was—as he'd described it—endless noise in his head that was a nightmare to make sense of, never mind quiet. He lived for the moments when he could stop all the chaos in his mind and just breathe. Just *be*. With all the chaos around him right now, it had to be absolute hell inside his head.

Julien drew back, and when he met my gaze, my breath hitched. He was so raw. So vulnerable. His eyes were pleading.

I didn't even know what he was pleading for, only that in that moment, there was nothing I wanted more than to give him whatever it was he needed. Anything to make his world better.

He clasped our fingers together. "Isaac. Tell me what to do."

"Tell you—" I blinked. How was I supposed to do that? *I* didn't even know what to do. This whole situation was overwhelming me and confusing the shit out of me and—

"*Isaac.*" The desperate words echoed in my head. "*Tell me what to do.*"

Oh.

*Ooh.*

This promised to be a *lot* of pressure—finding the right balance between giving him what he needed and asking too much of him—but I was damn well going to try.

I swept my tongue across my lips and ran my thumb alongside his. "Turn off your phone."

He immediately grabbed his phone off the table and powered it down. Once it was lying dormant beside mine again, he met my eyes and waited.

I tried to keep my nerves under the surface. Julien needed strength right now. He needed to lean hard, and I was determined to be sturdy enough for him to do exactly that. I was pretty confident I could be. But what he was asking for, it also meant pushing him, and that was daunting when he was this brittle. How far was too far?

I brushed his hair behind his ear. "You can always say no. To anything. You know that, right?"

His smile almost broke me. So sweet and genuine and deeply, deeply trusting. "I've always known that with you."

My throat tightened. The way he'd trusted me in the beginning had been mind-blowing, but the implicit trust now that I knew everything he'd been through—now that I knew everything he was going through—was... I didn't think there were words to describe it. I treasured the faith this man had in me, and I couldn't imagine ever doing anything to jeopardize it. Knowing what I did now, I was awestruck that he still had the capacity to trust anyone. The fact that he placed it in me... holy shit.

Swallowing my own emotions, I rose and gestured for him to do the same.

In silence, I led him up the stairs. I had no idea how far this was going to go, but I reminded myself that I always followed his lead. Even when everything was right in the world, I watched for his signals and only pushed him in ways I knew he wanted to be pushed. There was still pressure this time, though. Julien was the first to admit he could be reckless. His story about the blogger who'd hated him stuck out in my memory—a reminder of the things Julien could do that, in hindsight, might not have been healthy. Not that we were in danger of hate-fucking or anything like that, but there was always the possibility of Julien craving more than he could handle and only realizing it after the fact.

No pressure or anything.

I opened his bedroom door and gestured for him to go in ahead of me. Then, even though we were alone in the enormous house, I closed the door behind us with a quiet click.

Facing him, I said, "It's just us. Nothing out there"—I gestured at the door—"matters right now."

His gaze flicked to the door, lingered there for a second, and then met mine. Slowly, something seemed to settle in him. He rolled his shoulders, and they seemed...not relaxed, but less tense than they'd been even a few minutes ago.

My own shoulders were doing the opposite. Renewed tension was creeping in as reality made itself known. Julien was more vulnerable than he'd ever been in the months that I'd known him. I'd always been cautious about pushing him too hard or in the wrong direction, but the pressure to do right by him this time was... It was a lot. It weighed heavily on me and made me consider, however briefly, suggesting that this wasn't a good idea.

No. Julien needed this. How much he needed—if sex or pain would even enter the equation—was impossible to say at this point, but he needed something he trusted me and only me to give him. I wasn't letting him down.

Maybe what I needed right now was a little extra metaphorical padding. Just enough to play the game with the confidence that no one was getting hurt.

I stepped closer and curved a hand behind his neck. "I know I said nothing out there matters, but it still exists."

Julien winced, breaking eye contact.

"I'm not saying no or backing down," I went on. "But we should be careful."

"You're always careful," he whispered.

"I am." I paused, then slipped into a slightly gentler version of that commanding voice he so loved. "Julien. Look at me."

He did, eyebrows up.

I moistened my lips. "I'll do whatever you need me to do tonight. Or make you do whatever you need to do. And I don't even know how far you'll want to go, or... Anyway, the point is, I want to have a safe word this time."

His eyebrows climbed even higher. "You do?"

I nodded. "I don't think either of us will need to use it, but I'd feel better if it was there. For either of us."

Julien studied me, his expression unreadable. I thought he might balk at the idea. I even imagined him getting angry or hurt, as if I were telling him—now of all times—that I thought he was weak or that I didn't trust him. But as some more tension eased in his neck and shoulders, he nodded. "Oui. Yes. A safe word—that would be good."

Oh, thank God.

I caressed his cheek. "A lot of the books and websites say people use red, yellow, and green. Like traffic lights, I guess. Like 'red' means everything stops completely. 'Yellow' means pause and regroup. 'Green' means it's all good." I waved my free hand. "So...yeah. Traffic lights."

"Red, yellow, green." Julien nodded again. "All right."

I shouldn't have been this relieved that he'd agreed to it. I wasn't even surprised, really. As reckless as he'd been in the past, and as intense as he liked things like this, I'd gotten the impression for a long time that he craved *safe* even more than he craved pain and submission.

I pushed myself up and kissed him lightly. Then I let him go and moved to sit on the edge of the bed. Leaning back on my hands, I said, "Take off your sweatshirt and T-shirt." I gestured at the closet. "Hang them up neatly."

His eyebrow flicked up in an unspoken, *Seriously?* I understood. We both usually tossed casual clothes in the hamper.

But that questioning look only lasted maybe a split second before he did as he was told. He probably understood what I was doing. That this was a safe way to get us both into the headspace we needed to be in.

He obediently pulled off both shirts, then disappeared into the walk-in closet. Hangers squeaked and rattled. Then Julien emerged, shirtless with his sweats sitting perfectly on his hips. He was visibly getting hard, which didn't surprise me, and any other night, I'd have told him to strip off the rest of his clothes.

I was still feeling him out, though. Still getting a bead on where he needed this to go. Or *not* go.

I took a pillow off the bed and dropped it to the floor between my bare feet. A single downward nod summoned him across the room and put him on his knees in front of me.

The second he was kneeling, Julien closed his eyes and released a long breath. Though he still sat up straight, his shoulders drooped as if he were exhausted from holding them up for so long.

I ran my fingers through his hair, and that was the first time I noticed the faint dampness along his hairline. As if listening to Vince Alexander's statement had made him break out in a sweat. Maybe it had.

Without a word, I leaned down and pulled him in closer. For a long time, we sat like that, me cradling Julien's head as we both just breathed together. He rested a hand on my thigh. I stroked his hair.

"I love you," I whispered.

Julien exhaled, relaxing even more. "I love you, too."

Closing my eyes, still stroking his hair, I whispered, "We don't have to do everything tonight. We don't have to do *anything*." I kissed his temple. "Whatever you need or want, I'm all in, but I don't want to push you too hard."

"I *want* you to push me, Isaac." He lifted his head, and we separated enough to look at each other. "The last few days... I..." He sighed. "I've felt so damn many things that I never want to feel again, and right now..." He swallowed hard. When he spoke again, his voice wavered. "I don't want to feel broken tonight."

The words made my chest ache. "I don't want you to feel that way either. But I also don't want to break you more."

Julien was already shaking his head. "You won't. If there is one person on this planet who I know wouldn't break me, it's you. Even if..." He hesitated. "Even if we didn't work out together as a couple, you're not—that's not you. You don't have it in you."

"No, I don't." I stroked his long hair. "Which is why I want to be extra careful tonight. I would never set out to hurt you, but if you want something, and I give it to you, and we both realize afterward that it's too much for you..."

Christ. Just thinking about that had my eyes welling up.

Julien sat up and wrapped his arms around me. "I'll tell you. I promise. The safe words—I'll remember."

I ran a hand down his back. "So will I." As he released me and sat back on his heels again, I said, "How far *do* you need to go tonight?"

His eyes lost focus as he seemed to consider the answer. When he met my gaze again, the rawness and vulnerability were still there but with desire and determination mixed in. "Do you remember the first time, when I asked you to make me stop talking?"

Did I? God, that was a memory that would *never* fade. "I remember."

Julien ran his tongue along the inside of his bottom lip. "Make me stop *thinking*."

Oh *hell*—the goose bumps those words raised along the length of my spine.

I ran my fingers through his hair, reveling in his shiver because we both knew what he was anticipating. I teased at his hair, not *quite* pulling but letting the possibility fuck with his mind. "Is that what you want, Julien? For me to make you stop thinking?"

"Yes," he breathed. I didn't think French had ever sounded sexier than it did in that low, husky voice when he added, "S'il vous plait."

"Safe words?"

He opened his mouth to speak, but I closed my fingers around a handful of his hair just tight enough for him to feel it. He squeezed his eyes shut as a shiver rippled through him.

"Julien. Safe words."

He sucked in a breath and looked up at me, his eyes absolutely ablaze with need. "Red. Yellow." He paused for another breath. "Green."

"Good." I bent for a kiss, and Jesus, the way he moaned into it had me so turned on, my head spun. I was wrung out from the last couple of days, and Julien had to be too, but the way he kissed me back promised it would be well worth it if I found a second wind. And I planned to make it absolutely worth it for him, too.

Without giving him any warning, I tightened my grip on his hair. Fuck, that gasp and the helpless whimper—I could've powered a stadium with the surge of *need* they sent through me. I suddenly didn't care how wrung out I was; before tonight was over, I was making this man come undone.

I rose, hauling him with me, and Julien scrambled to his feet. His sweats were tented now with his fully hard cock, and when I teased him through the soft fabric, French curses tumbled off his tongue. He was trembling all over, especially his hands.

"Green?" I asked.

"Green." He met my gaze. "Fucking hell, Isaac. *Green.*"

I grinned. Well then. Game on.

Releasing his hair, I said, "Get the rest of those clothes off. Let me see you."

He obeyed immediately. With his sweats and underwear in hand, he paused. "Do I...?" He gestured at the hamper, then the closet.

I nodded at the hamper. He tossed everything in, and I drank in the sight of him, gloriously naked and hard and all mine. Still looking him up and down, I stripped off my own clothes, leaving them on the floor but kicking them out of the way.

Julien's gaze went to my cock, which was also hard, and he bit his lip. I didn't know if he wanted his face or his ass fucked, but lucky for him, he was probably getting both. Safe words permitting, of course—as hungry as we were for each other, I'd still be keeping an eye on him.

But he wanted me to push him. He wanted me to make his mind shut up.

So I did.

I put him onto his knees again and pushed my dick between his gorgeous lips, and when I was sure he was still into this, I rocked my hips and fucked his eager mouth. With a fistful of his hair, I kept him still, and none of the sounds he made were out of distress or even hesitation. No, he was all wanton enthusiasm. Horny and greedy. I hadn't been sure I had it in me to even get turned on right now, but it was impossible not to be rock-hard and dizzy when Julien was like this.

"So hot," I murmured. "Your mouth is so..." I ran out of words. Breath. Thoughts.

Right then, he looked up at me, tears dotting his long lashes, and I knew without a doubt those were nothing like the tears he'd shed over the past few days. This was all surrender and need. He was overwhelmed, and he wanted more, and I was damn sure going to give him more.

I loosened my grip on his hair so I could stroke it instead, earning me another moan as he took my cock all the way into his mouth. The sight of him... Was there anything sexier in the world?

"God, you're so beautiful," I growled. "Fuck, Julien..." My own words rang in my ears, and I was suddenly overcome with the need to show him how beautiful he was.

I grabbed his hair again and pulled him back. "On your feet." He didn't hesitate, though he did stumble a little as he got up. "You all right?"

"Oui," he panted. "I'm good."

"Mmm, yes you are," I murmured, and claimed a deep, hungry kiss. Julien melted against me like he always did. It was more than the arousal making my head spin now—it was relief. This was the closest we'd been to "us" since the Carolina game. We'd reconnected, of course, but Julien had been understandably off-balance. There hadn't been time or energy to come back to this, and even if I didn't have an orgasm tonight,

I'd go to sleep satisfied just from being this close to Julien again. From feeling him this close to himself again.

I broke the kiss and met those gorgeous eyes. Wow. There were still some fading bruises on his face from the fight with Travis, but he was living up to his tattoo: Now. Nothing mattered except now, and despite everything, Julien was—if his eyes were to be believed—absolutely in the here and now.

He thought he was broken. In some ways, he was—that was inevitable after a trauma—but not in as many ways as he thought. He wasn't defective. He wasn't weak. He was healing.

Paxy was right. Julien really was the strongest person I'd ever met.

I let go of his hair. "Get the lube."

Julien's eyes widened, but there was no fear or apprehension there. Excitement and maybe a little disbelief, but nothing to indicate any resistance.

Of course that didn't stop me from second-guessing myself. Was he really okay going this far? Should I err on the side of caution and go slower? Or was this exactly what he needed to really feel like himself again?

Unaware of my internal debate, he went to the nightstand and pulled out the bottle we'd been using. He pressed it into my hand, and his voice was shaky with hunger as he said, "Green, Isaac."

I grinned. That was all I needed to hear.

I gestured at the bathroom. Julien didn't ask any questions. We'd fooled around in the shower enough times, that wasn't exactly an unusual order.

We weren't getting in the shower this time, though. Not until I was finished with him, anyway.

Instead, I put the lube beside the sink, then wrapped my arms around Julien and kissed him. "Do you think you can come tonight?"

"I know I can," he said with no hesitation. "Crisse, Isaac. You turn me on so much."

"Likewise." I brushed my lips across his. "Especially because I see what you don't usually see."

His brow furrowed. "What?"

"You." I grabbed his hips, turned him around, and bent him over the counter. Shock registered on his reflection's face, and that quickly turned to renewed arousal as I slid my hand down over his ass. "I want you to see me fucking you." I kissed the back of his shoulder. "I want you to see yourself getting fucked."

Julien bit his lip and almost stifled a moan. "Please."

"Is that what you want?"

He nodded. "I want you, Isaac." As he held my gaze in the mirror, his expression shifted to one I recognized well—that hungry, feral look that meant he was out of his mind with need. Exactly the way I wanted him. And his voice echoed all of that when he pleaded, "Make me scream."

There was nothing in the world I wanted more in that moment.

I took a little extra time to make sure he was ready for me. When he was, I kept going just to make him beg, and when his pleas hit that strained, breathy sound that meant he was about to fall apart, I rewarded him with my dick. I fucked him over the counter, ordering him to watch us in the mirror until he couldn't keep his eyes open anymore. I pounded him over the side of the bed. His dresser. I was tempted to put him on the floor like I sometimes did, but neither of us needed rug burn on our knees or feet for tomorrow's practice or the next night's game.

And Julien...

Oh God, yeah, I made him scream. He pleaded and babbled in both languages, begging for more and telling me how good it was, and I gave him everything I had until I was sure one of us was going to collapse. Any other night, we'd have both come by now, but that must have been the stress and fatigue taking their cut. Fine by me.

I pulled him away from the chair I'd bent him over, let him go, and lay back on the bed. "Get on top," I panted. "Ride my dick."

Julien immediately did as he was told, and oh, wow, that was a sight. His hair was a mess, damp strings falling down over his eyes. Muscles stood out—his abs, his powerful thighs. His flushed skin gleamed, and sweat rolled like teardrops over the twining branches of the sleeve that immortalized so many people he loved. I brushed the sweat away with my thumb, my mind clear enough for only a few seconds to wonder if he knew that if he tried to include a tattoo for everyone who loved him, he wouldn't have the space for it. Not on his arm, not on his shoulder and back, not around the firebird symbolizing his survival—not anywhere on his body. There were simply too many.

But my thoughts scattered a moment later because Julien rolled his hips just right to draw a, "Holy fuck," from my lips. My back arched off the bed, and I reached back to grab the headboard slats to anchor myself. "Oh God, Julien…"

He slid his palms up my chest and gazed down at me, desperation written all over his face.

He was close.

I let go of the headboard and started pumping him. Julien threw his head back and cried out, and he clenched around me as he stiffened in my hand.

"You're gonna make me come." His voice was strained, the words fast and furious. "So close, baby. So close."

We fell into the frantic rhythm of trying to reach the finish, both of us breathing harshly and erratically, and in seconds, Julien gasped, shuddered, and shot cum over my hand and stomach. I wasn't far behind—watching and feeling him come always snapped my control, and I dug my heels into the mattress and thrust up into him as I came.

Julien slumped over me. I wrapped my arms around him and pulled him all the way down. I didn't care about getting cum on either of us; we were going to shower in a minute anyway.

Right now, all I wanted was to hold him while we caught our breath.

Still trembling and panting, Julien buried his face against my neck. I didn't know if I'd made him cry this time. Sometimes I did, sometimes I didn't.

But in my arms, he was more relaxed than he'd been in days. In his arms, I felt more like myself than I had since the Carolina game.

So I just closed my eyes.

And held him.

## Chapter 38

### Julien

I woke to the sound of birds chirping and soft light filtering in from the doors to the balcony. For the first time in—well, a long while—I felt well-rested and calm. Something akin to myself again. Oh, my brain immediately clicked through all that had happened recently, but the absolute pain in my bones and heart was more like a dull ache, and the panic I'd felt for so long was gone.

Closing my eyes, I soaked in the now. The here. This quiet moment with the man I loved sleeping next to me in my bed. When I opened them again, I let myself imagine the future a bit. Time up north with Isaac and my family. A lasting relationship.

Isaac's hair was mussed in sleep and curled against his temples, but even asleep there was strength in his features, in the arm he had tucked under the pillow.

He thought he didn't deserve me, that I deserved more than him, as if there could be anyone more perfect for me than he was. Both of us were flawed—me far more than Isaac—but one of the things these past few months had taught me was that our idiosyncrasies complemented each other. Our passion. The care we had for each other.

I shifted, and he stirred and opened his eyes.

"Hey," he said, his smile sleepy and warm.

"Hi." He was so stunning like this. People thought me beautiful. They had no idea. I brushed his hair from his eyes, then trailed my fingers over his jaw. "How are you feeling?"

"Me?" His laugh was soft. "I'm the one who should be asking that."

I shrugged. "I put you through a lot last night."

His brow creased. "You...put *me* through a lot?"

I huffed and stole a kiss. "Asking you to fuck me like that, after everything, that wasn't easy on you." I'd needed the pain and the pleasure and the physicality of sex to shut down the storm in my mind. "I put a lot of pressure on you, I know." I pressed a finger to his lips to stop him from speaking. "Thank you for suggesting safe words, because it let me know that *you* knew I wanted what you gave me."

He nipped at my finger.

"Ow!" I shook my hand.

"Oh come on, I've bitten you harder than that!" Isaac gave me a gentle shove.

Laughing, I rolled onto my back, and he straddled me, his powerful thighs gripping my hips. I slid my hands up his arms. "You have. But I was trying to comfort you, not turn you on."

He leaned down and whispered one of the most cheesy lines he'd ever managed. "Baby, you always turn me on." The kiss that followed was on the edge of dirty.

I groaned when he relented. "We have practice." My dick was well on the way to becoming hard, and I wanted to reel Isaac down and spend part of the morning losing my senses as he drilled into me. But my stint away from the ice had me worried about timing and conditioning. Tomorrow's game would be a challenge, for so many reasons.

"We do." Isaac sat back. "Guess we have to be professional." Then he slipped off me and out of bed, heading for the bathroom.

I threw my legs over the side and sat on the edge. "Isaac..."

Pausing at the doorway, he looked over his shoulder and met my gaze.

"I know you think you should be more for me, but I want *you*, not some ideal. You're wonderful. You're *enough*."

He turned to face me, and slumped against the doorway. "You're amazing."

I stood and closed the distance. "I'm really not."

"Yeah, you are." He rose on his toes to kiss me. "I'm not the only one who thinks so, either."

Maybe I needed to listen to those voices for a change. So I let Isaac kiss me, and tried to believe what he and so many others told me about myself.

---

Before we left the house, I turned on my phone. On the way to the garage, I unlocked it, then handed it to Isaac. "I don't think I can face this right now—would you mind checking to make sure no one sent me anything I absolutely have to deal with?"

The order to turn it off had been incredibly freeing. Though I didn't wake up at all last night, leaving it downstairs meant that even if I had, the screen wasn't there for me to gaze at. Nor was it there first thing in the morning.

Maybe I needed to buy an old-fashioned alarm clock.

Once I'd gotten us onto the road, I glanced over to Isaac. He was frowning at the screen.

"What is it?"

"There's a text from your sister, but it's in French...and I can pick out a word or three... She asks how you are, but after that..."

I huffed a soft laugh. "Text her back so she doesn't worry. Ask if I need to answer now."

Isaac tapped away on the phone, then read out what he'd written. "Hi Marie, it's Isaac. I had Julien shut his phone off last night. Was overwhelming. He's driving us to practice. Is it okay if he answers you later?"

Sounded good to me. "Hit send."

He did, and about the time I turned onto the highway, Marie answered. Isaac read that out loud, too.

"Hi Isaac! Good idea about the phone. Was just wondering how he was and sent a little story about the kids. Can wait until later. All my love to both of you."

I couldn't help smiling. Even in Isaac's voice, that was my sister, through and through. I was still a little surprised she hadn't shown up on my doorstep. Marie was protective of both me and Mathieu, but especially of me.

"Can you tell her I love her, and I'll call soon?"

Isaac tapped away. "Done." He paused. "There's a bunch of stuff from numbers not in your contacts."

"I'll go through them later." Not a task I relished. I suspected a bunch of them were reporters.

"Or I can," Isaac said. "Might be easier if I did it."

I tapped my fingers on the wheel and didn't reject the offer out of hand. All those questions and all the other shit people threw at me were hard to stomach. Having someone else go through it first might be smart. Not sure if it needed to be Isaac, though. "Maybe." I glanced quickly at him. "Let me think about it?"

"Of course." He turned off the screen. A couple minutes later, we were pulling into the parking lot by the players' entrance at the rink.

Things were more normal this time, with the staff and the

guys and the coaches, at least until Larry—who always took a couple laps on the ice without all his pads before gearing up—came back in. "It's, um, a lot more crowded than normal out there."

The room quieted, and I knew everyone was looking at me. "In a good way, or a bad way?"

He chuckled. "Good. It's good, Lans. You'll see. Just—be prepared."

Coach had been lacing up his skates. "It'll be good practice for St. Louis tomorrow. Lots of eyes on all of you boys."

And on me. Especially on me. I should've felt the pressure, should've been a wreck of nerves, but neither of those emotions touched me. I was—excited to get back to it. Hockey had always been a joy, even during the worst of it—I could lose myself in the game. Focus on the puck. Clear my mind and react to the players, the shifts, the sounds of blades on the ice.

I wanted that back, and I never wanted to give it up, so I finished dressing, and headed out to the sheet.

Once on the ice, my brain stuttered to a halt, and I glided a few feet, utterly stunned at what I was seeing. Larry had warned me, but "more crowded than normal" was an understatement. The stands were *packed*, and a roar went up so loud, I almost thought we were at the arena.

The stands could get crowded for practices sometimes, especially if there was a youth tourney in the building, but I'd never seen it like this. Not a free seat, and anywhere there was space to stand, there were fans.

A sea of jerseys sported thirteen—that happenstance unlucky number that I'd turned into luck for myself all those years ago.

There were also *signs*. So many signs. With messages that made my heart ache.

*Je t'aime, Julien!*
*We Love Landry*
*I #StandWithLans*

If this was practice, what would the game tomorrow be like? Holy hell.

Of course, it was Nikki who knocked sense back into me. He skated past, checking me in the shoulder. "You brought me your fan club!"

Then he skated around the rink waving at people.

I rolled my eyes and laughed, and I skated after him. "You asshole."

I took my warm-up lap and waved like I did when my family had been here—except there were so many more Landrys in the stands. Part of me wanted to cry, but mostly I choked up on gratitude and happiness. I tossed some pucks to kids—they had to have been cutting school, even though their parents were there too—then headed over when Coach blew the whistle to start practice.

The loud atmosphere made for a fun practice. We worked with our skills coach on some offensive tactics, then on the power play. Lots of drills and movement. Stuff I loved. Give me a puck and a task, and I'm happy. Hearing that place erupt when I snuck a puck past Larry? Fantastic.

I saluted the crowed, then gave Larry a tap on the pads. "No offense."

"Hey, you do that tomorrow against the other guy and I'll be a happy man." He grinned at me.

By the end of practice, I felt like my timing was nearly back to normal, as were my legs. I slid in between Nikki and Elias, who were shooting the shit with Isaac by the benches. "Want to race?"

Nikki got his comedic thoughtful look. "Backward or forward?"

"Forward. None of you can handle backward."

"Hey," Isaac said. "I can skate backward. These losers might not be able too, but—"

Elias shoved him. Not hard, but there was a competitive spark in his eyes. "Don't get above yourself, rook."

Isaac raised an eyebrow and Nikki cackled. "Skating backward. You're on. If we beat you, you're buying the next dinner on the road for all of us." He gestured to our group.

"Does 'we' mean beating you and Elias, or does that include Julien?"

"Ah, no," I said. "I love you, but you're on your own for this. Besides, I'm going to win, so..." I shrugged.

"Fair enough." Isaac gave Elias and Nikki a cocky-ass look I recognized. Isaac with swagger was sexy as hell. "What about you gentlemen?"

"Same wager," Nikki said. "You beat the two of us, dinner for the four of us."

Elias nodded.

"Okay." Isaac grinned. "If I win, can I call you Nikki?"

"Ho!" Nikki's voice echoed across the ice.

Elias got a look I couldn't describe for the life of me. I don't think anyone else caught it, because it lasted maybe a second, if that. "Maybe you should stick to dinner," I said.

"No," Nikki said. "I like this. You're on, rook."

So that's how the four of us ended up racing around the rink, backward, to a huge crowd of onlookers. Paxy and Larry were the judges.

As I'd predicted, I won, but not by as much as I thought I would. With the stands screaming at my victory, Isaac barely came in second to Elias's third, with Nikki laughing as he slid in fourth.

Isaac clapped both Elias and Nikki on the back. "I'll still buy dinner."

Laugher all around. Isaac and Nikki were still chirping

each other as they headed back to the locker room, so I caught Elias's elbow. "Hey, you okay with that?" I nodded after them.

"Of course," he answered smoothly. "Why wouldn't I be? Besides, it's Nisha's choice."

"I don't want you to be angry at Isaac."

The laugh I got was genuine, and spontaneous. Elias gripped me by the shoulder and ushered me toward the locker room. "I am not mad at him at all." He sobered. "He's going to be a great leader someday."

Okay, so I wasn't the only one who saw that spark in Isaac. The intensity and talent along with his easygoing nature, coupled with his hockey sense. The raw building blocks that would take him far.

I couldn't wait to see it.

As I undressed and showered, I caught sight of the script on my wrist. *Now.* For so long, that had been the only safe place for me. Still was where I needed to be on the ice. But for the first time in my life, I wanted to imagine beyond that and let myself dream.

Something was off when I entered the lounge, though. A little somber, a little tense. I had a fairly good idea the source, since Isaac had that look that he got, the one that said he wasn't sure how I'd react to something.

I grabbed food and settled in at our usual table. "So, what did that asshole do now?"

"Not him," Nikki said. "Carolina."

"They put Canterbury on unconditional waivers. To terminate his contract for cause." Elias sipped his water.

Oh, there was more there, from the absolute fury in his eyes. I turned to Isaac. "What else?"

Isaac's brow furrowed, and he looked down at his plate. "There's a rookie on Carolina's team."

Ah shit. The bitter taste of despair, then anger surged through me. "That motherfucker."

"I know him. The rookie. We played against each other in college. Great player. Tough as nails on the ice. Saw him at the All-Stars. Said he was having a hard time adjusting to the league, but I didn't..."

I found Isaac's hand. "Don't you put any of that on yourself." I glanced around the table at all of them. "You guys won't let me blame myself, so I'm not about to let any of you take the blame for him either."

Nikki nodded, and we ate for a while in silence. I poked at my food. "The crowd at practice," I said, then looked up. "That was something. I—is the game going to be like that, do you think?"

It was Elias who answered, his smile like dawn in the summer. "Oh, I suspect the game will be nothing at all like practice."

Isaac blinked. "You—do?"

A nod. "Wait and see."

---

Elias was right.

When I stepped out on the ice third from last, the roar that erupted in the arena was so deafening it blotted out the music. I felt it in my bones. I swear I'd never heard this place that loud, even during playoffs. Then they started chanting my name, and I couldn't make it through the first part of my warm-up routine because my heart was on fire.

As there had been at practice, there were signs, but not just on the glass, not only on our end of the sheet, but *everywhere*. I'd only ever seen something like this in videos of superstars when they came back from an injury that took them out for a season. This wasn't that.

I wasn't a generational talent. I doubted I'd ever make the Hall of Fame. I was just me, a kid from Saguenay who loved hockey and had gotten into a horrible situation during his rookie year. I'd survived, maybe even thrived, and I wondered if that's why Travis had never left me alone.

I raised my stick in the air, and saluted the crowd, well aware that the big screen had every single one of my emotions on display. I'd never been able to keep my passion off the ice, and right now the gratitude in my heart was enough to make my eyes well. Everyone there saw that.

It was Isaac who slid up to me first. "Hey, are you okay?"

I nodded. Then I was shoulder checked gently from behind. Didn't even need to turn to know who'd done that. I laughed and flipped Nikki off—well, as best I could in hockey gloves—but he knew. "Time for warm-ups, King."

"Eh." Elias joined Isaac and me. "Soak it up." He met my gaze. "People love you, Julien. Never forget that."

Fucking hell. I slipped my glove off, and rubbed at my eyes. "I know. I won't. But Nikki's right. We need to warm up."

Elias clapped me on the shoulder, and got back to it.

I studied where everyone was in their various routines, and fell back into the flow. Being the best player I could be tonight was something I could give this amazing crowd. In the back of my mind, I tinkered with an idea of what I could do in the future, too. But that could wait.

We had a game to win.

# Chapter 39

## Isaac

I'd always heard there was nothing more grueling, stressful, or exciting than the playoffs, and holy crap, did that turn out to be true. Even my college level playoffs didn't prepare me for this. The pressure. The way so much was riding on every minute of every game. How every goal felt like it was literally making history. The grueling travel and media scrums and *more* travel in between.

But I loved it. Every goddamned minute of it.

Okay, not every minute. I'd always hated the superstition about not shaving during the playoffs. The longer we held our own, the fuller my playoff beard became, and I couldn't wait to shave it off. Mine was itchy and annoying. Julien's was thicker than mine, and it got in the way when I was kissing him—I was seriously looking forward to him shaving too.

So yeah, the playoff beard thing sucked, but it was what it was, and having an annoyingly full beard while my teammates looked like lumberjacks on ice meant we were still in the running for the cup. I could live with it.

We'd very nearly lost during the semifinals. To Carolina, no less. And though I'd never have said it out loud to my teammates, I think I'd have been *almost* okay with that loss, if only because their would-be game-winning goal had been scored by Chad Weyland.

I still felt guilty for not seeing the writing on the wall about him. For not making the connection between his asshole teammate and his discomfort over my relationship with Julien. Yeah, I'd thought he was straight, but goddamn, I should've erred on the side of caution. We'd talked some since that whole thing had gone down, and he was doing good. He was working on getting some therapy, same as Julien.

I'd also found out later that during the time when Carolina had been silent about Travis after Julien's statement, Weyland had pulled aside his team's captain and alternates and told them about his relationship with Travis. He'd been so freaked out, thinking no one would believe him or the team would side with their veteran player over the idiot rookie, he'd literally had to stop in the middle of the conversation to throw up.

In the end, rumor had it the only reason Travis still had any teeth at all was that he happened to be in a hearing with some lawyers right then. Otherwise the team's leadership had been ready to curb stomp him. Travis had walked out of that hearing to a team refusing to speak to him and unanimously informing their brass that, "It's either him or us—he plays, we walk." And they'd meant it.

Going public had been traumatic for Weyland, same as it been for Julien and the others, especially since he'd still been in the thick of things with Travis, but the support had worked wonders. His hockey did a one-eighty almost overnight. Everyone still asked him if he'd scored in his first game after that to spite Travis. Whenever they did, he grinned, shrugged, and said he was out there playing for his team, not his ex.

"*You can't focus on the past in this game,*" Julien had told me a lifetime ago. *"When you're out there, the numbers don't matter, and neither does the past."*

Words to live by. Weyland must have agreed, and he'd played his ass off alongside his team now that his abuser could no longer touch him. When Carolina had secured the first place spot in their division, Weyland hadn't just been a rookie tagging along with the big boys—he'd earned it right along with them.

And then there was Julien. He'd been an amazing player for years, but his post-Travis hockey was nothing short of glorious. It was like he'd been kicking ass all this time while dragging a huge weight behind him, and now that he'd finally cut away that anchor chain, he was unstoppable.

At the first semifinal game, Weyland and Julien had shared a handshake and a hug at the red line during warm-ups. They'd both been through a lot. God only knew how much abuse Julien had saved Weyland from, and Weyland's gratitude had almost moved Julien to tears that night.

But once that puck dropped, they were on opposite sides, and neither team was giving up without a fight.

It was a battle, and in the seventh game of the series, when Weyland scored in the waning three minutes of the third period, everyone—both teams, the crowd, the commentators—were sure it was all over. Carolina was heading to the finals. The absolute elation on Weyland's face, the way his team had celebrated with him—it was almost enough to make me okay with letting go of our shot at this year's cup.

Almost.

With a minute to go, Nikki tied up the score again.

And with single-digit seconds left on the clock, Elias tapped one in after an assist from Julien and Paxy.

Weyland bought me and Julien beers later that night. Clinking his bottle against ours, he said to Julien, "It's always disappointing to lose, but I don't think I'd have made it this far if you hadn't done what you did."

I would never in a million years forget the way Julien smiled on the way out of the bar after that.

The playoffs weren't over, though, and we'd barely had a chance to catch our breath before we were on our way to play against the Western Conference champions—Los Angeles.

There was hockey against a really good team, and there was hockey against a really good team who was so close to winning the cup they could taste it, and Jesus fuck, that second option was *hard*. Nobody wanted to lose. Nobody wanted to give up an inch of ice, never mind a goal. We never did, but when there was a cup on the line, the competitiveness was wild.

Tonight, it was cranked up even more.

Because tonight...someone was taking the cup home.

The league had even paraded it out onto the ice before the game, as if to whet our appetites even more. I was genuinely surprised no one was openly salivating on the benches. Though maybe I just couldn't see it since our faces were hidden behind these stupid beards.

Now we were down to the wire, and it wasn't looking good.

The second period ended. We were trailing three to two. Paxy was benched for the rest of the game after he'd made a diving save in front of our goal; he'd kept the puck out of our net, but wrenched his hip in the process. Elias's nose had finally stopped bleeding after he'd taken an elbow to the face, and we'd be starting the third period short-handed thanks to Nikki throwing a punch at the owner of said elbow. We were lucky the refs had only called it roughing.

My hands were shaky as I retaped my stick in the dressing room. It didn't even need it, but it was something to do with all this nervous energy. So much pressure. So. Much.

We needed a minimum of two goals in twenty minutes. Needed to find the path of least resistance. As I ran through the replays of the game over and over in my head, a path started to come into focus. One of their defensive pairs was weaker than the others tonight. I couldn't tell if it was a lack of communication, fatigue, or what, but they couldn't stop turning over the puck. And I'd noticed a few times that they'd been leaving their goalie's right side more exposed than they should have. Especially since that was this goalie's weaker side.

"What are you thinking, Rivs?" Ozzy appeared beside me. "You've got that look like you're strategizing."

I tore off the tape and set the roll down on the bench between us. "I have an idea."

We grabbed Julien and Benson along with Jackal, who was filling in for Paxy, and an assistant coach. As they all leaned over me, I put a small whiteboard flat on my lap. With a few circles and lines, I explained what I had in mind.

"Their offense has been on point all night," I said, "offensively *and* defensively. But if we can break away and get into their zone with *just* this D pair and the netminder"—I tapped the board with my knuckle—"then we've got a shot."

The guys all nodded. We discussed a few potential strategies for getting everyone where they needed to be, though a lot of that would have to happen on the fly depending on where players on both teams were situated when the opportunity arose.

The period started shortly after that. We killed the penalty, though it was close a few times, and my line went in to relieve Elias's. Julien caught my eye and gave me a nod, and I realized the weak defensive pair was on the ice. This was our chance.

It was risky, but Julien and Jackal let their forwards go a little deeper into our defensive zone before relieving them of the puck. Julien battled it out with one of the wingers, sent the puck to Jackal, who sent it to Ozzy, who was waiting for it in the neutral zone. He made a run for their end with Jackal and me on his heels.

Just as I'd predicted, the defense didn't have their shit together. Ozzy danced around one. I went around the other just in time to catch the pass from Ozzy and send it to Jackal, who shot it at the goalie's weak side and—

Right into the glove.

Damn it.

I tried not to be demoralized. No play worked every time. Their coach might've gotten on their cases about the weak defense. All wasn't lost. We just had to get at least two goals in...

I looked up at the clock.

Fifteen minutes.

My line went back to the bench.

"Rivs." That was Julien, calling me from a few places down. I leaned forward to make eye contact with him. "The play." He gave me a sharp nod. "It's a good one. Next shift..." He jerked his head toward the other team's goal.

My heart, still pounding from my minute or so on the ice, seemed to speed up. I nodded back.

We both sat back, and I watched the action on the ice, looking for more weak spots to exploit. I peered down at one of the iPads to watch the video of our failed play.

A roar of excitement rose from the crowd.

My head snapped up, and in an instant I was on my feet with the rest of my team as Nikki tore across the ice. Two of LA's forwards were on his heels, but Nikki was still mad about his time in the box, and there was no stopping him when he was pissed.

The goalie was ready for him. Twitching left, right, trying to anticipate.

Nikki faked left.

The goalie didn't buy it.

Nikki was ready for that—he faked again to the right.

The goalie hesitated.

Then he dove.

But it was too late.

The crowd drowned out the goal horn. Nikki got a hug from Elias that nearly knocked him off his skates, and both were grinning from ear to ear as they came by the bench for fist bumps.

The whole vibe of the team and the crowd shifted. The game was tied. There was still time. We could *win* this motherfucker.

No one was giving up, though. As we got down to the last four minutes, I had a feeling we were going into overtime.

When we hit the last two...yeah, probably overtime.

But then as my line went out for another shift, I noticed the weak defensive pair.

Maybe...?

I skated up to Julien. "Try the play again?"

He did a sweep of the ice with his eyes, then met mine and nodded. "Let's do it."

We shared a fist bump, then skated off to pass the word along.

The play flopped again, *but* one of their defensemen flubbed a pass and sent the puck over the glass. While a fan snagged a souvenir, we got the opportunity for a faceoff in the offensive zone.

On my way to the circle, Julien stopped me with a hand on my arm and spoke in a hushed voice. "We're on the netminder's weak side. This D pair is trash on faceoffs." Looking right in my eyes, he added, "Get me the puck."

For a split second, I froze, wondering if there was still time to do a line change. Elias was *way* stronger in faceoffs than I was. I was good, but maybe not "the cup is riding on me winning this one and getting the puck to the right guy" good.

Julien's eyes said he absolutely believed in me, though. He wouldn't risk a cup just to massage my ego. If he believed in me, then who was I to say I couldn't?

So I nodded and put my mouthguard back in.

Then I went to the circle. I glanced over one shoulder, then the other, making sure I knew where everyone was. In particular, where Julien was. He was hanging back slightly from where he'd usually be. There was more space between us for someone to grab the puck, but he was in a better position to capitalize on the goalie's weak side.

I turned to Ozzy and gave him a pointed look and a nod in the general direction of the other side of the goal. The defenseman nearest him bought it and closed some of the distance between him and Ozzy...leaving more space for Julien. Taking the focus off him too. Perfect.

The puck dropped. The other center and I both fumbled a little for it, sending panic through me for a heartbeat, but then he lost control just long enough for me to snatch it away.

From the corner of my eye, I saw the defenseman lunge to cover Ozzy, but I'd already put the puck right on Julien's tape.

The crowd knew. I knew. I could *feel* it.

With thousands of fans roaring around us, Julien faked.

The goalie lunged.

And Julien scored.

The crowd went ballistic. He pumped his stick in the air, absolute joy radiating off him.

I reached him first and threw my arms around him. "You did it! Holy shit!"

"You're brilliant!" He hugged me back, and my God, it was a struggle not to steal a kiss from him right here on the ice even as our teammates crushed us. Maybe later. This wasn't over yet. We were ahead now, but that could still change, and I wanted Julien to have his game-winning goal.

The rest of the team wasn't going to deny him that either, and when the buzzer went off...

Holy shit.

We'd won.

My first year as a pro, and we'd won the fucking cup. I had the assist on the game-winning goal, which had been scored by the man I loved. Just... wow.

Elias's line had been on for the final minute, and we all flew over the boards to celebrate on the ice. I'd never imagined being more ecstatic than I'd been when my college team had won our championship, but right now...wow. Just...holy crap. There weren't words to describe the utter joy and relief and excitement and I had no idea how many other emotions that hit me the second the buzzer sounded.

We'd. *Won*.

In between hugs and back slaps, I found Julien in the crush of teammates, his face full of all the same emotions that were overwhelming me. He had tears running down his cheeks. So did I. So did half the team, really.

Just looking at him as he shared a hug with Nikki, though, I was even more overwhelmed.

He'd made it. He'd been through hell, and he'd landed here—surrounded by fans who adored him and teammates who'd walk through fire for him. He'd gone from believing he'd lost everything because of Travis to scoring the game-winning goal in the cup finals.

Maybe it was weird, a rookie being this ridiculously proud of a veteran player, but there I was.

And then he looked at me.

And oh God, if I hadn't been in tears already...

I skated closer to him and hugged him again, ready to come apart from all these feelings crashing through me. I didn't know what to say. Maybe there wasn't anything *to* say.

He drew back, taking a breath like he was about to speak, but when he met my eyes, he stopped.

After a second, he grinned, and right there on the ice, he kissed me. I wrapped my arms around him, not even caring that both our beards were scratchy and annoying.

The roar of the crowd shifted to an "Awww," and I laughed, breaking the kiss. I didn't have to look up to know we were on the big screen, but I did anyway. So did he.

Then we both shrugged, and I lifted my chin to kiss him again, prompting another "Aww" from the fans, which made us both laugh again.

"You know what's the best part of winning the cup?" I asked.

His eyebrow arched. "What?"

I grinned and touched his bearded face. "We can finally *shave*."

Julien laughed, unaware of what that did to my heart. "Oh, come on." He gestured at himself. "You don't like it?"

"Oh, I do. But when it's out of the way, I have a much easier time getting to your mouth."

His eyes were instantly huge, and he gulped.

"So." I gave him a challenging look. "Shave?"

"Uh-huh." He nodded. "Shave."

"That's what I thought."

Eventually, the cup was presented to Elias, who held it up over his head and skated along the boards, his expression full of the same sheer joy and triumph as the rest of us. He passed it to Nikki. Nikki passed it to Julien, and in the moment they exchanged the cup, they both looked like they might break. Nikki watched Julien skate a circle with it, a flurry of emotions in the big Russian's eyes that I couldn't quite parse. Pride, warmth, and maybe even a spark of sadness.

I skated up next to him. "You good, Nikki?"

He looked down, and he smiled as he gave my shoulder a

firm clap. "Of course." Nodding toward Julien, he added, "Always hoped I'd see him like this. Wondered sometimes if I ever would." His smile warmed as he watched Julien hand off the cup to Paxy, who was skating a little gingerly but wouldn't have missed this for the world.

I understood. Nikki had seen Julien through more of that awfulness than I had. He'd been there for the worst of the aftermath. Without him, there was no telling what would have happened to Julien.

Thank God for Nikki. Thank God for Elias.

And thank God for Julien.

The best friend and boyfriend I could ever ask for. The man who'd not only emerged from the ashes like the firebird on his hip, but had also set fire to the predator who'd tried to destroy him and others. Because of Julien, the other victims could rise again just like he did. He was stronger than he'd ever truly know, more resilient than he ever should have had to be, and more amazing in every way than anyone I'd ever met. He was everything.

And I was determined, then and there, to spend the rest of my life showing him how beautiful he was.

# Epilogue

## Julien

My therapist said that joy and grief were two sides to the same coin, that one often followed the other. In the days after winning the cup, I found this to be so true. Elation and joy swamped me. My entire family had been in the arena for that last game, as had Isaac's parents and Darian. There'd been hugs and kisses. I'd found myself in Isaac's arms whenever we came close to each other. Laughter and tears. We'd done it. Hoisted the proof above our heads.

But Marie had sobbed when she'd held me. Longer and harder than even our mother. Grief twined with jubilation. She'd had me crying too. The road to that moment had been fraught and painful and I'd hidden so much from those who loved me.

So many loved me. I knew that now. Family. Teammates. Elias and Nikki.

Isaac. God, *Isaac*. In the locker room, after the beer and champagne and drinking from the cup, he'd pulled me onto his lap, and I'd sat there, the room spinning around my inebriated head. I didn't know what the future held, but I did know that I'd be by Isaac's side. So many people had saved me, but Isaac had drawn me back to myself, over and over.

The city threw us a parade, and it felt like half the state poured into Pittsburgh. I'd thought I'd had an inkling of what to expect, but nothing prepared me for the joy we'd felt, or the way the fans turned out and cheered. Even Elias cut loose, whooping it up, drunk off his ass.

I wanted to do it again. Desperately. I think we all did. But that was work for autumn and winter. After the grand party in the city, the team scattered like parade confetti for our shortened off-season.

As I'd suggested, Isaac and I rented a house for three weeks on Lac Saint-Jean, one big enough to house my whole family. While there were plenty of days of Landry chaos, there were also times when it was only Isaac and me. I needed the quiet as well as the noise. Sometimes sorrow caught me—my wounds would always be there. I was slowly working through all that had happened. Therapy helped my mind. Training helped my body. The quiet helped my soul.

Isaac was my heart. He seemed to know when to let me wander down to the lake to skip stones until my eyes blurred from the tears and then when to join me, to help me back to the present, to the *Now* that was inked on my wrist.

We made love. Sometimes it was intense and painful in every way I wanted. Other times so gentle I could only weep in gratitude. Occasionally, I'd kneel at Isaac's side, and he'd hold me.

I hung up a lot of clothes that summer.

My day with the cup took place while we were up north, and I shared that with as many people as I could. The kids at my old rink. My parents' neighborhood. Folks at a local hospital. I'd ended up misty-eyed by the end of the day.

I also spent some time researching and talking with my

financial advisor about starting a foundation. I wanted to provide some kind of support for athletes who, like me, had been abused. I didn't know what form that would take, but I knew I had to start building something. I planned to reach out to other organizations, too. See where there was a need, and go from there.

It was a start, anyway.

After the trip north, we returned to Pittsburgh briefly to check on the status of the swimming pool. Elias and Nikki had been sending me updates while they were in town, but both the contractor and I wanted to talk before the next stage began. Then we'd fly to Oregon to visit with Isaac's family and friends and for his day with the cup.

Kelly had texted me about a package that had arrived at the arena for me and said it contained something I should've had a long time ago. So, I wasn't that surprised to find a shipping envelope from her waiting with the rest of the mail. Once I'd torn into the envelope, I discovered another opened one that contained a folded note and a square black box—one exactly the right size to hold a hockey puck.

The original envelope was from Charlotte, North Carolina.

My breath caught and I wavered on my feet. Oh fuck. I knew what was in this box. I'd only ever held it once. Thought it was gone forever. Grief and joy twined together and squeezed the air from my lungs.

Isaac caught my elbow, concern lacing his voice. "What is it?"

"I need to sit down." Words tasted like chalk.

With Isaac at my side, I lowered myself onto the couch. Then, with a trembling hand, I lifted the lid off the box.

As expected, a hockey puck with the league emblem sat inside. The familiar words in English and French, Rondelle de Match Officielle—Official Game Puck—stared back. White tape wrapped the edge and I knew even before I lifted the puck from the box what would be written there.

*Julien Landry. First Goal. From Elias Karlsson.* The date and time of that goal, so many years ago.

I remembered that moment clear as day, the way I saw the lane opening and the puck coming toward me at the blue line. How it felt to wind up, then follow through. The sight of the puck streaking past players and the goalie to hit the back of the net. The elation of my teammates and the fans. Skating to the bench for fist bumps. The team media folks snapping photographs afterward, me holding the puck with its inscription.

The crushing horror when I realized Travis wasn't giving it back after I'd handed it to him.

*Hey Julie, let me see that.*

I'd been so fucking naïve.

"Holy shit," Isaac breathed out.

I rotated the puck in my hand, and read the inscription. "He took it from me. Came to my room later, asked to see it, then—took it. Said it was his, since I wouldn't have scored it without him. Fucker wasn't even on the ice when I put it in the net." I set the puck down on the coffee table, then wiped the tears off my cheeks, throat tight and raw. "My family wanted to see it. It's something most players in the league have eventually, you know? I had to lie and say that I'd lost it."

Isaac pulled me into a hug and held me. Didn't say a word.

After a few moments, I picked up the paper and unfolded it to discover a handwritten note:

*He had one from each of us. I thought you'd want yours back. Thank you for everything.* —Chad

I slid the note onto the table next to the puck. "I hope the others got theirs back, too."

"I'm sure they did," Isaac said.

Emotions were so strange. Joy brushed up against me. There, on the table, was a piece of my past, once more in my possession. Not everything had been lost from that year.

This puck was here. *I* was *here*.

I had mementoes from other important moments tucked away. "There are other pucks. Sticks. Photos. I've never displayed any of that because this one was missing."

"Now it's not." Isaac slid his fingers between mine. "And you'll have a little mini cup soon."

Giddiness rose through the sadness. "We won the cup," I whispered. Still couldn't quite wrap me head around that. The Pittsburgh Griffins were champions—and so was I.

"Guess we should buy a case? Figure out where to display all of it?"

Isaac chuckled, then stole a kiss. "Yeah, we should."

Wasn't until a couple days later, while on the flight to the West Coast, that I realized both Isaac and I had made assumptions that we'd not spoken about.

"Hey," I squeezed his hand. "Do you want to move in with me?"

His laughter had most of first class peering at us. "You're building me a waterfall. Half my clothing is in the house. Of course I want to move in with you."

Heat touched my cheeks. "Your apartment is pretty nice, though."

"It is." He kissed my knuckles. "I may keep it. I don't know yet." Then he stared into my eyes. "I want to be where you are, and your house is your oasis. You're doing all you can to make it mine, too."

"Ours," I said. This time there was only joy. "It'll be ours."

There was nothing more beautiful in the world than Isaac's smile.

I'd only ever been to the Pacific Northwest for away games. This time, we spent three weeks there in a little rental on the coast. We visited with Isaac's family, with Darian and his other friends, and trained with some of his hockey buddies, including Chad Weyland, who'd ended up at the same facility. We welcomed him into our group, and he worked as hard as anyone.

Toward the end of our time there, he finally managed to deke me out and score.

"Great," Isaac said, smiling. "You've made him *better*. How are we going to beat them now?"

I shrugged. "That's the fun of it, isn't it? Besides, I didn't teach him everything..."

Chad laughed outright at that, and my heart soared.

As we packed our gear after our last practice, I pulled him aside. "Thank you," I said. "For the puck."

He nodded, then met my gaze, his eyes suddenly shining. "Thank you for beating the snot out of that fucker."

I laughed, then pulled him into a hug that had us both sniffling. Grief and joy.

A few days later, Isaac and I were back in Pittsburgh, unpacking, when my cell phone rang.

"Ah, fuck." It took me a minute to find it under the clothes I'd tossed onto the bed from my suitcase.

I froze as soon as I saw the number, a chill running to my feet. Mother*fucker*. This was going to end, right the hell *now*.

I answered and spoke. "Hello, Travis."

Isaac fumbled hanging his suit, and the jacket crumpled to the floor. The hanger followed when he whipped around and stared at me.

Silence on the line. Silence in the room. Then the voice

that had haunted my thoughts and nightmares spoke. "Julie. You answered. You never answer."

"I did this time." I shrugged, even as my ire rose and rose. "And my name is Julien."

"You're such a little prissy thing," he sneered. "You fucking ruined my life."

The laughter that poured out of me was ugly and raw and ended with me snarling back. "You complete *asshole*. You ruined your own miserable life."

"I—"

I spoke over that piece of trash. "It burned you, didn't it? That I kept going. Kept working. Even after you cast me off, even as broken as you left me, *I kept going*. Kept skating. I didn't leave. Yeah, I had to face you, but you had to face me, too, starting to thrive, despite everything you did to keep me down."

"You liked—"

Fire raged through me. "Go fuck yourself." My throat hurt from the venom inside me.

Once more, there was silence in the room and on the line, then his damn voice again. "My name's going to be on that cup with yours. We're tied together, you and me."

This time my laugh was high pitched. "They didn't tell you?" I hadn't noticed because I purposefully hadn't looked. It was Mathieu who'd pointed it out. "They stamped out your name. Both years. Just a line of Xs now. So, no, we won't share that. It'll only be me."

No more words from the other end, just labored breathing.

"Goodbye, Travis. I hope you never know a moment's peace for the rest of your life." I pulled the phone away from my ear, and jabbed disconnect. Then I finally blocked that asshole's number, lobbed my phone onto the pile of clothes on my bed, and screamed.

Joy. Rage. Relief.

"Julien?" Isaac whispered.

I turned to him, tears sliding down my face. "Oh my God, Isaac." He was in my arms a moment later, then steering my trembling body to the edge of the bed so I could sit. I didn't know whether to laugh or sob, so I ended up doing both "Oh my God," I repeated. "I did it."

"You did." He smoothed my hair, brushed strands from my face, and kissed me on the cheek. "That took a lot of guts."

I buried my face against his shoulder, my whole body shaking with adrenaline. "I feel like I should run around the neighborhood a dozen times. I'm so—" Relieved. Free. "Happy."

Isaac tightened the hug. "What do you need me to do?"

I pulled back and looked into his eyes. "You're going to think this really strange, given everything..."

He raised an eyebrow.

And that's how we ended up in the driveway, on rollerblades with hockey sticks and a ball, playing two on two street hockey with Elias and Nikki until I was hungry and exhausted and full of so much joy that I collapsed into a happy heap on the lounge chair that sat on our newly constructed patio out by the pool.

Elias had been quite happy to discover I'd had beef patties delivered with my grocery order and that the new grill was ready to go. He and Nikki were chatting about something or other over by the grill. I was staring up at the blue sky, listening to water flow into the pool while my whole body relaxed against the cushions. "I can't wait for the season to start."

Isaac nudged me over, sat down on the lounger, and offered me a bottle of water. "It's almost your birthday."

I'd be twenty-eight. My ninth year in the league. Isaac's second.

"Yeah." I paused and watched as Elias laughed at something Nikki said, then pulled Isaac down next to me. "I want this. You. Our friends. A pool party. Nothing fancy."

"Twenty-some odd pro hockey players playing street hockey in our driveway?"

"Why not?" I nuzzled Isaac's neck. "What the worst that could happen?"

Isaac gave me a gentle shove. "Never ask that question!"

I chuckled as I curled around him. Thank goodness we'd gotten very wide patio furniture. "I love you."

His eyes practically sparkled. "Love you, too."

Isaac in my arms. Elias and Nikki bickering playfully in the background. The sound of water trickling over stone. I was still a patchwork of emotions, still had room to heal and grow and learn, but the future looked so bright. And now?

Now was *perfect*.

The End.

## Coming Next

Thanks for reading Rookie Mistake! We hope you enjoyed Isaac and Julien's story. There's more in store for the Pittsburgh Griffins.

At nearly thirty-one years old, Pittsburgh Griffins captain Elias Karlsson's hockey years are numbered. Everything is changing around him, including his eleven-year friendship with Nikolai Sidorov. Elias would give anything for Nisha to be with him, but their once bedrock-strong bond has broken into a million pieces, and Elias doesn't know why. More than anything, Elias wants his friend back, but if that isn't an option, maybe it's time for him to look outside of hockey for someone to be there with him when hockey isn't an option anymore.

Nisha's world is splintering apart. He's been in love with his two best friends for years, but now one of them has someone. The other, Elias, is searching for everything Nisha wishes he could give him... but he's looking for it in anyone *but* Nisha. The farther his friends slip away, the deeper the loneliness sinks in and the bleaker his empty future looks. What can he do but numb the pain in the only ways he knows how?

On the eve of the season opener, Nisha's unexplained absence threatens the cohesion of the team and puts him and Elias on a collision course of strong wills, broken hearts, and shattered trust. In the end, they may lose the one thing that matters the most to them both: each other.

## Also by Anna Zabo

### Close Quarter

Close Quarter

Slow Waltz (a Close Quarter short story)

### Takeover

Takeover

Just Business

Due Diligence

Daily Grind

### Twisted Wishes

Syncopation

Counterpoint

Reverb

### Standalone Works

CTRL Me

Outside the Lines

Weave the Dark, Weave the Light

Cinnamon Roll

# Also By L.A. Witt

The Right to Remain

The Venetian and the Rum Runner

The Husband Gambit

Name from a Hat Trick

**The Gentlemen of the Emerald City Series**

Luca

Cole

Bryce

Marco

Andre

Hunter

**The Pucks & Rainbows Series**

Rebound

Assist

Shot on Goal

**The Hitman vs. Hitman Series (written with Cari Z)**

Hitman vs. Hitman

Sniper vs. Spotter

Killer vs. Kingpin

# About Anna Zabo

Anna Zabo writes queer contemporary and paranormal romance. They live and work in Pittsburgh, Pennsylvania, which isn't nearly as boring as most people think. They can be easily plied with coffee or a tickets to see the Pittsburgh Penguins.

Anna has an MFA in Writing Popular Fiction from Seton Hill University, where they fell in with a roving band of romance writers and never looked back. They also have a BA in Creative Writing from Carnegie Mellon University.

Anna uses they/them pronouns and prefers Mx. Zabo as an honorific.

Website: annazabo.com.

Facebook Group: facebook.com/groups/AnnaZabo

 twitter.com/amergina
instagram.com/amergina
bookbub.com/authors/anna-zabo

# About L.A. Witt

L.A. Witt is a romance and suspense author who has at last given up the exciting nomadic lifestyle of the military spouse (read: her husband finally retired). She now resides in Pittsburgh, where the potholes are determined to eat her car and her cats are endlessly taunted by a disrespectful squirrel named Moose. In her spare time, she can be found painting in her art room or destroying her voice at a Pittsburgh Penguins game.

Website: gallagherwitt.com

Facebook Group: facebook.com/groups/1633167680026803

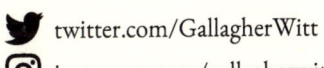
twitter.com/GallagherWitt
instagram.com/gallagherwitt

Made in the USA
Middletown, DE
13 August 2022